USA Today bestselling author **JO SEGURA** lives in the Pacific Northwest with her doggo, who vies for her attention with his sweet puppy dog eyes whenever she's trying to write. Her stories feature strong, passionate heroines and draw upon aspects of her life, such as her love of good food, her Mexican heritage, and her fascination with archaeology. When she's not writing you can find her practicing law, shaking up a mean cocktail, or sitting out on the patio doing BuzzFeed quizzes (though she doesn't care what the chicken nugget quiz said—her favorite fruit is *not* banana).

VISIT JO SEGURA ONLINE

JoSegura.com
X JoSeguraBooks
⊙ JoSeguraBooks

ALSO BY JO SEGURA

· · · · · · · · ·

Raiders of the Lost Heart

TEMPLE of Swoon

Jo Segura

PIATKUS

PAITKUS

First published in the US in 2025 by Berkley,
An imprint of Penguin Random House LLC
Published in Great Britain in 2025 by Piatkus

1 3 5 7 9 10 8 6 4 2

A CIP catalogue record for this book
is available from the British Library.

ISBN 978-0-349-43870-2

Printed and bound in Great Britain by Clays Ltd, Elcograf S.p.A.

Papers used by Piatkus are from well-managed forests
and other responsible sources.

MIX
Paper | Supporting
responsible forestry
FSC® C104740

Piatkus
An imprint of
Little, Brown Book Group
Carmelite House
50 Victoria Embankment
London EC4Y 0DZ

The authorised representative
in the EEA is
Hachette Ireland
8 Castlecourt Centre
Dublin 15, D15 YF6A, Ireland
(email: info@hbgi.ie)

An Hachette UK Company
www.hachette.co.uk

www.littlebrown.co.uk

For Rachel and Brandon.
We started as friends. Now, we're family.

TEMPLE of Swoon

CHAPTER
One

DR. MIRIAM "MIRI" JACOBS RACED THROUGH THE WILD, CHAOTIC jungle, whipping around obstacles and ducking from danger. *You can make it. You can make it.* She repeated the mantra in her head as her bag pounded against her back in sync with her sprinting footsteps, the ground seeming to give way beneath her feet. She was weaving. Sliding. Careening past creatures of all shapes and sizes. Sweat dripped down the side of her face, but she wasted no time or energy to wipe it away, focusing her strength on reaching her destination before it was too late.

Almost there!

She reached for the silver handle, her fingertips grazing the metal before . . . *Whoosh!*

"Wait!" The imaginary backdrop faded as the bus pulled away from the curb, splattering dirty street water onto Miri's brand-spanking-new water-resistant Patagonia hiking pants.

But her voice was no match for the roaring engines in the bus depot or the plane jets overhead, and a second later, the last bus of the day from the Aeroporto Internacional de Manaus to Manacapuru, Brazil, was rounding a corner and out of sight.

Crud. Day one of her new gig—an expedition to search for the Cidade Perdida da Lua, the Lost City of the Moon—and she was going to miss the kick-off meeting. Not exactly the start she was hoping for, especially with her career hanging on this whole thing. *Way to make a good first impression.*

It was a miracle that she'd been selected for this expedition. Sure, her mentorship with the famed archaeologist Dr. Socorro "Corrie" Mejía at UC Berkeley helped, but until this point, Miri had only been on a handful of digs, all in already-discovered sites. When she'd decided at the age of eight that she wanted to become an archaeologist, she thought she'd be traveling all over the world, unearthing ancient skeletons and finding hidden treasures. She didn't think her archaeological dig experience would be summed up as Human Brush, cleaning dirt off *other* archaeologists' discoveries. Yes, every archaeologist had to begin somewhere, but Miri never seemed to move past the starting line. Unlike just about every other professor on staff at the UC Berkeley Anthropology Department, Miri had absolutely nothing remarkable to pad her résumé.

Professors like Dr. Mejía, who became a world-famous bad-ass archaeologist because she took risks and didn't shy away from danger. Being handpicked by her for this assignment gave Miri instant street cred, as if the association alone meant she must have mad skills like Corrie.

Too bad Miri's top skills were memorization and reading maps. Though, despite the need for wearing glasses, she sometimes seemed to have laser vision and could notice things that others often overlooked. Like a book that was out of place on a shelf. Or a single misplaced brick in a wall. Or a man's fly being down.

She *always* seemed to notice *that*.

Cold, wet liquid seeped through her pants as she glanced down to assess the damage and sighed. *Awesome.* There went a hundred bucks. *Note to self: water resistant does NOT equal waterproof.*

Perhaps not Miri's wisest decision—splurging on a new wardrobe at REI that would almost certainly get destroyed by this trip—but she wanted to at least try to look the part of tough, rugged archaeologist. Her normal go-to dig outfits consisted of little more than yoga pants and a few Columbia hiking shirts she found on the clearance rack at T.J.Maxx. Something not far off from her regular everyday attire, come to think of it. But she had big shoes to fill, or rather, big shoes to impress. That, and she couldn't help but want to emulate her idol, who always looked effortless, hard-core, and hot as hell.

Miri slung her backpack around to the ground and crouched beside it, searching the pockets for a wet wipe, when a figure appeared alongside her.

"Shit!"

She glanced up toward the voice and— *Holy moly, was everyone in this country a supermodel?* The man looked like he could star in an ad with the likes of Alessandra Ambrosio or Marlon Teixeira, and Miri would buy whatever products he was selling—surfboards, cologne, men's underwear, you name it. He stared down the empty street in the direction the departed bus had gone, seemingly oblivious to Miri, one hand on his hip, the other rubbing his forehead below the hairline of his luscious . . . shiny . . . wavy . . . to-die-for jet-black locks. His gray Henley stretched across his chest, outlining every ripple beneath the thin fabric. With the sleeves pushed up, she could see the flexing muscles in his forearms—taut and beckoning for her touch. He had to have been six-foot-two, six-three, judging by the location of his knee in relation to her crouched view. Hard to tell by his towering position, and when preoccupied by his incredibly good looks.

Miri gulped before ordering herself to stop staring, but his presence commanded her attention. This. This was why she didn't date. Because she got all deer-in-the-headlights whenever she saw someone she found attractive. And then they'd stare at her like there was something wrong with her. And then she'd gasp like a fish out of water. And then their faces would contort with confusion, trying to figure out whether she needed help. And then her face would turn the brightest shade of crimson on the color scale. And then they'd leave . . .

The entire scene unfolded in Miri's mind, distracting her from the can of sour-cream-and-onion Pringles rolling out of her bag toward the man's foot.

She watched as his head shifted downward toward the dull *thump* against his boot, and she quickly dipped her head, scrambling to snatch up the runaway snacks. But as she reached over, the rest of the contents of her backpack cascaded onto the sidewalk—a couple of KIND bars, a bag of trail mix, some cheddar-cheese-and-cracker Combos, peanut butter M&M's, and much-needed Altoids for her sour-cream-and-onion breath.

He crouched down to assist her, but Miri hurried to gather up her belongings.

"Don't mind me. Just a regular ole convenience store over here," she said with strained laughter in her voice.

But all she got in return was "the stare."

"Oh! I'm sorry," she said, realizing that she probably sounded like a silly American talking gibberish. He must not have understood her. "Inglês?"

With a quick shake of his head, the man seemed to snap out of a daydream. "Uh . . . yes. Yes, I speak English."

Miri detected a hint of an accent, though not quite the Portuguese accent she'd expected. She also detected a slight flutter in her stomach at the way his rich brown eyes scanned her face.

"Sorry," he continued. "I was distracted checking out your goods."

Never mind. *Now* she had a flutter.

He waved his hands. "Not *your* goods, but *the* goods. From your convenience store, I mean. It's quite the selection."

"Nothing beats snacks from home when traveling internationally, right? What'll you have?" She fanned her hands over the bounty in an offering.

"Oh, no. I can't." He held up his hands in protest.

"I insist. Just not the Pringles."

"Why is that?" He ticked his head to the side, eyeing her curiously.

"Because you know what they say—'Once you pop'—and I've popped and now cannot stop," she said. Instantly, she regretted the level of dorkiness infused in her attempts at banter. *Here it comes again . . . the stare. And his departure.*

Why? Why couldn't she react like a normal human being?

To her surprise, however, the man palmed his ridiculously handsome, smiling face as he playfully shook his head. At least her silliness hadn't caused him to retreat like people usually did whenever she made jokes at the department holiday parties. And summer picnics. And weddings. And bars . . .

"Then I'll take these," he said, snagging the M&M's. "Thank you."

"Thank *you* for shopping." She tipped her head, then shoved her things back in her bag, this time cinching the top to avoid further escape attempts.

His lightheartedness faded away as he checked his watch. "Pretty sure I already know the answer, but was that the bus to Manacapuru?" He nodded in the direction the bus had gone.

"Yup. We both missed it by maybe twenty seconds?" It wasn't a question, but she hoped her inflection might soften the blow.

"Twenty sec . . ." His voice trailed off with a heavy sigh. He whipped out a cell phone and began furiously texting. Must be missing some important modeling gig. Though models probably didn't travel by crusty old bus. Miri took her time wiping off her pants and hands as she watched his frustration. Finally, with a grunt and an exaggerated press of his thumb, he tucked his phone in the front pocket of his charcoal pants and scanned the passersby.

"Excu— I mean, perdona?" He reached his arm out to an older gentleman, who sneered and kept walking. He grumbled something unintelligible under his breath.

Hmm. Maybe he wasn't Brazilian after all. Or at least not from around here. "It's 'com licença,'" Miri offered. "They speak Portuguese here."

"Oh, right. Thanks."

"Com licença," he asked another person. "Billetes?"

Close enough. Fortunately for him, the person understood his Portuguese-Spanish mashup and pointed him in the direction of the ticket office. She thought to warn him that heading to the ticket office would be a waste of time. That the bus they'd missed was the last one to Manacapuru for the night. But it wasn't any of her business. Maybe he was going somewhere else, Manacapuru merely being a stopover before his final destination.

Or *maybe* he'd be so grateful for Miri's assistance that he'd ask if she wanted to grab a coffee. And coffee would turn into a stroll through downtown. Which would turn into happy hour. And then dinner. And then they'd . . .

"Thanks again," the man said with a smile, waving the bag of M&M's at her as he disappeared inside the airport—snapping her out of her fantasy.

Sigh.

Though the exchange with Mr. M&M's provided Miri a pleasant escape from her problems, she had important things to deal with, such as changing out of her dirty street-water pants and finding her own alternative transportation to Manacapuru. But she'd consider their encounter a win in Miri's *How to Interact with a Hottie* book—even *if* it meant saying adeus to her M&M's.

With every ounce of energy left over after her sprint, she lifted herself and her bag from the ground, taking one last glance at Mr. M&M's heading toward the ticket office and admiring his swagger, and headed in the opposite direction toward the bathrooms. She propped her bag up on the counter, then stared at herself in the mirror, instantly recoiling at her appearance.

Yikes. No wonder she'd left Mr. M&M's speechless.

Her cheeks were beet red from racing through the airport.

Her light brown wavy hair stuck out in complete disorder, except for her bangs, which were matted with sweat against her forehead. Her thick, yellow-framed glasses had smudges of who-knows-what on the lenses. And her clothes? Soiled, sweat-stained, and—she ducked her head to take a whiff—oof. Stinky.

Yeesh. She'd definitely looked better.

Then again . . . she'd definitely looked worse! Score for Miri! Nothing could beat that time she'd crashed into the janitor's mop bucket as she ran down the hall, late for her dissertation defense.

She wasn't sure which would be more damaging to her career: showing up to the team kick-off meeting looking like this or not showing up at all. Maybe being delayed wasn't such a terrible thing.

With a heavy sigh, she set her glasses on the counter, peeled off her T-shirt, then twisted her hair into a messy ball on top of her head. She turned on the water, splashing it on her face and her armpits, then took a few pumps of soap and cleaned up as best she could. *Whelp . . . this'll have to do. Get yourself together. You can be a badass like Corrie Mejía. You can do this. Find a ride. Get a good night's rest, and—*

The bathroom door opened and in walked none other than Mr. M&M's himself. His eyes widened at the sight of her standing in front of the mirror in nothing but her bra and pants.

Miri yelped, then grabbed her dirty shirt from the counter and held it in front of her chest.

"Excusez," he choked out as he averted his eyes. And as quickly as he'd come in, he departed.

Annnnnd I should probably put on some clothes.

She glanced down at her bra, wincing at the boring unsexiness of it all—a plain navy T-shirt bra that did little to boost her barely there B cup. Okay, fine . . . A cup. B on a good day. Why hadn't she put on a cuter bra this morning?

Oh right. Because she didn't own any. Cute bras were for showing off. Miri hadn't had a reason to show off her bra since . . . since . . . well . . . Hmm. When *was* the last time?

Pushing thoughts of her nonexistent romantic endeavors to the back of her mind, she finished getting dressed, peeking out the door to make sure the coast was clear before finally emerging from the bathroom. Not that any of this mattered, but she didn't particularly care to have a hot guy seeing her in such an unflattering state. Last thing she needed was a look of pity from Mr. M&M's. She had already given herself enough of those to last the remainder of the day.

Now . . . time to figure out how the heck she was going to get to Manacapuru tonight. Looking around the station, her eye caught on the taxi stand outside with one, and only one, taxi parked in front of it. Phew. There was still a chance that she'd make it before the team dinner.

"Com licença, fala inglês?" she asked the driver in passable Portuguese.

"Um pouco."

The tension in her shoulders relaxed. "Can you take me to Manacapuru?"

"Sim. Trezentos."

Miri looked down, trying to recall her Portuguese numbers and do the math in her head. *Tre . . . trezentos in Brazilian real. What is that . . . Fifty . . . fifty-four-ish U.S. dollars?* Certainly more than the bus ticket had been, but at this point, Miri didn't care. One way or another, she needed to get to Manacapuru before nightfall.

She pulled her wallet out of the money belt tucked in her pants, counting the U.S. bills she hadn't had a chance yet to exchange. *Forty-five, fifty . . . fifty-two.*

"Will you take fifty-two in U.S. dollars?"

The man shook his head. "Não. Three hundred *Americano*," he said, exaggerating.

Miri's eyes about popped out of her head. "Three . . . three hundred *U.S.*?" She choked on the words.

He nodded.

"That's outrageous!"

He shrugged.

"Please. I need to get to Manacapuru tonight. Could you make an exception this one time?"

"Trezentos."

Shoot, shoot, shoot. *Think, Miri. Think. What would Corrie Mejía do? WWCMD?*

Well, Corrie probably wouldn't have been in this situation in the first place. And even if Corrie hadn't been able to outrun the bus—which was unlikely—and was stuck begging cabbies for rides, they'd take one look at her and practically *beg* to drive her. For free. Miri, not so much. Even on her best day, Miri looked like a plain house sparrow compared to the beautiful, sexy, elegant swan that was Corrie Mejía.

Sparrows were cute, too, though, right?

"What if . . . what if I give you fifty-two now, and the rest when we get there?" Surely, the crew would help her make up the difference.

The man scoffed. "I take you, then you disappear. No deal."

"No, I promise! I won't run," she said, clasping her hands in a pleading position in front of her chest. "Once we get to the hotel, I can get the money from my boss."

This time, he gave no response. Simply a grunt as he pulled out a cell phone and leaned against the car, paying her no attention.

"Fine. Fine, then I'll find someone *else* to drive me." As if he cared.

He gave her body a quick glance up and down, then snorted. "Good luck."

Miri cocked her head back. "What's that supposed to mean?"

"No one will drive a street urchin for less."

Street urchin? Ouch. She looked bad but she didn't look *that* bad, did she?

"Listen, buddy, I'm no worse than that filthy hunk of junk you consider fit for transporting actual human beings!"

Wrong answer.

The man turned his back to her without so much as a scoff. Well . . . that did it. She'd messed things up this time. Letting her shoulders fall, she tucked the fifty bucks back in her money belt. As she debated whether she should save the little cash she had or splurge and try to find a cheap hotel for the evening, a light wind brushed past her.

Mr. M&M's.

He waltzed straight by Miri toward the cabbie. "Can you take me to Manacapuru tonight?" he asked.

The driver glanced at a defeated Miri standing off to the side.

"Sim. Three hundred. Americano."

"Fine." Mr. M&M's handed over the cash and the two of them circled the taxi, with the driver popping the trunk as he got inside. Mr. M&M's dropped his bag into the trunk then lifted his hand, motioning to Miri. "You coming?"

Miri stood straight, then turned both ways to check her surroundings. She placed her hand on her chest. "Are you talking to me?"

"Yes, Pringles. You're heading to Manacapuru, aren't you?"

"Uh-uh. Not that one," the driver called out the window, glaring at her.

"She's with me," Mr. M&M's said, sending a wave of heat over Miri's face. *She's with me.* She liked the sound of that.

"She called my car a filthy hunk of junk."

Mr. M&M's craned his neck to look inside, then turned up his nose. "Well, it *is* filthy." But before the driver could protest again, Mr. M&M's added, "I'll give you an extra hundred."

"What? No, I can't let you do that," Miri called out, but it was too late. Mr. M&M's was already placing more money in the driver's palm out the window, signaling their agreement.

"Call it payment for the M&M's," he said with a sexy smile. "Now, are you coming, or what? Déguédine. The money's been spent no matter if you join me."

Miri's mind raced, creating elaborate scenarios of how this could end, ranging from romance to kidnapping. Wait . . . was this real life? Because only in her fantasies did men like him even notice her. Gorgeous face. Fantastic hair. Long limbs. Large hands. And that accent? Miri pinched the soft webbing between her thumb and index finger to make sure she wasn't dreaming. Nope. Awake. Wide awake.

WWCMD?

Not stand here like a bump on a log, that's for sure.

What *should* she do?

Debate her other options (none). Analyze her chance of failure (eh . . . inconclusive). And finally, trust her gut (which should *probably* not be trusted given the amount of whirling and fluttering going on inside her as she eyed Mr. M&M's in all his handsome glory). No, shouldn't trust the gut when the choices amounted to little more than hot guy versus sleeping in the airport and possibly getting fired.

"I'm in."

CHAPTER

Two

GLOBAL GEOGRAPHY WOULDN'T LOVE LEARNING THAT RAFAEL had splurged on a three-hundred-dollar cab ride, but when he'd texted his boss that he'd missed the bus, he'd told him, "Do what you need to do" to get to Manacapuru. He figured that gave him free rein to spend *GloGeo*'s money as he best saw fit. Spending an extra hundred for some random stranger to tag along, though? Yeah . . . But what was he supposed to have done? Leave her there? By the look of things, her day had been even worse than his. It's what any Good Samaritan would have done and had nothing to do with the fact that he was thoroughly charmed.

Okay, fine. It had everything to do with that.

He hadn't meant to stare when he'd first crouched down to pick up the errant Pringles, but her sapphire eyes entranced him from behind her glasses. And as the playful words gushed out of her mouth like a faucet that couldn't be turned off, clearly not an attempt to impress him, well . . . he'd been downright captivated. Something about her whole nerdy-glasses-and-messy-bun combo was doing it for him.

Not that he was in Brazil looking for romance. But given the unwelcome hellish couple of weeks he was in for on this trip, he deserved a momentary distraction.

"Here." The woman handed over a wad of cash from the pouch underneath her shirt. "I have fifty-two dollars, but I can get you the rest when we get to Manacapuru."

He waved her off. "Seriously, don't worry about it. Consider it an apology."

She tilted her head to the side.

"For the bathroom earlier," he clarified, and her terrified look of mortification flashed through his mind. "Don't worry. I didn't see anything."

Her cheeks flushed. "You promise?"

"Promise. You've got lightning-fast reflexes."

"You didn't see me trying to run down the bus that we both missed," she said, half chuckling, half wincing.

"Was it smooth?"

"Oh, the smoothest." She smiled and ducked her head, pushing a loose strand of her light brown locks behind her ear. "Thank you, by the way. I'm Miriam, or you can call me Miri," she said, extending her hand.

"Rafael. Or you can call me Rafa." His hand enveloped hers and he fought the urge to stare. "American?"

"Is it that obvious?" Her face twisted, and he snickered.

"I can say no if you'd like."

She let out a breath, blowing her bangs up. "What gave it away? Super posh accent? Stylish clothes? General lack of awareness when changing in a public bathroom?"

"Fanny pack." He tried to keep a straight face when he said it, but he couldn't help his lips quirking.

"Hey, this is a money belt, thank you very much," she said as she puffed up her chest and smiled.

"Exactly." That smile was something. The woman was wearing a fanny pack, yet he found her utterly adorable.

"I take it *you* aren't American?"

He shook his head. "Canadian."

Her eyebrows lifted. "Canadian, aye?" It came out more like a pirate than a Canadian.

"Quebecois," he responded, his gaze homing in on her. "Grew up in Montreal, though I live in Washington, DC, now. Avez-vous déjà été?"

"Oh." She clearly had no idea that he'd asked if she'd ever been there, but her hungry eyes shot to his lips, as was customary—and as he intended—whenever he opened his mouth and released his French-Canadian je ne sais quoi. Every. Time. One didn't look and sound like Rafa and not know how it affected women.

Or use it to their advantage from time to time.

"I thought you may have been a local when I first saw you at the airport," she continued.

"First time here. Though my mother was Brazilian."

"Are you here to visit family?"

He paused for a moment, debating how to respond. Stranger or not, no one was supposed to know he was in Brazil, and *especially* not what he was doing there.

The reasons for his travels were to be kept top secret: document a private archaeological expedition in the Amazon to find the lost Cidade da Lua. His employer—top world culture, travel, and exploration magazine *Global Geography*—had learned of the excursion from the team financier, some wealthy businessman named Eugene Larity, who wanted to chronicle this momentous occasion. Or, at least, *potentially* momentous, seeing as dozens of explorers had undertaken this very same quest to no avail. But *GloGeo* had been involved in many great discoveries, and somehow Mr. Larity was familiar with Rafa's work as both a prize-winning journalist and an accomplished photographer.

Too bad he wasn't familiar with the fact that Rafa had recently tried quitting his job.

But this was it. One last mission and then he was done. Or he would be, once he could convince his dad that leaving *GloGeo* to pursue writing novels *wasn't* the career suicide his father made it out to be.

So, fresh off his prior assignment and with less than a week's notice, Rafa had packed his bags, done some rudimentary research on the Moon City, and set off for his next—and hopefully, final—adventure.

Tchau, DC, olá, Brazil.

All that to say, though the chances were slim to none that Miri would A) know what the hell he was talking about or B) care enough to do anything about it, he didn't need her making even a casual reference to her friends and family about the *GloGeo* journalist she'd met who was on his way to the Cidade da Lua.

"Yeah, meeting my uncle and some cousins," he answered before the pause came off as too suspicious. "And, hopefully, exploring a bit of my mother's homeland while I'm here."

Was that believable? Though, honestly, it would be nice to finally get up close and personal with his heritage. He knew so little about the maternal side of his family tree, only the things his father told him, which wasn't much given his parents' whirlwind romance. Many years ago, Rafa had tried tracking down whether he even *had* relatives in Brazil, but, unsurprisingly, ancestry websites weren't all that useful when the only thing he had to go on was his mother's first name: Andressa. No birthplace. No former addresses. Not even a last name, since it seemed she'd used a fake one on his birth certificate.

But now that he was here . . . well, maybe he'd finally be able to get some answers.

"That's awesome," Miri said, interrupting his thoughts. "I always wanted to do that—visit my parents' birthplace."

Phew. He let out a breath, thankful for his convincing delivery. Lying wasn't really his forte, although it would be good to start getting in some practice before the expedition heated up.

"And where would that be?"

"Poulsbo, Washington. I mean, not nearly as sexy as Brazil, but I hear it's beautiful. They met there in the seventh grade and, well, you know how the saying goes."

He quirked his brow.

"*The rest is history,*" she offered. "Sorry, maybe they don't say that in Canada?"

"Yes, we say that in Canada," he said with a chuckle. "So, what's stopping you? From visiting Poulsbo, I mean."

"Oh, you know. The usual. Time. Money. Motivation."

"Yet you're in Brazil? Some would say that's the opposite of the usual." He said it with a smile, but her face instantly fell, and her cheeks blushed.

"I, uh . . . I'm here for work, so that doesn't count."

"What kind of work do you do?"

"Oh . . ." Her eyes shifted. *Hmm.* "I, uh . . . I'm a consultant," she said.

"What kind of consultant?"

"Um . . . I . . ." she murmured, twisting her hands in her lap. "I, uh, am a . . . a backpack consultant."

Backpack consultant? Rafa cocked his head. "Is that an actual job?" he asked.

She snapped, "Yes, it's an actual job." Her eyebrows knit together.

"Sorry, I didn't mean to insult you. I've never heard of a backpack consultant before, is all."

"There are consultants for everything."

He nodded. "I suppose that's true. What does a backpack consultant do?"

"Oh, you know . . ." She raised her head, looking everywhere but at him.

No, clearly he *didn't*.

"We test out backpacks for manufacturers and tell them what works and doesn't work."

"You're going to be backpacking through Brazil?"

"Yep."

"Alone?" The Amazon didn't exactly seem like the most hospitable place for a test run, with its giant green anacondas, red-bellied piranhas, electric eels, and a whole host of poisonous bugs, frogs, and snakes. Not to mention poisonous Amazonian plants and Cannonball trees, dropping giant bowling ball–sized fruit from the sky onto unsuspecting tourists' heads. Traveling in a group expedition was dangerous enough. Rafa didn't want to imagine encountering these dangers alone.

She tilted her head and offered an overly confident smile. "Don't think I can handle myself? Need I remind you of my lightning-fast reflexes?"

He had to hand it to her. She certainly had spunk. "I retract my last question."

Where had this woman come from? Maybe this was a sign.

A sign of what, exactly, he had no clue. But visiting this country had been a pivotal moment in his dad's life. It had been the place he'd found purpose. Found . . . love.

Rafa glanced at Miri, and then he quickly wiped the ridiculous thought away. Was he seriously daydreaming about love four thousand miles away from home and hours before he was scheduled to set foot in the Amazon on an uncharted adventure? He'd only just met this woman. *Arrête d'être niaiseux.*

"Address?" the driver called out, stealing Rafa's attention.

"Here," Rafa said, pulling out his phone and pulling a text up on his screen. "Hotel dos Sonhos."

"Wait," Miri said, placing her hand on Rafa's forearm, sending a pleasant jolt through his body. "That's where I'm staying."

He turned toward Miri. "You're . . . you're staying at the same hotel?"

"Unless there's more than one?"

"Only one," the driver called out.

This is definitely *a sign.*

No . . . no. Rafa waved off the absurdity of it all. He'd taken this job for a reason, and he couldn't disregard it simply because this woman had made him smile half a dozen times in less than thirty minutes. Besides, not to judge a book by its cover, but Miri didn't quite seem like the type who partook in casual rendezvous with strangers. That she could barely look at him without blushing didn't exactly mesh with his usual *meet me in my room in an hour* routine he'd grown accustomed to on the job.

And yet, Rafa had a tough time accepting that the universe put the two of them on the same bus platform, hitching a ride to the same hotel in Brazil, for shits and giggles.

"So . . ." Rafa patted his hand against his thigh, debating his next move. Time slowed to a near standstill. Now what? Would they spend the next hour riding together in silence before she'd eventually thank him for the cab fare? Then would she wish him a nice life and a good visit with his family, to be followed by him spending the next who knows how many weeks in the fucking rainforest, drenched, miserable, with nothing but the memory of her sapphire eyes keeping him warm at night, leaving him to regret passing up the opportunity to spend more time together when it presented itself?

He erased the thought from his mind. That didn't seem right. It didn't need to end with a handshake, even if his job had to take priority and even if she didn't seem like his typical hookup companion. Or maybe . . . maybe he needed to let the universe play its course.

And to quit making assumptions about whether Miri fit some preconceived mold Rafa had concocted. Maybe she was a backpack consultant during the daytime, but a bedroom consultant at night.

Hmm . . .

They sat staring at each other for another few moments as Rafa weighed the pros and cons of his next couple of words.

"I've got this thing tonight, but—" he started as she simultaneously said, "Did you know the Amazon is home to—"

They paused. *Fuck.* Guess he'd read that wrong. "You go," he said.

"No, you first. I insist."

Aside from an awkward taxi ride, what did he have to lose?

"I was going to say, I've got a thing I have to go to this evening, but I was wondering if maybe you wanted to grab a drink afterward? What were you going to say?"

"I . . . I . . ."

Rafa's body tensed at her hesitation. What . . . *was* this sensation? He'd never been nervous around women. On the rare occasion that a woman passed on his advances, it never bothered him. And he certainly didn't get anxious when he awaited a reply.

"I was going to ask if you knew the Amazon is home to some amazing bars and if you'd like to get a drink this evening?"

He exhaled internally. "No, you weren't," he said, smiling at her. But cute that she'd tried.

"You're right." She smiled back. "Technically, I was going to ask if you knew the Amazon is home to two point five million insect species. But I'd . . . I'd like to get a drink . . ." She blushed. "Unless after this car ride you decide you can't handle all this awesomeness. And by awesomeness, I mean, this," she said, motioning her hands over her fanny pack like Vanna White on *Wheel of Fortune*.

Rafa burst out laughing, garnering a raised eyebrow from the driver in the rearview mirror. *Mind your business.*

"I'm *only* coming if you wear that, Pringles. And bring your snack bar."

"Well, you're in luck, my Quebecois-nian friend. This thing doubles as a snack pouch."

He bowed his head to partially conceal his smile.

"Sounds great."

He may be there for work, but he could still have a little fun after the team meeting. Who knew how long it would be before he had another chance to let his hair down, so to speak?

But after that, he'd focus. Because Rafa was here for one purpose and one purpose only—to sabotage any attempts Mr. Larity's archaeological team had at finding the Lost City of the Moon.

Three

THERE WAS A SURPRISING AMOUNT OF SECURITY DETAIL FOR this expedition.

ID check. Pat-down. Password. Why not include a secret handshake while they were at it?

A lady with a clipboard checked Rafa's name off a list after confirming his details in a folder marked "R. Monfils," then handed him a name tag. "Write your full name, job title, and where you're from."

Name tags? Seemed a little more mixer and less top-secret archaeological expedition, but he wasn't there to argue, so he filled out the white sticky tag and slapped it on his chest:

Name: Rafael Monfils
Occupation: Journalist/Photographer
Institution: *Global Geography*

He glanced around at the others' name tags: archaeologists, field crew, archaeological technicians, historians, equipment techs—all from various universities and museums from around the world. He was the only person not associated with some sort of archaeological institution, which wasn't unusual in his several years of experience working at *GloGeo*, though usually he wasn't the one writing the story *and* taking pictures. Clearly, they wanted to keep their numbers down. More people meant more rumors. Rafa took good photos, but he certainly wasn't as skilled as the photographers usually hired for these things. And he'd never documented an entire expedition from start to hopefully (or rather, unhopefully) finish. He was in it for the long haul, though. This excursion could take weeks, or it could take months.

There were at least another dozen people on the hotel roof deck, minus the staff setting up the dinner buffet. He overheard the clipboard lady (ANISSA DAVIES, PROJECT COORDINATOR, ARCHAEOLOGICAL INSTITUTE OF AMERICA) telling the staff that once the crew sat to eat, all hotel personnel would need to leave. Guess they were serious about this whole secrecy thing.

The rooftop was set up with a few tables facing a rolling cart in the front with a laptop and a pull-down screen alongside it. *Great*, he thought, grumbling to himself. Sure, a presentation would be helpful and all, but he hoped this meeting didn't take too long, so he could still make it on time to meet Miri in the hotel bar later. He didn't quite know what to make of this supposed backpack consultant, but he couldn't remember the last time he'd smiled so much from talking to a woman.

He shook his head to himself. God, he couldn't believe he'd whipped out the Quebecois on Miri. He'd have to apologize later for coming off like a smarmy prick.

"*Global Geography*, huh?"

A voice pulled Rafa's attention. He turned to face its source;

an early-fortysomthing guy dressed like Crocodile Dundee, hat and all. This guy couldn't be serious. Weren't people over the whole archaeological cosplay thing by now?

Name: Dr. Bradley Quinn
Occupation: Archaeologist, PhD, and Professor of
    Archaeology
Institution: Joukowsky Institute for Archaeology and the
Ancient World at Brown University

A tad overkill, don't you think, Dr. Quinn? Rafa tried not to make snap judgments, but the *dinosaur*-tooth necklace—on an archaeologist, no less—didn't bode well.

"Hi, yes, Rafa Monfils," he said, extending his hand.

"Dr. Bradley Quinn. Archaeologist."

Yeah, buddy, we got it.

"Where's the rest of your crew?" Bradley asked, scanning around the rooftop.

"You're looking at it."

Bradley froze and furrowed his brow at Rafa. "No cameraman? I was hoping to talk to him about some shots I'd like to get of the expedition."

Rafa rolled his eyes internally. "I'll be doing all the camera-*person* work." He swung around the camera bag slung over his shoulder to show him. And Rafa didn't take direction from his subjects. "Are you the project lead?"

Bradley stood taller as the start of a smile formed in the corners of his mouth. "Actually . . ." He paused as if realizing he was about to say something he shouldn't before continuing, "I have a good eye for this sort of thing, that's all."

And Rafa *especially* didn't take direction from try-hard

nobodies like Bradley. If the project lead had a special request, Rafa might try to accommodate it so long as it didn't look staged, but not for this guy.

"Good thing I've got an eye for it, too. I'll let you know if I ever need help."

In other words, *never.*

Bradley's eyes narrowed at him. Probably not the best idea to make enemies right away, but Rafa also didn't care to launch this job with Dr. Quinn here setting unrealistic expectations. Things usually worked out better when Rafa didn't tell people how to do their jobs and vice versa. Because, guaranteed, Rafa knew way more about photography than *Brad* the archaeologist.

"All right, everyone," Anissa announced loudly. "Please grab a plate and then take your seats so we can get started."

"Later," Rafa said, slapping his hand against Brad's arm and heading over to the buffet.

The group formed two lines, one on either side of the buffet table, loading their plates with delicious local fare. Rafa was famished, having eaten nothing except a packet of airline snack mix on the plane in the last several hours—he was saving Miri's M&M's for an emergency. Or maybe for sharing with her later.

He piled up his plate, focused on the food in front of him and ignoring all the chatter of the team and their clattering plates as they worked their way down the line. Potatoes, skewers of meat, empanadas, rice alongside some dark, thick sauce . . . he wanted it all, despite already sensing the meat sweats coming on. But he needed to set a solid base if he was going to be getting drinks with Miri. Last thing he needed was to get hammered on an almost empty stomach.

"Jeez, Miriam. Take a little longer, would ya?" a man's voice called out.

Miriam?

Rafa glanced up and found himself staring at the woman who seconds earlier had invaded his thoughts. Freshly showered, with her wet hair pinned in the back of her head, she wore a dark blue T-shirt that matched the color of the bra he'd lied about not having seen. And held a plate of food that rivaled his own. She made a face at the person beside her—Brad, of course—took a ladle of the brown sauce, and brought it over to her plate.

"Miri?" Rafa spoke.

She looked up and froze upon seeing him. "Rafa?" Her hand slowly turned, pouring the contents of the ladle onto the floor and missing her plate entirely.

"Watch what you're doing!" Brad cried out, and Miri quickly returned the ladle to the metal catering pan as several others handed her napkins to help clean up. The flurry stole her gaze from him, but not without one last questioning glance.

Well, that explained things.

With Miri sufficiently distracted, Rafa moved through the rest of the buffet, his appetite suddenly diminished, and he found a spot at one of the tables. His eyes stayed on Miri the entire time, hoping she'd finish quickly and snag one of the other three seats at his table, but no such luck. Others took the seats before she had the chance, and she eventually took the last open spot on the opposite side of the rooftop—directly in his line of vision. The conversation around him continued as if he wasn't there. However, while he kept his gaze on her, trying to get her attention, her eyes shifted everywhere *but* in his direction.

She was avoiding him. So that was how this was going to be?

"Where are Dr. Mejía and Dr. Matthews? I thought they

were leading this expedition?" The others at the table carried on, but Rafa couldn't care less.

"Maybe they're already out scouting in the field?"

"I can't wait to meet them. Did you see their interview on *Good Morning America* last month?"

"They're so cool."

"Hey, you gonna eat that?"

A light tap on Rafa's forearm tore his gaze from Miri. "What?"

"I asked if you're going to eat that?" a slender, youngish Black man asked, pointing to one of the empanadas on Rafa's plate. "They ran out, but they're sooo good."

"It's all yours," Rafa said, pushing his plate over to the man.

"Thanks, man. I'm Felix."

Rafa glanced at his name tag:

Name: Felix Richardson
Occupation: Equipment Tech
Institution: Field Museum, Chicago, IL

"Rafa."

"You know anyone else here?" He chomped into the empanada, staring at Rafa and waiting for an answer.

Rafa glanced in Miri's direction, this time catching her staring back at him before she quickly looked away. "Not really. You?"

"Nah. Though my boss back at the Field Museum is friends with the leads, Dr. Mejía and Dr. Matthews. He talks about them all the time. Can't believe I'm going to get to work with them. It's going to be fucking sweet."

Rafa hadn't been given the names of the project leads in advance, otherwise maybe he would have looked them up when he'd been researching the Moon City. Now he regretted not insisting on more details from his boss when he'd practically pushed him out the door on this job. Everyone was talking about Drs. Mejía and Matthews like they were a couple of celebrities.

"What's the deal with those two?" Rafa asked.

Felix cleared his throat. "They're, like, the most famous archaeologists in the world right now. Did you hear about that dig gone to shit down in Mexico about a year and a half ago? It was all over the news. With the smugglers and the ancient remains of that Aztec warrior?"

Come to think of it, Rafa did remember hearing about it. He'd been on assignment at the time in northern Nova Scotia, so he hadn't gotten deep into the press, but he recalled thinking it sounded pretty wild.

"Yeah, that was them. And Dr. Mejía is a total babe," the other guy said.

Rafa raised an eyebrow.

"Real professional," Rafa said, wrinkling his forehead. The man's face turned bright red. If he was looking for others to engage in locker room banter, Rafa wouldn't be one of them.

"Everyone, everyone," Anissa said from the front table. "I know you are all ready to hear more about the assignment from the project leaders. They aren't here at the moment, but they've sent a recording that I'm going to play for you now."

Rafa glanced over at Miri, catching her gaze for a fraction of a second. His cocked head and lifted brow asked the words his lips could not: *Are we pretending like we've never seen each other before?* But her expression gave no answer.

Her eyes fixed to the screen along with everyone else's, determined not to give him any clues, and he sighed internally. Guess he should probably pay attention, too.

"Good evening, team. I'm Dr. Socorro Mejía and this is my partner, Dr. Ford Matthews . . ."

Hmm. A rather attractive duo stared at them from the video, and now Rafa understood everyone's obsession—Dr. Mejía *was* hot. Smokin' hot. And he wasn't embarrassed to admit it, but Dr. Matthews was pretty fucking good-looking, too.

But *Rafa's* mind was still focused on a certain pair of sapphire eyes.

"You're probably wondering where we are, and we'll get to that shortly. But first, we want to explain a bit more about why you are here," Dr. Mejía continued. "The twelve of you have been selected to comprise an expedition team to search for the Cidade Perdida da Lua—the Lost City of the Moon."

A few hushed murmurs carried among the group. Interesting. Guess not everyone knew about the assignment in advance.

"We assume everyone has at least heard of the Cidade da Lua, but in case you haven't, here is a primer," Dr. Matthews said. "For centuries, explorers all over the world have searched for this fabled ancient land. No one knows its exact location, but according to the stories, the Moon City is located somewhere in the Amazon. Legend says that the city glistens under moonlight.

"The earliest accounts of the Moon City date back to the early fifteen hundreds. It was a city full of riches—precious metals, gemstones, ceramics, and textiles. The people who lived there flourished in the mid-to-late fifteen hundreds but abandoned the city without reason or explanation and fled to nearby lands. Possibly descendants of the Inca, or even the ancestors of the Yanomami or Kayapo. No one knows—"

"Because," Dr. Mejía cut in, "no one truly knows whether the Moon City existed. We want to be clear: this expedition could end up a bust . . ."

Yeah, especially if Rafa was able to succeed. He'd heard these stories, too, from his father. *You must protect it, son. You must protect the Cidade da Lua and your mother's legacy.*

His father's voice echoed in his head, warning him of the desecration of the holy city if the Western world got its hands on it. The city had been abandoned for a reason—to protect its riches from the invasion of the Spaniards. To protect it from people like Mr. Larity, Dr. Mejía, and Dr. Matthews. He couldn't let them destroy it. But more importantly, he couldn't let his father down.

It had always been only the two of them. Rafa and his dad. His father had shared his fascination with archaeology and his penchant for world travel with Rafa at an early age, even pulling strings and getting him the job at *Global Geography*, a dream job by any journalist's standards.

He'd been to more than one hundred countries. Seen the Seven Wonders of the World. Some more than once. Marveled at the earth's beauty. Almost cried the first time he watched the sunset in Hạ Long Bay, Vietnam. And for years, it seemed he'd hit the career lottery. Who *wouldn't* want to do all these amazing things?

But as Rafa's frequent-flyer status ticked up, his enthusiasm for being a world traveler slowly ticked down. For every country he'd visited, he'd had to miss a friend's party. For each expedition he'd gone on, he'd had to cancel a date. He lived out of suitcases and subsisted on microwave dinners and takeout on the rare occasion he was off-assignment. When it was all said and done, the only person he ever had to come home to was his father. And even then, with all his father's philanthropy endeavors and various boards and committees, half the time when Rafa came home, he didn't even have *him*.

Rafa was tired. Tired of traveling. Tired of returning to an empty apartment, sometimes only for a few days at a time. The occupation that once invigorated him now made him restless. He wanted *a life*. Friends to make plans with. Possibly a woman he could take out more than a couple of times before he'd disappear again for weeks or months on end. A job he got on his own, and not because his dad was on the board. Even if it meant starting over.

His resignation wasn't supposed to have been countered with a call from his boss to his father, and, from his father, a special request:

Rafael, it's time you knew the truth about your ancestry. Os protetores da lua have been protecting the Cidade da Lua since it was abandoned hundreds of years ago. They are the only people who are said to know the true location of the city. But they are everywhere. Living normal lives. Out in the world, listening. Watching. Waiting for the next explorer to set their sights on the Moon City. And your mother . . . she one of them.

I'm counting on you. You must save it from these treasure hunters. For your mother.

Finally, a chance to discover who he really was.

"Now, as to our whereabouts," Dr. Mejía continued, focusing Rafa's attention back to the screen. "We had every intention of being there, guiding you through the Amazon rainforest—"

"And darting from black caimans and electric eels," Dr. Matthews said, giving a loving glance to Dr. Mejía as she playfully elbowed him in the ribs, causing him to wince.

"But . . ." The camera panned out, revealing Dr. Matthews's arm in a cast. "Ford had to go and get himself injured yesterday. Seriously, only Ford could manage to topple off a three-foot-high retaining wall and break his arm mowing the lawn," Dr. Mejía said with a good-natured eye roll.

"Hey, it was my first time," he teased back.

Hmm . . . how was this going to work?

"You're probably wondering, how is this going to work?" Dr. Mejía said.

Mind readers. Maybe they *were* superstars.

"Given the demands of an expedition in the Amazon," Dr. Matthews said, "we didn't think it was prudent for me to accompany this search."

"And seeing as Ford is a walking catastrophe right now—"

"Catastrophe?" he said, making a face at her.

"Babe, you stubbed your toe getting out of bed this morning."

A few snickers carried through the group.

"Fair," he said.

"As I was saying," Dr. Mejía continued, "this is where I need to be right now. Where we *both* need to be."

They stared at each other with affection. Rafa had never had someone look at him that way.

"Fortunately, the team we curated is brimming with talent," Dr. Mejía said. "And we've selected our replacements from the lot of you. Allow me to introduce Dr. Bradley Quinn . . ."

Rafa fought to keep his eyes from rolling as *Brad* stood and gave himself a couple pats on the back—literally—completely taking the spotlight from the video still playing with Dr. Matthews explaining Brad's qualifications and background. Rafa folded his arms. Lead or not, Rafa still had no intention of taking direction from Brad.

"But while Dr. Quinn would probably make a fine lead on his own, every good archaeologist needs a partner. Someone to bounce ideas off—" Dr. Matthews said.

Brad's shoulders deflated, sending a satisfied grin across Rafa's face.

"And to check them when they are wrong," Dr. Mejía said,

nudging Dr. Matthews in the side. "We also want to introduce Dr. Miriam Jacobs, doctor of archaeology and my colleague from UC Berkeley."

Everyone's eyes shot toward Miri as her's grew to the size of oranges. Whereas Brad's reaction evidenced that he must have been forewarned about this sudden change of events, Miri sat frozen in her chair. No, this wasn't planned. And by the look of things, her sudden promotion perhaps wasn't a welcome one— not for Miri, nor for Dr. Brad.

Brad's gaze narrowed at Miri. But Miri didn't seem to notice. Her eyes shifted from face to face, then to her surroundings, as if she were looking for an escape route. She didn't want this. No . . . that nervous, quirky chatterbox Rafa had spent an hour and a half with in the car wanted no part of this.

And when her eyes finally connected with his, he saw the fear in them. Fear that she wasn't ready for this responsibility.

It killed him that he'd have to prove her right.

HE'S NOT GOING TO COME.

Miri twirled her gin and tonic in her hands, wiping the condensation down the glass. Could this day get any worse? Muddy bus splatter. Flashing a hottie. Nervous oversharing. Finding out the hottie she'd flashed, overshared with, and *lied* to was somehow a participant on this expedition, while pouring a cup of brown goo all over her hiking boots. *God, those are gonna* reek *in a few days.* That was all pretty bad. Then, getting completely ambushed by Corrie into being a co-lead on this excursion?

And now getting stood up? She had to be breaking records on terrible, horrible, no good, very bad days here.

Even taking the whole Moon City expedition out of the equation, the fact that Rafa had asked to meet for a drink in the first place was still mind-boggling. *He*, someone who by the look of things must succeed in the dating department, had asked *her*, someone whose dating prowess could be summed up as *went on numerous impressively bad dates—several years ago—and not a single one since.* Though . . . *was* it a date? Officially? Maybe Rafa'd been asking out of politeness, seeing as they were staying in the same hotel and all.

Miri closed her eyes and shuddered. *Riiiiiiight. That makes more sense.* A pity invite.

One thing was certain: he hadn't bothered confirming their "date" before departing the team meeting. Not that she could blame him. She'd barely looked at him throughout that entire disaster of a dinner, unwilling to acknowledge that they knew each other. After avoiding Rafa for the evening, of course he wouldn't think she'd show. No, he'd flown out of there like a bat out of the Amazon—much like Miri *wished* she could do.

The barstool next to her scooted out, and Miri's heart kicked up a notch—only to realize it *wasn't* Rafa.

"Hey, Anissa," she said, dejected.

"Ouch. Nice to see you, too," Anissa said, taking the seat next to her.

"Sorry, I was just . . ." *Getting stood up?* "Never mind." It was too embarrassing to say it out loud.

"Well, don't worry. I'm not staying. The minibar in my room wasn't stocked, so I'm grabbing a couple provisions." Anissa waved down the bartender and placed her order—a few bottles of red and a bottle of cachaça. "I'm stocking up for later," she clarified.

Miri smiled and shrugged. "Hey, I don't judge."

"And this is why we are friends," Anissa said, stealing a sip from Miri's drink while she waited. "Drowning your sorrows?"

"What do you mean?"

"Corrie's announcement? You looked a bit deer-in-the-headlights up there."

"Oh . . . that." Sigh. Was it that obvious? "Yes, I mean, no.

Deer in the headlights, yes. Drowning my sorrows? Not exactly." Not how Anissa intended the question, at least.

"So you're excited, then?" Anissa said. "Personally, I think it's awesome. You've always wanted to lead an expedition." She snacked on a couple of cocktail peanuts sitting in a dish on the bar like it was no big deal.

Because, yeah, leading—co-leading—an expedition to a *lost city* was nothing. Not when you'd never even led an excursion into a metropark, let alone the freaking Amazon rainforest.

Miri wasn't ready for this responsibility. She'd never been the lead on a dig—or *any* job for that matter. Even her invitation for this assignment was a result of being Corrie's mentee. And now Corrie was throwing her to the wolves—Dr. Bradley Quinn.

She'd heard plenty of things about Dr. Quinn. *Assertive. Skilled. Genius.*

In other words, the opposite of Miri. How was she supposed to get her voice heard over Dr. Quinn's? Miri was no Corrie Mejía.

She dropped a cocktail peanut down her shirt, and it skated right by her B cups—okay, *okay*, A cups—and straight through to the floor.

Yeah . . . she was *nothing* like Corrie Mejía.

"Yeah, no, it's great," Miri said. Unconvincingly, by the skeptical look on Anissa's face.

"Miri, we've known each other for, what? Seven years? I can tell when you're bullshitting me."

"I'm not bullshitting! Seriously. I'm genuinely excited!" Miri proclaimed with every ounce of bubbly energy she could muster. "See? I'm celebrating." She lifted her glass and took another sip. "Mm-mm. So pumped."

Anissa laughed. "You are *such* a bad liar."

Miri's shoulders sank. "Fine. I was waiting for someone, but it looks like I got stood up." She twirled the glass in her hands again.

A devilish smile formed on Anissa's face. "Ooooh, girl! Now *that's* what I'm talking about! Are you getting your freak on before we hole up in the jungle?" Anissa stuck out her tongue and waggled her brow.

But like she'd said—they'd known each other for seven years. Anissa should know by now that Miri did *not* get her freak on. Not now. And certainly not in the time they'd been friends.

"Ah, yes, because you know me. So much freaking happening."

"Gah!" Anissa said, excitedly yanking on Miri's arm. "It's about time! My girl's finally gonna pop her cherry."

"I'm not a virgin, Anissa," Miri said, tipping her head down and folding her arms.

Anissa pursed her lips and raised her brow. "Could have fooled me."

Miri would have protested had Anissa not already been well aware that Miri suffered from a chronic case of no-date-itis.

"So when did you have time to meet this mystery man?" Anissa continued. "Didn't you just get here this afternoon?"

"I met him at the airport."

Simple. Truthful. That's all she needed to say.

"And he ended up in Manacapuru, too?" Anissa cocked her head to the side.

"Yeah, well, it doesn't matter, because clearly he's not going to—" Movement caught her attention in the mirror behind the bar. Rafa. "You came," she said into the reflection and not to Rafa walking up behind her.

"So did you." He pulled out the stool to the other side of her, opposite Anissa, whose lips pulled in a tight line, clearly *dying* to say something, and he motioned for the bartender as Miri's heart rate increased. She stared at his strong profile, accentuated by the soft hue of the red lights overhead. Thank God for this lighting and its ability to mask her blushing, because seeing him up close again sent a fire roaring over her skin. *Especially* with the cat-ate-the-canary look Anissa was tossing her way.

Anissa shifted her eyes back and forth between the two of them, anticipating Miri's acknowledgment that *he* was the one she was waiting for. Thankfully, their seven-year friendship also afforded them the ability to speak with eyebrows only, and Miri used hers to signal, *yes, now please get the hell out of here.*

The bartender came over with Anissa's order to go, then turned to Rafa.

"I'll have what she's having," he said, gesturing toward Miri. The bartender gave a quick nod, then walked away to prepare the drink.

"And *I'll* take this as my cue to leave. Have fun, you two," Anissa said, barely able to keep that goofy-ass grin off her face.

Just as Anissa turned away, Miri addressed her one last time by eyebrows—*I'm going to kill you.*

Anissa simply blew her a kiss, then whisked off toward the hotel lobby. Leaving Miri and Rafa in awkward silence.

"I thought you weren't coming," Miri said once Anissa had gone.

"And I half expected you to be on a plane back to the States right now," Rafa responded.

She winced.

"Can we not talk about that?" she asked.

"You mean not now, or never?"

"Give me a few minutes at least."

The bartender slid a drink in front of Rafa and he picked it up, raising it to Miri. "All right. Shall we drink to something, then?"

She picked up her glass. "To fanny packers anonymous."

He wryly chuckled. "To fanny packers anonymous."

They toasted and took sips in unison. Awkward silence then settled between them. So many questions swirled through her head. Questions about who he was. Questions about who *she* was, as if he held the answers. Questions about what they were doing there. In the bar, that was. On a . . . date?

"I take it you're not actually a backpack consultant?" He broke the ice with a smile, instantly calming Miri's nerves.

Miri laughed and ducked her head. "Oh jeez, was that a ridiculous response or what?"

"You had me convinced for a minute there. Who knows? It might be a real job. *Someone's* got to test out backpacks, right?"

Miri put her hand on his arm, which sent a jolt through her body. "See? I'm right, aren't I? It *has* to be a real job."

"But not *your* job." He tipped his head to her with a knowing look in his eye.

"Correct. Not *my* job. So then . . . should I assume you're not here meeting your uncle and cousins?"

"Also correct. Although, my mother was Brazilian, so that part was true."

"What is it that you do? What is it that you're going to be doing on the expedition, I mean?" She leaned forward and propped up her head with her arm resting on the bar.

"I'm a journalist for *Global Geography*. I'm supposed to document this expedition from start to finish."

"And when we met, had you already learned what you'd signed up for? For the"—she leaned in and brought her voice to a whisper—"search for the Lost City of the Moon?"

He took another sip. "Yes, I knew. But I was told not to tell a soul."

"Same. Though I had no idea that I'd—" His eyebrow quirked, and she paused. No. She didn't want to talk about that. Not yet. "I'm sorry I lied to you."

"You don't need to apologize. We were in the same boat. And if it makes you feel better, I didn't *want* to lie to you."

Warmth washed over her cheeks. "I didn't want to lie to you, either."

"Well, at least we're not a couple of dirtbags, then, who get off on lying to other people."

"Unless *that's* a lie, too," she said.

He smirked. "Fair point. Okay . . . ask me anything and I promise to tell the truth."

"How will I know if you're lying?"

Rafa shifted in his seat, like he was suddenly uncomfortable. "You won't. You'll have to use your intuition."

Miri laughed to herself. Her intuition? *Ha.* Her intuition hadn't thought he'd show.

Though she *had* sensed something wasn't quite right when he'd said he was in Brazil visiting family after that long pause in the taxi.

"All right. How long have you worked for *Global Geography*?"

"Seven years."

"Have you ever been on an expedition like this before?"

"Exactly like this? No. But I've been assigned to plenty of unusual and somewhat secretive jobs."

"Such as?"

"Let's see . . ." he said, looking up to recall and keeping count on his fingers. "An ivory-poaching story in Africa. A climate change piece down in the Antarctic. A prehistoric settlement discovered in northern Europe."

"Where were you born?"

He looked at her. "São Paulo."

"But you live in the States?"

"Yes."

"Are you really French-Canadian?"

This time he paused for a moment to take a sip. "Oui," he said.

"Say something else in French so I know."

"Do you understand French?"

"No. But I think I'll be able to tell."

"Okay," he said, moving closer and never taking his eyes off her. "J'aimerais pouvoir vous emmener dans ma chambre."

She hadn't the slightest clue what he'd said, but it didn't matter. Hearing the words roll off his lips sent a tingling sensation down to her core. *Get a grip, Miri.* Oh, but she'd gotten a grip all right. She clenched her thighs as if holding the wooden stool beneath her together with the tension in her legs. She pictured those soft, luscious lips next to her ear, whispering French words like *oui*, *bonjour*, and *croissant* against her lobe before traveling down her neck with soft wet kisses. And his large, strong hands grabbing hold of her ass, pulling her pelvis toward him. And her hips rolling against his abdomen because, dang, this man is tall. And his fingers trailing up the back of her shirt, twisting the clasp of her . . .

Plain, boring, navy T-shirt bra. Her gaze had fallen to his hands before she snapped back to him as she regained focus.

"Did you lie when you said you didn't see anything when you walked in on me in the bathroom?" she asked.

He brought his hand in a fist to his mouth as he choked on a sip of his drink and cleared his throat. "Yes."

She gulped and forced herself not to stare at his entrancing lips any longer.

"And what did you see?"

"I saw exactly what you think I saw." She gulped again. "Now . . . let me ask you a few questions."

She bit her lower lip as he stared intently at her. "Okay." Her heart pounded. *Please don't ask what's happening in my panties.*

"How long have you been an archaeologist?"

She let out a breath. "Four years."

"And are you still not ready to talk about what happened tonight?"

Maybe asking about her panties wouldn't have been so bad after all. But if they were going to be stuck together for the next few weeks, she needed to get comfortable around him.

"I suppose we might as well."

"I take it you didn't know you'd be assigned lead?"

"Nope."

"How do you think that happened?"

"Dr. Mejía—she's my mentor. I think she's trying to help me build my résumé. Give me opportunities that she didn't have."

"And does that frighten you?"

"It terrifies me."

"More than seeing me across the buffet table?" His eyes homed in on her, kicking up the temperature a few thousand degrees. *Not wasting any time poking the elephant in the room, I see.*

"That didn't terrify me."

"Oh yeah? Then what was that reaction?" His finger glided along the rim of his glass.

Was he analyzing her or flirting? She'd had so few experiences flirting in recent years that she honestly couldn't tell the difference.

"Oh, you mean the slop on the shoes? That's my usual *oh hey, good to see you again* move." She smiled, and he flashed one in return, shaking his head at her comment. "I'm sorry . . . I say weird things when I get nervous."

"I quite enjoy your quirky quips. Besides, what's there to be nervous about?"

"You know."

He stared at her, signaling that, no, he didn't know. Or at least he was good at playing coy. She paused, waiting to see if he would respond before asking, "I mean . . . what are we doing here, exactly?"

Rafa lifted his drink and twirled the glass in the air. "Appears we're having a couple gin and tonics."

She rolled her eyes with a playful smile. "You know that's not what I mean. What did you *think* was going to happen when you invited me out for drinks earlier?" Her heart pounded in her chest at her forwardness. But she had to know.

"Well, I thought we'd be having caipirinhas, since we're in Brazil." His lips turned up in the corner.

"Now you're teasing me," she said, turning away from him.

"No, I'm trying to make you laugh. Trying to soften the *terrifying* blow you received this evening. You've got nothing to be worried about. Dr. Mejía said it herself—there's a decent chance this entire expedition ends up a bust. No one is going to blame you if you don't succeed."

"Wow, you're great at pep talks. You should be a motivational speaker. 'Don't worry . . . you'll probably fail, but that's okay. Gold stars for everyone!'" she said in a voice that sounded more used-car-salesperson than motivational speaker.

"Hey, don't knock it. I could get paid big bucks with a speech like that. And then I could afford all the fanny pack snacks in the world."

"I told you, it's a money belt."

"Sure it is." He smiled, popping a couple of cocktail peanuts into his mouth.

She couldn't help but smile in return. "Well, thank you. If you were trying to ease my nerves, then you've succeeded. Partially."

"Anytime, Pringles."

"Am I ever going to live that one down?" she asked with a smile, finally turning back toward him.

"Nope."

She dipped her head to hide her ridiculously wide grin. Aside from the shortened name *Miri*, she'd never had a nickname or a pet name. *Pringles* wasn't exactly flattering, but she quite liked it, even if she'd never admit it aloud.

"What do you know about the Cidade da Lua?" he asked, pulling her out of her thoughts.

Miri leaned back in her chair and looked up. "Oh . . . let's see. I mean, I suppose the same things everyone knows—lost ancient civilization that disappeared without a trace. Supposedly the structures glimmer under moonlight. The people who lived there weren't part of any other tribe or group. They managed to keep to themselves and avoid conflict with other people living in the Amazon and surrounding areas during that time. The rumor is that it's because the Moon City peoples would trade their abundant riches to avoid any kerfuffle. But those riches were eventually their downfall."

"How so?"

"Others wanted their gold and gemstones and tried to find

ways to infiltrate the city, following its people home if they were ever spotted. Legend has it that slowly the people of the Moon City stopped returning to avoid detection, ultimately resulting in its abandonment."

"Seems pretty extreme, don't you think?" he asked.

"To us, sure. But to them, they felt their home needed to be protected. They say there are people still protecting it to this day: os protetores da lua."

Rafa shifted in his seat when she said those words, his discomfort palpable.

"Have you heard of them?" she asked.

"No, I don't think so," he said, turning and watching her intently.

She smiled at his apparent interest in the topic. This. This was one of Miri's favorite parts of her job. Hypothesizing with others about ancient worlds and civilizations. Talking about the people who lived there and how to honor and respect their traditions. So often Miri was left out of these conversations. Few of her colleagues ever sought her opinion.

"Oh, well, they think they're the descendants of the people from the Moon City," she said, excitedly. "From generation to generation, they've passed down the city's secrets. Posing as tour guides and throwing unsuspecting explorers off its scent whenever they get too close—"

"Sounds like some secret grail society nonsense straight out of *Indiana Jones and the Last Crusade*, if you ask me," Dr. Quinn said, interrupting their conversation and sending a wave of nausea mixed with annoyance over Miri's body.

Perfect. Just what she needed. Not that she necessarily *wanted* to be a lead on this expedition, co-lead or otherwise, but it probably didn't look good that instead of studying up on the

Lost City of the Moon, she was out getting drinks with the hot photojournalist.

"I was hoping to find you," Dr. Quinn continued, sidling up not to Miri, but to Rafa.

"We're in the middle of something," Rafa responded, earning an internal fist pump from Miri.

"This is *work* related. I'm sure Miriam won't mind the interruption."

Miri gritted her teeth.

"Well, we were *also* talking about work, so if it's work related, then why don't we all have a seat?" Miri asked.

"Oh, I wouldn't want to bore you," Dr. Quinn said. "I want to ask him about cameras and lenses."

"I mean, that might be interesting."

"Picked up a photography hobby in your free time?" Dr. Quinn asked.

"Does an iPhone count?"

Dr. Quinn narrowed his gaze and gave her a disapproving glance. "Let's see what you've got, then," he said, motioning toward her phone sitting face down on the bar top.

"Oh, well, I . . ." she said, picking up her phone and opening the photo app, trying to remember the last couple of things she took pictures of. "Um . . . let's see."

She scrolled through the photos with Dr. Quinn craning his neck over her shoulder to see. The most recent was a photo of the brown sauce on her boots.

"Very artsy," Dr. Quinn said.

Miri made a face he couldn't see, then moved to the next pics. One of a pretty—yet blurry—bird sitting on the wrought-iron railing on the balcony of her hotel room. Another of the folded towel swan on her bed. Then a pretend selfie of her in hotel elevator mirror that was really a ploy to capture Rafa at the lobby desk in the background before the doors closed.

She tensed, realizing Rafa could see her phone, too. She glanced at him, and he smiled—*shit*—then she quickly closed out of her phone before jumping from her chair. "You know, I just remembered, I told my parents I'd call when I got here. I'd better get going."

"You really don't need to go," Rafa said, also lifting from his seat, but she motioned him back down.

"No, no, it's fine," she said as Dr. Quinn was already settling into her seat and ordering *a glass of your finest red wine—but nothing over fifty Brazilian real.* "I was going to head to my room to do some research anyway. Prepare for tomorrow, you know? Besides, I've got some Pringles calling my name."

Rafa's eyes pleaded for her to stay, but she knew what she had to do. If she was going to be taken seriously and ever come close to being a badass like Dr. Mejía, she needed to stop playing fantasy with Rafa.

That's all it would ever be anyway, right? A fantasy? Sure, they seemed to hit it off like a real rom-com, but instead of the leading lady, Miri would inevitably play the role of the dorky best friend and *not* the one who'd get the hot guy. And she had the experience to back up that theory. Like when she'd thought she and her high school chemistry lab partner, star quarterback and homecoming king Bobby McMillan, had *a connection* but the only connection they actually had was the correlation between their extra study sessions and the boost in his GPA.

Surely with Rafa she'd misinterpret one of his gestures and wind up with her eyes closed and lips puckered, kissing nothing but air. She'd open her eyes and he'd be staring at her with a pitying look and say, *Miri, I think you've got the wrong idea.* And then they'd spend the next several weeks engaging in awkward small talk, all while pretending it never happened.

Things were better when Miri didn't let her crushes crush her.

Besides, now that they were working together and now that she was lead, she needed to focus on more important things. Like figuring out what the hell she was doing.

She flashed Rafa an apologetic smile before saying her goodnights and heading up to her room. Time to concentrate. Formulate a game plan she could run by Dr. Quinn. And hopefully get a good night's sleep.

"Senhorita," the hotel desk clerk called out as Miri crossed the lobby approaching the stairs. "Something arrived for you this evening."

"Me?"

The clerk nodded, then turned toward the wall of wooden mail slots, pulling out a large rigid envelope and handing it over the counter. The envelope was marked "RUSH DELIVERY" and it was addressed to her, with the return label to Dr. Corrie Mejía in New Haven, Connecticut.

She thanked the clerk, then trudged up the two flights to her room, curious about what Corrie had sent her. Once in the privacy of her room, Miri plopped on her bed and tore open the envelope. Inside was another manila envelope with CONFIDEN-TIAL: *For Dr. Miriam Jacobs's eyes only* in Corrie's handwriting. The envelope had some bulk to it.

Miri glanced around her room as if she was being spied on, then got up to close the curtains before settling back onto the bed and ripping open the second envelope, revealing a hand-

written letter and a small roundish object wrapped in a piece of
burlap and tied with string. She held the object, judging its heft
using her hands like a scale, before setting it on the bed and
unfolding the letter:

Miri—

*I'm sorry. I'm sorry for springing this job on you without
notice. I'd wanted to tell you in advance, but you were
already en route by the time plans changed. But you're the
only person we can trust to lead this expedition.*

*Yes, I know Dr. Quinn is also there, due to his alleged
expertise on the subject. But you know I've never been a fan
of that pompous asshat. The only reason I didn't fight his
inclusion was because I figured Ford and I would be able to
put him in his place at the outset of the expedition.
Unfortunately, that's not an option now. Also unfortunately,
with his expertise and background, had we not made him a
co-lead, people would have been suspicious. As shitty as it is,
there would have been too many questions if we made you
lead on your own with your lack of lead experience.*

Ouch.

*But I know you can hack it, Miri. Wrapped in the cloth
are instructions on how to find the Cidade da Lua and a key
to its location . . .*

Miri paused from reading the letter, and again scanned the
room to confirm that this wasn't some sort of prank or a *Punk'd*

reboot before picking up the object and slowly untying the string around the fabric. With careful, delicate movements, she spread open the cloth, setting the piece on the bedspread. Inside was another piece of paper and a large gold medallion on a chain. Miri lifted the necklace, dangling it in front of her face. It appeared to have originally been a disc, perhaps three inches in diameter, although about a third of it had been broken off. The piece was substantial and heavy, solid gold about half an inch thick. She took the necklace over to the nightstand and flicked on the bedside lamp to inspect it. One side had carvings—a temple with a moon above it. But the other had strange holes in a random pattern. Constellations, perhaps? Or simply weathered by the elements?

Miri set the pendant on the nightstand, then unfolded the paper that was with it. Corrie wasn't kidding—it was a list of various landmarks.

Mesa de pedra. Rocha cara de macaco. Lágrimas de jaguar. Lago de nenúfar. Trilha de árvores gigantes. Ponte de videiras. Porta do coração da árvore. Miri's Portuguese was spotty, but she was pretty sure she'd pieced it together:

A stone table.

A rock that looked like the face of a monkey.

A waterfall that looked like the tears of a jaguar.

A lake of water lilies.

A trail of giant trees.

A bridge made of vines.

And a doorway through the center of a tree.

The only thing missing was a dotted line showing how to get there. This list wasn't so much a map as it was a scavenger hunt.

No freaking way! It couldn't be this easy.

Miri continued reading the letter from Corrie:

The investor, Eugene Larity, spent two decades searching for the Cidade da Lua, and a team under his direction found this necklace in an abandoned settlement during an expedition to the Amazon last year. Regrettably, Mr. Larity had been working with Pierre Vautour, the smarmy piece-of-shit scumbag who was responsible for the fiasco in Mexico and for those pictures of me being leaked . . . but I digress. He wasn't aware of Vautour's notoriety, and Vautour managed to steal a copy of this list.

Mr. Larity believes Vautour has invested in lidar technology to locate the Moon City now that he knows what landmarks to look for. But as I'm sure you can imagine, there are thousands of spots in the Amazon that might fit these descriptions. That's where the medallion comes in. We don't know how, but somehow it's the key to finding each of the landmarks on this list. The mesa de pedra is the gateway to the Cidade da Lua. This was the trading post for the Cidade da Lua, so it's likely located near a waterway. Find the mesa de pedra, and this medallion will point you to the Moon City.

I'm sorry I can't give you more help. These instructions are more of a guide than a map. There's no "X" marking the spot. Just your intuition and keen eye . . .

Again with her intuition.

You must find the Cidade da Lua before Vautour does. Lord knows what he'll do if he gets his hands on it first. Tell no one about this, Miri. I mean it—no one. Vautour has spies everywhere and is an expert at manipulation. There's no telling who he might have gotten to.

We're counting on you. You've got this.

Now go kick some ass.

—Corrie

Fuck.

CHAPTER

Five

FUCK, FUCKITY, FUCK.

Rafa took a sip of his cafézinho at the sidewalk café across from the hotel the next morning while he scribbled in his notebook, debating how the hell he was going to get out of this mess. This wasn't how things were supposed to go. That wasn't how the *evening* was supposed to go. Rafa had planned to wrap up his sting operation with the archaeological crew where *no one* would recognize him, then he'd waltz over to the hotel bar, buy him and Miri the "backpack consultant" a couple of caipirinhas. Laugh a little longer. Flirt a little more. And perhaps end up in one of their rooms for the night before saying goodbye forever.

Miri was *not* supposed to be working alongside him for the next who knew how many weeks. And she certainly wasn't supposed to be assigned lead.

He couldn't tear his mind from her lips. They were cute, delicate, and appeared to be impossibly soft. The kind of lips that would swell after a proper make-out session. Lips that looked in desperate *need* of a proper make-out session. But more than that, he couldn't stop thinking about them because the words flowing out of those lips made him smile.

He'd been mesmerized as she talked about the expedition, even though he worried for a moment when she brought up os protetores. But he needed to know what *she* knew. Needed to know how far he had to push his interference.

And now Rafa would be personally responsible for her failure.

Fuck my life.

At least he hadn't lied to her. Maybe he didn't tell her the whole truth (though, what was a *whole* truth anyway, Jack Nicholson?), but skipping a few details here and there was fine. So long as she never found out the bits he omitted. He *had* planned to order caipirinhas. And, yes, he *had* used his accent to impress her.

But that was before everything changed.

She didn't need to know the rest of his plan or his true intentions. Because it no longer mattered. He *couldn't* sleep with Miri. *Wouldn't.* He wouldn't fuck her over on the job *and* in her bed.

Rafa hadn't been looking for romance before, and he certainly wasn't in need of it now that Miri was effectively off-limits.

He took another sip, when his phone buzzed beside him with an incoming call from his dad, he closed his notebook.

"Hey, Dad."

"Did you make it to Manacapuru?"

His father launched right in, but he was a busy man. He didn't have time for meaningless pleasantries, something Rafa never took personally. Jean-Luc Monfils was a man with a purpose: to do great things. Whether it was serving on a committee to raise money to save baby harp seals, teaching at a university abroad as an adjunct professor for a semester to open the minds of impressionable young adults to the dangers of deforestation, or sitting on the board of *Global Geography* to ensure the whole world knew about the Earth's most precious biomes and fascinating civilizations, his father never ceased to amaze him. But the one thing he always had time for, no matter where he was in the world or what philanthropic endeavor was on his plate, was Rafa and his well-being.

Even if he didn't have time to say the word *hello*.

"All in one piece," Rafa responded.

"Good, good. And how are things with the expedition?"

"Fine. Though there have been a few changes of plans."

"What do you mean, changes of plans? What happened at the team meeting last night?" his father asked worriedly.

"Well, I met the crew at the meeting. They put on a slide-show with information about the Moon City. Got drinks afterward with each of the new leads—"

"New leads? What do you mean, new leads?" his father asked, his voice kicked up another octave. "Socorro Mejía and Ford Matthews are supposed to be the leads."

Confusion and another emotion Rafa couldn't quite put his finger on vibrated through the phone.

"How did you know that?" Rafa asked, casting a curious glance at the phone. Or, better yet, how did everyone seem to know about the leads except Rafa? There sure were a lot of loose lips on this supposedly top-secret expedition.

"Your blabbermouth boss, of course. I've told you, Rafael, you can't trust that man with a secret to save your life."

Rafa rolled his eyes. Didn't he know it. He still couldn't believe his boss had called his dad to tattle about his resignation.

"Well, Dr. Matthews broke his arm," Rafa explained, "so he and Dr. Mejía aren't heading the expedition anymore. They put two other archaeologists in charge instead."

"Who? Who did they put in charge?" his dad demanded.

Hmm . . . maybe it was anxiousness?

"Drs. Bradley Quinn and Miriam Jacobs."

"Who the hell is Miriam Jacobs?" his dad asked.

The tenor in his dad's voice threw Rafa off. Busy as he was, most of the time Jean-Luc was still an amiable old man who enjoyed reading the paper in the morning with a cup of tea at his favorite café while he chatted with other regulars. A cultured widower who everyone wanted to rub elbows with. A father who was always a voice of reason when Rafa needed to vent.

But there were two things his dad didn't like: surprises and talking about Rafa's mother. They brought out the worst in him—anger and sadness—and Rafa learned long ago to avoid those things if he could. Unfortunately, this expedition involved both.

"I'm sorry," his dad quickly resumed. "This is unexpected, that's all."

"It's okay," Rafa said, knowing his dad didn't mean to yell. "Dr. Jacobs is a colleague of Dr. Mejía's."

"Jacobs? Jacobs?" his dad mumbled to himself as if racking his brain. "From UC Berkeley?"

"Yeah, how did you—" Rafa started to ask, but caught himself—his dad knew everything *and* everyone.

"What's the situation with this Dr. Jacobs?" his dad asked, not even bothering to entertain Rafa's prior half inquiry.

But good question. Rafa had been wondering the same thing all last night. While Quinn had talked his ear off until almost midnight. While he'd lain awake in bed until well past two in the morning. While he'd slowly walked through the hotel before heading for coffee, not *not* hoping for a chance encounter with Miri in the hallway. While he'd . . .

A loud crash across the street at the hotel stole his attention. Two enormous ten-passenger vans were parked on the street, each with loads of gear being strapped to the top; or at least *some* of the gear had made it onto the roof. Several bags rested in the roadway, having toppled over during loading—and were now lying beside Miri's feet.

Speak of the devil.

"I'm not . . . I'm not sure," Rafa answered while his eyes remained on Miri, who was arguing back and forth with the driver. What was it with Miri and drivers?

"Hmm . . . I'll need to check her background. What does she know about the Moon City?" his dad continued, oblivious to the commotion on Rafa's end of the call.

"I don't know. I don't think much. Though there was a memo under my door this morning that was directed to the entire team saying to be packed up and ready to go at nine a.m."

"Packed? Where are you going?" his father asked.

"Not sure."

"Well, as long as you stay along the Amazon River, you should be okay. Just remember, keep them away from the Serra da Mocidade."

His dad's voice registered in Rafa's ears, but he was too distracted watching Miri to answer. He couldn't hear what Miri and the driver were saying, but based on the pointing and arms flailing about, it appeared she was being blamed for the bags falling over. With a final flourish of his hands, the driver turned and walked away. Her gaze shifted from the bags to the roof rack before Dr. Quinn walked over to assist.

No . . . wait . . .

What's he doing?

Quinn shoved his own bag into Miri's chest, then departed.

"What a dick," Rafa unintentionally said out loud.

"Excuse me?"

Rafa snapped his attention back to the call. "Sorry, looks like we're loading up. I have to go."

"Send me updates . . . and find out what you can about Dr. Jacobs."

"Will do," he said.

He hung up without waiting for his dad's goodbye as his eyes fixated on Miri. *What is she doing?* Miri strung a rope through the handle loops on the bags, then flung the rope over the top of the roof. She then backed up several feet and ran toward the van, hurling her body to reach the roof rack.

Her body slammed against the back of the van with a painful sounding *kerchunk*, causing Rafa to wince.

With the grace and precision of a giraffe walking on ice, she swung her legs every which way, trying to loop her ankle around the roof rack before struggling to pull herself up. Once on top of the van, she pulled the rope, heaving her entire body into it without success as the weight of the bags inevitably fell back to the ground.

Attempt number two wasn't any more successful. She swatted her bangs out of her face—*sure, Miri, that's it . . . it's the bangs getting in your way*—and tried, and failed again, this time landing on her back atop the other bags on the roof.

Okay, he couldn't sit there any longer and watch her struggle. He drained the contents of his mug and then made his way across the street. The tension in the rope tightened again as soft grunts came from atop the van and the bags lifted from the ground once more.

"I've got you. Don't . . . let . . . go," Miri grunted to herself, clearly unaware of Rafa's presence below her.

He smiled at her utter adorkableness. She groaned again, clearly straining to pull the bags all the way up, when Rafa lent a hand and pushed the bags over the lip of the roof.

"What the—?" Miri said as she scrambled to the edge of the van to investigate the sudden ease with which she'd succeeded. One look at his face, however, and hers turned a bright shade of pink. "How long were you down there?"

"Only a few seconds. You seemed like you could use a hand," he said.

"Well, here . . . help me tie this down."

They circled the van, tossing the rope back and forth and looping it through the rack to secure the load.

"Why are you the one doing all this?" he asked.

"The driver got annoyed when I told him he'd smashed my chips, so he said he'd like to see if *I* could do a better job, and what was I supposed to do? Can't decline a challenge."

Rafa snickered. Of course. "And the chips?"

"Did you happen to see how many times I dropped the bags? I'm fairly certain they're nothing but dust at this point. But it's the principle that counts," she said, pointing toward the sky with a cute and unintentionally sexy smile.

She finished securing the bags, then looked around, apparently searching for a way to dismount. "Here," he said, reaching his hand up to hers. "I've got you."

She ticked her head to the side with another smile. "Are you making fun of me?" She scooted toward the edge of the van and placed her hands on Rafa's shoulders.

"Of course not," he said, reaching his hands to her waist. "Just don't . . . let . . . go." His exaggerated grunts could barely hold in his laughter as he easily lifted her down from the van, her own snickering unable to be controlled. Her boots hit the ground as she buried her laughter in his chest, and Rafa looked down at her, her sapphire eyes staring back at him from behind her yellow-framed glasses. "Morning, Pringles."

"Hi," she said in an almost whisper as her cheeks turned a brighter shade of red.

"Hi." It came out like the words of a person in a drunken stupor, but how else could Rafa explain the emotions overcoming him? Lost in the sapphire sea of her gaze, forgetting all the things he told himself about staying away from her.

The space between their bodies closed a fraction of an inch, sending a heat wave over his skin and pulling him out of his fog. He released his hold on her like she was a hot potato . . . which, come to think of it, wasn't a bad assessment. But he hadn't yet popped the top of this hot little can of Pringles. He still had a chance to stop before he did something he couldn't take back.

"So, uh . . . what's the plan today?" he asked, clearing his throat and taking a few steps back. "I got the memo under my door saying to be packed and ready by nine a.m."

She smoothed her clothing out, then responded, "We're heading into the rainforest to an eco-resort called Florestacasa. It will be our new base camp for a few weeks."

Hmm . . . *eco-resort* and *base camp* didn't exactly sound compatible. It also wasn't on the itinerary as of last night. No, the schedule Anissa had handed out had them staying at the Hotel dos Sonhos for another three nights before their first trek into the rainforest.

How was he supposed to keep the team off the trail if he didn't know where they'd be going?

"Funny, but I didn't imagine I'd be glamping on this expedition," he said.

"I use the term *resort* rather loosely. Imagine rustic cabins on stilts."

"Cabins don't exactly sound like we're going to be roughing it."

"We're only moving the jumping-off point. Once we have a better sense of where we're going, we'll be in the rainforest."

"Any particular reason we're starting somewhere new?"

"I . . . I, uh, stayed up late doing research last night and think we need to start closer to Serra da Mocidade. And I found a resort that's a few hours' boat ride downriver on the Rio Branco from Caracaraí that's got plenty of availability due to the impending rainy season, so they cut me a deal."

Serra da Mocidade? Shit. How had she figured that out?

Rafa was going to be sick.

"I thought we were heading west? That's what Quinn said last night," he said.

Despite having tuned it out a few minutes earlier, his father's warning had been loud and clear. Rafa hadn't thought he had anything to worry about. Not with the original route Quinn had told him about over drinks.

"We are," she said, as she started to walk back toward the hotel. "But my . . . research is pointing us more northwest toward Serra da Mocidade, so we're changing course a bit."

Rafa trailed behind her, trying to keep up. No, no, no, this wasn't supposed to happen.

Rafa needed to fix this, and he needed to fix it fast.

"I thought you didn't know anything about the location of the city," Rafa said.

"I told you. I studied up," she called over her shoulder.

Something wasn't adding up. If all one had to do was a couple hours of *studying up*, the Lost City of the Moon should have been the Not-So-Lost City of the Moon ages ago.

"And in the less than twelve hours since I last saw you, you suddenly became a Moon City expert and pinpointed a new starting place that dozens of explorers have searched for unsuccessfully for the last couple hundred years? You sure we shouldn't stick with the original plan and head west along the Amazon first?"

Miri stopped short, causing Rafa to almost crash into her backside before she whirled around to face his chest. Her eyes went wide, taking in his pecs, before traveling up to his face. She pulled in a deep breath.

"You know, they put me in charge for a reason. Give me a little credit that I might know what I'm doing, would ya?"

Rafa stared back at her, stunned. Her voice was firm, albeit a little shaky. But her eyes were determined. Her finger, pointed. And her nipples, hard.

Whoa . . . that was hot.

She spun back around, and he watched her saunter with confidence inside to the hotel lobby. Under those nerdy glasses, subtle features, and klutziness stood a boss waiting to be unleashed. And it was fucking sexy as hell.

Fine. He'd let her lead them to Caracaraí and on this little boat ride through the jungle. He'd give her this win, but that didn't mean he'd make the rest of the expedition easy.

Then he'd get serious about this sabotage business.

THE INSTANT THE BATHROOM DOOR CLICKED SHUT, MIRI LET OUT the breath she'd been holding. Her interaction with Rafa had run the emotional gamut—embarrassment, attraction, annoyance, and . . . what was that last one she'd felt when staring at his hard chest and smelling that fragrant coffee aroma laced with bodywash lingering around him? Lust?

She glanced at her reflection in the hotel lobby restroom mirror, noticing her rosy cheeks and hard nipples through the thin fabric of her unlined bra and T-shirt. *Oh god.* Had Rafa noticed? Was that why he was staring at her like that?

Heat shot between her legs, and she fought the urge to relieve the pressure. The thought had already crossed her mind when his hands had wrapped around her waist as he'd lifted her down from the van, and the only thing she could focus on was wondering what they'd feel like against her bare skin. And popping the button on her pants. And dipping beneath her pale pink cotton briefs and sliding along the folds of her—

Knock, knock, knock, knock!

Miri jumped at the heavy pounding on the door, snapping herself out of her daydream and pulling her hands away from the button of her pants, where they'd unwittingly gone.

"Miriam, are you in there? We're all waiting," Dr. Quinn called from the other side of the door.

"Yes," she squeaked out, then cleared her throat. She glanced in the mirror again, her cheeks even more flushed than before. "I need another minute, and then I'll be right there." She swatted her sweaty bangs from her forehead and splashed cold water on her face.

"Well, hurry up. I'd like to know what the hell is going on before the rest of the team." The anger in his voice couldn't be masked.

This was bad. This was really bad.

When she'd woken Anissa early this morning to change their itinerary, she hadn't yet cleared everything with Dr. Quinn first. Perhaps she should have—they were co-leaders after all. But she'd tried calling his room and knocking on his door to no avail, and she needed to get everything set in motion. Waiting to fill in Dr. Quinn would have only slowed them down.

Yet she had still planned to give him the rundown before they set out for Caracaraí. It wasn't her fault that he'd decided to be a grouchy louse when shoving his bag at her. *Since you're clearly taking charge, you can also take this. Come find me when you're done—you've got a lot of explaining to do.* And she still would have tried again if Rafa hadn't completely zapped her brain of all functioning activity.

Functioning activity she desperately needed if she was going to succeed on this mission.

Ever since her very first visit to a natural history museum, Miri had been enthralled with archaeology and ancient civilizations. If only archaeological society was as enthralled with her. She hadn't written any noteworthy articles, gone on any high-profile expeditions or digs, or scored any sizable grants based on her research. She was still seven years away from making tenure, something the head of the Anthropology and Archaeological Science Department reminded her of more times than she could count. He'd given her a warning before she departed for this adventure: *Dr. Mejía may have asked for you, but this is your last chance, Dr. Jacobs. If you're unable to turn this expedition into something tangible—journal articles, funding sources, or a discovery worth bragging about—you won't make it to tenure. Not here, at least.*

Sure, UC Berkeley wasn't the only archaeology game in town, but you didn't leave Berkeley without a damn good reason. And getting fired? Well, it was a reason, all right, but not one Miri particularly cared to experience or explain in any future job interviews.

This was everything she'd worked for. But no matter how hard she tried, Miri always faded to the background.

So, now that she was in charge—sort of—she'd scoured her notes and every bit of research she could find on the Moon City. Analyzed the landmark list and compared it to the various rainforest biomes. Studied the least-explored areas in the Amazon. And after a sleepless night, Miri had placed the Cidade da Lua as being potentially located near Serra da Mocidade and the stone table possibly somewhere near Rio Branco.

It was a long shot, but why couldn't she be the one to make the actual discovery? Just because others had failed didn't mean she needed to as well. Being smart wasn't all it took. What about tenacity, determination, and . . . intuition?

Miri had those things, or at least Corrie believed she did.

WWCMD?

Get out of this bathroom. Stand tall. And be a badass.

I can do those things . . . I can be a badass.

I can puff up my chest—sort of.

I can get out of this bathroom!

She swung open the door, ready to take charge, and was immediately confronted by Dr. Quinn.

"Take your time, why don't you?" he snapped.

Her instinct to apologize started to kick in when *WWCMD* rang through her head.

"I didn't realize there was a time limit on bathroom privileges," Miri quipped back.

Her voice quaked a bit as her heart pounded, unused to speaking with such authority. *Twice in one day and it's not even nine a.m.!*

"Excuse me? You can't talk to me that way."

"But you can lurk outside of the bathroom, banging on the door like a toddler throwing a temper tantrum, instead of giving me privacy?" Miri said, folding her arms.

His brow furrowed as he sneered. "I don't like your insinuation."

"And I don't appreciate yours. Now, I want to be partners here—" she said, trying to relax her tone, but Dr. Quinn interrupted her.

"You call this being partners? Completely changing the itinerary without even consulting me?"

"I tried calling and I stopped by your room—twice—to give you a heads-up, but you didn't answer."

"So you went ahead and did your own thing anyway? Some partnership."

Now Miri was the one furrowing her brow. "I'm sorry . . .

but weren't you the one dismissing me last night so you could 'talk work,'" she said, using air quotes, "with Rafa?"

"You mean when I interrupted your flirting?"

Miri gulped. Shoot.

"We weren't—"

"Oh, you weren't? Because it looked to me like you and *Rafa* were getting pretty cozy." Suddenly, his face softened, as if something clicked in his head. "Look, Miriam, I get it," he said, calmly. "You're young. He's attractive. Sometimes these things happen on digs. I mean, look what happened with Dr. Mejía and Dr. Matthews."

Miri blinked several times. Was he reading her WWCMD mind? "I don't . . . I don't know what you're talking about. That's not what this is." And Miri didn't like Dr. Quinn's *insinuation*, as if Corrie and Ford were just a couple of horny teens who couldn't differentiate between work and play.

Dr. Quinn sighed. "I know you haven't been doing this long. What's it been? Two? Three years?"

"Four."

"See? You're still practically a baby archaeologist," he said, like he needed to coddle her.

Miri gritted her teeth, biting back her anger.

"I'm sorry," he continued, "I don't mean to upset you. It's just that I know you're inexperienced, and sometimes that leads to our minds focusing elsewhere. I understand if you're enamored by him. There's no rule against fraternization between the two of you, after all. But if you're going to be distracted and making irrational decisions simply with an intent to impress him, it might be better if you let me do the decision-making."

"Nothing is going on between me and Rafa," Miri said. *And even if there was, it would be none of your damn business.*

"Besides, I'm not here to create a scandal. Corrie trusted me to lead this expedition, and that's what I intend to do."

"*Co*-lead," Quinn said, his calm demeanor starting to fade. "I'm curious, though. Tell me, Miriam, why do you think that is? Frankly, you're lucky to even be here, if you ask me. It must be nice to have your friend giving you favors, but some of us have actually earned our spot on this expedition."

Miri opened her mouth to fight back, but nothing came out. What could she really say anyway?

"Dr. Jacobs? Dr. Quinn?" Anissa called from the other end of the hallway, interrupting their conversation. "Everyone's packed and the vans are ready to go."

"Great. We'll be right there," Dr. Quinn called back before returning his attention to Miri and lowering his voice. "This discussion is over. No more going rogue. No more surprises. I'll respect you if you respect me. I'll be waiting for you in van number one and you're going to fill me in on the drive. And after today, all decisions need to be agreed upon in advance."

. . . .

THEY HAD A LONG DRIVE AHEAD OF THEM, SO THE GROUP SPLIT INTO the two vans, all twelve of them being unable to fit into one. Miri and Dr. Quinn's van led the convoy, with Rafa in the front beside the driver, guiding them with the GPS. They sat in the back row so they could talk without distraction as they went over the updated itinerary, but her mind wandered every few minutes, shifting from the expedition to her job, and then to the secret she kept tucked in the side pocket of her cargos.

Each bounce of the van refocused her attention to Dr. Quinn with various shades of greens and browns blurring in the background of the windows. She hadn't looked up the directions to Caracaraí in advance, but she hadn't expected to be so deep in the rainforest so soon. She also hadn't expected it to be so bumpy.

Hmm . . . I wonder if there's a spa at Florestacasa . . .

Maybe a glamping resort wouldn't be so bad after all. Rafa's hearty laugh from the front passenger seat stole her attention and sent a flurry of butterflies to her stomach. A massage package for two, perhaps? With champagne—ooh! No, with caipirinhas and—

"Eh-hem." Dr. Quinn cleared his throat, staring at Miri staring at Rafa.

She quickly wiped away the silly grin she'd had plastered over her face and returned her focus to Dr. Quinn's narrowing gaze.

"Sorry," she said, pushing her glasses back up her nose. "I was . . . was thinking about how I spilled that brown sauce all over my boots last night. Funny, right?"

"Hilarious," he deadpanned. "Anyway, now that I have a better idea of the plan, when we get to Florestacasa, I'll go over the specifics with the team while you sort out the reservation details."

Miri's eye twitched. "Or you can wait for me. Co-leads, remember?"

Dr. Quinn sighed, closing his small leatherbound journal in his lap, and turned ever so slightly toward Miri before placing his hand on her forearm. "Why don't you let me take things from here? You're clearly distracted, and your panicked expression at the announcement last night didn't exactly instill confidence in the rest of the team."

She pulled her arm away, trying not to cause a scene in the

packed van. Fortunately, the others carried on as if Dr. Quinn and Miri weren't even there, paying little attention to the conversation they'd been having. But Dr. Quinn wasn't her boss. And he certainly wasn't her dad. So it was time he stopped treating her like he was.

"We were all expecting Corrie and Ford to lead this excursion. Forgive me for appearing surprised to learn that wouldn't be happening. My reaction was no different than anyone else's. Yours included."

Dr. Quinn chortled. "I already knew about Drs. Mejía and Matthews. I knew because Anissa had already informed me that I'd be taking over. That surprised look on my face was in response to learning that I'd be mentoring you in addition to ensuring that this expedition is a success. So, no, Miriam. My reaction was *not* the same as yours."

"What happened to 'I'll respect you if you respect me'? I thought we were making decisions together?" Miri asked.

"We are making this decision together right here and now. It just makes more sense if I'm the one who heads the discussions with the team, is all. Perhaps you didn't realize this, but I *am* the world's foremost expert on the subject."

"Yet Corrie and Ford still thought you needed a partner. Why do you think that is?" Miri cocked her head to the side as she stared pointedly at him.

His eyes homed in on hers. "I don't need your help."

"Well, too bad. Because you're going to get it."

"We'll see who's running the show in the next few days when this little detour you've taken us on proves a waste of time. I mean, Serra da Mocidade? Really?" he questioned, rolling his eyes. "I've been studying the Moon City since before you were in high school. I think I would have figured that out by now.

The only reason I'm even entertaining this diversion is so the rest of the group sees what you are."

"And what's that?"

"A nobody. A fraud." He glared at her.

Miri fought the urge to pull out the medallion and wipe that smug grin off his face. She may not have been *the world's foremost expert* on the Cidade da Lua, but there was a reason Corrie had trusted *her* with the clues and not Dr. Quinn.

It was time to put Dr. Quinn Medicine Man in his place.

"I don't appreciate—" Miri started, but was quickly interrupted by a commotion at the front of the van.

"Watch out!" Rafa yelled at the driver.

"Porra, porra!" the driver called back, sharply jerking the steering wheel.

Miri's and Dr. Quinn's heads snapped toward the front of the van as the driver cursed and swerved, tossing the rest of passengers around like balls in a bingo caller machine. Miri glanced over at Dr. Quinn and saw his face twisting in horror.

"We're all going to die!" he screamed, creating panic among the rest of the group.

She clenched her hands atop the bench seat in front of her as she looked ahead out the windshield at the dense forest in their path as they skidded off the dirt road. Straight toward a giant kapok tree. *Oh no, oh no, oh no!* She squeezed her eyes shut, bracing for impact, when the engine cranked and sputtered before the van came to an abrupt, jarring halt. Miri slowly opened her eyes, as if opening them quickly would somehow be worse. They'd stopped mere inches from the tree.

"Is everyone okay?" Miri called out.

Yeses accompanied by moans and groans carried through the van cabin as the crew re-situated themselves in their seats.

"Let's get out and have a look. Everyone, we'll be okay. Don't worry," Dr. Quinn called out, suddenly recovered from his distress.

Before the team made it to the door, however, it swung open with Rafa on the other side, already out of the passenger seat and assessing the damage.

"Is everyone all right?" he asked in a panic. "Did anyone get injured?"

One by one, he helped the others from the van, quickly pulling them out and away from the puddle of mud and muck surrounding them. As Miri, the last to exit, approached the door, Rafa reached in and put his hands on Miri's face, checking her for bumps and bruises. His warm hands and the concerned look in his eyes sent a flash of heat over her entire body. Five other people were in that van, but none he seemed as concerned about as her.

"My God, are you okay? I'm so sorry," he said, unable to take his hands away. Not that she wanted him to. Had a man ever touched her like this? Been so attentive to her well-being?

I could get used to this. And to those dark brown eyes . . . mmm . . . He has nothing to be sorry for.

"It wasn't your fault, but yes, I'm all right," she said. "What happened up there?"

The driver walked over. "I'm sorry. I lost control."

The other van rolled up, with Anissa immediately hopping out and running over to find out what had happened. Rafa finally took back his hands and hung his head. Darn. Miri almost *wished* she'd gotten injured—moderately. Like a scrape that he could tend to.

Or a bump that needed a kiss to make it better.

"It was my fault. I thought I saw a warthog," Rafa said.

"There aren't any warthogs in the Amazon, you idiot!" Dr. Quinn snapped, marching up to Rafa. "You could have gotten us killed."

"It was probably a tapir. I'm sure it wasn't intentional," Miri said, trying to defuse the situation.

"Where the hell are we, anyway? This doesn't look like the road to Caracaraí," Dr. Quinn continued, clearly having no interest in defusing anything.

Miri glanced around at their surroundings, the rainforest completely enveloping them. Lush vegetation covered the ground on either side of the dirt road. Ferns, orchids, and palms were scattered throughout the understory, overshadowed by the towering mahogany and ceiba trees covered in moss and vines. *Hmm . . . Dr. Quinn is right.* She was no expert on Brazil, but the road to Caracaraí should have been an actual paved road. A straight shot from Manaus, not some jungle dirt trail like the one they had been traveling on. Had they taken a turn when she wasn't paying attention?

"Senhor Monfils thought this was a shortcut," the driver explained.

"A shortcut? Through the fucking Amazon?" Dr. Quinn yelled, turning back to Rafa. "Did you flunk geography in school or something?"

"Oh, I'm sorry. I didn't realize you knew exactly where we were supposed to be going to find this centuries-old *lost* city," Rafa snapped back.

"Well, where the hell are we?" Dr. Quinn asked.

Miri, the drivers, Dr. Quinn, and Anissa took the GPS from Rafa while he stood close behind. *I'm sorry*, he mouthed, and she waved her hand at him, signaling that it was okay. Though once the GPS was up, Miri quickly realized things were the

opposite of okay. Instead of being on the main road to Caracaraí, they'd somehow gotten off course and were on a dead-
end dirt road in the middle of the jungle not far from the Rio
Anauá, a tributary to the Rio Branco, but still hundreds of miles
from Florestacasa.

"This is on you, Miriam." Dr. Quinn pointed his index finger at her. "I knew you had no clue what you were doing."

"Hey—" Rafa started.

But Dr. Quinn cut him off. "Oh, here we go. Coming to defend her honor, Mr. Shortcut? I thought you were using the GPS?"

"I was, but it looked like this road went through," Rafa responded.

"Went through?" Dr. Quinn said incredulously. "And what's
your excuse, you nitwit?" he asked, turning to the driver. "I
thought you were from around here."

"No, senhor. I'm just a driver."

"There's no reason to be calling people names," Rafa said to
Dr. Quinn. "It was my fault. He was only taking directions
from me."

"You're damn right it was your blunder. Look at this," Dr.
Quinn said, waving his arms at their surroundings. "Where are
your cartography skills now?"

Rafa took a slight step forward, and Miri rushed and put up
her hands between the two of them.

"Okay, okay, let's all settle down," she said.

"Good idea. I apologize, everyone," Dr. Quinn said, turning
to address the group, who had been observing this interaction,
"for letting this screwup get the best of me . . ."

Miri caught a slight shift in Rafa's stance as if he wasn't yet
ready to back down, but she placed her hand on his forearm to

stop him from whatever was building inside him. *He's not worth it*, she told him with her eyes.

He pulled his lips in a tight line and gave her a slight nod as if saying *fine*.

"And that's not the leader I am," Dr. Quinn continued, gently placing his hand on his heart and giving the crew a quick nod.

"*Co*-leader," Miri mumbled under her breath. This time, Rafa gave her a knowing glance with a smile and slight tick of his head.

Touché.

"Now, let's put the mistakes aside and hit the road. How about you back out of this mud slop so we can climb in?" Dr. Quinn said to the driver.

"Yessir," the driver responded as the rest of the group backed away to give the van some space. But as he put the van in reverse and revved the engine, the only movement came from the tires spinning and whirling, and little more.

"Try rocking it. Or press harder on the gas," Dr. Quinn called out.

"I am. It's not budging," the driver yelled out the window.

"We should call for help," Rafa said. "We need a winch."

Dr. Quinn scoffed. "Nonsense. I've maneuvered countless vehicles out of stickier situations than this."

Miri rolled her eyes to herself. Stickier than a ten-person passenger van getting stuck in the mud in the middle of the Amazon? Unlikely.

"Come on, Quinn, this is silly. What are you trying to prove?" Rafa asked.

"Prove?" Dr. Quinn cocked back his head with an exaggerated flourish. "Excuse me, I'm trying to get *my team* out of the mess that you and your little girlfriend over here created."

Little girlfriend? Great. Things were even worse between her and Dr. Quinn than Miri had originally thought.

"Whoa!" Rafa said, putting up his hands. *Yeesh. Didn't have to sound* so *mortified by the idea.* "You're out of line."

"And you're in my way. I'll show you all how it's done," Quinn said, pushing past the group.

"Dr. Quinn, maybe we need to take a few minutes for everyone to calm down," Miri said, trailing behind him as he searched the ground for something to wedge underneath the tire. "We should wait until we can get a tow."

"Out here?" he said, bringing his hands up and signaling to their surroundings.

"We have a satellite phone."

"And do you know the number to a tow company?"

Hmm. Good point. "What if we send the other van to find assistance?"

"That's a waste of time," Dr. Quinn said, dragging a few logs toward the van. Miri didn't have experience maneuvering countless vehicles out of sticky situations, but those pieces of wood were little more than glorified sticks. "You'll see. We'll be out of here in ten minutes tops."

"Maybe we can find something to use to pull it out of the mud with the other van. Or we can hike back to the main road and flag down help," she said, scanning the area for something, anything, that could help get them out of this mess.

Dr. Quinn stopped what he was doing and faced Miri, placing his hands on her shoulders. "Look, Miriam. When you're a leader, you must take charge and make things happen. You can't wait for others to come along and save you. But me? I don't need saving. The only person I can count on is me, myself, and I. Numero uno. My favorite number. Watch and learn."

Miri was sick of his tone. She wasn't some baby intern who needed a lesson. She'd earned her title the same way he had—by busting her rump in grad school and paying her dues on digs and in the lecture hall. She may not have accumulated a bunch of awards and accolades, but she had enough bumps, scars, and worn-out hiking boots to prove it. Besides, some Moon City expert he was. Had he ever even *been* on an expedition in the Amazon? Miri was seriously beginning to question the "countless" sticky situations he'd actually faced in his life.

"Being a leader also means admitting when you don't have all the answers," she said, folding her arms in front of her chest.

"I couldn't agree more. Which is why I'll be taking over from here."

"This is a bad idea," Rafa whispered to Miri.

"Why don't you let me handle formulating the ideas, okay?" Dr. Quinn said, scowling back at Rafa. "Now, driver, when I say 'go,' I want you to floor it," he called out so he could be heard over the idling engine. On his hands and knees, Dr. Quinn finagled a log under the tire.

"Say what?" the driver called back.

"Go!" Dr. Quinn angrily shouted back to the driver, then from his spot by the wheel, turned to the rest of the group and said, "And just like that, easy-peasy, lemon squeeze—"

"Look out!"

CHAPTER
Seven

MIRI WASN'T KIDDING ABOUT HER LIGHTNING-FAST REFLEXES. One second, they were standing there, watching Quinn barking out orders—and, frankly, being a jackass—and the next, Rafa was lying with his back flat on the ground, several feet away from the van.

And with Miri resting on top of him.

It had all happened so fast. Rafa wasn't even sure his brain had registered what was happening when someone yelled to look out before he was on the ground, followed by a sharp snap and a howling scream.

Rafa lifted his head at the same time Miri lifted hers off his chest. "Are you okay?" she asked.

Everything else ceased to exist. Those sapphire eyes stared at him with concern, silencing the world around him. God, she was beautiful. More beautiful than he'd realized before. Like a painting in a museum that appears unassuming at first, but when you get up close, you notice all its nuances and specialness and suddenly, you can't look away. And the longer you stare at it, the more you see.

Such as the faint, scattered freckles on her cheeks. The length of her full lashes. The slight upturn of the tip of her nose. And even that tiny chicken pox scar below her right eyebrow. But most importantly, the dip of the cupid's bow in her lips, pointing straight to her barely open mouth. Those lips. Glistening. Beckoning. Daring him for a taste.

Rafa fought the urge to touch each feature—you can't go pawing a Monet, after all. But he didn't fight the urge to stare. Because she deserved to be looked at. To be admired.

Rafa steadied her body in his arms, holding her tightly as all her weight rested atop him. It felt so natural having her this close. For the second time in one day.

He could get used to this.

"Yeah, I think so," he finally answered, begrudgingly taking his hand away from her hip and rubbing the back of his head. "What happened?"

"I . . . I don't know. I heard 'look out' and reacted," Miri said.

They twisted their heads toward the van, and the disorder came into focus. People on the ground groaning, dusting off, and inspecting their bodies for bumps and bruises after apparently also having taken nosedives away from the van.

And beside it, Quinn. Writhing in the mud and clutching his hand tightly against his chest. It wasn't the time for *I told you so*s, but . . .

"Somebody help me, goddammit!" Quinn yelled. "Except you, you buffoon," he said, elbowing the driver away from him.

"You said 'go,'" the driver pleaded.

"I said *when* I say go!"

Shit. Rafa closed his eyes for a second, willing it all away. *Maybe this is a dream. Yes, that's it. A dream.* But as Miri hopped off his body and rushed over to Quinn, Rafa snapped back to reality, instantly missing the touch of her skin against his.

"Dr. Quinn, Dr. Quinn, look at me," Miri said, squaring in front of him to check his head wound. "I think a bag fell and hit you on the head. How many fingers am I holding up?" She raised two fingers, but he swatted her away.

"Your powers of observation are severely lacking. There's nothing wrong with my head. Can't you see *this*?" He lifted his bloody hand to her face before wincing and tucking it back into his chest. "That clumsy jackass ran over my hand!"

Bummer that the knock on his head hadn't done a number on his personality.

But Miri didn't back down from assessing Quinn. "How many fingers?" she asked, again raising two.

Quinn squinted, then his upper body started to sway. "Three."

Miri turned to Anissa. "I think he's got a concussion."

"I don't have a commotion. I need an aid first kit, s'all." Quinn went to stand but immediately faltered. Rafa hurried to catch him before he fell. "Oh . . . 'm not feel s'good."

With a swift turn, Quinn leaned over and vomited onto the ground, barely missing Rafa's shoes.

"We need to get him out of here," Anissa said.

An eerie stillness settled over the group as their eyes shifted to one another and their surroundings. The gravity of the situation finally sank in. Twelve people. One ten-passenger van. Hours from their intended destination. They could *maybe* squeeze into the one van if they left their equipment. If Rafa had to put a quick estimate on it, he'd say the equipment alone was worth a couple hundred grand. Not something to leave un-attended in the rainforest, even if they hadn't seen a single other vehicle in the last two hours they'd been traveling. And to have Quinn prone on a full bench, taking up at least three seats, that *really* didn't leave much room for the rest of the team.

New rule—choose non-injury-inducing sabotages.

Nothing was going to Rafa's plan. They were supposed to have had a nice, long detour. Get to the end of the road. Realize they'd made a wrong turn (*whoopsies, my bad*). Tack on another several hours of travel. The first in a series of delays. Delays that would ultimately tire out the crew. Frustrate Quinn and Miri. And soon they'd be on their way back to the States, empty-handed, like every other explorer who'd traveled to this damn jungle searching for a happily ever after to the fairy tale of a lifetime.

Unfortunately, Rafa hadn't considered the driver catching on so soon. When he'd asked to take a quick look at the GPS, Rafa had only sought to distract him momentarily by calling out for him to avoid a nonexistent warthog. How was he supposed to anticipate that the driver would run them off the road? Or that there weren't any warthogs in the Amazon.

Nous sommes baisée.

Yes, they certainly were fucked. No one was supposed to get hurt, even *if* Quinn deserved a swift kick in the ass. The way Quinn kept belittling Miri was pissing Rafa off. The fact that he refused to call her "Dr. Jacobs," treating her like she hadn't earned her title just as he'd earned his, showed a complete lack of respect. Rafa had noticed it last night with the way he dismissed Miri at the bar, but the insults were even more pronounced today. Call it karma, but Quinn had it coming.

He didn't deserve more than a minor injury, though. Karma

or not, Rafa didn't want Quinn to get seriously injured because of his little detour.

Rafa held Quinn safely in his arms while Miri and the rest of the group were going over their options.

"I can see why she likes you," Quinn said with a hum and a singsong voice.

"What are you talking about?" Rafa pulled Quinn up to keep him from slipping.

"Mari-um," he slurred. "You're strong. And hamsom. Vautour knew she'd like you."

Vautour? Who the hell was Vautour?

"I don't know who that is or what you're talking about," Rafa said.

"Well, he knows you. And I'm sure he knows your secrets."

Rafa tensed. "My secrets?"

"Mm-hmm. About who you *really* are."

No. It wasn't possible.

"Okay, relax, Quinn. You've got a concussion. In fact, you should probably stop talking," Rafa whispered in Quinn's ear, hoping no one else could hear his gibberish.

But Quinn didn't stop talking. "He's coming. You'll see."

"Who are you? Who do you work for?"

Quinn chuckled like a drunkard. "Do we ever really know who we work for? Like truly, really? *Glogal Geograbic*. Brown Unibersary. Just words on a résumé. But deep down, s'all same. He owns me. Who knows. He probby owns you, too."

What the hell?

Rafa opened his mouth to ask another question, when Quinn started to cry.

"I'm fucked," Quinn said, his humor now gone. "I dimmit mean it. Help me. Please don't let him take everything. I'm sorry.

I'm so sorry." Quinn tugged on Rafa's shoulders, pulling him down like he was trying to drown him in his pool of self-pity.

"Okay, we've got to get going. Quinn's delirious," Rafa called out to Miri.

But she didn't flinch. Instead, Miri stared off in the distance. The scene unfolding in front of Rafa's eyes was like an adventure movie gone horribly wrong. People crying. A mysterious forest awaiting them. The decision-makers incapacitated.

This can't be happening. What have I done?

"Miri . . . Miri . . ." Anissa said, giving Miri a soft tug on her arm, snapping her out of whatever trance she'd been trapped in. "We need you to make a decision," Anissa followed up.

"Well . . ." Miri paused, and for a moment, Rafa worried that she was going to zone out again, but she quickly rallied and scanned the group, appearing to calculate her options in her head. "We've got a ten-passenger van—"

"How many people will that fit?" Felix asked.

Miri shot a glance to Rafa. "Ten," she responded with a straight face.

Relief overcame Rafa as he snickered under his breath. Glad she still had her sense of humor through all this.

"But we won't all fit. Not with all our gear," she continued.

"So we leave the gear," someone chimed in.

"Do you want to be responsible for hundreds of thousands of dollars of equipment left on the side of the road?" Miri responded.

Beneath all those nerves, Rafa had to admit—Miri had sass.

"How about this? I'll stay with the gear while the rest of you take that van." She pointed to everyone. "Then you can take Dr. Quinn to the hospital, drop the crew members at the boat launch so you can still get to our base camp tonight, then send someone to get me and to pull this behemoth out of the mud pit. If you hit the road now, hopefully I can still make it to base camp by this evening."

Rafa straightened. Leave her here? Alone? "That's a terrible idea," he said.

"Do you have a better one?" Miri said, placing her hands on her hips.

"Send a few people with Quinn," he said, lifting Quinn in his arms as if needing to remind everyone of his condition, "and they can send help to the rest of us."

"And what if they're delayed? We can't all sleep out here overnight," she said.

"Imma stayin'," Quinn mumbled.

"No, you're going to the hospital," Rafa said.

"An leave *her* m'charge?" Quinn said, thrashing his arm in Miri's direction. "She'll just fu-gid all-up!"

Miri's nostrils flared. "You mean, like how *you* fucked up your hand playing Captain America? You're leaving," she said, pointing at Quinn, "I'm staying, and that's the end of it."

"Then I'm staying with you," Rafa said. "It's not safe for you to be out here alone."

Before Miri could protest, Anissa chimed in. "He's right. What if something were to happen?"

"I can stay, too," Felix chimed in.

"Same," Logan offered.

Miri glanced at Rafa as if cycling through a variety of scenarios, sending a few running through his head as well. Picturing them alone in the jungle, keeping each other warm by the campfire. But something flickered in her expression, and as if brushing the thought away, she shook her head.

"All right," Miri said, walking around Rafa and Quinn to

address the group. "Felix, Logan, Rafa, and I will stay here. The rest of you, load into the van and get to the hospital. You've got the other satellite phone, right, Anissa?"

Anissa nodded.

"Okay, then keep us posted if there are any other hiccups or delays. Otherwise, we'll be waiting here until you send help."

Marching orders settled, the crew set off in a flurry. Rafa pulled out the camera to document the ordeal: unloading and reloading vans to redistribute weight and equipment; carrying Quinn to the van and making him comfortable; hooking up the GPS so they wouldn't get "lost" again.

Rafa climbed in the van once more to speak to Anissa. "Make sure he doesn't sleep," he said, motioning toward Quinn. "And he was talking total gibberish earlier. Just ignore everything he says."

Rafa, Miri, Felix, and Logan stood in silence as they watched the other van drive away from the side of the road. Leaving Quinn alone with the crew was a potential liability. Who knew whether Quinn actually had any dirt on Rafa? But it was a risk Rafa was going to have to take. The other option—leaving Miri—was out of the question.

The Amazon wasn't a place for the faint of heart. In all Rafa's years and all his wild adventures with *GloGeo*, he'd never had one quite like this. At the very least, all his other escapades had had a concrete destination.

And in all those other undertakings, his goals had been the same as everyone else's. This was uncharted territory for Rafa.

"I need to go to the bathroom," Rafa said, though what he really needed was a moment to himself to figure out how the heck he was going to get out of this mess.

He walked twenty feet into the forest and rounded a tree to go relieve himself, when a giant tarantula scurried out in front of him. *Nope*, he thought to himself, changing direction. When he finally found a spot that looked clear, he took his break and allowed his mind to spin as he sorted through his options. Not that Rafa ever had a solid plan, but being stuck out in the middle of nowhere certainly wasn't part of it. Though, the more he thought about it, maybe he didn't need a plan at all. Perhaps all he needed to do was convince Miri that the accident and Quinn's injury were a bad omen.

He made his way back to the van to find Felix and Logan rolling a couple of downed logs out of the dense forest toward the clearing by the road to sit on.

"Where's Miri—I mean, Dr. Jacobs?"

Felix responded without even looking in Rafa's direction as he fumbled with the log. "She said something about taking some measurements. She went that way," he said, pointing toward the opposite direction from where Rafa had been.

Rafa set out into the jungle, quickly losing sight of the road. Jeez, where the hell had she gone? Didn't she realize how dangerous it was to wander off in the rainforest alone? The dense forest was full of plants he'd never seen in real life. Bromeliads. Açai palms. Trees taller than imaginable. He walked in what seemed a straight line, but quickly realized there was no going straight when trekking through the rainforest. *Shit*. He spun around, unsure which direction he'd even come from, when he heard a faint voice coming from beyond a stand of trees.

" 'Fuck it all up,' " Miri said, talking to herself and clearly unaware she had an audience. " 'Leave *her* in charge?' " Her tone was mocking as she paced around, pantomiming.

"That's right, Dr. Dipshit," she continued. "Look who's in

charge *now*. I'm a fucking badass!" she proudly proclaimed as she sprinted toward a vine hanging from a tree, grabbing the woody rope and swinging from it like Indiana Jones. But with a quick *snap*, the vine broke, sending Miri crashing to her ass.

"*Oof!*" she grunted.

Rafa flinched for a moment, ready to jump to her aid, when she quickly stood and brushed off, then looked up at the vines again. Searching for another option.

This time, she reached up and tugged on a vine first, then walked back a few feet before running and attempting the stunt again. She soared through the air, then let go of the vine for a dismount and landed flat on her face. *Ouch*.

"Fuck!" She pushed herself up onto all fours and growled.

She brushed herself off more forcefully this time, then huffed before trying yet again. And landing this time on her knees on dismount.

What exactly was she even trying to do? Win an award in the Most Ungraceful Vine-Swinging Competition? From his observation, there wasn't anywhere for her to go. Nothing for her to accomplish. Swinging around the jungle wasn't exactly a skill that needed to be mastered. But whatever her goal, she certainly had tenacity, never giving up. Just like her van antics earlier in the morning. Rafa admired her gumption and spirit. Had to admit—Miri was one of a kind.

Rafa pulled out the camera, documenting her attempts. Observing her through the lens, focusing on each subtle movement of her face and the determination in her eyes. He couldn't help but smile as he watched her.

Attempt number five: Miri let out a gibberish raspberry and shook every part of her body like Elvis gyrating onstage. "Here we go," she said, taking off on the vine and calling out like Tarzan.

Rafa laughed softly under his breath.

Miri's head snapped in his direction, catching him capturing her on camera.

Shit. He lowered the camera, and their eyes connected as she set her feet to the ground.

"Are you taking pictures of me?" She narrowed her eyes at him, one hand on her hip, the other clinging to a vine overhead.

Rafa glanced at the camera in his hands. Okay, sure. It didn't look good. But he hadn't intended to stand there for so long. It wasn't his fault that he was so captivated by her. Besides, it was his job to document the expedition. And candid photos were always better than the posed ones.

"I was looking for you," he said, standing from his crouched position behind a fern and tucking the camera behind his back.

"From the other side of the camera lens, hiding behind a fern?"

"Yes?" He was questioning himself more than anything.

"You know, Rafa, some would say it looked like you were spying on me. Again." She stared at him pointedly as she pursed her lips.

He cocked his head. "First off, this morning I was simply enjoying a cup of coffee when you decided to audition for *Brazilian Ninja Warrior* across the street from me. And second, I wasn't spying. If I was spying, you wouldn't have seen me. Trust me, Miri, I know how to conceal myself. If I didn't want you to see me, you wouldn't have."

"You should have announced your presence," she said.

"You're right. But candid shots are more impactful."

"You can't use those!" she protested, letting go of the vine and walking toward him.

"Why not?" he asked, ticking his head to the side.

"Because I probably look ridiculous. I don't want you putting a photo of me face down in the dirt in *GloGeo*," she said, reaching for the camera.

He stepped back, pulling the camera tighter to his chest. "Why would you assume that's the photo I'd choose?"

"Because . . . because I'm a joke." She hung her head. "It's only day two . . . and you heard Dr. Quinn. I've already fucked everything up."

Rafa's heart ached for her. Sure, he wanted to convince her to scrap this whole thing and pack up the team. But he didn't want her to blame herself. It wasn't her fault this expedition was a flaming fiasco.

"I wouldn't put too much credence into what Quinn thinks," Rafa said, rolling his eyes at the thought of Quinn. "That man is a grade-A asshole—"

"Who happens to be a well-respected archaeologist. Once he gets better and tells people about what's happened out here, I'll be a laughingstock. And those pictures will only solidify that fact. I can already see your article now. 'Failure in the Amazon: How Dr. Miriam Jacobs Fucked It All Up,'" she said, waving her hands in the air like reading a movie marquee.

Rafa burst out laughing. "That's a terrible title," he said, covering his mouth. "And it would never pass copyedits."

"See? I'm not even good at describing how colossally bad my botch jobs are!" she said.

"Maybe that's a good thing," he said with a smile. But the worried look on her face didn't seem to buy it. He softened his eyes at her. "You can't blame yourself for what happened to Quinn. No one asked him to try to be a hero. You didn't put his hand under the wheel."

"But I put us out here—"

"No, *I* did. If anyone's responsible for our current situation, Pringles, it's me."

Miri shouldering the guilt didn't sit right with him.

"Had I not changed course, though—" she started.

"And what if you're right?"

Shit. Shit. Shit. The words came out so quickly without a second thought. What was he doing? Was he *helping* her?

She looked up at him, her pretty sapphire eyes sparkling from behind the lenses of her glasses. "You mean that?" she asked.

A tingling sensation fluttered in his stomach as he stared at her. Her eyes were hopeful—someone believed in her, even if she didn't believe in herself.

He wouldn't—no, he *couldn't*—be the one to break her down.

"Of course I do. Hey, it's a lost city. No matter which direction you take, it can't be any worse than the last person who tried, right?" he said, trying to deflect. "And if you're worried about the article, think of it this way—I promise, if this ends up a bust, I'll make sure you get a title worth bragging about."

She smiled, sending another wave of warmth over his skin. "Thank you," she said.

His resolve faded as he gazed at her mouth. She shifted her stance into a beam of light poking its way through the tree canopy, casting a glimmering sheen across her lips like a beacon calling his name. The call from a paradise tanager stole his attention as it flitted through the trees, and he cleared his throat.

"Look, if you're bothered by the photos, I'll delete them," he said, bringing the camera up and turning it back on. "It's not like we were doing expedition-type stuff anyway."

"Can I see them first?"

"What? The pictures?"

She nodded.

"Okay." He turned his body toward her and lifted the camera so they could both see. Her arm brushed up against him as she leaned in, and for the briefest moment, they glanced at each other, sending a pleasant jolt through his body.

One by one, he scrolled through the photos. Frankly, if he hadn't witnessed it with his own eyes and the photos were the only thing to go on, one would think Miri *was* that badass vine-swinging adventurer she'd been trying to emulate.

"Hmm . . . I look rather good," she said, causing Rafa to laugh. "What, you don't agree?"

Her smile was wide and charming, and . . . damn. She was getting to him again.

"I appreciate the confidence, that's all," he said.

"Well, I mean, I'm sure it has more to do with your skill as a photographer than my acrobatic prowess, but Tarzan better watch out. There's a new swinger in town!"

This time, Rafa burst out laughing.

"You laughing at my talents?" she said with a grin.

"No, I'm laughing at you calling yourself a swinger."

"Swinger, schwinger," she said, shrugging.

He hung his head and chuckled. "That's not any better."

"Whatever. I'd like to see *you* try," she said, handing a vine to him.

"If you want to fill me in on what exactly you were trying to do out there, I'd be delighted to try," he said, laying on the playfulness.

"I was *trying* to swing and then launch into the air and land like this," she said, demonstrating a crouched position on the ground straight out of *Lara Croft: Tomb Raider*.

"All right. Here," he said, lifting the camera strap over his head and handing it to her. "Watch me and weep."

Not that he had any experience with vine-swinging in the jungle, but he couldn't resist her goading. He yanked on the vine, making sure that it would hold his weight, then with a quick intake of his breath, he backed up, then ran and lifted himself from the ground, tucking his feet beneath him before swinging his legs through and launching himself in the air, landing on the ground in more of a Spider-Man stance than Lara Croft, but, hey, it was pretty damn good for a first attempt.

"What the hell?! How did you do that?" she said as she lowered the camera from her face.

"Now, hold on a minute," he said with a smile, "were you taking pictures of me?"

She brought her shoulder to her chin with a coy smirk. "It's only fair, don't you think?"

He laughed and walked over to her to inspect the photos. Though while Rafa's vine technique was a solid nine-point-five to Miri's six-point-two, the pictures told a different story. Judging by these photos, Rafa's skill looked more like it would be something that would end up on *America's Funniest Home Videos* than *American Ninja Warrior*.

"These are horrible," he said with a hearty laugh.

"Horribly amazing, you mean," she said with a grin.

"Maybe don't quit your day job, that's all."

She playfully shoved him in the stomach.

Warmth washed over his face. Had a woman ever touched him like this? So playfully? Teasingly? Delicately? He couldn't recall, but man, he liked it.

"Show me," Miri said. "Teach me how to do that jump thing you did."

"I don't even know exactly what I did."

"Yeah, well, it was better than what I did."

"Okay, here," he said, walking over to set the camera on a rock then returning to Miri. "So what you want to do is when you get off the ground, tuck your legs up like this," he said, demonstrating by pulling himself up on the vine then returning to the ground. "And then when you're getting close to completing your arc, bring your legs back like this, then launch yourself into the air. Go ahead and try."

She took a deep breath, then brought back the vine before trying again.

And she fell straight down.

"Dammit!" she said, throwing her hands to her sides. "What am I doing wrong?"

"You're not swinging through. Here, like this." He took the vine and pulled himself up again, showing the follow-through with his legs. "Just try that right here. Lâche pas la patate," he said, walking back to her and holding the vine in his hand.

"What does that mean?"

"It means 'Don't give up the potato.'"

Miri stopped mid-grab and burst out laughing, placing her hands on either side of her head and resting it on his chest. With a natural ease, he held her for a moment as she giggled in his arms. He couldn't help but smile as he looked down at the top of her head, taking in the moment.

"No, it does not," she said as she lifted her head away from his body. He smiled, knowing she'd like that saying, before finally releasing her from his arms.

"Literally, yes. Figuratively, it means don't give up. Now take it," he said. He handed the vine back to her, and she lifted herself up and tried the swing, but nope. Still didn't work.

"Okay, let me help you. Pull yourself up," he said, standing beside her.

She tried again, but this time he placed his hands below her ass and assisted her swing through. She sucked in a sharp breath, as if his touch sent that same familiar jolt through her body as hers had done to him. As if she wasn't used to this feeling. Used to being touched this way. Or at all. And as if just realizing what he'd done, Rafa let her go and took a step back.

"I'm sorry. I shouldn't have—" he started.

But Miri put her hand on Rafa's forearm to stop him from apologizing. "Can we try again?"

Her deep blue eyes summoned him, almost as if they were saying something else. Inviting him into her space. She took a step forward, facing him head-on, then reached her arms above her head, her eyes never straying from his face. He circled around her body to her side, but this time she made no effort to lift herself, clearly waiting instead for him to assist.

He placed one hand under her thighs, then lifted her off the ground. So close he could take in her scent. She smelled like lily of the valley: sweet, delicate, and with a hint of lemon. Even with remnants of dirt on her face from her earlier falls and a few pieces of twig and leaves in her hair, he'd never wanted to kiss someone so badly in his life. But not only that. He wanted to brush his lips against hers, taking in her nervous breaths through his every sense before pressing his mouth to hers. Run his tongue along the opening of her mouth until she let him in, commingling her tongue with his. Slowly massage their lips together. Savor every part of that kiss.

"Like this?" she said brightly, bringing his attention back to their practice session.

He cleared his throat. "Yep, that's it." He moved back and refocused his energy. "Now go ahead and try the whole thing."

With a deep breath, Miri took several steps back, then ran

and did the routine in one seamless movement with a perfect landing.

"Oh my God! I'm queen of the jungle!" She jumped up and down, cheering for herself, giddy and cute as all get-out. As he watched her dancing around like she'd kicked a game-winning football goal, a sense of pride overtook him. Witnessing her succeed, even at something as silly as completely pointless vine-swinging in the jungle, warmed his soul.

It was then that Rafa realized Miri wasn't the only thing falling in the jungle.

Forget what he'd said earlier. *They* weren't fucked. He was.

MIRI COULDN'T IMAGINE A SINGLE INSTANCE IN HER LIFE WHEN she'd need the skill of swinging from a vine and landing in a crouched position, but boy did it feel great to stick that landing.

Almost as good as it felt having Rafa's hands on her body.

When was the last time she'd experienced that warm, full-body tingling sensation? Had she *ever* experienced such a sensation?

After their jungle rendezvous, they eventually found their way back to Felix and Logan. Several hours had passed since Anissa, Dr. Quinn, and the rest of the crew had taken off, but it felt like they'd been out there for days. She glanced over at Rafa sitting beside Felix and Logan. Who was he? Where had he come from? In all her thirty-one years of life she'd never met someone she'd had such a strong physical attraction to as Rafa. With his looks, surely she wasn't the only person drawn to him like a magnet. It was hard not to stare at him. Wonder about his life story. Imagine what he looked like with his shirt off.

Probably had an eight-pack hidden under there. Firm. Hard. Soft to the touch. She pictured her hands running along the ridges of his shoulders, slowly making their way to his pecs with a smattering of dark hair before traveling down to the ripple of his abs. He'd flinch at the delicate glide of her fingertips, but only for a moment. Stepping into her, he'd press his warm flesh against her, placing his hands behind her back and pulling her in. He'd stare down at her as he lifted her chin. His eyes would shift from her lips to her hungry gaze, waiting to taste him. His mouth would open as he leaned in, and—

"You all right over there?" Felix called out.

Miri jumped, realizing she'd been staring intently at Rafa. He eyed her curiously, then tossed her a mischievous smile as if he could read her thoughts. No. That wasn't possible.

Was it? God, she hadn't said anything out loud, had she?

"What do you mean? Of course I'm fine," she told Felix, calming her voice as best she could.

"If you're worried about the van coming back to get us, I'm sure they'll be back soon, that's all," Felix said.

She released the breath she'd be holding, thankful that she hadn't been over there acting out the scene playing in her head. Miri looked up at the pink-and-purple sky as it quickly vanished, taken over by a creeping darkness. Darn it. She'd hoped the other van would make it back before sunset. It should have only taken them five or six hours to get Dr. Quinn to the hospital, drop the rest of the crew at the port to catch the boat to the resort, and make it back to pick up Miri and the others. At this rate, it might have been faster—and easier—to take a boat from Manacapuru up the Rio Negro and onward up the Rio Branco. If that had actually been an option.

Without warning, Rafa stood from his position between

Felix and Logan, who'd already resumed their conversation, and meandered over to Miri before plopping on a log beside her. *Oh God. What is he doing? What is he going to ask me?*

"What?" she asked.

"What, what?" he retorted.

"What are you doing?" She eyed him suspiciously, trying to figure out his motive.

"You're here all by yourself. I came over to keep you company . . ."

It had been ages since a man had *kept her company*.

"You're not actually worried about the van, are you?" he asked.

She shook her head and pulled out the satellite phone from a bag alongside her. "They would have called by now if there was an issue." She shook the phone as if it proved there wasn't a problem. Because, sure, a little wave solved everything.

"Got any snacks in there?" he asked, leaning over and peeking in.

She pulled the bag away and smiled. "Finished your M&M's already?"

"Nope. I'm saving them for an emergency. Got any more Pringles?"

"I told you, the Pringles are mine."

"I know, but I'm a huge Pringles fan." His words hung in the air, and suddenly she wasn't sure they were talking about snacks anymore.

"You are?"

"Mm-hmm," he murmured, pressing his lips together.

"What kind?" she asked, staring at his mouth.

"It doesn't matter. Ever since yesterday at the airport, however, I can't seem to get them out of my mind."

She gulped as her eyes shifted all over his face, though his eyes never left hers.

"What . . . what is it that you like about them?" she asked.

He shrugged. "What's not to like about them? It's no ordinary chip."

"Some might say they are kind of boring."

He laughed. "Boring? Hardly. So are you going to give me a taste?"

Miri's eyes grew wide. "Here?"

"Why not here?"

"I mean, as in right now? In front of Felix and Logan?" she asked, shifting her gaze between them.

Rafa furrowed his brow. "Why would they care about us having a snack? Unless you don't want to share," he then added in a whisper.

Miri's face turned bright red. No, purple. He was talking about *actual* Pringles, not her. And now he likely thought she was an even bigger weirdo than he'd probably thought before.

She opened her mouth to backpedal, when the satellite phone rang in her hands. "I've got to—" she started, waving the phone at him before giving up entirely on trying to produce an excuse and answering the phone. "Hello?"

"Hey, Miri. It's Anissa."

Please tell me you have good news.

"I'm afraid I have bad news," Anissa continued.

Shit.

"What is it?" Miri asked. Might as well get on with it.

"I'm unable to find anyone who can make it out to you tonight. The earliest I have found is someone who can pick you up tomorrow morning," Anissa said.

"Tomorrow?!" Miri blurted out. Rafa, Felix, and Logan all

shot worried glances at her. Maybe they *should* have crammed into the other van with as much equipment as it could have reasonably held.

"I know. I've tried everything, though," Anissa said.

"Why can't you come back with the other van?" Miri asked.

"Because when I told the car company owner, Carlos, what happened, he refused to let us take the van again. He said he doesn't want to chance us messing up another vehicle."

"Well, what about another company?" Miri asked. "There has to be *someone* who can get us."

"By the time I called others, word had gotten around. Those who hadn't already talked to Carlos called us 'os caçadores de tesouros.' Treasure hunters."

Miri hated that term. The archaeologists she knew were scholars. Historians. Preservationists. They weren't in it for a quick buck—the cost of graduate school alone thwarted any argument to the contrary. But Miri had lost count of the number of times someone had asked her about searching for treasure. A lost civilization wasn't treasure. It was a key to the past.

A clue to life's greatest mystery: Where had humans come from?

Miri's search for knowledge and the answers to that question had led her to this field. The last thing she was looking for was gold to line her pockets. Anyone who thought otherwise clearly wasn't familiar with the cost of student loans.

"No one seems to want to help us," Anissa continued. "They kept saying they didn't want to get in trouble with the protectors, or something like that. Even the company I *did* find is charging us quadruple their normal price. I'll keep trying to find someone sooner, but chances are looking slim, so you might want to get comfortable."

Miri sighed. It wasn't ideal, but they had food and supplies. They could make it work if they really had to.

Which, as it turned out, they did.

"How is Dr. Quinn?" Miri asked.

"His hand is broken, or as the doctor said, 'shattered.' There's no way he can continue this expedition," Anissa said. "Plus, he's got a serious concussion. He was talking all sorts of nonsense. Saying he needed to call his boss about the unfortunate turn of events or he'd lose his house. He was begging me for his phone, even though I told him I'd already let Mr. Larity and Drs. Mejía and Matthews know what had happened. Honestly, I can't even make sense of half the words he's saying between his slurred speech and talking about agents and bad guys coming after him."

"Bad guys?" Miri repeated, wrinkling her nose.

The others' ears perked up again.

"I know, right?" Anissa said, almost with a laugh. "He clearly hit his head harder than we thought. You would have thought he was talking about the plot for the next Indiana Jones movie. They had to sedate him so he'd calm down."

Anissa continued talking, but she might as well have been speaking in Portuguese. Miri's mind went in circles, from Dr. Quinn to inventorying how much food they had to sleeping arrangements—which then led her mind straight to Rafa, who was watching her intently.

"—and so I'll call you when I have a better estimate of what time they'll be showing up tomorrow," Anissa said, snapping Miri back to reality. "You'll be okay, right?"

"Yes, I'm sure we'll survive. I mean, how much trouble can we really get into out here?" Miri asked.

"Do you really want me to answer that?" Anissa responded.

"It's the Amazon, Miri, and we've already had a few mishaps today."

Good point.

She hung up with Anissa and fidgeted with the phone in her hands for a moment, trying to think of a way to put a positive spin on their situation.

"So . . . I take it you already know what I'm going to say?" Miri said, tugging on her earlobes.

"We're stuck here overnight," Felix said, very matter-of-factly.

Miri scrunched her face and gave them a shaky nod. "But it's not all bad. At least this way we'll get to know the rainforest a little better," she said with an upbeat flourish. "Did you know the Amazon is home to over two point five million . . ." Miri let her voice trail off as Logan and Felix stared blankly at her. Okay, so maybe they weren't interested in getting to know the insect species up close and personal.

"What are we supposed to do out here all night?" Logan asked.

Miri fiddled with the phone some more. "Hopefully we can find a couple of books or a pack of cards in someone's bag to keep us entertained?" she said.

Logan sighed, then turned to Felix and said, "Let's gather some firewood." The two of them headed into the forest, leaving Miri and Rafa alone again.

"What were you saying about bad guys?" Rafa asked.

"Oh, it's nothing," Miri said, tucking the satellite phone back in her bag. "Anissa says Dr. Quinn is delirious, is all."

"Delirium doesn't sound like nothing," Rafa said, lifting his brows.

"You know what I mean," she responded, waving it off.

"Not really. Is Quinn okay?" he asked.

"He's definitely got a concussion, and his hand is broken, so he won't be coming back. But otherwise everything is fine."

"You have an interesting definition of 'fine,'" Rafa said, tilting his head. "Not sure I'd classify being stuck out in the middle of the Amazon rainforest with a broken-down van as everything being fine."

"It's only for one night. I'm sure we're not in any danger," Miri said.

"*Are* you sure about that? Bad guys? Do you even know anything about Quinn?"

The chirps, hoots, and howls from the forest seemingly stopped as Corrie's warning popped into Miri's head. *Tell no one about this.*

Surely Corrie didn't mean Dr. Quinn. He was a renowned archaeologist. A legit scholar.

Wasn't he?

Fuck. She needed to know.

"I'll be back," Miri said, hopping up from the ground and heading over to the van without waiting for a response from Rafa so she could read Corrie's letter again. See if it had any other clues.

She rounded the van once Rafa couldn't see her, then she ducked inside, digging through her bag for Corrie's note. *Vautour has spies everywhere . . . There's no telling who he might have gotten to.*

Dammit. No clues.

Miri carefully folded the paper and tucked it back into her satchel. With a sigh, Miri scanned her surroundings as if this broken-down hunk of junk or the rainforest would give her a sign. *You're being ridiculous*, she thought, rolling her eyes at herself.

Bad guys? Seriously?

Shaking her head at her gullibility, Miri started to back out of the van when she saw it.

Dr. Quinn's bag.

His bag must have fallen on the floor during the collision. And with all the ruckus to get him to the hospital, it must have gotten overlooked.

Maybe Miri could take a quick peek inside.

Usually Miri wasn't one to go snooping into other people's belongings. Something she'd learned the hard way at fourteen years old when she thought it would be funny to look through her older sister's diary and read, *God, why is Miri so WEIRD?*

Capital W-E-I-R-D weird.

There was nothing like reading *that* to make Miri feel like even more of an outcast than she already was. She and her sister eventually came to understand each other now that they were adults, but, oof. Miri could have done without the almost two decades of that voice in the back of her head.

So did she *truly* want to know what was in Dr. Quinn's bag? Did she really need confirmation that all this talk about bad guys and spies was really the ramblings of a concussed fool?

Unless . . . unless Dr. Quinn had something to hide.

Miri scurried between the seats to retrieve his bag, reaching under the bench and giving it a quick yank. But it didn't budge.

Crap.

It was stuck on something.

She crawled under the seat, stretching her arm around the strap of his pack. Tugging. Pulling. Grunting as she wrenched it in her hands.

"What are you doing?" Rafa said from behind her, causing her to startle.

"Nothing," she said as she quickly let go of the bag and lifted her head, hitting it underneath the seat. "Ouch!"

But now she couldn't move. Dammit. She was stuck on something.

"Are you okay?" he asked.

"No . . . I . . . I'm stuck," she said, twisting her arm around atop her head and trying to wriggle herself free. "My hair . . . ow."

What a disaster.

"Here, stop moving," he said, inching into the van beside her. "Let me help you."

"It's okay, I can get it," she yowled.

"You're making it worse."

His body snaked beside hers. There was barely enough room for Miri on her own. With Rafa in the mix, they were like a couple of sardines in a tin can. If the twisting of Miri's hair weren't causing extreme pain, she might have actually enjoyed this.

He finally made his way under the seat face-to-face with her. "I see what it is. Your hair is caught around this metal thing. Hold still and I can probably get it," he said, lifting his hands into her hair.

She pulled her bottom lip into her mouth, scrunching her face to keep from yelping.

"What were you doing under here?" he asked as his fingers plucked at pieces of her hair. "And don't say nothing," he quickly followed up, flashing her a gentle but telling smile.

"I was . . . I was trying to get Dr. Quinn's bag."

Rafa wrinkled his brow, then tipped his head to check for Dr. Quinn's belongings before turning back to her. "What's in there?" he asked, continuing to work on her hair.

Miri opened her mouth to reply, when Rafa pulled on a piece of hair too tightly and she hissed. "Sorry," he said. "I've almost got it, though."

For a moment, Miri debated not answering Rafa's question. But clearly she'd been snooping. There was no hiding it.

"I was checking to see if Dr. Quinn had any clues," she said.

Rafa stopped for a moment, eyeing her curiously, before continuing again. "Clues about what? About the location of the Moon City?"

Miri shrugged, at least as best she could. "I don't know. Bad guys, I guess? Now that I'm saying it out loud, though, I realize how ridiculous that sounds."

"It's no more ridiculous than thinking you saw a warthog in the Amazon," he said, giving her a wink. "There, I think I got it."

Miri lowered her head and rubbed the spot where she'd been stuck, still tender from the pulling. "Thanks," she said.

"No problem. Does it hurt?"

"A little."

"Here," he said, reaching over and massaging his fingers through her hair. His fingertips danced along her scalp, sending a tingling sensation throughout her body. "Better?"

"Mm-hmm," she purred, not realizing how dreamy she sounded. "I mean, yes. Yes, it's better. Thank you."

He smiled at her, then tucked his arms underneath his head as they lay on their sides staring at each other.

"So," he said.

"So."

"What are you thinking about?"

What was she thinking about? She was thinking about the

way his fingers felt between the strands of her hair. How dangerously close his body was to hers and the fact that he wasn't doing anything to expand that distance. How this was the third time today their bodies had made contact.

All those things swirled through her mind, though lingering in the back of it—and in her peripheral vision—was Dr. Quinn's pack.

"Do you think Dr. Quinn was up to something?" she asked.

He tipped his head a bit to the side. "What do you mean?"

"I don't know. Anissa said something about how he was looking for his phone and was going to lose his house. I know he has a concussion and all, but something isn't sitting right with me."

"I'm not sure. Personally, I didn't know anything about Quinn before this trip. It does seem a little strange, though. Maybe this is all a sign or something," he said.

"What do you mean, a sign?" Miri asked.

"Like that we shouldn't be out here. Maybe this is the Moon City's way of telling us it doesn't want to be found."

"What?" Miri said, shaking her head. "No, that's not what I'm getting at."

"Let's face it, Pringles. We're not exactly off on the right foot here."

"We need to get to base camp is all, and then everything will be back on track."

Rafa opened his mouth in an apparent protest when the hum of a vehicle in the distance caught all their attention.

"Do you hear that?" Miri asked.

No way. No way could they be that lucky.

They twisted and turned to pull themselves out from the

van—though not without Miri noticing how firm Rafa's abs were when she wriggled out from the tight space—and they walked up to the road to see where the noise came from at the same time Logan and Felix emerged from the forest. A white pickup truck caked in mud came barreling along the road right toward them.

They waved their arms to get the truck's attention, as if it could miss them. Four people on the side of the road deep in the Amazon wasn't an ordinary occurrence. Thankfully, the truck slowed down and pulled up beside them. Miri prepared to butcher her way through some Portuguese to explain their situation, when the tinted window rolled down to reveal two white guys in baseball caps—one Red Sox and one Nationals.

Odd.

"Everyone all right?" Red Sox asked.

Americans.

"Um, yeah. I mean, no, not really. Our van," Miri said, thumbing back to the van as if it wasn't already obvious. "It got stuck."

The men craned their necks to peek. "Anyone on their way to get you?"

"Not until tomorrow," Miri said.

"We're stuck out here," Logan chimed in.

"Any chance you got a winch?" Rafa asked.

"Nah, man. Sorry," Red Sox responded. "Not much out this way, though. Where are you headed?"

Miri hesitated for a moment before answering. "To an eco-hotel downriver from Caracaraí."

"Well, hot damn. If that isn't a coincidence. We're heading that way ourselves," Red Sox said.

Well, that *was* a coincidence. Miri glanced over at Rafa, noticing his eyes narrowing at the men in the truck. Clearly his wheels were spinning.

"I looked. There aren't any ferries that go up that way from here," Miri said.

"We chartered a boat. Got a local guide waiting to take us upriver past Caracaraí. If you want, you can come with us," Nationals said.

"What are you doing out here?" she asked.

"Boys' trip," Nationals said with a wide toothy grin. "A little private Amazon tour."

"Where are you from?" she asked.

"Boston, originally. Though this one had to go and move to DC. Traitor," Red Sox said, tossing a sarcastic glance at Nationals. "By the way, I'm Hunter and this is my buddy Kevin."

Kevin waved two fingers in a salute near the brim of his baseball cap.

"So what say you? The river's not too far, but we gotta get going before the boat decides to take our money and ditch us," Hunter continued. "We'd planned to make it to Caracaraí by midday tomorrow, so we can drop you off on the way."

"I say heck yes," Logan said.

"Hold on," Miri said, turning to her crew. "We can't leave our equipment."

"Toss it in the bed," Kevin said. "You can squeeze in in the back seat here," he said, pointing to the extended cab.

"Sounds great," Logan said, rushing over to the van to start unloading the equipment.

"Sweet," Hunter said, throwing the truck in park and hopping out to help.

"What do you think?" Miri whispered to Rafa as the others started loading the truck.

Rafa rubbed the back of his neck, turning his face so the others couldn't see him speak. "I don't know. Something about this feels off. A little *too* coincidental."

"I was thinking that, too," she said. "I guess it's *possible* these guys are just your everyday Good Samaritans."

"Is that really a thing? An everyday Good Samaritan?" Rafa asked, cautiously eyeing the others. "I mean, we haven't seen a single vehicle the entire time we've been on this road. What if *these* are the bad guys Quinn was talking about?"

"Or what if *this* is a sign that we *shouldn't* quit now? It'll get us to base camp sooner than if we wait for the pickup tomorrow."

And it would save the expedition the quadruple payment.

"All this nonsense about bad guys is getting to us, that's all." *Right?* She continued, "Besides, there're four of us and only two of them."

"Are you saying you can take them?" he asked, raising his brows.

"Are you saying that you can't?" she retorted with a playful smile, trying her damnedest to bring a little levity to the situation.

"I don't know, Pringles, but I really don't want to find out the hard way," he said, clearly not buying what she was selling. "I've got a bad feeling, is all."

She'd be lying if she said she didn't share the sentiment. But she'd played it safe her whole life and look where it got her: on a fast track to the archaeologist's graveyard. The place where nobodies like her went to wither away cataloging artifacts in a crusty old basement while other archaeologists—*real* archaeologists—explored the world.

Archaeologists like Corrie.

WWCMD?

"Don't worry," Miri said to Rafa. "Like I said earlier. Everything will be fine."

Nine

"**A**LMOST THERE," HUNTER CALLED TO THEM OVER THE ROAR OF the engine and the wind whipping though the cab of the truck.

Miri may not have been worried about these guys, but Rafa sure was. The only reason Rafa agreed to go on this detour was because he figured if they *were* in on something with Quinn, they probably wouldn't have let them stay back at the van if they'd tried. Well, and because Miri was clearly dead set on going with them, and Rafa wasn't going to let her out of his sight.

Cooperation was key in situations like this. Rafa knew that from firsthand experience, like that time his *GloGeo* team had unwittingly walked into an inhospitable encampment in the bush. Fortunately, they'd been able to talk their way out of any trouble, but only after playing *very* nicely and being *very* agreeable.

At least they'd called Anissa to make sure she knew their whereabouts, though that provided little solace.

Miri, Rafa, Logan, and Felix were crammed in the back seat as the truck careened down the bumpy dirt road. Rafa had to put his arm around Miri to make enough room. He would have done the same thing if Felix or Logan had been beside him.

That's what he told himself, at least.

Her side nestled softly into him, her lily of the valley scent now permeating its way into his clothes. Every so often she'd lean forward to ask Hunter or Kevin a question, resting her hand on Rafa's knee to steady herself. She did it so casually, like she'd known him for longer than the little more than twenty-four hours since they'd first met at the airport. He didn't mind. He quite liked it, in fact.

Was it intentional? Did she even realize she'd done it?

One thing was certain: *Rafa* realized it. Every part of him was aware. His entire body tensed under her hand, wanting to move but not wanting to draw attention to it in case she stole it away. It took all his strength to focus on the oddity of what was happening in the truck and not Miri.

Given the road's condition, Rafa's original detour plans probably wouldn't have fooled anyone much longer. This wasn't a road meant to be traveled on with any regularity. The closer they got to the river, the narrower the drive width became. Soon the forest seemingly swallowed them whole, encroaching into the travel lane.

Thwack! Branches slapped against the windshield then scraped the side of the truck, screeching as they dragged across the metal. Had they taken a wrong turn or something?

"So, why are you taking a boat rather than driving straight to Caracaraí on the highway?" Rafa asked.

"What's the point of being in the Amazon if you're going to drive everywhere?" Hunter said. "This is more of an adventure."

Rafa watched Kevin messing with something in his lap. Kevin elbowed Hunter and flashed him a message on his phone, and Hunter gave him a simple nod before looking in the rear-view mirror and catching Rafa's glance.

Something still wasn't sitting right with him.

"Where in DC do you live?" Rafa asked Kevin.

"Huh?" Kevin responded, tossing him a curious look over his shoulder.

The hair on the back of Rafa's neck rose and, unfortunately, this time it *wasn't* because of Miri's touch.

"DC. That's where you live, right?" Rafa called out to Kevin again.

"Oh. Yeah. I'm over by, uh, the ballpark. Gotta be close to my team, am I right?"

Time to see how *right* Kevin was. Having lived in DC for the last seven years, Rafa was more than familiar with the city. "Oh, so you're in Columbia Heights?"

"Yep. Columbia Heights. Great 'hood." Kevin said.

"Cool. I haven't been," Rafa responded, "but I hear it's pretty sweet being able to see the Lincoln Memorial from the ballpark, too, don't you think?"

"Totally. Makes me emotional every time I see it. So powerful."

Wrong.

This was bad. This was very, very bad.

Rafa tapped his thumb on Miri's shoulder, casually trying to get her attention. She looked at his hand and smiled, then at his face. But Rafa wasn't smiling. He shook his head with the most minuscule movement possible. Without words, she ticked her head in their direction and lifted her brows with the subtlest of movements as if asking, *Are you sure?* Oh, he was sure all right. Nationals ballpark was in the Navy Yard neighborhood, miles away from Columbia Heights. And the Lincoln Memorial was nowhere near the stadium, certainly not within viewing distance. He nodded, but his solemn eyes said it all—they were in trouble. She pulled her mouth in a tight line then returned a nod with the same amount of movement, signaling that she understood.

"How long is your trip in the Amazon?" she called out to them.

"Two weeks," Kevin replied.

"When did you get here?"

"Yesterday. It's gonna be wild."

Miri glanced into the back of the truck bed, likely thinking the same thing Rafa was. "Then where are your bags?"

Kevin and Hunter exchanged the tiniest glance. "Oh, uh, they're already at the boat. Speaking of, here we are."

Hunter rolled up about thirty feet from the edge of the river, and sure enough, there was a ramshackle fishing vessel waiting for them. The thing looked like it was barely waterproof. Mismatched boards. A cracked window on the small captain's cabin. Rafa wouldn't be surprised if duct tape held it together. To put it as nicely as possible, it was a hunk of junk. And completely out of place in the Amazon.

Dusk was upon them, bringing the wildlife out in full force. Birds hooted and called. Bats flew overhead. A splash in the distance signaled the caimans weren't far. Rafa seriously regretted his choices earlier in the day. This was not a place to be stuck all night, that was for sure.

"All right, let's get everything loaded up," Hunter said, hopping out of the truck. "There's the captain. Olá, Sérgio! We found some stragglers who need to hitch a ride upriver," he called to the man.

"Sim, senhor," Sérgio said as he tipped his straw hat at Miri and Rafa, then continued prepping the boat for their journey.

"Can that thing even hold us?" Rafa asked Hunter.

"Good point," Hunter said. "Let's load the most important stuff first. You might have to ditch some of your things here. Come on."

Hunter, Kevin, Logan, and Felix started carting stuff back and forth between the truck and the boat, while Rafa and Miri stayed back, pretending to be sorting through a few of the bags.

"I don't like this," Rafa said under his breath.

"I don't, either," she said. "I'm sorry . . . I . . . I shouldn't have insisted." Worry—and guilt—read all over her face. If they were going to play the blame game, though, Rafa would win by a landslide.

"Not as sorry as I am for bringing us this way in the first place," he said, rubbing her shoulders. "I don't know who these guys are, but he's not from DC, that's for sure."

"What should we do? Should we tell them we changed our minds and ask if they would let us take the truck back to town?"

"Something tells me they won't agree to that."

"Maybe Sérgio can help us?"

"Sure. Unless they're working together."

Miri and Rafa looked over toward the boat, checking for any other crew members. Only one—Captain Sérgio.

"Do you think he's in on it?" Miri asked.

"I have no clue."

If these were the men Quinn was talking about, then Rafa was in deeper shit than he thought.

"You guys get the last of the things," Hunter called over to Felix and Logan as they headed back toward the truck.

Once they were near, Miri pulled Felix and Logan by their arms and huddled everyone together. "Something isn't right," she whispered. "I think they're up to no good. I don't think we should go with them."

"We were about to say the same thing. Hunter . . . he whispered something to Kevin about the Cidade da Lua," Logan said.

"Let's get our things and tell them we changed our minds," Miri said.

They all stood up to face the boat, but the boat was no longer docked. Instead, it had pulled away from the riverbank, with Hunter and Kevin watching them from the bow.

"So long, suckers. Mr. Vautour thanks you for the gear," Hunter called out, one leg up on the edge of the boat like Captain Morgan.

Vautour? They worked for him, too?

"Hey! Wait! Give us our stuff!" Miri said, running toward the riverbank.

"Nah, we're good. Besides, you won't be able to carry it all back to your van anyway," Hunter yelled back at them.

"Then give us the keys!" she yelled, pointing at the truck.

Hunter raised a set of keys above his head and jingled them in his hand. "What? These keys? I think we're good." He tossed the keys in the air then placed them on a crate on the boat.

Shit! How could they have been so foolish?

Rafa opened his mouth to scream profanities at Hunter and Kevin when the sight of Miri hurling her body over the river swinging from a vine in the direction of the boat stole his attention. "Miri! What are you doing?" he screamed.

Shit. Fuck.

She was just short of the boat, her legs flailing about in the air. She let go and plummeted into the water. Rafa went running

along the river after them, with Logan and Felix close behind.
The boat thankfully hadn't picked up enough speed yet, and
Miri reached a rope ladder in the back, pulling herself onto the
stern of the boat. Rafa couldn't hear what they were saying over
the puttering of the engine, but he watched everything like it
was in slow motion.

Pringles, what are you doing?

Rafa looked down the current and saw a fallen tree hanging
over the river braced against another across the way, almost like
a bridge over the water. "There!" he said, pointing out the tree
to Felix and Logan. "Hurry!"

Rafa raced toward the tree, running up its trunk like a
champion parkour athlete, and launched himself into the boat.
He landed with a thud and was instantly met with a punch in
the face. With a quick shake, he jumped up only to be faced
with another swing from Hunter, though this time Rafa ducked,
barely missing Hunter's fist. Rafa and Hunter circled each other,
trading punches, before Kevin joined.

"Two on one? Really?" Rafa said, squaring up for the fight.

"This is real life, dickwad, and life's not fair," Hunter said.

Right as Hunter geared up for another swing, Miri jumped
on his back, beating him with her fists. He growled at her, desperately trying to get her off him. Miri was a scrapper. For a
moment, a sense of satisfaction—and a little pride—overcame
Rafa as a smile escaped from his lips. But Hunter rammed into
the boat cabin, pinning Miri with a dull thud before she crumpled to the deck.

"Leave her alone!" Rafa said, lunging for Kevin and pushing
him over the side of the boat, where he dropped into the river
with a splash.

"Enough!" Hunter called out, pulling out a knife from

behind his back and pointing it right at Rafa. "Both of you, over there," he said, motioning to the deck's handrails with the blade. "Don't try being a hero."

Rafa's heart pounded as his stomach sank. This was it. This was how they were going to die. How could he have been so stupid to get into that truck and risk their lives?

This was all his fault.

"Look, all we want is our stuff," Miri said with her hands raised to her chest, palms facing out. Her voice trembled, but she spoke calmly. "Give us our things and then you can go."

"Why are you talking like you're the ones in charge here? Like you have any negotiating power. I'm the one with the knife, if you haven't noticed," he said, waving it around like it was nothing more than a rubber movie prop.

Something caught Rafa's attention behind Hunter—Felix and Logan climbing over the side of the boat, completely unbeknownst to Hunter.

"Senhor! Watch out!" Sérgio called out.

Hunter spun around just in time to catch the force of Felix and Logan wrestling him to the floorboards. Rafa dove for the knife and twisted it out of Hunter's hands before Felix and Logan picked him up and tossed him overboard. Rafa then pointed the knife at Sérgio.

"I suggest you jump as well," Rafa growled at him.

Without hesitation Sérgio launched himself off the boat. Rafa rushed over to the steering wheel and put the boat in full gear to speed away from Hunter, Kevin, and Sérgio crawling their way back up on the riverbank.

"If you think this is the last you've seen of us, you've got another think coming!" Hunter screamed. "See you at the Moon City!"

Rafa shot a look at them as Miri flipped them the bird.

"Don't forget these!" she yelled, dangling the keys to the truck overhead before flinging them into the dark, murky river off the front of the boat.

Between the piranhas, caimans, and electric eels, something told Rafa they wouldn't be finding those keys anytime soon, if ever.

Once they were a safe distance away, Rafa let off the throttle. With all the rattling and clanking happening, they had no clue how far this boat would make it. Even with the distance between them and those jackasses, his heart still raced. He'd had some wild adventures, but nothing like this.

I can't believe I pointed a knife at someone.

He stared at the blade resting on the dash panel. He hadn't actually planned to use it on Sérgio, but if things had gone differently with Hunter or Kevin, who knew what would have happened? Rafa didn't want to think about it.

He didn't want to look at it, either.

"Is everyone okay?" he called out to the main deck. Felix and Logan nodded, squeezing the water out of their clothes.

"That was close," Miri said, startling him out of his thoughts and entering the captain's cabin.

"*Close*?" he asked in disbelief. *Close* was them almost catching the bus yesterday and barely missing it. Or her failing to pull the bags on top of the van this morning. Her calling what had happened *close* after he'd only minutes earlier threatened to stab someone set him off. "What were you *thinking*? We could have been killed."

She ducked her head, twisting her hands together in front of her. "I know. But I . . . I wasn't thinking. Or at least I wasn't thinking about that."

"Then what *were* you thinking about?" he demanded, alternating between watching where they were going and Miri standing in the doorway.

"I was thinking about the equipment." She moved closer as she tried to explain. "I mean, we've got hundreds of thousands of dollars' worth of equipment here. I've already messed so much up on this expedition. I didn't know they had a knife, otherwise I wouldn't have gone after them. But I couldn't . . . I couldn't let them take everything."

"So what? All that equipment isn't worth your life, Miriam."

He stared at her, her hands trembling at her sides and her eyes welling with tears. Shit.

Sure, he was angry, but not because he was mad at her. If anything, he was terrified of how badly things *could* have turned out.

"Come here," he said with a sigh, reaching one arm out to her while the other held the wheel steady. She stepped into him and folded into his body, letting him wrap his arm around her. She buried her face in his chest. "Are you okay?"

She nodded. "I was so scared once I realized what I'd gotten myself into."

"I was scared, too."

She looked up. "You were?"

"Of course I was. When I saw you swinging over the river, my heart froze. I don't think I've ever been so scared in my life."

"I don't know what I was thinking. In my head, I thought I'd swing on that vine and touch down on the deck with the perfect footing. And then I'd give them a stern talking to like a badass and they'd flee."

"Yeah, but like you said, this isn't exactly Hollywood out here. In real life you don't always land feet first."

"Well, in all fairness to my skills, even movie stars often eat their landings, too," she said with an air of humor in her voice.

Rafa smiled at her, and she smiled back, burying her face in his chest once more. "I'm glad you're okay," he said.

"I'm glad you're okay, too."

"Minus a couple of sore ribs. And I don't even want to look in a mirror. My face feels like it's about ten times bigger than normal," he said, reaching his hand to gently touch his face.

"It still looks pretty to me."

Rafa looked down and her eyes went wide.

"I mean, pretty good. Like, it looks normal. Or mostly normal at least. You have a cut on your lip, that's all. Well, and a bruise above your cheek. But you still look good. I mean, normal. You still look normal," she rambled, and God, it was adorable. "We should probably get that cleaned up, though," she said, pointing to his lip and releasing him.

He watched as she wiped a tear from her cheek and tucked her hair behind her ears before searching the cabin for a first aid kit. But while she banged around cabinet doors and bins, Rafa brought his hand up to his lip and winced, tasting blood. Shit, that hurt. Rafa had gotten in some solid jabs, and they may have won the fight, but not without a few injuries of their own.

"Don't touch it," Miri said, opening a first aid kit beside him.

Rafa glanced down at her hands sifting through the supplies. Her knuckles were bloody. She'd put up one hell of a fight herself.

"We should get you cleaned up first," he said, motioning toward her hands.

"Oh. Right. I suppose you don't want dirty hands tending to your wounds," she said, smiling.

"Here, take the wheel." He found some antiseptic wipes and tore open a square. One hand at a time, he swiped the cloth over her knuckles as she steered the boat with the other hand.

"Sssssss," she hissed, pulling her hand away and wincing. "Sorry, it stings," she said.

"Need me to kiss it to make it better?" He smirked, and she playfully elbowed him. "Hey, watch the ribs. Here, give me your hand."

She gave it to him again, but this time she fought through the pain. "You were pretty ballsy back there, taking on two men by yourself," he said.

"I've never punched someone before. Man, that hurts."

Rafa snickered. "Yeah, it's not pleasant."

"Have you ever been in a fight like that?"

"You mean a fight on a boat in the Amazon with two guys trying to steal our stuff at knifepoint? Of course. That's a regular Friday night where I'm from," he said with a smile. "I've been in my fair share of fights, though."

"Fair share?"

"Not recently. More when I was in my teens."

"Were you a troublemaker?"

"I don't know if I'd say trouble*maker*, but all boys go through a period where trouble seems to find them whether they created the trouble or not."

"Oh yeah? What's the dumbest thing you ever got in a fight about?"

"Let's see . . ." Rafa looked up, trying to recall his youth. "In secondary school we had this assignment where we had to write a funny poem. I thought it would be hilarious to write about William Tremblay, the soccer team captain, splitting his shorts on the field at the championship game. Seemed a good idea until we had to read the poems out loud in front of the entire class."

Miri burst out with a laugh. "You didn't?"

"Oh, I did. That assignment earned me high marks and a black eye," he said with a wink, quickly bringing his hand to his eye at the sting and wincing. "Apparently, I'm good at earning those."

His face hurt, but he still couldn't help but grin picturing the look on Will's face when he'd read that poem. The shiner had been worth it—the poem was damned good.

"What a talent," Miri said, laughing. She had a nice laugh. The kind that made you want to keep saying funny things just to hear it over and over.

"Well, I suppose I was asking for it with that one, so maybe I should take back what I said about not being a troublemaker."

"Did he let you off the hook after that? William, I mean?" Miri asked.

Rafa's smile fell with the memory. Oh right. He'd forgotten about that part.

"Not really." He crumpled up the wipe, tossing it on the dash, and ripped open another one before setting back to work on her scrapes and bruises. "He stole my writing notebook from my locker and copied some of my stories. He and the soccer team then taped them up on the walls at school. Spent the next week taking them down before another would pop up."

That first day when he'd shown up at school, seeing everyone crowded around a photocopy of a page from his notebook, was etched in his brain, buried deep in the crevices, but so clear. So vivid. How could he have forgotten?

His private writings exposed, out there for everyone to see. Stories that weren't supposed to be read by anyone. Declarations on death. Loneliness. Heavy reflections on life and love by a sixteen-year-old kid who still didn't understand what those things even meant.

That week had been hell. Or, at least, it would have been if it weren't for his dad.

"That's shitty," Miri said. "I mean, I get that you pissed him off with that poem, but sharing someone's work without their permission?"

Rafa shrugged. "It wasn't all bad."

"How so?"

"Well, at first, I was worried that my dad would find out and be angry about the things I wrote. Stuff about my mom and her death. Things we just don't talk about. But when the principal called and told him what happened, my dad enrolled me in a creative writing program. He didn't know how to talk to me about it, so I guess he figured me writing about it was the next best thing. And now, here I am, writing for a living." Rafa paused, then added with a devilish smirk, "Plus, the entire soccer team got suspended."

"Okay, that's pretty amazing," she said.

Yeah. It was. Rafa smiled.

"So, do you know what ever happened to William Tremblay? Please tell me his pants-splitting saga lives on in infamy and follows him wherever he goes."

Rafa chuckled. "You know, I have no idea."

"Then we *have* to look him up whenever we find internet access again."

"You really want to waste precious internet data in the

Amazon to look up what happened to a secondary school soccer captain?" Rafa asked, unable to control his smile.

"Absolutely. When I learned that the mean girls from my high school got arrested in this whole shoplifting–Poshmark resale ring, I savored the sweet satisfaction that all their glitz and glam was phony."

"Mean girls, huh?"

"Oh yeah." Miri chortled. "They did their best to make my high school experience true misery."

"Why?"

Miri made a face. "Because, well . . . well, look at me."

Rafa was looking at her, all right, but all he saw were her sparkling sapphire eyes. Her spunk. Her sassy spirit.

"I mean," she continued, clearly unaware of her charms, "I know *you* think my money belt is cool, but it wasn't the most fashionable of accessories back in high school."

God, she was doing it again, bringing out his goofy, uncontrollable grin.

"Pringles, I hate to break it to you, but no matter how many times you say it, you're never going to convince me it's not a fanny pack."

She punched him playfully in the arm as he turned away laughing.

"Okay, all better," he said, balling up the trash in his hand.

"Your turn," she said.

They traded places, with Rafa resuming his spot at the ship's helm. Miri brought an antiseptic wipe to his lip, and now it was his turn to hiss.

"Man, you were right. That smarts," he said.

"Need me to kiss it to make it better?" she mocked.

But the instant the words came out of her beautiful mouth,

the air in the cabin shifted. They stared at each other for a moment. Was that an invitation? More than a playful ribbing?

The thought of kissing her flashed through his brain. Could he? Should he? She lifted her hand up once more, slowly dabbing the blood and dirt from his face, staring intently into his eyes. She moved, putting her body between his and the wheel. Yes, he did need her to kiss it to make it better.

"I think I do," he said.

"Okay . . ."

Rafa leaned down, pressing Miri's back against the wheel as she sucked in a breath. Waiting for him. Wanting him.

And he wanted her.

"So, what's the plan?" Logan said as he and Felix burst into the cabin.

Miri and Rafa quickly separated, creating so much distance between them that you'd think they'd gotten in trouble for not making enough room for the Lord at a school dance. He cleared his throat and ran his fingers through his hair, hoping it wasn't too obvious what they'd interrupted.

"Um, well, first things first, we need to figure out where we're at. Does someone know where the GPS is?" Rafa asked.

"Here," Felix said, handing it over.

They checked the GPS and compared it to a few of the maps in the cabin, determining that they were several nautical miles from the base camp at Florestacasa. At the pace they were going and assuming they had enough fuel, it would take them the better part of a day. Rafa showed them each how to operate the boat. Not that he was an expert, but he and his dad had gone boating several times during his childhood. This way, they could take turns and get some sleep. It was going to be a long night. But at least now they had a plan.

"Who were those guys?" Logan asked.

Miri shrugged. "Don't know. We're lucky, though. Had they gotten away with all our stuff, the expedition would have been over."

Rafa tensed as it all finally hit him.

He'd sabotaged his perfect chance at sabotage.

LOOK WHAT I FOUND," MIRI SAID, WAVING A TUBE OF PRINGLES and sitting next to Rafa, who had his back against the front of the captain's cabin while Logan and Felix were on steering duty.

The moon had poked out above the tree line, casting an eerie glow on the river. Fortunately, the boat had lights, so they could keep going through the night. It wasn't ideal, but they had no idea whether Hunter and Kevin scored another boat and were hot on their tail.

All sorts of worst-case scenarios cycled through Miri's head—getting the boat stuck in the mud, giant boa constrictors dropping onto the deck from an overhanging branch, Hunter and Kevin catching up to them—but then her mind would drift back to that moment when Rafa had her pinned between the ship's wheel and his large, hard, utterly delectable body, and . . . well, her imagination wiped everything else clean. They had been close—*so* close. He had been about to kiss her. Kiss her and make it all better. Because if anything could improve their current predicament, it had to be Rafa's lips.

And hands.

And eyes.

And thirty-four pack.

And—

"Wow, they made it?" Rafa asked, closing his notebook and taking the tube Miri held before him in midair.

Food. Right.

With a quick shake of the head, Miri returned to the present, blinking a few times to get reality back into focus.

"Yeah. My satchel apparently made it."

Though, unfortunately, none of the rest of her stuff did. Luckily Logan's bag made it, so they could change into clean, dry clothes. Logan's cargo shorts and men's medium hiking shirt, however, weren't doing anything for Miri's figure.

Though Logan's men's medium Teenage Mutant Ninja Turtles T-shirt was doing *wonders* for Rafa's.

Had she known the Ninja Turtles could be sexy before this moment?

She *did* always have a bit of a crush on Michelangelo.

Rafa popped the top of the can and offered the first Pringle to her. They each took one, then tapped them together in a cheers before eating.

"Mmm. I needed this," Rafa said, closing his eyes as he relished the snack.

Miri wet her lips, staring at him savoring that chip.

"God, I love Pringles," he said, moaning to himself. "Thank you for sharing," he said.

Miri wouldn't mind sharing a few other things if he was interested.

"Of course. After a day like today, we needed a little home

comfort," she said, trying to take her mind off Rafa's satisfied moans.

They took turns reaching into the can, nibbling in relative silence minus the calls from the birds and the hoots from the monkeys. It was almost better that they couldn't see too far into the forest surrounding them. Miri didn't want to know whether there were jaguars or panthers watching them. If this was going to be their demise, she'd rather not see it coming.

From where they sat, Miri couldn't see Logan and Felix inside the cabin, but it sounded like they were laughing and telling jokes. Hopefully they weren't *too* traumatized by what had happened. It had taken a while for all of them to settle down, but thankfully everyone seemed to be doing okay. This wasn't what any of them had signed up for, and Miri certainly hadn't made matters any better by taking unnecessary risks.

They'd called ahead to the rest of the group at the base camp, giving Anissa a warning about Hunter and Kevin. Something told Miri it wouldn't be the last they saw of them, but at least they'd have greater numbers once they made it to Florestacasa. What they were going to do with the boat once they got there, however, was beyond her. Surely Vautour and his cronies would come looking for it. Looking for *them*. For now, they were safe. But Miri had no idea for how long.

"Do you know who this Vautour guy is that Hunter mentioned?" Rafa asked, breaking into the silence.

Miri's shoulders dropped, stopping her snacking mid-chew.

She was starting to wonder if Dr. Quinn's ramblings to Anissa weren't quite as rambly as they'd thought. It didn't seem possible that Dr. Quinn, a world-renowned archaeologist, would fraternize with the likes of a criminal like Pierre Vautour, but if what he'd said about losing his house was true, perhaps Dr. Quinn was in some financial trouble and Vautour was his ticket out of that mess. It wouldn't be the first time Vautour had taken advantage of someone with money problems. Ford had apparently witnessed that firsthand.

But they were in it now. If Vautour was involved, the stakes had just gotten a lot higher.

And since they were in it together, she decided to tell Rafa what little she knew.

Mostly. She couldn't spill *all* the beans simply because she got twitterpated in Rafa's presence.

"He's a notorious artifact thief," she said. "Corrie and Ford encountered him in Mexico last year when he posed as the landowner of the site where they were searching for Aztec artifacts. And when Ford got suspicious and refused to keep up the dig, Vautour extorted him by threatening to release photos of him and . . ." Miri paused for a moment, her cheeks heating up at talking to Rafa about what Corrie and Ford were doing in those photos. "Photos of them being intimate."

"Nude photos," Rafa said, as if he'd already heard the story.

"Yep."

"That was him?"

She nodded. "He was the brains behind the whole scheme. He has a penchant for getting others to find what it is he wants, and then he takes it from them."

"Hence his name, I take it?"

"Huh?" Miri cocked her head.

"Vautour? It means 'vulture' in French. It can't possibly be his real name. I mean, you've got to hand it to him. He's bold if he's going around convincing people to work for him with a name like that."

Hmm. Maybe I should have paid more attention during French class.

"Well, I think he might be searching for the Moon City, too," Miri continued. "And that maybe Dr. Quinn was working for him."

Rafa cocked his head and gave Miri a quizzical look. "What makes you think that?" he asked.

"Just some things he said to Anissa at the hospital."

"Such as . . . ?" His brow rose as he waited for her to answer.

"He mentioned needing to call his boss or he'd lose his house. I'm thinking he made some sort of deal with Vautour. He's got a knack for finding people in dire straits."

"Did he say anything about working with anyone else?" Rafa almost seemed nervous, which was understandable. Miri was nervous, too. Who knew how many other people Vautour had working for him and where they might pop up next?

She shook her head. "Anissa didn't say. Though maybe he was working with Hunter and Kevin? The timing of their arrival was too coincidental otherwise. They clearly knew we were out there." Given Dr. Quinn's present state, however, how they knew was a mystery.

"This doesn't make any sense. What are the odds that not one, but two expeditions are out here searching for the Cidade da Lua at the exact same time? It's been lost for centuries. So why now? And what makes this Vautour guy so sure he's going to find it?"

"He's using lidar."

The words escaped her mouth without warning. Shoot. Miri hadn't meant to say that.

Rafa's forehead wrinkled and he cocked his head. "What do

you mean he's using lidar?" he asked, turning his body toward hers.

"I mean, lidar isn't some guarantee or anything," she said, like it was no big deal. "You still need to have a general sense of where to look. Corrie told me about it before we left. So long as we find the Moon City first, it shouldn't matter."

"Shouldn't matter?" He laughed as if saying, *You've got to be kidding me.* "We're racing against someone who's using lidar to pinpoint the Moon City's location. Someone who has a team of men with knives scouring the jungle, probably looking for us as we speak. A guy who has a *reputation* for being a notorious criminal, but you think we'll be fine so long as we get there first?" Rafa peppered her with facts she couldn't rebuke.

"They're down one knife, at least," Miri said with a smile.

"I'm serious, Pringles," he said, his tone firm and solemn. "This is . . . this is dangerous. I don't think we want to be messing with this guy. You need to call whoever it is that's in charge of this expedition and tell them we need to call the whole thing off."

"What?!" she said, shooting up. "No. We can't!"

"This isn't a game," he responded, still from his seated position on the boat deck and staring at her. "We had a knife pointed at us earlier. *I* pointed a knife at someone. If we don't call it now, someone could end up getting hurt. Or worse."

"I doubt they would have actually hurt us. It was only a knife. And it wasn't even that big."

Even as the words came out of her mouth, she wasn't sure she believed them. But give up? On day two? She doubted her boss's ultimatum included a bad-guys-and-knife-fights exception. The archaeological world had plenty of crooks and criminals hoping to score their next priceless find. If all archaeologists quit at the first whiff of trouble, countless artifacts would have likely succumbed to illicit trading.

See Corrie, case in point. WWCMD? Well, she certainly wouldn't back down because of a measly three inches of steel. In fact, she *didn't* back off when placed in a similar situation.

Miri couldn't be a wuss.

"And you know that how?" Rafa asked. "Look, this was a perilous job already with just the environmental factors, but sorry, I'm not going to risk my life out here running from bad guys and con men, too."

"Rafa, no. We can't let Vautour get there first."

"Why not? Who cares?"

"I care! Do you know what he'll do to it? He'll loot it. Take what he wants. Discard—and destroy—anything and *anyone* in his way. And then he'll sell those things on illegal markets, keeping a few special pieces for himself in his private collection. And no one will know who the Moon City people were."

Rafa eyed her curiously. "And what about you? What would you do if *you* were to find it first? Protect it? Because it seems to me that the very act of finding the city will undermine any attempts to do so."

"No, I want to preserve it. Study it. Find out what happened to the people who lived there. Find out why they left."

"Why does it matter?"

"Because we can learn so much from the people who came before us. And we can do that by honoring them, not leaving them to fade away in history."

His gaze fixed on her, studying her face. There was no telling what was going on in his head, but his attention was starting to make Miri uncomfortable. She wasn't used to men looking at her for so long. Examining every feature. She bit the inside of her mouth, impatiently awaiting something—anything—from him. Any indication that he was on her side.

They couldn't give up. Not now.

"Fine," he finally said. "If you're not going to call it off, then I'm going to call my boss at *GloGeo* and tell him what's been going on. Maybe he can knock some sense into whoever is paying for this expedition."

Rafa snatched the satellite phone that had been sticking out of the side pocket in Miri's—or rather, Logan's—cargo shorts, and started dialing, but Miri lunged to stop him, snagging the phone from his hands and quickly hitting the end button.

"Give that back," Rafa demanded. He grabbed for her arms, which she had raised above her head.

"No," Miri said. "I'm not going to have you telling your boss and then writing some article about the ridiculous Dr. Jacobs who fumbled her way through the Amazon."

Rafa narrowed his eyes at her. "Don't presume to know what I'm going to write."

"Don't presume to think I'm an idiot," she said, glaring right back at him. "You leave now, you write a story about the Moon City fuck-up brigade."

"So, what? You're holding me hostage now?"

"If it stops you from going back to the States before we've found the Moon City, then yes!"

He let out a full-throated laugh. A teasing laugh that said, *Try me.*

They stared at each other for three solid beats before launching into a full-on wrestling match for the phone on the deck of the boat, their hands whirling around each other with frantic energy, twisting and turning until she was able to brace herself with one leg on either side of his body.

"Pringles, what are you—" he said, tussling with her to get the phone back when suddenly she lost her balance and fell forward, landing with her mouth pressed against his. The struggling stopped.

In fact, the entire universe stopped.

Their eyes both went wide, and she quickly pulled away, covering her mouth with her hands. Miri couldn't tell who was more shocked.

"I'm sorry. I didn't mean to—" she mumbled through her fingers, but he stopped her, taking her hands and lowering them from her lips.

"Miri?" he whispered.

"Yes?"

"Kiss me."

Miri released the tension in her legs and settled into his lap, straddling his waist. Rafa stared up at her with his beautiful deep brown eyes, waiting for her kiss. Wanting *her* lips. With one hand holding hers, his other raised to the back of her neck, then gently pulled her closer. She closed her eyes in anticipation, and when they finally connected, she melted into his arms as their mouths melted into each other.

For someone with hands as firm as Rafa's, his lips were impossibly soft. Like tender pillows Miri wanted to nestle into. He took his time exploring her mouth, planting slow, delicate kisses against her lips before opening his mouth, gliding his tongue against hers, and seeking an invitation to be let in. An invitation Miri readily accepted.

He tasted of Pringles. Maybe she'd have to start calling *him* that as well. But his tongue twirled around hers as if he enjoyed the taste of her as much as she enjoyed him.

She needed more. Wanted more. She pulled their bodies closer, grazing the apex of her thighs over his pelvis as a low moan escaped from his throat, rumbling into her mouth. A jolt of arousing electricity from the friction and his satisfied groans raced through her body and sent a pleasant shiver across her skin.

"Are you cold?" he asked with his mouth still pressed to hers.

"Uh-uh," she said, smiling against his lips. "The opposite."

Even with her eyes still closed, she could sense his smile before he dragged her bottom lip between his teeth, then returned to kissing her. A kiss that sent a fire burning straight between her legs. His length hardened beneath her as she rocked her core against him. Desperate to have all of him. He caressed her mouth, showing no signs of stopping, when the screeching howls from a monkey in the tree branch above them broke their kiss apart.

"I think someone's jealous," Rafa said, smiling at her and tucking a strand of her hair behind her ear.

"What makes you so sure?" Miri said.

"Because I'd be jealous if someone else was kissing you, too."

Miri's cheeks grew warm, and she tried hiding her bashful grin. But it was no use. Not with Rafa holding her in his arms— and with her body straddling his.

"Miri," he said with concern in his voice, tearing her focus away from their kiss. She was afraid to look at him. Afraid to acknowledge the worry that was most certainly evident on his face. "Miri," he repeated. "You know it's not safe to be out here. Those guys? They're going to come looking for us. We stole their boat."

"Then we'll ditch it."

"They know where we're heading. They'll find us."

"Right, and once we're at Florestacasa, we'll have a dozen other people to stop them. This sort of thing happens all the time," Miri said, waving her hand like it was no big deal. "Looters looking for an easy payday, spying on expeditions so they can raid them as soon as they have a chance."

"*All* the time?" he asked, raising his brow.

"Okay, maybe not *all* the time. But sometimes."

"That doesn't mean *this* time needs to be one of them. Have you ever been on an expedition being tracked by thieves?"

Miri twisted her mouth. "No, but Corrie has."

"Corrie's not here."

Thanks for the reminder.

But Corrie would never back down from a fight. And certainly not when Vautour was on the other side of it.

"Look, I know you think this is a bad idea, but Vautour will desecrate the city. Don't you think their descendants deserve to know what became of them?"

He squinted at her. "What makes you think they don't know already? You said it yourself yesterday. Os protetores serve to protect the city. Maybe they don't *want* it to be found, by Vautour *or* us."

"Maybe you're right," she said, relaxing her shoulders. "Maybe os protetores *aren't* real. But until I have some evidence of that, I can't just give up. That's not how archaeologists work."

"Quinn is an archaeologist—" he started, but Miri wasn't having any of it, tensing up again.

"Do *not* compare me to Dr. Quinn," she said, glaring at him. "I actually care about what I do and why I do it."

"You don't think Quinn cared before he got himself mixed up with the wrong people? What if you were in his position?"

"I wouldn't ever be in his position." She folded her arms.

"I'm sure Quinn never imagined he'd be in this situation, either, but things happen, Miri. People fall on hard times. Or . . . trust the wrong person," he said, almost as if he had first-hand experience. "All I'm saying is that until you've found yourself in a bad spot, you never actually think those things could happen to you." Rafa untwisted her arms and took her hands, gently rubbing his thumb over her knuckles.

"Fine. You're right. I have no idea what I'd do if I were in Dr. Quinn's shoes. But I'd like to think our character speaks for itself, and Dr. Quinn is an ass. And if that's what you think of me then that's on you for kissing me."

Rafa half chuckled, then lowered his chin, shaking his head slightly. "You really are something," he said.

"Given the present discussion, I'm not sure if I should take that as a good or bad thing." She smiled at him, hoping it would ease the tension.

They stared into each other's eyes, questioning everything. What more was there to say, though? Miri had laid her heart out there. She was done fighting. What Rafa chose to do with it was all up to him.

So she let him have the phone, but not without one last plea. "Please, Rafa. I need this."

Rafa stared at the phone and then lifted his head to the sky, closing his eyes before letting out a long exhale. Miri sat silently atop his lap, biting her bottom lip as she debated what, if anything, to say. Rafa didn't move, taking slow, measured breaths. Then, with a swift movement, he rolled her off his lap and hopped to his feet.

"Come on," he said as he reached down for her hand.

"What are you . . ." Miri started as she put her hand in his and he pulled her up to his level.

"If we're staying out here, then I've got two conditions: One, you need to tell the rest of the crew what happened so they can make their own decisions as to whether they want to stay."

Miri nodded. "Fair enough. And what's condition number two?"

"You've got to learn how to throw a decent punch that's not going to leave you cofounding a broken-hand support group with Quinn," he said, causing her to snicker.

"All right. Deal."

"Great. Now come here," he said, motioning for her to stand next to him. "First, you need to ball your fists. Curl your fingers and then tuck your thumb like this," he said while demonstrating and tucking his thumb over his middle finger. "Do not put your thumb on the inside of your grip or you might break it."

Miri mirrored his fists. "Like this?"

"Yes. Like that. Okay, next, you need to get in the right stance. You should turn your body to the side so that your dominant punching side is away from your opponent. You're going to want to stand with most of your weight on the balls of your feet and a slight bend in your knees. Then bring your hands up to your cheeks so you can defend yourself like this. Now you try."

Miri stood next to Rafa and tried mirroring his stance, but it looked twice as awkward when she did it. He walked around to the other side of her and twisted her hips.

"I'm sorry . . ." she said, putting her hands to her side and squaring to face him, clearly frustrated. "Are you really able to just move on and not say anything about it?"

He cocked his head to the side. "Say anything about what?"

Miri groaned. "About me kissing you. Look, I'm sorry if I made things awkward—"

"Hey," he said, stopping her from going into another spiral. "You have absolutely nothing to apologize for." Rafa looked over to the captain's cabin, seeing Felix and Logan watching through the window, seemingly amused by this showing. Great. It wasn't the time for this conversation. Though, thankfully, from Rafa and Miri's earlier seated position, the guys likely hadn't seen them kissing, and they couldn't decipher their words over the boat's motor.

"Now, get back into the fighting stance," he continued as he helped reposition her hands, "and then you're going to extend your dominant arm like this and rotate your palm, so it faces down as you aim for a vulnerable area on your opponent like the nose, eyes, or ears. Imagine that you're punching *through* your target and use your hips to maximize power. Watch me."

Rafa threw a few punches in slow motion before speeding up his motion for a full demonstration. Miri wasn't one for watching fights, but there was something so sexy about the way he threw his weight.

"Okay, now you try."

But she didn't. Instead, she stood there in a slack fighting stance, staring at him and trying to read his mind. "Come on. Just throw a few punches," he said.

Miri sighed and threw a few punches, but she didn't need a mirror to know that unlike Rafa, her moves were lackluster, possessing little, if any, oomph.

"Your technique is good, but you really need to make sure you *pack*"—he exaggerated as he demonstrated again—"the punch."

"I feel silly punching the air."

"Then, here," he said, moving in front of her and putting up his hands. "Aim here."

Miri let up her stance. "You want me to punch you?"

"My hands, yes."

"Full force? What if I hurt you?"

"You're not going to hurt me," he said with a bit too much of a snicker for Miri's liking.

She narrowed her eyes at him—*Is that so?*—then got back into fighting stance and threw a punch, connecting with his palm.

"Good. That's better," he said. "Just make sure you follow through. Don't stop just because your fist connected with your target."

Her mouth pulled in a tight line as she sent another throw his way. This one stung a bit more. Maybe she *was* getting the hang of it.

"Great. Now feel free to go a little harder. Don't worry about hurting me," he said.

Her eyes looked as if a fire had just been set behind them as she swung her arm again, growling, "I'll show you, Ninja Turtle," before her fist could connect with his.

But he grabbed her fist and brought their hands together between them, stopping her momentum like a needle scratching a record player.

"Hey, hey, what's going on?" he asked.

"What's going on? I can barely even look at you right now!"

Rafa raised his brow. "Because I'm wearing a Teenage Mutant Ninja Turtles shirt?"

Her mouth twisted, fighting to hold back the words on the tip of her tongue, before she blurted out, "Yes, actually. I mean, look at you, wearing that teeny tiny T-shirt, which leaves absolutely *nothing* to the imagination," she said, casting her eyes down almost as if talking to herself. "It's downright ridiculous, yet it's the hottest thing I've ever seen, so it's kind of hard having you stand in front of me right now, forcing me to stare at all the ways that shirt should be R-rated, *especially* after I kissed you and *especially* when you've so easily moved past it. So, yeah, what's going on is that I feel silly. Silly while you're so clearly indifferent about what happened. And so while you're ready to move on like it never happened, I'm over here wishing I could rewind ten minutes and do everything differently."

He smiled, brushing the pad of his thumb over her knuckles. "Pringles? I liked it."

Her head ticked up. "Wait . . . what?"

"The kiss."

"You did? Like it, I mean?" she asked.

Rafa smiled.

"Of course I liked it. I like just about everything about you." She bit her bottom lip. The lip that she wanted nothing more than to be all over Rafa's. "And when we're alone," he said, pulling her closer by a fraction of an inch, "I'm going to kiss you again. But for now, we have an audience." Miri glanced over her shoulder as he motioned with his head toward Felix and Logan. "But at least this way, it looks like nothing more than me trying to teach you to fight."

"So is this lesson just a ploy to touch me?"

His gaze homed in on her. "Maybe. And possibly also to distract myself so I'm not just thinking about kissing you for the next who knows how long."

"And are you? Focused, I mean," Miri asked as her eyes stayed on him.

His gaze went straight to her lips. Oh, he was focused, all right. But . . . he was right. Kissing would have to wait.

"Yes. And if you really want to be a kickass jungle warrior, then I need *you* to focus on learning these moves."

He flashed her a smile and gave her arms a shake, changing the energy.

"Okay, but next I want you to teach me the proper way to kick a guy in the groin." She shook her limbs and returned to fighting stance.

Rafa snickered. "Fine. But *that* one I'm not letting you practice on me."

A SOFT GLOW FILLED THE SKY AS A MACAW FLEW OVERHEAD. A light fog settled atop the river, casting a serene, almost peaceful stillness on the rainforest. Which was funny seeing as there were probably a few hundred thousand various plants, insects, and animals that could kill them lurking beyond the tree line. The puttering boat at least provided a steady hum of white noise to drown out the creatures lurking at the riverbanks. Creatures they couldn't see but Rafa knew were there, stalking them in the night.

The temperature had dipped, casting a chill over their bodies, but Miri's quiet, gentle kisses radiated enough heat to stoke the inferno raging through Rafa's body. With the team taking turns at the helm, there was always someone else beside them—thankfully fast asleep. Lucky for Rafa, he was adept in the art of covert kissing.

He knew he shouldn't have invited that first real kiss. He *knew* it was a bad idea, that once he'd had a taste, he'd want more. But it was the first time in his life that he could remember going for something that he wanted that hadn't been someone else's suggestion. His hobbies. His career. Those were his father's hopes and dreams for him. Thinking back, Rafa wasn't sure he would have made those same choices had his father not pushed him in those directions. Even that creative writing course had led to his career as a journalist, not as the fiction author Rafa so desperately wanted to become.

He couldn't picture a situation where he allowed himself to veer. Allowed himself to want something so badly that he was willing to forgo common sense.

And when he'd tasted Miri's lips, well, she'd kissed him silly. He was giddy as a schoolboy, riding high like it had been his first kiss. He couldn't stop smiling. Smiling at how delightful her lips felt, at how haphazard it was, just like each of their interactions, at how much he didn't care about anything except wanting to kiss her again and again.

So he did. All night. And once they were satiated by each other's lips, she eventually allowed herself to drift to sleep in the safety of his arms, his body molded to the curvature of hers.

He lay there most of the night contemplating his next move until it was his turn to captain the boat. Though he slept for only a few short hours—if even that—he felt more rested than he'd felt in a long time. It was amazing Rafa had managed to sleep at all given the danger they were in, and after sleeping on a wooden deck with no pillows or blankets and only each other to provide comfort. But oh, did Miri provide enough comfort for Rafa to forget about everything else.

Such as his promise to his father. He'd yet to figure out how to explain this situation to him.

For now, however, Rafa took in the sights and sounds of the Amazon. This might be the last time he did something like this—well, hopefully it would be the last time he traveled by stolen boat running away from criminals in the Amazon—but really he was thinking about being out in the wild. Exploring the world. He couldn't say he hadn't enjoyed his time working at *GloGeo*, but sometimes even good things had to come to an end.

Sometimes they needed to end to make room for better things.

"Morning," Miri said as she entered the captain's cabin, stealing his thoughts. Speaking of.

"Morning, Pringles," he said, unable to hold back his smile at the sight of her.

Her hair stuck out from her ponytail, glasses askew on her face. It only added to her charm. Even swimming in Logan's clothes, she was beautiful.

She let out a huge yawn, then said, "Man, what I wouldn't give for a cup of coffee."

"Well, it's not coffee, but I did find this," Rafa said, handing Miri a half-drunk bottle of cachaça.

"Do you drink this straight?"

"I did. Helped to wake me up."

"Won't this make me sleepy?"

He chuckled. "Maybe if you drink the whole thing, but I don't think a little nip is gonna knock you out."

Miri opened the bottle and took a whiff. The scent of alcohol alone seemed to awaken her senses, but she took a quick nip at the bottle anyway. Rafa imagined the subtle, almost fruity flavor hitting her taste buds and sending a jolt through her body as it did his.

"Not bad, right?" he said, taking the bottle back.

"It's surprisingly good. Though, seeing as the only thing

we've eaten in the last twelve hours was a few chips, not sure I
should have much more than that."

"Well, I found this, too," he said, lifting a ratty bench cushion on the side of the cabin and revealing a random assortment
of food: some fruit, nuts, bread, meats, and cheeses.

"Jackpot!" Miri dove toward the box, digging in and grabbing a banana. She quickly peeled the small banana variety and
took a bite, closing her eyes and groaning at its sweet flavor.
"Oh my God," she mumbled into the fruit. "Mmm . . . I could
put this whole thing in my mouth right now."

Rafa's jaw slackened as he watched her devouring the banana halfway in her mouth. *Oh God.* It hadn't been *that* long
since he'd been with a woman. But watching her eat that phallic
fruit sent his mind back to that first kiss last night. A kiss he had
no business enjoying as much as he did. And no business wanting more of, particularly given the predicament they were in.

But, oh, did he want it. Want *her.* All of her.

He pictured that pretty little mouth of hers wrapped around
his cock, those sweet sapphire eyes staring up at him behind her
yellow glasses. Imagined her twirling her silky tongue and delicate fingers along his shaft. Taking him in like she was taking
that goddamn banana.

She opened her eyes to find Rafa examining her. Upon meeting her gaze, he quickly cleared his throat and snapped his attention straight ahead.

"You must really like bananas," Rafa said, hoping she didn't
notice the bulge growing in his pants.

Miri swallowed and covered her mouth as she finished
chewing, then said, "Actually, it's a banana maçã. Apple-banana.
Have you ever tried one?"

"I don't think so."

"Oh, here." She broke off a one-inch piece then brought it to his mouth. He stared at her hand for a fraction of a second before wrapping his lips around the fruit, his tongue grazing her fingertips with the subtlest of touches.

"Mmm . . . that *is* good," he said.

Now Miri was the one clearing her throat and averting her attention as she snapped her jaw shut and backed away. "I know. I wish you could find them in the States more easily," she said. "Do you think it's okay if I eat something else?"

Rafa laughed. "Sure. I don't think Sérgio will be expecting that we left his stash alone," he said with a wink.

Miri smiled, then dug into the box again, this time pulling out a guava. She bit right into the skin, again groaning at the deliciousness and settling onto the bench. Did she not know what those groans were doing to him?

"God, why is fruit *so* much better here?" she asked, her eyes practically rolling into the back of her head.

Rafa laughed again. "Let me try it."

Miri hopped up and brought the fruit to his lips while licking her own. This time, he took her wrist in his hand, steadying her hold, then sunk his teeth into the juicy fruit while his gaze firmly focused on her.

Time slowed as the juice seeped from the fruit and dribbled down his chin, and he paid no attention to the fact that her hand was dripping with the guava's sweet nectar. With Felix and Logan still sound asleep, they were finally alone. They lowered their arms and took a few steps toward each other. He pulled her close, then leaned down to kiss her.

"Wait!" Miri said, stopping him and lifting her hand to cover her mouth. "I have morning breath."

He smiled and then took the guava from her hand, placing it on the steering panel. Then, one by one, he took her fingers and placed them in his mouth.

"After spending half the night kissing you," he said as he lapped up the delicious juice from her pinky, "I'm surprised that you think I'd care about a little morning breath."

Miri's chest heaved as he sucked her fingers. Tasting her. Savoring every bit of that fruit on her and then some. Maybe it was simply the boat rocking on the river, but Miri's knees buckled, and she lost her balance.

"Whoa," Rafa said, quickly wrapping his arms around her. "I got you."

Her hands gripped his biceps, and she looked up at him. Oh, he had her all right.

Though, with the way her eyes seemed to search his soul, maybe it was the other way around. She'd taken hold of him. And as his entire body swelled like a thunderous wave crashing into the shore, he wasn't sure he ever wanted her to let him go.

"Morning," Logan said as he and Felix entered the cabin.

"Everything okay?" Felix asked upon noticing Miri in Rafa's arms.

Rafa quickly released her from his hold and returned to the ship's wheel.

"Yep, lost my footing is all," Miri said, smoothing out her clothes and hair.

"Oh! Where'd you get that?" Logan said, rushing over to the guava sitting on the dash and sinking his teeth in. "Mmm, so good," he said with his mouth full.

"Some might say finger-licking good," Rafa said, winking at Miri. "Goes great with Pringles."

"You've got Pringles?" Felix asked excitedly.

"Sorry," Rafa said. "I don't share." He tossed Miri a suggestive glance, and her mouth slackened.

"Er," Miri stammered, her cheeks flushed, "but there's more stuff in there."

She lifted the bench lid, then immediately scrambled out of the way to avoid getting bowled over by Felix and Logan as they lunged for the food.

"Score," Felix said, passing food back and forth with Logan and sharing bites.

With the two of them thoroughly distracted, Miri circled behind Rafa, then stole a quick kiss. Nothing but a peck, really. But there wouldn't likely be another opportunity for a while, so he'd take whatever he could get.

"So, what's the plan?" Logan said, mouth half-full with a piece of bread.

"Looks like we've got another half day on this boat," Rafa said, handing a map over to him.

"And after that?" Felix asked.

After that? Oh, Rafa had grand plans for the evening.

Nice hot meal. Nice hot shower, perhaps *with* Miri. And maybe, just maybe, Pringles for dessert.

. . . .

THEY PULLED UP TO THE BASE CAMP BY MIDAFTERNOON. ALMOST like a village in the trees, the resort campus was a collection of thatched-roof huts on stilts, connected by wooden platformed walkways, with a larger structure connecting them in the center. It looked like the body of a spider with all the individual cabins webbing away from its legs.

The structures sat in the middle of a wide clearing

surrounded by strangler figs and giant Brazil nut trees, but Mother Nature had already started to reclaim the resort. Lianas covered in moss and epiphytes grew from the nearby tree branches, twisting and winding their way around the boardwalk railings. Bird nests hung from beneath the huts. Although the rainy season was coming, the resort hadn't yet flooded. But in a few short weeks, the ground would be completely submerged, overtaken by the adjacent river, necessitating the raised walkways. A family of capybaras watched them from the other side of the river, surely waiting for an opportunity to poke around the grounds for some food scraps. Every inch of this place was a reminder that *they* were the intruders. The forest was only allowing them to visit.

The expedition team gathered to greet them at the river's edge. They may have been strangers, but Rafa had never been so happy to see a group of strangers as he was now. Anissa quickly whisked Miri away with her clipboard in hand, but not without Miri tossing Rafa one last sweet, sexy smile, signaling that they'd meet up again soon. That look gave Rafa the boost he needed to get through the rest of the day. Because as soon as night fell, he'd find an opportunity to get Miri alone, and hopefully this time without Felix and Logan sleeping beside them.

Rafa tied the boat to a stump on the edge of the river as the rest of the crew helped unload. Once they finished, he set off to his cabin for a shower and a change of clothes. Each cabin had its own bed and bathroom but was otherwise bare bones. They didn't need much. And hopefully, they wouldn't be here long. Fortunately, his bag seemed to have made it with the other van and was already waiting in his room when he got there. After cleaning up and doing an inventory of his belongings, he headed back out to the resort grounds to start working on documenting the expedition. Sabotage or not, he still had an article to write, after all.

He meandered through the group, listening to their stories and taking notes. Most of it wouldn't make its way into the piece, but a journalist didn't always know what details would necessarily be important later, so he jotted everything down, weaving in and out of conversations. Word had spread fast. He heard lots of whispers and rumors. Questions about what had happened with Quinn. Worries about Vautour.

Maybe Rafa didn't have to do anything to sabotage this expedition. The expedition seemed to be sabotaging itself.

It sure would make things easier between him and Miri if that were the case.

Right then, Felix came running up to him, waving the satellite phone in his hand.

"Rafa, there's a call. It's for you," he said.

A call? On the satellite phone?

"Are you sure it's for me?" Rafa asked.

"He says it's your father."

His father? How in the—?

Rafa glanced around, almost as if he half expected his dad to pop out from behind a fern and yell, "Surprise!" No, that was absurd. He took the phone and walked several feet away from Felix.

"Dad?" Rafa asked, wrinkling his brow.

"Rafael?"

"Where are you?"

"What do you mean, where am I? I'm at home."

"In Montreal?"

"Of course. Where else would I be?"

"Well, is everything okay? How did you get this number?" Rafa asked.

"I called your boss."

"But why?"

"Why? Son, I was worried about you. I'd heard a rumor that Dr. Bradley Quinn got injured, and that your crew had gotten off course, and when I hadn't heard from you, I feared something had happened to you."

"Dad, I'm in the Amazon," Rafa said, pinching the bridge of his nose. "Cell service isn't exactly 5G out here. How did you even hear about Quinn?"

"Protecting the Cidade da Lua has been my life's work," his father said matter-of-factly. "I know people."

Wasn't *that* an understatement. Rafa had witnessed his dad's connections firsthand. People spilling their secrets. It was amazing his dad wasn't involved in politics.

"We're fine. There were some guys in the jungle who were trying to steal our equipment, and we got into a fight with them," Rafa explained.

"Were you hurt?" his dad asked with worry in his voice.

"No, but we managed to get away."

"You should have let them take the stuff. That might have solved all our problems."

"Yeah, I realized that afterward," Rafa said, rubbing the back of his neck. "But it all happened so fast. One second these guys were waving goodbye with all our stuff, and the next Pring—I mean, Dr. Jacobs—she went after them without a second thought." Rafa smiled thinking about it, picturing Miri taking on those guys as if she didn't have a fear in the world. "She was pretty amazing," he unwittingly said, immediately snapping his mouth shut once the words came out.

Fuck.

"Mmm . . . Dr. Jacobs," his dad said. "I looked her up after you told me about her. She's quite pretty."

"Yes, she is."

"Sounds like you might have a soft spot for her."

"I suppose I do." There was no use denying it. Besides, he couldn't lie to his dad. That was one thing they promised never to do. No matter how bad things got. No matter how terrible things seemed to be. Their relationship depended on trust.

It was bad enough he hadn't told his dad how he felt about his job at *GloGeo*.

"Hmm," his father murmured, as if deep in thought. "That might be a problem, then."

"Why?"

"Because you can't let her succeed, Rafael. She can't find the Cidade da Lua. That's not what you're there for."

That may have been the plan, but Rafa didn't want to be the reason for her failure. It didn't feel right. Not anymore.

"Well, I don't think it matters anyway," Rafa said, trying to refocus his dad's attention away from Miri. "Seems there's another team out here looking for it, too."

"Another team?"

"Yes. Have you ever heard of Pierre Vautour? His guys are the ones that attacked us."

"Rafael," his dad said after a beat. "Pierre Vautour is a dangerous man."

"You know who he is?"

"Of course I do. I met him in Brazil many years ago, searching for the Cidade da Lua."

"Why didn't you mention him when we were talking about this expedition last week?"

"I had no idea he'd still be out there looking for the city de-cades later. If he's there, then you need to stay out of his way."

"And how am I supposed to do that? It's not like I know where he is."

"You do that by keeping Dr. Jacobs and her team from mak-ing any further progress."

"But then what about Vautour? Won't that make it easier for him to find the Moon City? If he's as bad as everyone says he is, shouldn't we try to get there first? To protect the city, I mean," Rafa said, echoing the words Miri had said to him.

But she'd changed his mind. Opened his eyes. All he needed to do now was convince his dad that her way was the right way.

"No!" his father yelled. He'd yelled so loud, in fact, that Rafa jumped. It was amazing no one else had heard. "I'm sorry, Rafael. But you must convince Dr. Jacobs to leave. The Cidade da Lua cannot be found."

"But what if I convince Dr. Jacobs to leave and then Vautour finds it anyway?"

"We leave Vautour to os protetores da lua."

"I don't get it, Dad. Why send me out here if all we had to do was rely on os protetores da lua? Couldn't they have stopped both teams?"

"Because os protetores da lua will stop at nothing—and I mean nothing—to protect the Moon City. Vautour has done many terrible things. And unlike Vautour, Dr. Jacobs and her team are innocent people. They don't deserve what os prote-tores da lua would do to them. What they'd do to *you* to get back at me."

Get back at him? "Dad, what are you talking about?" Rafa said, holding his head to think. "I thought Mom was one of them? Why would they be trying to get back at you?"

"Rafael," his father choked out. Rafa could feel the tears in his father's eyes although he couldn't see them. "Rafael, it's time you knew the truth about your ancestry."

The truth? Rafa already knew the truth.

"What more is there to say? You've told me this already. Mom was a member of the protectors. She'd heard about a man in Manaus asking questions about the Moon City—you—so she posed as a guide, intending to throw you off the scent, but then you fell in love."

Rafa recited his parents' love story as if it were old news he'd heard before. Why was his dad bothering him with this now?

But his father let out a long sigh.

"That's only part of the story," his father said. "All of that is true, but what I didn't tell you is that . . . your mother . . ." He paused.

Okay. *Now* Rafa was starting to worry. *What the hell is going on?*

"Your mother," he continued, "she was sent to lure me to os protetores so I'd be killed."

"What?!" A knot formed in the pit of Rafa's stomach. The protectors were murderers? And his mother was one of them?

His father had *lied* to him. Lied all these years, tricking him into believing in this fairy-tale love story that didn't exist.

"I know this is hard to accept," his dad explained. "Os protetores da lua will stop at nothing to protect the Cidade da Lua. It's no coincidence that several expeditions to the Moon City resulted in people never returning. Whole teams lost, never to be heard from again."

"Why didn't you ever tell me this?"

"I'd always planned to tell you someday, but the moment

was never right. Because I didn't want you to think ill of your mother. She wasn't a bad person—"

"She was going to let them kill you!"

"No, no, son." Rafa could almost picture his father coming to his side to comfort him. "She couldn't do it, but os protetores . . . they are dangerous people."

With shaky legs, Rafa shuffled to a nearby tree and sank to the ground. With the tree at his back, he looked up at the dense canopy.

His father continued. "Your mother—she showed me the error in my ways. Taught me that the Cidade da Lua needed to be protected. Even though your mother had changed me, os protetores were angry with her for leaving with me. But more than that, they were furious at *me*. I was someone who'd wanted to take what was theirs."

"So why should I help them?"

"Because I promised her—I promised your mother that I wouldn't let anything happen to the Cidade da Lua if I could help it. But I'm old now. I wouldn't last a day in the Amazon. So it's on you. I'm asking that you do this, Rafa. Please, do this for me. All you need to do is stop Dr. Jacobs from reaching the city."

Rafa dragged his hand slowly down his face, wishing more than ever that he hadn't taken this job.

"Which brings me to that problem I mentioned earlier."

"What problem?" Rafa asked.

"The soft spot you have for her." His father sighed again. "Rafael, I know this isn't what you wanted. To be on another expedition, away from home. Away from your life. I know we said we'd talk about your career and your future when you got back but . . . she isn't it."

Rafa wrinkled his brow even though his father couldn't see it. "What do you mean?" he asked.

"I'm sure you have lots of feelings about what's happening to you right now. Being there, in the very same jungle where I fell in love with your mother. But Dr. Jacobs can't be that for you."

The buzzing and chirping of the rainforest stilled, as if creating silence for Rafa's father to hear his thoughts. His dad was right—there were all sorts of feelings swirling through his head, things Rafa couldn't make sense of.

But it had been *two* days. He wasn't in love. He couldn't be.

"Dad, I don't know what you're even talking about. Just because I enjoy being around her doesn't mean I—"

"She wants to destroy everything your mother wanted to protect," his father said, cutting him off. "Destroy the very memory of her."

"No, Miri isn't like that. She cares about protecting the city."

"By revealing its location to the rest of the world? How can she protect it once it's been found? If you care about her, you need to convince her to leave before os protetores find you."

"She'll hate me if she finds out. I don't want to be the reason she quits."

"And I don't want to lose you!" His father's voice boomed through the phone. Long, slow breaths reverberated on the other end. Almost as if he were angry. "I won't have you die for a woman you barely know," he continued after calming down. "I've already lost your mother. I can't lose you, too. You're all I have left."

Rafa hung his head. His father was right. Two days ago, Miri was nothing to him. Was he really willing to risk everything—his job, his father's trust, his *life*—for her?

"Okay," Rafa said.

"Okay, what?"

"I'll do it. I'll find a way to get the team out of here."

His father let out a breath. "Thank you. Be safe, my boy. And remember, I'm with you. Always."

'M SO GLAD YOU'VE ARRIVED," ANISSA SAID, TAPPING HER CLIP-
board on a small side table in Miri's cabin.

Miri turned away from the window perched high above the
river after counting the team members down by the boat. Eight
of them total.

There should have been nine.

"So am I," Miri said.

She'd never been happier to see her friend. Or an actual
bed. Although the furnishings in the huts were simple, after the
night they'd had, this place felt like a five-star hotel. If she
hadn't still been wearing Logan's clothes, dirty from sleeping on
the deck of the boat, she would have already nestled into that
cozy-looking bed.

"Is that everyone?" Miri asked, nodding her head down to
the group then turning back toward Anissa.

"Erm . . ." Anissa said, twisting her face, "about that. We
had someone quit in Caracaraí."

"Quit?" Miri blurted out. Shit, shit, shit. "What happened? Why didn't you tell me when I called earlier with our update?"

"I didn't want to worry you."

"Worry me? Anissa." Miri said her name very matter-of-factly.

"I know, I know," Anissa said, raising the clipboard to cover her face. "But with those guys attacking you and with you being out in the middle of nowhere, I figured you didn't need *another* thing to worry about."

"Funny that you thought I wouldn't worry about it no matter when you told me," Miri said. "So what happened?"

"It was Dr. Quinn and all his gibberish nonsense. He kept saying, 'He's coming. Pierre Vautour's coming, and he'll destroy all your lives like he did mine.'"

"He mentioned Vautour?"

Anissa nodded. "Yes, that asshole who fucked with Corrie and Ford in Mexico. And after I confirmed that another team with lots of gear arrived in Caracaraí a few days ago, Frank said this wasn't what he signed up for and left."

Vautour. The other crew had to be his.

"Great. Well, when we find the Cidade da Lua, we can send them a postcard," Miri said.

"You mean, *if* we find it."

Miri waved Anissa off. Now wasn't the time for casting doubt.

"What about the men who attacked us? Were you able to figure out who they were?" Miri asked.

"No. Just a couple of dirtbags working with Vautour, I suppose."

"And presumably Dr. Quinn?"

Anissa stopped in her tracks and turned to face Miri. "You think?"

"How else did they know how to find us?"

Anissa looked at the floor as if trying to recall the events of the last day. "I mean, I chalked up most of the crap he was saying to the concussion, but now that you mention it . . ." Her voice trailed off as she considered Miri's suggestion. "Oh, by the way, that's your stuff."

Anissa motioned to a couple of bags in the corner of the room.

"Oh, thank God!" Miri said, diving toward the bags and pulling out a clean pair of underwear and clutching them to her chest.

"You must really love your panties," Anissa said with a snicker.

"You try sleeping in river-soaked undies and men's cargo shorts and then see how excited *you* are for a clean pair of underwear. Mind if I shower really quick?"

"It's your room. Go for it."

Miri grabbed her toiletries and a fresh set of clothes, then headed to the bathroom and started the shower. God, she'd never looked forward to a shower quite like this. It was amazing Rafa wanted to get close to her given how she probably smelled.

The water hit her face and instantly she felt rejuvenated. Sort of like the way she felt kissing Rafa. His lips awakened something in her, something she didn't know existed. A desire. A passion. A sexiness she didn't know she possessed.

He made her feel beautiful. Special. It had been a long time since anyone had made her feel wanted. He'd been so warm and comforting last night. If only Felix and Logan hadn't been there. Who knew what would have happened?

Perhaps she'd find out tonight once everyone went to bed.

"How were things sleeping on the boat last night?" Anissa called from the other side of the bathroom door.

Speaking of.

Miri wiped the soapy water off her face and called out, "Good."

"Good? Hmm . . . Might that have anything to do with the company you kept?"

The suggestion in Anissa's tone couldn't be missed, but after her goading the night before, Miri didn't need to spill the tea. She'd never hear the end of it.

"Yeah, we all got along well," Miri said, pausing to await Anissa's reaction.

"I'm sure you did," Anissa said saucily. "I noticed how quickly Rafa volunteered to stay back with you, and how quickly you agreed."

"Well, it was silly of me to think I should stay out there alone. He was just trying to be helpful. Besides, Felix and Logan offered to stay behind, too," Miri said.

"Okay, Miri. And so how'd things go at the bar the other night?"

"Fine, until Dr. Quinn showed up." Miri rolled her eyes thinking back on it, then remembered his phone. "I have his phone, by the way," she called out.

"You do?"

"Yeah, it was in his bag under the seat of the van. But I haven't looked at it yet."

"Where is it?" Anissa asked.

"It's in the cargos I was wearing. They're in here. You can come in."

Anissa opened the door and dug around for the phone while Miri continued showering.

"Shoot, it's locked," Anissa said. "What do you think his password is? It's only three numbers."

"Probably something pompous."

Dr. Quinn's voice echoed in her head. *Me, myself, and I. Numero uno. My favorite number.*

No? He couldn't be *that* pompous.

"Try one-one-one," Miri said.

She waited a moment, then Anissa called out, "Oh my God, that actually worked. How did you know?"

"Lucky guess." She *did* always have a knack for picking up on things others may have missed. "See anything interesting?"

Anissa was silent for a few moments. "Hmm . . . there's a text string between him and someone named V."

It could only be one person.

"What's it say?" Miri asked.

"Let me scroll back. Hmm . . . well, Dr. Quinn was bitching about you changing course and talking about how you must have figured something out. And then this V person said to stop you, and Quinn said . . . er . . . never mind."

Miri scrunched her face, pausing for a second in the shower. "What do you mean, 'never mind'? What did he say?"

"Well, um, he said you have no idea what you're doing and not to worry because he'd put you in your place."

"Put me in my place?" Miri pushed the shower curtain around her face so she could see Anissa. "Fucking asshole!"

"Is it awful that I'm a smidge *glad* he got injured?" Anissa asked, twisting her face to soften the dig.

"A smidge glad? I'm fucking elated!" *Hope you're enjoying your place in that hospital bed, Captain Save-a-Dick!*

How men like Dr. Quinn managed to score journal articles and prestigious speaking engagements while Miri was exiled to jobs like dig cleanup duty would forever remain a mystery.

"Oh my God, did Corrie ever tell you about that time when he said she was a 'good archaeologist for a woman' during that speaking panel?" Anissa said, resting her behind on the sink and holding the phone by her thighs.

"No, he didn't!"

"He did. I mean, are you even surprised?"

Unfortunately, not really.

"So what did she do?" Miri asked.

"She said, 'Well, you're an *okay* archaeologist for being a prick.'"

"No!"

Anissa nodded proudly. "You know she did. Someone even caught it on video. Seriously, she was *pissed* when Larity insisted on Dr. Quinn being here. She said the only way she'd agree was if she got to pick the rest of the team."

Miri smiled and pulled the curtain back in place to finish rinsing off. Damn, what it must be like to command such authority.

"So, what else do the texts say?" Miri asked, unable to stop grinning thinking about Corrie's badassery.

"Hmm . . . well, looks like they were talking about Rafa."

And instantly, Miri's smile fell. "What about him?"

"Oh, you're not going to like this . . ." Anissa said. "Quinn said he saw the two of you getting cozy over drinks."

"What?!"

Miri hopped out of the shower and snagged a towel, not bothering to fully wrap it around her wet body before snatching the phone out of Anissa's hands.

"Damn, girl," Anissa said, smirking at Miri's bum hanging out.

Miri waved her comment off, then haphazardly pulled

the towel the rest of the way around her body with her free
hand while scrolling through Dr. Quinn's texts with her other.

QUINN
This journalist from GloGeo seems like an arrogant prick.
He looks familiar. Is he working for you?

V
No. What's his name?

QUINN
Rafael Monfils.

V
The name sounds familiar. I'll look into him.

A few minutes passed between texts.

V
Seems his father is Jean-Luc Monfils. He's a GloGeo board
member.

QUINN
That charity do-gooder?

V
Yes. I wouldn't worry about him. Silver spoon baby.

QUINN
Explains the arrogance.

V

He should be a non-issue.

QUINN

You sure? Jacobs probably would have gone to his
room if I hadn't interrupted. What if they're working
together?

V

I doubt that. Seems Jacobs is just following in the
footsteps of her mentor.

QUINN

How so?

V

Just another female archaeologist whose mind isn't on
the expedition. Fire her.

What the hell?

QUINN

Fire her? For what?

V

You don't want another scandal like what happened in
Mexico, do you?

QUINN

Weren't you the one behind that?

V

I had nothing to do with Mejía and Matthews frolicking in
the jungle.

QUINN

Well, I don't have the authority to fire her. And it's not a
fireable offense anyway.

V

Then you call someone who does have the authority. Tell
them she's not taking the job seriously. THAT is fireable.

QUINN

And what about when Dr. Mejía finds out that I got Jacobs
kicked off the job? She'll have my head. What if we make
a call to GloGeo instead and get Monfils tossed?

V

No. I told you. He's not the problem. It has to be her. She's
the one who needs to be stopped.

QUINN

Fine. I'll see what I can do.

V

You'd better figure out a way. Need I remind you what's at
stake? That loan I gave you wasn't free.

QUINN

Will figure something out.

Miri lowered the phone a fraction of an inch. "I think I'm going to be sick," she said. "I can't believe this is happening."

"A year and a half ago, I would have said the same thing. But now, after everything that happened to Corrie, well, I . . . I . . . shit. Fuck!"

Miri paced in the three-foot-by-three-foot bathroom, staring at the floor, debating their next steps.

"Should we call Corrie?" Anissa asked.

"What? No!" Miri said, perhaps a little too forcefully. But WWCMD? She certainly wouldn't call herself. "I just . . . need a few minutes."

Anissa stood in the bathroom doorway as Miri tried to come up with a plan, but her mind kept going back to the texts.

"God! Bradley Quinn, of all people," she blurted out. "Acting all high and mighty, calling me a nobody, and look at him. Can you believe him?" Miri paused to look at Anissa before continuing her ramblings. "Plotting against us? And did you see the way they were talking about me and Rafa, like we're horsing around at high school band camp?"

Anissa tossed her a sympathetic glance. "Oh, who cares what they think? Besides, like Quinn said—it's not fireable. You can fuck whoever you want."

"But we're *not* fucking!"

"Which is a shame, if you ask me," Anissa said, pursing her lips.

"I'm serious, Anissa!"

"So am I." Anissa looked at Miri straight in the face to ensure the message was clear. So Miri returned the stare. Two could make this standoff.

Anissa folded her arms and ticked up her eyebrows. *So we're going to play this game, are we?* they said.

Miri pulled her face tight, glaring at her friend. *If that's what it takes.*

A few more seconds went by, when Miri finally gave in. "Oh, whatever. Can we focus here?"

"Fine. What else does it say?" she asked, nodding her head toward the phone.

Despite her strong desire to take the phone and toss it into the depths of the Amazon River, Miri begrudgingly snatched it up and resumed scrolling.

There was a gap in the time stamp for the texts, then hours later:

QUINN
Got into a car wreck.

V
?

QUINN
Van ran off road. Doesn't look like we'll be going anywhere soon.

V
Where are you?

QUINN
GPS PIN DROPPED

V
I thought you said you were heading toward the Serra da Mocidade. This is nowhere near there.

QUINN
That idiot journalist got us lost. Jacobs trusted him to
navigate. I think I can use this to take over as lead.

V
Do it.

Ten minutes passed between texts.

V
Update?

Another five minutes.

V
Update?

Ignoring me isn't going to get you out of this.

I'm sending Hunter and Kevin out to find you. Remember
our deal. Break it and you'll regret it.

That was the end of it.

Miri set the phone on the edge of the sink near Anissa, then
she walked out of the bathroom and collapsed on the bed, lowering her head to her hands with her elbows braced on her knees.
Her mind raced. Surprisingly, confirming Dr. Quinn's involvement didn't make her feel any better.

This was a disaster. A complete fucking disaster.

So much for not creating a scandal.

"Well, that was something," Anissa said, joining her after
turning off the shower and sitting on the bed across from Miri.

Not that Miri was looking at her. No, Miri's eyes were squarely focused on the wide wooden planks of the floor. Maybe if she counted the striations in the wood grain everything else would fade away?

Miri lowered her hands and pinched the webbing between her thumb and index finger. *Ouch.* Nope. This was all real. Very, *very* real.

"At least now we know how those guys found you," Anissa continued. "I can't believe Dr. Quinn was working with Vautour the whole time. Dropping our coordinates? Now I'm *definitely* more than a smidge glad about his injury."

"I hope he never gets to go on a dig ever again," Miri said.

"Well, he won't get the opportunity once you tell everyone what he did. You should get *his* ass fired!"

"I can't."

"You can't what?"

"Tell people about this. Not yet."

Anissa eyed Miri curiously. "Why not? That guy's an asshole! After the Joukowsky Institute finds out that he fraternizes with the likes of Pierre Vautour, he'll lose his job. Don't feel sorry. He deserves whatever's coming to him."

"It's not that. Once we find the Moon City, I'll have no problem taking down that pompous sack of shit. But until then, no one else can know. I already had to convince Rafa not to tell his boss at *GloGeo*."

"Oh really?" Anissa said, waggling her brow. "Convince him how?"

A wave of heat washed over Miri's cheeks. "I told you. It's not like that," she said. Though by the shit-eating grin on Anissa's face, she clearly wasn't fooling anyone.

"And I told you, you're a terrible liar."

Miri sat still. *Maybe if I pretend I didn't hear her . . .*

"Don't pretend like you didn't hear me," Anissa followed up. "Tell me what happened between you two!"

Miri groaned. "Fine! We kissed."

"Oh my God, yes! I knew it!" Anissa said, covering her mouth and giggling. "How was it?"

"It was . . . it was amazing," Miri said with a sigh.

"Of course it was."

"Well, it won't be happening again." Miri pulled the towel up under her armpits, then got up to get her clean clothes from across the room.

"Why?" Anissa cocked back her head. "Because of those texts? Seriously, who the fuck cares? Quinn's gone. And you're both adults. You can do what you want."

Miri furrowed her brow. "But they were right. I'm distracted. And, I don't know, Vautour seems to know *a lot* about Rafa. Why would he know who he is?"

"I mean, if he's some rich guy's kid, then it would make sense that people might know who he is. Not people like us, maybe, but people like Vautour—they make it their business to know things. And he wasn't exactly pulling strings for him."

"But he also wasn't trying to get him fired, like he's trying to get me."

"Sure, but what would getting Rafa canned accomplish? You're the one who's looking for the Moon City, not him."

"Okay, then I need to *actually* look for it and focus on this expedition, not on some guy."

"Who says you can't do both? Look at Corrie and Ford. They took the dig seriously *and* fell in love at the same time."

"Fell *in love*?" Miri couldn't mask the incredulity in her voice. "You're talking about *love* now?"

"Yeah, so what?"

"So what?" Miri started pacing. "Anissa, I've known the guy for a total of forty-eight hours and you're already comparing my relationship with him to Corrie and Ford's!"

Anissa smirked.

"What now? What are you smirking about?" Miri asked.

"You said your 'relationship.'"

"Oh my God, Anissa!" Miri tossed her head back and threw the towel at Anissa. "It's just a word! Besides, I've never been in love. I don't even know what love *feels* like. This is . . . this is lust. That's all."

Yeah. That was it. It couldn't be a relationship. Miri hadn't been in a relationship in well over five years. Definitely not since getting her PhD.

"Okay, and what is it about him that you find attractive?" Anissa rested on her side, propping her head up under her arm.

"Well, he's funny, and kind, and brave, and patient, and—" Miri stopped and stared at Anissa sitting there looking quite satisfied. "What? Why are you looking at me like that?"

"Oh, hon. You like him," Anissa said, staring at Miri with tenderness in her eyes. "Like, you *really* like him."

"Oh, I do, do I? And how do you know that?"

"Because you listed all these reasons why you like him, and *none* of them have anything to do with how he looks. That's not lust. That's"—*Don't you dare say it. Don't you dare say the L-word.*—"affection." Anissa sat up. "Look, Dr. Quinn's not even here anymore, so you don't have to worry about someone tattling on you, if that's what you're worried about. I'm certainly not going to say anything. And honestly, Miri, if this *is* only lust, you could probably stand to get laid."

Miri's jaw dropped.

"What?" Anissa asked all innocently. "You know it's been a while."

"There's no way you could know that." Miri crossed her arms.

"Girl?" Anissa said, leaning back on the bed and propping herself up on the side. "I know." Her lips pursed as she gave Miri the side-eye.

Miri's mouth twisted as she fought to come up with a retort, but how could she argue? The last time the two of them had gotten together in Chicago for the Chimalli exhibit at the Field Museum and they'd grabbed some drinks at the bar, Miri had pretty much confessed her dry spell over a couple of G and Ts. The gin had been doing most of the talking—okay, so maybe it was Miri's proclivity for buzzed ramblings, or ramblings in general—but *damn, Anissa*! This had to be breaking some sort of friend code.

"Well, whatever." *Nice comeback.* Miri almost rolled her eyes at herself for her unwitty response. "None of this matters anyway, because with Vautour out there clearly looking for the Cidade da Lua, I don't have time for distractions."

Anissa sighed. "I mean, if that's what you think you need to do."

"It is," Miri said with feigned confidence.

Though she wasn't sure she meant it.

Miri peered out the window, watching the crew standing around talking, waiting for further instruction. Laughing. Joking. Carrying on not knowing the danger that awaited them.

And there was Rafa. He was a few hundred feet away, but

she could make him out clearly. The reminder of his lips warmed her body, giving her momentary pause.

But that was the exact reason she needed to pull away. She couldn't afford to pause. She couldn't afford to waste any more time thinking about anything other than what she came here for. The Cidade da Lua.

Corrie would be so disappointed in her.

She needed to do this. She needed to stop this *not*-relationship and *definitely-not-love* before it turned into something more.

Tonight. She'd call things off tonight.

But first, she had to meet the terms of their deal.

· · · · · · · · ·

TING, TING, TING, TING, TING.

Miri held her wineglass high, tapping a butter knife on the side to get the group's attention at dinner in the open-air cabana.

"Can I have your attention for a few minutes, please?" Miri said.

Annnnd, nothing. Forks and knives clattered against plates. Conversations continued. Barely even a flinch.

Let's try this again.

Miri flipped the butter knife so the heavier end could tap against the glass. *Ting, ting, ting, CRACK!*

The glass shattered, spilling red wine down Miri's arm and onto her shirt. Thankfully the stem she'd been holding hadn't cracked with it, but still. All eyes shot to her.

But hey, at least she'd gotten their attention.

She scanned the tables, spotting Rafa with Logan, Felix, and a few other guys, before connecting with his gaze. So many questions swirled in Miri's head. Wondering what he was thinking about. What, if anything, in Vautour's messages was true.

Whether she was making a mistake by deciding to end things with Rafa, not that they'd ever really started. But with the way her heart skipped just at the sight of him, the answer to at least that last question was clear.

Anissa whispered into Miri's ear from behind, "What was it you were saying about distractions?"

The words zapped Miri back to the task at hand, finally tearing her focus from Rafa and back to the rest of the group, staring and waiting for her to speak.

"Now that I've got your attention, I want to fill everyone in on where we're at with this expedition. First, Dr. Quinn is no longer with us . . ."

The entire team gasped in unison. Their hands quickly shot to cover mouths, and their faces contorted with worry.

Anissa palmed her face. *Oh. Oh dear.* They had the wrong idea.

"No, no, no," Miri said, quickly waving her hands. "Not that. What I meant to say is that he's alive"—the others instantly relaxed—"but his hand is broken in multiple areas, and he has a concussion, so it's not safe for him to rejoin us here in the middle of the jungle in case his condition worsens."

"But isn't Dr. Quinn the expert on the Cidade da Lua? How are we supposed to find it without him?" someone called out.

Oof. Talk about a punch to the gut. They doubted she could handle the situation without a more experienced lead. But Corrie trusted her for a reason.

And Miri had the medallion. All the experience in the world couldn't have been better than that, right?

If only she knew how to use the medallion to find the landmarks.

"Dr. Quinn is *an* expert," she continued, "but I think you'll be surprised. I happen to know a few things about the Moon

City as well." She smiled and puffed up her chest, then paused as if waiting for the team to cheer her on. Crickets.

Okay, so maybe knowing "a few things" wasn't all that impressive.

"I mean, I know a lot of things," Miri continued, her voice shaky and hurried. "More than Dr. Quinn, in fact. And I was handpicked by Dr. Mejía. And I've been on a bunch of digs. Like to Guatemala, and Belize. Oh! And I did this really cool field study in Greece. And another in Italy. I mean, I wasn't really digging, but . . ."

Faces turned from concerned to skeptical. *Sigh.* The regurgitated résumé was probably unnecessary.

She scanned the cabana, looking for support, but none came. "Anyway, there's more. Yesterday, Felix, Logan, Rafa, and I were, well, perhaps they've already told you, but we were attacked."

More gasps, now some murmuring. Okay, so maybe they *hadn't* already mentioned it. Shit. This wasn't going at all how Miri had imagined it.

"Hold on a second. Please, please let me explain," she said, pumping her arms to try to calm them down. "Yesterday after we all split up, a couple of men found us on the side of the road and offered to help. But we eventually realized that they weren't there to help us. They were there to stop us. They're working for Pierre Vautour, and it appears he has another team out here looking for the Cidade da Lua."

"Isn't that the guy who was behind that whole debacle with Drs. Mejía and Matthews?" someone asked.

Miri nodded. "Yes, that's him. Some of his cronies attempted to steal our equipment and they . . . they . . ."

How was she going to explain this without scaring everyone off?

"They pulled a knife on us," Logan blurted out.

The group clamored again as rapid-fire voices shot at Miri.

"A knife!"

"I didn't come out here so I could get stabbed."

"Where's Dr. Mejía when you need her?"

Ouch. Their comments were valid, though that last one stung a little.

"Listen, listen," she said, trying to regain their attention. "I get it. You all thought you were going on an expedition led by Drs. Mejía and Matthews, and now you're stuck in the Amazon with me. I'd be disappointed, too. But we're going to be an effective team, I can feel it—"

"Searching for a place that no one knows ever even existed and, even if it did, no one has seen in hundreds of years," someone responded very matter-of-factly.

"Yeah, and possibly getting killed while we're at it," another pointed out.

The team peppered her with questions, standing and shouting over each other with demands for more information and assurances. Miri's attention shot from one person to another as she tried her damnedest to answer their questions only to be met with more pressure and inquiries. Control was fleeting.

"Dr. Jacobs?" Anissa said, lightly tugging on Miri's arm.

Miri slowly rotated her head toward Anissa, trying to wake from her fog, before her gaze flashed over to meet Rafa's. Despite what she'd planned to tell him later, she hoped he'd at least give her a supportive smile, but all he offered was an apologetic twist of his mouth.

"I'm sorry . . . I just . . ." she said, shifting her attention to Anissa before shaking it off and then turning to address the group again. "Listen!"

Her commanding voice silenced the team.

"I need you to trust me," she continued. "We may be strangers, but we're here for the same thing. We all want this expedition to be a success, and we can't do that without a little trust. But, again, I get it. This isn't the expedition you signed up for, and if you want to leave, I totally understand. You'll be bound by the NDA you signed, but you're free to leave if that's your choice.

"But for those of you who are up for an adventure, we start tomorrow morning. I want to be packed and ready to leave by seven a.m. As you are already aware, we don't know where exactly we'll be going and there isn't going to be an official trail to follow. So we'll pack light and hike in and out from camp each day until we find what looks like the right way and then we'll load up for a longer trek."

"How are we going to know we're going the right way?" someone called out.

Miri paused and the crew fell silent waiting for her answer. Her eyes shifted as she tried to figure out what to say. She glanced at Rafa again, then quickly averted her gaze.

"Dr. Mejía gave me a clue to the location of a landmark. The mesa de pedra," she responded.

Rafa's eyebrows raised and he sat straighter in his seat while the rest of the group continued murmuring.

"Once we find it, I'm sure the rest will be easy," she continued, struggling to convincingly say the words without wincing. "Look, I can see everyone is tired. How about we finish dinner, get a good night's rest, and in the morning we can start fresh?"

A few more grumbles, but no one outright refused. She'd take it as progress.

"Great!" she said, like they were answering a question.

"With that, guess I'd better change." She motioned to her wine-soaked clothes, then followed up, "See you at seven!"

Miri hurried away before they could ask more questions she couldn't answer. Plus, now she'd met Rafa's conditions. If anyone decided to leave at this point, then it would be of their own volition.

Back in her cabin, she searched her bag for yet *another* clean, dry shirt. It was only day three and she'd already soiled a quarter of her wardrobe. She peeled off her hiking shirt down to a tank top and rushed to the sink to try to wash the red wine out of the fabric. Last thing she needed was to ruin *another* outfit.

Knock, knock, knock.

Miri shot her gaze up to the vanity mirror and blew her bangs out of her face. Seriously, what now? She didn't have any desire to give further explanation. Couldn't whatever this was wait until the morning?

She paused for a moment, willing the visitor away, but when another knock rapped against the door, she succumbed to the fact that there was no getting out of this. So she stood straight, dried off her hands, and tucked her hair behind her ears before swinging the door open.

"Rafa?" she choked out.

He stood on the other side of the door, his head dipped to the side. Seeing him now standing in front of her, she no longer wanted to have *the talk*. And not simply because he looked utterly delectable. And it had *nothing* to do with the fact that there was a soft, cozy bed positioned a mere six feet away. But the sheepish look on his face told her he was equally torn by whatever reason he had come for.

"What are you doing here?" she asked, crossing her arms like an invisible barrier.

"I was hoping we could talk."

He wanted to talk, too? Nope. She couldn't do this now.

"Oh, well, I was about to go to sleep." Jeez. She *was* a terrible liar.

His gaze traveled the length of her body still in her day clothes, then he craned his neck to look around her room. "Doesn't look that way," he said.

She uncrossed her arms and stood straighter. "I'm finishing up a few things, and *then* I'm going to sleep."

"Are you trying to avoid me?" He eyed her suspiciously. "Because if that's the case, you can say so."

"No!" she said, perhaps a tad too emphatically. "I'm tired, that's all. It's been a long day."

"You're not just saying that because you're trying to get rid of me, are you?"

"What? No, why would you think that?"

"Oh, I don't know. Maybe because you're practically shutting the door in my face?"

Miri blinked quickly and took a step back, just now realizing she'd unconsciously begun closing the door on him. She looked at the door as if it had magically closed by itself. *When did that happen?*

"Look, if this is about what happened on the boat—" he started.

But Miri swiftly cut him off. "It's not about the boat."

"So, then, the reason you're acting weird doesn't have anything to do with the fact that we kissed?"

She furrowed her brow. "Weird? I'm not acting weird."

"Pringles," he said matter-of-factly. "You're being weird. The only reason you haven't locked me out is because my foot is in the way."

She glanced down at his foot, and sure enough, the toe of his hiking boot barely broke the threshold barrier, keeping her from being able to shut the door completely. She released the pressure she'd placed on the doorknob, instantly giving way to his foot, and opened the door wide.

"Fine. You want to come in and talk?"

She turned her back to him and walked a few feet into the room, letting him follow. *Shit, now what?* Her thumbs tapped together with her hands folded in front of her waist as she debated what to say.

Rip off the Band-Aid.

Cut him loose.

Get your head back in the game.

The door clicked behind her, and she spun around, blurting out, "I think we need to cool the jets," at the same time he said, "I don't think we should take things any further between us."

A pit formed in Miri's stomach. He wasn't supposed to reject her. She was supposed to be rejecting *him*. Though *rejection* wasn't the right term. Either way, however, it didn't matter who rejected who. For the first time in a long time, she'd met a guy who'd seemed to like her as much as she liked him. She'd sure read that situation wrong.

And it fucking sucked.

"Well, okay then," he said, standing a few feet inside the door. "Seems we're on the same page."

She bit her bottom lip. It wasn't that she *wanted* to cry. She'd known the guy for two days, for fuck's sake. But being on the same page meant closing the door on the possibility. After spending the last decade believing love was an *im*possibility, Miri couldn't help but be disappointed. Hurt.

But it didn't matter. This was the right decision—and it seemed it wasn't her decision, anyway. So she forced the next words to come out of her mouth with as much confidence as she could muster. "Oh, good. I was worried things were going to be awkward between us."

"*Riiiight*," he said, unconvinced. "Because things *totally* won't be awkward now."

Miri scrunched her face and shook her head. "Nope. Not at all. It was just a kiss."

"Or twenty. But, hey, who's counting?"

"Twenty?" she said skeptically, cocking her head to the side. "That's a bit of an exaggeration, don't you think?"

"Okay, but there were a lot," he said with a sweet smile that gave her hope that maybe things *wouldn't* be awkward.

So she played up the frivolity. They were just people, after all. Two people who'd kissed in the heat of the moment. And a dozen more times later that evening. And the next morning. It was no big deal when she really thought about it. Not like she hadn't kissed a guy before.

Even if it *had* been a while.

"It's fine. We were caught up in the excitement," Miri said, waving her hands all footloose and fancy-free. "With Hunter and Kevin, and the whole boat thing, and then with the knife . . . it just got our danger-boning hormones going, that's all, and—"

Rafa burst out with a laugh. "I'm sorry, our what?"

Oh, God. Had she really said that out loud?

Just play it off. Don't make things awkward.

"Danger boning. I mean, it's a common action and horror movie phenomenon." He looked at her like he had absolutely no idea what she was referring to, so, naturally, she needed to explain even though he technically didn't ask. "You know, like in a movie when there's a couple in serious danger, like they're-about-to-get-*killed* level of danger, yet somehow they still have time to get it on even though it defies all common sense?"

"I didn't realize there was a term for it," he said, clearly amused.

"Oh, absolutely," she continued even though her brain screamed to stop talking. "Like, oooh, the movie *Scream*? *Classic* danger-boning scene in that one." He stared at her blankly. "Oh, I suppose you probably don't have time to watch movies."

He snickered. "I watch movies, Pringles."

"Oh. I guess I figured maybe with all the traveling and assignments . . ." She trailed off, fearing she'd lost him with her tangent. "Anyway, so, yeah, that's all this was. We got caught in the thrill of the danger. At least we stopped it before things went any further. I mean, could you even *imagine* what would have happened if we hadn't stopped ourselves, or if Felix and Logan hadn't been there?"

An uncomfortable laugh escaped her lips right when another knock rapped against the door, saving her from continued mortification. Rafa turned to face the door as Miri called out, "It's open."

Anissa poked in her head, immediately grinning at the sight of Miri in the room with Rafa. "Well, hello!" she said, a little too excitedly. "I can come back if you're busy." She was hardly able to contain her smile.

I'm going to kill her.

"Actually," Miri said, "we were wrapping up."

He glanced back at her, his eyes like lasers trying to figure her out.

"So we're good, then, right?" Miri asked, not really waiting for him to say otherwise.

"Yeah, we're good," he said, walking to the door and nodding at Anissa as they switched places. "Oh, and, Pringles? To answer your question, yes, I *can* imagine it. And I suppose that's the root of the problem. 'Night."

T HEY WERE GOING AROUND IN CIRCLES. LITERALLY.

It had been two weeks since they'd arrived at Florestacasa, and they were no closer to having discovered the Cidade da Lua.

Or whatever this mesa de pedra Miri had talked about was.

First, critters had ransacked their food supplies, leaving them with little prepackaged food to take on day hikes.

Then, some of the mapping equipment had mysteriously broken.

After that, the red string they'd been using to mark their way like breadcrumbs had seemingly vanished, resulting in significant detours. Fortunately, they'd made it back to Florestacasa that night using GPS.

So, naturally, a day later, the GPS went missing, necessitating a whole new system for tracking their whereabouts.

The following day, a pit viper blocked their path.

And then the rain came.

Round and round they went, each day encountering a new obstacle. All thanks to Rafa.

Well, maybe not the viper. Or the rain.

But everything else was one hundred percent Rafa. His father would be so proud. With each sabotage, Miri grew weary, inching closer and closer to her tipping point (assuming she had one). So why didn't it feel good? Why did Rafa feel like a sack of shit when he went to bed each night?

"Maybe an animal keeps taking the string," Anissa chimed in after their fiftieth wrong turn one particularly taxing afternoon.

"Or maybe it's os protetores," Rafa followed up with a casual shrug, clutching the bundle of strings deep in his pants pocket. He'd have to remember to dispose of them later.

His comment earned him a perturbed eye roll from Miri before she pressed onward. Perturbed or not, however, her simple acknowledgment of his existence sent a flutter through his stomach.

Because Rafa was going around in circles, too. Figuratively speaking.

He did somersaults trying to avoid her. He tried to stay away. He really did. But his mind and body had other ideas. He gravitated toward her. Sought out her proximity. Watched her. Photographed her. It *was* his job, after all. For the article, of course. And he had to make sure he stayed on top of the mission. He needed to keep an eye on her, to make sure she hadn't made some important discovery.

But he knew it was bullshit. The night they'd mutually agreed to end things had done nothing to dissuade his affection. If anything, her ridiculous chatter only further cemented that Miri was special. And that any guy lucky enough to get to spend the rest of his life with her would never grow bored.

It just wouldn't be him.

He'd traveled the world. Witnessed some of Earth's most magnificent wonders. Yet none of it was as fascinating—or beautiful—as Dr. Miriam Jacobs.

Miri's reason for pulling away was unclear. He hadn't expected that, to be honest. He had thought he'd show up at her room, she'd think he was there to finish what they'd started on the boat, and he would crush her when he informed her instead that they needed to back off. The fact that she almost beat him was a punch deep in his gut.

She'd rejected him.

And yet there had been uncertainty in her voice. In *both* their voices. Almost hesitant, waiting to see if the other would take it back.

Though neither of them did. But that little glimmer of doubt. That speck of uncertainty. It gave Rafa hope that maybe she was still thinking about him, too.

False hope, seeing as it wasn't like there was anything he could—or rather, would—do about it. But he liked imagining that she saw something in him like he'd seen in her.

For the fifteenth day in a row, they set out into the rainforest, taking a different path than they'd taken the prior days. Not that it mattered. Most days they somehow still ended up in the same place: always at the rim of a ravine at least half a football field wide and thirty feet deep, bounded by a steep wall of vegetation, leaving them with no place to go but back from whence they came. By the look of things, this morning wouldn't be any different.

"Haven't we seen this tree before?" Jerry, one of the equipment techs, called out, wincing as he lugged a giant bag on his back on the trail bordering the ravine.

From the outside, it seemed a silly question. After all, how could a person tell one tree from another in the Amazon, full of millions of trees? But this particular tree—a walking palm with a hearty network of stilt-like roots towering almost seven feet high—stood out among the crowd.

And they had one hundred percent walked by it at least a half dozen times in the last couple of days. Rafa could identify it by the row of bromeliads growing along one of its branches, which he had noticed days ago.

"You say that about every tree," Felix said, coming up beside Rafa and rolling his eyes as if to say, *Can you believe this guy?*

Rafa snickered. He, Felix, and Logan had formed a bit of a friendship over the last couple of weeks. It was too bad they didn't live near each other in the States. And that Rafa was lying to them.

"Well, how about *you* try carrying this bag sometime, and *then* see how you feel about circling the same trees day in and day out?" Jerry said, stopping and letting the bag fall to his feet.

"How about you try not complaining every day?" Felix said, spinning around.

Miri may not have had a tipping point, but it sure seemed the rest of the team did.

"Hey, hey," she said, pushing through the crowd already gathered around Felix and Jerry like they were ready to spar. "We're not going to do that. I'm not going to have people fighting on my watch."

A group of monkeys started howling at the disturbance.

"Great," Miri said, throwing up her hands. "Now look what you started."

"Yeah, you'd better watch it," Rafa said. "You don't want Dr. Jacobs going *Ninja Warrior* on you."

Miri rolled her eyes, but not without first flashing him the sexiest smile, and then she turned to head back on the trail—right before tripping on a root sticking out of the ground and losing her balance. She stumbled sideways a few steps, straight toward the path's boundary at the rim of the ravine.

"No, no, no, no, no!" she called out as she fell over the lip.

"Miri!" Rafa yelled as he reached for her, but it was too late.

Rafa leaned over the edge, witnessing Miri flailing her arms through the air as she dropped. She grabbed on to one of the vines hanging from the trees, her momentum swinging her to the other side of the ravine and straight toward the steep wall of vegetation. Anything could have been on the other side of that greenery. A sheet of rock. A tangle of trees. Another drop-off. It was virtually impossible to tell from this vantage point.

Helpless, Rafa watched from above as Miri braced herself for impact.

Whoosh!

One moment she was there, and the next she was gone, swallowed by the greenery.

The group froze, all except Rafa, who took a tentative step forward, his arms straight out to his sides to keep the others from falling into the ravine.

"Miriam!" he yelled at the top of his lungs, his heart pounding so hard he could barely breathe. "Miriam! Answer me!"

Hearing nothing, Rafa rushed into the ravine, sliding down the dirt, when a riotous sound resonated through the forest. He paused. Was that . . . laughter?

"Miriam!" he called out again. "Are you okay?"

"Yes!" she called back, instantly settling his heart. "Come quick! I think I found something!"

Rafa looked over the vast expanse of the ravine—it would

take a while to trek through the thick understory—then he climbed back out, took hold of a vine, slung his camera around to his back, then said to the team, "Meet you over there," before throwing himself over the edge and swinging toward the thick curtain of leaves and vines. His body stiffened as he reached the barrier, clenching his eyes tight and praying with all his might.

Swoosh.

Leaves and twigs scraped across his skin as he broke through the vegetation. Once through, he opened his eyes to a giant, flat stone slab in the shape of a round table.

His body swung over the stone and he let go of the vine, landing on the table with finesse and precision just like he and Miri had practiced.

Once his feet were firmly planted, he took in his surroundings, looking up at the wall of stone protecting the slab from the elements and visibility. Water seeped from the wall, with bromeliads and orchids growing in the cracks.

He hopped off the stone, then turned back to it, running his hand along the top. The surface was partially covered in moss, but in the places where it was bare, an almost luminescent rock glistened, shimmering in the light peaking through the thick tree canopy above.

"Whoa," Rafa said, gazing at the space and looking up toward the sky.

"'Whoa' is right," Miri said, sidling up beside him.

He glanced down at her, but she was already staring at him. Beaming. Adorably proud of herself. She took his hand in hers, wrapping her other hand around his arm, then she looked at the stone slab, admiring her find.

Now Rafa was the one staring, unable to stop smiling. The heat of her body pressed against his, creating a fiery inferno between them. But it was her smile, from her contentment, that filled every inch of him with warmth.

He missed her touch. Missed being near her. Sure, they were together, hiking with the others through the rainforest day in and day out, and he watched her from behind his camera lens, but it was the first time in more than two weeks they'd been alone since that night in her cabin before Anissa interrupted. The first time he could take in her lily of the valley scent, even underneath the sweat and ever-present twigs in her hair.

She hugged his arm, then glanced up at him again.

"Hi," he said.

"Hi," she responded, her eyes sweet and her mouth curled into an almost impossibly cute smile.

"Hi," he repeated involuntarily.

How did she do it? How did she manage to turn Rafa, a man who was, by all accounts, known for being good with words, into a bumbling doofus?

"What do you think?" she asked.

What do I think? He was thinking about how much time they had before the others made it through the ravine. Wondered whether any would take the shortcut on the vines. They likely only had minutes. Maybe seconds. It took everything for Rafa not to spin her into his arms and kiss her. What harm could a little kiss cause, after all?

"Beautiful," he said.

"I know! And I fucking found it!" Miri said, releasing his arm and bringing him back to reality. The *exact* place where harm awaited.

Miri screamed with excitement, her scream quickly becoming laughter. She turned around, inspecting the stone. It was more of a boulder with a flat top. Even with the moss, dirt, and grime caking its surface, it really was quite beautiful. Even if it wasn't what Rafa had been referring to.

"What is this place?" Rafa asked as he circled around the stone, examining each angle. With slow, steady movements, he brought his camera to his eye, snapping photos of the stone and its surroundings.

"I . . . I think it might be the mesa de pedra," she said. "This is it. This is the first landmark on the way to the Moon City."

He scanned the stone. Whatever gemstone it was made of was magnificent, but in the end, it was only a rock. A large rock, yes, but just a rock. The placement of it was what was most spectacular, though, tucked back in this hidden botanical trove.

"And what exactly is that?" he asked. "The mesa de pedra."

"It literally means 'stone table,' but many think this is the spot where the people of the Moon City would come and trade with other people in the Amazon. It was the farthest location from the city that they would regularly travel, and the closest they would allow others to come to the Moon City," she explained.

"But isn't that Portuguese? Mesa de pedra?"

"Well, yes. The people who lived in the Cidade da Lua likely spoke some other language. Perhaps some form of a Tupian or Arawak language. Their word for this place would have likely been lost over the centuries, though. So the landmarks are known by more common Portuguese terms."

"What do you mean, landmarks?" Rafa lowered his camera and shot a confused glance at Miri.

Her eyes widened a bit, and she pulled her bottom lip between her teeth. "Oh, I mean, there are probably other markers on the way toward the Moon City, don't you think?" she said. But she was holding something back.

She quickly looked away, clearly trying to avoid eye contact. What wasn't she telling him?

He couldn't let her off that easy. Rafa was taking a step forward and opened his mouth to ask follow-up questions, when the wall of vines rustled behind them, stealing their attention. Dammit.

"Whoa! What is that thing?" Felix asked as he emerged from the other side of the vegetation.

"It's the mesa de pedra," Miri responded confidently, as if she'd somehow gotten confirmation in the last thirty seconds. "I found it."

Now wasn't the time to point out that her "find" was a complete accident. But it was *her* clumsiness that led them here. Too bad for all the previous explorers and their coordination. Who knew all you had to do was trip, swing on a vine, blast through a sheet of foliage, and voilà!

The rest of the group pushed through the vines, filling the small space and inspecting the stone table and its surroundings.

"What's the mesa de pedra?" Logan followed up.

Miri filled in the team, repeating the facts she'd recited to Rafa but elaborating further on the details. Explaining how the people of the Moon City brought their goods and wares to this spot. How it was likely selected for its distance, the stone table possibly containing similar mineral properties as the stone found in the city itself.

"How can you be sure?" Jerry, the skeptic, asked.

"Well, I . . . uh . . ." Miri struggled, looking around for a sign. Something—anything—that could confirm this was the place.

"I mean," she continued, "what else could it be?"

"Um, maybe just a rock?" Jerry said.

Truthfully, there was nothing spectacular about this place. It was, after all, a giant boulder in the middle of the Amazon. Probably one of hundreds like it. Nothing remarkable that would differentiate it from any other slab of stone.

Didn't mean Rafa didn't want to punch Jerry for pointing out the obvious.

"Fuck!" Miri called out, seemingly unexpectedly. The team stopped scouring the area to watch her, all waiting for her next move. "Dammit!" she then followed up, kicking a stone at her foot. "It's just another rock."

Rafa glanced over at Jerry, who was bolstering himself up a bit as if proud that Miri agreed with him. Smartass prick.

Anissa walked up beside Miri, placing her hand on her shoulder. "Hey, we don't know anything yet. We only just got here."

"And so what if this isn't the spot?" Rafa chimed in, hoping to make her feel better. "It's still pretty cool, and you're the one who found it. None of the rest of us can say that."

Miri shot a glance toward Rafa and smiled. He could almost feel her hand squeezing his arm, needing his encouragement.

"No, you're right," she said, turning back to Anissa. "We can't rule anything out yet." Miri spun around to the rest of the group. "Maybe this *is* just a rock. Or maybe it's something more. We'll come back tomorrow and do some excavating. See if there are any clues. And *then*," she exaggerated, glancing at Jerry, "we'll determine whether this is just some old rock."

. . . .

THE CREW SAT AROUND THE FIREPIT THAT NIGHT, PASSING AROUND A bottle of who knew what, laughing and joking around for the first time in over a week. There was still a bit of tension in the air, everyone uncertain about what would happen when they returned to the site the next day. For all they knew, their excavation would confirm it was nothing but another wild goose chase. Yet another detour in a series of mishaps.

But as the liquor flowed, everyone loosened up. Talking. Drinking. Horsing around. Rafa sat back and observed, for the most part. He always found the dynamics and camaraderie of crew members on jobs to be fascinating. People who might not have any connection or even like each other in the outside world became the best of friends. He'd made a lot of pals on these types of gigs.

Rarely did they last beyond that.

Rafa snapped a few pics of the group, always having liked including candid shots of crew being regular people with his stories. The fire provided nice lighting for the photos. Highlights of oranges and reds on the otherwise shadowy figures. Miri looked especially beautiful across the fire from him chatting with Anissa, her delicate features emphasized by the soft glow.

The fire crackled with a *sizzle-pop*, and Miri turned her attention to the blaze—and beyond it, at Rafa. She smiled, then said something to Anissa before standing and walking toward him.

"Mind if I sit?" she said, towering over him, his back against a downed log.

"By all means," he said, brushing the dirt beside him with his hand, as if it could possibly clean the space.

She lowered to his level, sitting close enough that their shoulders touched even though there was plenty of room on the other side of her. They sat in silence, watching Felix and Rahim, another team member, get into a faux wrestling match after a friendly debate over the proper way to say *Neanderthal*. Their tussle commanded everyone's attention as they rolled around on the ground, laughing and ruffling each other's hair.

"Thanks," Miri said as Rafa snapped a picture of Logan giving Felix a noogie.

"For what?" Rafa asked, setting his camera down at his side.

"For making me feel better earlier." She twisted her hands in her lap.

"Hey," he said, nudging her in the side, "no matter what, it was a pretty cool find."

"I know, right?" she said excitedly, turning slightly toward him. "And did you happen to catch my landing?"

"Sorry, I missed it. How did it go?"

"It was rad."

Rad? Rafa snickered and covered his mouth.

"What?" she said with a smile, tugging his arm away from his face.

"Nothing. Just trying to picture your landing." He couldn't help but reciprocate the smile.

"Well, it was *perfect.*"

"You must have had a good teacher," he said with a wink. She ducked her head, trying to conceal her smile.

"He was all right," she said, nudging his shoulder and sending a tingle through his body.

A flutter he quickly pushed away. *If you care about her, you need to convince her to leave . . .* His father's voice repeated in his head. He needed to get up. Sit somewhere else. Somewhere far enough away that he couldn't engage in pleasant, carefree conversations or feel her heat.

"Ahhhh!" Jerry screamed from across the way. "Get it off me!"

Felix and Logan pinned Jerry down while Rahim plucked the largest spider Rafa had ever seen from his back and tossed it away from the campfire circle.

Miri tsked. "It's just a goliath birdeater," she said almost under her breath.

"Um . . . a what?" Rafa asked, vigorously rubbing his chest.

"It's a tarantula. Practically harmless," she said.

Nothing about something called a goliath birdeater sounded *harmless*.

"Well, I've got the creeps just thinking about it," he said, craning his neck to check his back.

"I'm pretty sure you would feel it if you had a foot-long spider on your back."

He shuddered. "You say it like it's nothing."

Miri looked over at him and snickered. "Well, he's over there acting like he was about to get his head bitten off by it. At worst, it would be like the sting of a wasp."

"Which, in my opinion, *also* sounds awful."

Miri smacked her lips again in disagreement. "I swear, it's like Jerry doesn't want to be here, you know? Always complaining. Getting in his unsolicited comments."

He could hear the annoyance in her voice.

"You can't blame him for being tired and frustrated. It's a hard job," Rafa said. "Ninety percent of the population wouldn't last a couple of days out here, and we've been here for over two weeks."

"Ugh," Miri said, tossing her head back and resting it against the log, looking up at the sky. "Don't remind me."

"Of what? Of how long we've been out here?"

Miri tipped her head back and twisted her shoulders to face Rafa. "I just don't know how much longer this crew has it in them if we don't find something more definitive soon, you know?"

"Something like what? Like another landmark?"

She froze and her eyes widened.

"Come on, Pringles. What do you know?"

"I . . . I . . ."

Yes. She was going to tell him.

Right then, Felix plopped beside Rafa, out of breath. Damn.

"Did you catch a shot of that big-ass spider?" Felix asked.

Before Rafa could answer, Jerry came over, pointing his finger. "If you did, you can't put that in the magazine," Jerry said.

"Don't worry. I got your good side," Rafa said. He could feel Miri's smile. A bit of vindication for Jerry's whining.

Jerry opened his mouth to protest, but Felix butted in. "Have you been getting many decent shots? I mean, not that we've really done anything yet," Felix asked.

Rafa noticed Miri's shoulders deflate out of the corner of his eye.

"A few," Rafa said.

"Can we see?" Felix asked.

Rafa handed the camera to Felix. "You can hit the arrow there and scroll through. Though, like you said, we've only just begun."

A more-than-buzzed Logan started belting out the Carpenters' "We've Only Just Begun," while swaying back and forth in Rahim's arms. *What a bunch of goofballs.* But at least they were lovable goofballs. Rafa smiled as he watched them, feeling sorry that their time together would likely be short lived.

"You've sure got a lot of pictures of Dr. Jacobs in here," Felix said, snapping Rafa out of his thoughts.

Shit. He *did* have a lot of pictures of her. No, not a lot. A shitload.

Rafa tossed a glance at Miri, who was already looking at him. Great. Did the guys not realize that she was sitting *right there*?

"Um, well, she is the lead. Of course she's in a lot of the

photos," Rafa said, pulling on the back of his neck and trying to play it off.

And *desperately* avoiding eye contact with Miri.

"I don't know. This one doesn't really look like an *I'm taking pictures of her because she's the lead* sort of pic," Felix said, turning the camera around so Rafa—and everyone else, Miri included—could see the photo he was referring to on the little view screen.

A photo of Miri up close. Smiling bashfully at the camera. Or rather, smiling bashfully at Rafa.

"Ooooh," a now-drunk Logan whistled. "Do you have the hots for Dr. Jacobs?" he asked about as quietly as any liquored-up buffoon could.

In other words, loud enough to get all of Florestacasa's— and all of the Amazon's—attention.

Other team members who'd been completely engrossed in their own conversations suddenly turned their heads, their ears wide open. Fuck. He didn't need everyone getting into his and Miri's business, even if there wasn't any business to be gotten into anymore.

"Give me that," Rafa said, reaching over and trying to take back the camera. But Felix spun around, shielding himself so he could continue scrolling.

"Man, Dr. Jacobs looks *good* in some of these," Felix murmured under his breath, unlike Logan, as he twisted away from Rafa's clawing hands.

Rafa stifled a frustrated growl.

"Dr. Jacobs looks good all the time," Rafa said, finally managing to finagle the camera back. And then he immediately froze and shut his eyes.

He pulled his lips into a tight line as he held his eyes closed. Why? Why did he say that out loud?

"Oooooh!" Logan said, shaking Rafa's shoulders. "Someone's got a crush on Dr. Jacobs!"

More drunken, teasing *ooh*s and *aah*s followed. Rafa was afraid to turn and look at Miri.

Please. Please let this end.

"Maybe *this* is why we've been going in circles," Jerry chimed in.

What was *that* supposed to mean?

"What are you talking about?" Felix asked.

"Oh, come on. Like it isn't already obvious they're all googly-eyed for each other," Jerry said, rolling his eyes. "I thought we'd be out here, oh, I don't know, making big archaeological discoveries. I didn't realize I'd actually signed up for sleepaway camp, instead."

The snaps and crackles from the bonfire and the chirps and howls of the forest were no match for the deafening silence among the group. Rafa's back was to Miri, but all eyes were seemingly on him. Slowly, he turned around, finding Miri standing in the same spot they'd been sitting in, having a delightful conversation only minutes earlier.

The orange flames shining upon her did little to hide the redness in her cheeks. She stared straight at him, her eyes wide, before glancing among the crowd. A few people looked away, unwilling to meet either of their gazes. Others watched with curiosity behind their smirks. Rafa had been on a lot of jobs and had witnessed lots of drama—but none where he was one of the main culprits.

"Miri . . . I—" Rafa said, reaching out his arm like he could touch her even though she was a solid ten feet away by that point. But the words got stuck in his throat.

I'm sorry?

I didn't mean it?

I hate to inform you, but behind those googly eyes are my attempts to subvert you on this expedition until you give up?

Time slowed to a near standstill until someone snickered, snapping Miri and Rafa back to reality. With that, Miri spun around and ran into the darkness toward the cabins. Rafa set his camera down and started after her as Felix and Logan cheered, covering their mouths like they had just witnessed the biggest Hail Mary in all of sports. Perfect. He'd never hear the end of this.

"You're an asshole," Rafa said to Jerry before running toward Miri.

"Miri, wait!" he called out as she reached the bottom stair on the way to the raised walkway.

With a swift movement, she spun around and placed her hand on his chest like a school crossing guard. He glanced down at her hand. *What the—?*

"Don't," she said.

"Don't?" He furrowed his brow.

"I need you to back off, Rafa."

"Back off?" Rafa asked, cocking back his head. "What do you think I've been *doing* these last two weeks?"

"Who do we think we're kidding here? You heard Jerry."

"And that's somehow *my* fault?"

"I can't do this right now," she said, rubbing her temple. "Go back, Rafa. And please don't follow me."

With that, she raced up the stairs, leaving Rafa standing in the darkness by himself. *Fuck this shit.* He debated following her anyway. But when he glanced back at the group, he saw them all watching him. Watching *them.* The last thing he needed was to give them a show. So instead, he headed back to the fire circle and plopped down next to Rahim before snagging the bottle and taking a swig of whatever the guys had been drinking.

"Sorry about that," Felix said, casting Rafa an apologetic look. "We shouldn't have behaved that way."

"It's fine," Rafa said. Well, not really, but by the looks on their faces, the guys certainly seemed remorseful.

"Is Dr. Jacobs pissed?" Felix asked. "Because she *looked* pissed."

"Nah," Rafa said, waving his hand. As if it wasn't already obvious. "I'm sure she knows it was all in good fun."

"So has this been going on since the boat?" Logan asked.

"What do you mean, the boat?" Rafa said, taking his camera, which he'd set on a tree-stump-turned-seat, quickly turning it off and regretting ever handing it over in the first place.

"In the boat. You two were kissing, right?"

Rafa shushed him and put out his hands as if tamping down the discussion. "Keep your voices down."

"So then you *did* kiss Dr. Jacobs?" Logan asked.

"I didn't say that," Rafa growled. God, why couldn't they leave it be?

"So, then you *didn't* kiss Dr. Jacobs?" Rahim said, scratching his head. "Wait, I'm confused."

Rafa rolled his eyes and laughed. These guys. He couldn't tell if they were lovable fools or just drunken jokesters. But they stood waiting with bated breath, wanting to know the answer.

"I didn't say that, either," Rafa said.

"Ohhhh," the guys cooed, throwing their arms around his shoulders and giving him a playful shake. He couldn't help but smile at their genuine interest in his romantic affairs.

"How was it?" Logan asked.

"Yeah, is she a good kisser?" Felix followed up.

"Uh-uh. *That* I'm keeping to myself," Rafa responded. He'd never been much of a kisser and teller.

"All right, all right. That's respectable," Rahim said.

"Yeah, Dr. Jacobs seems cool. You wouldn't know it by looking at her, but when she went after those guys on the boat? That was . . ." Felix said, unable to find the right word.

But Rafa knew the perfect word for Miri.

"Badass," Rafa said, almost as if to himself.

"Yeah, badass," Logan said, nodding his head like everything made perfect sense. "So, what? Are you two a thing now?"

Rafa shook his head. "It's not like that. We were caught up in the moment."

"Danger boning," Rahim said.

Wait? That was a real thing and not just something Miri had made up?

Rafa, Felix, and Logan turned their heads to Rahim in unison. "Danger what?" Felix asked.

"Danger boning. When you're in trouble and emotions are high, so you get caught up in the moment and then, *BAM!*" he said, smacking his hands together, causing all three of them to jump. "You fuck. *That's* danger boning."

The guys laughed, but Rafa managed to clarify, "I'm familiar with the concept, but, no, that's not quite what happened. Besides, I think it's time to move off this subject. I don't think Dr. Jacobs would appreciate knowing that her crew was gossiping drunkenly about her."

"If we're drunk, then you'd better catch up," Rahim said, handing over the bottle.

If it got them off this topic, then fine. Rafa took the bottle again, this time taking a much larger swig.

They continued passing the bottle around, talking about who knew what. Rafa didn't care. His mind kept wandering to Miri's directive, growing more annoyed with each sip. Honestly, he was a little pissed at her for saying that *he* was the one who needed to back off, when *she'd* been was the one holding on to his arm today. And sitting beside him at the campfire.

He'd been trying his damnedest to sabotage this mission. *He* was honoring the agreement they'd made in her cabin two weeks ago.

If only she'd get with the program and give up already. That way, he could forget she ever existed. This assignment nothing but a blip on his radar.

Another sip.

Yes, that's all he needed. To put this experience behind him.

"You have to admit, though. It *was* pretty wild when she went after those guys," Logan said, staring off into the fire.

Seriously? Were they still talking about this?

Rafa glanced at his watch, but the face was a little blurry and he couldn't make out the numbers.

"How bad was it?" Jerry said, worming his way into their conversation. There was something off in his voice. What was it? "Like, are we really in danger out here?"

Huh. Miri was wrong. It wasn't that Jerry didn't *want* to be there. Jerry was *scared* to be there.

Rafa opened his mouth to speak, but Logan beat him to it. "I mean, those guys looked serious. They weren't messing around."

"Well, I didn't come out here just so I could get murdered by a couple of loose cannons," another guy said. What was his name? Brian?

Another swig.

"I don't know, that Vautour guy sounds like who we really need to worry about," Rahim said.

Rafa stared into the fire, half listening as the group carried on, debating various theories about what Vautour and his henchmen were doing while they were out exploring. Who knew what Vautour was planning? Sure, they had eight on their crew, including Rafa. But they didn't have weapons. And looking around the group confirmed that they didn't have muscle, either.

Rafa brought the bottle to his mouth to take another drink, when Brian, or whatever his name was, spoke. "Maybe we need to back off this expedition." Rafa paused with the bottle at his lips.

Back off. Pfft. *Miri* needed to back off. She was the one leading them all into danger. And for what? It wasn't like this would be her *only* opportunity to lead an expedition. But it would certainly be her last if she got herself—or anyone else on this expedition—killed. What about the rest of the crew? Rafa would be doing her a favor by shutting this all down.

"I don't think we need to worry about Vautour," Rafa said, cutting through the discussion like a knife. "What we *really* need to worry about is os protetores da lua."

CHAPTER

Fourteen

*B*ANG, BANG, BANG!

Miri pounded on the door to Rafa's room, not caring that half the team was still asleep. Nor caring that she was still in her pj's—a white tank top and shorts combo set with a pink candy print that said "Sweet Dreams" all over it. But after Anissa gave her the news this morning, Miri didn't have time to change.

If Rafa thought he could scare off her crew, then he had another think coming.

She should have hashed this out with Rafa last night. If she had, maybe none of this would have happened. But since she hadn't, she needed to confront Rafa now.

A groan came from the other side of the door. Good. She hoped her pounding hurt his hungover brain.

"Just a minute," Rafa grunted.

Miri crossed her arms and tapped her toe. Just a minute? Well, this minute was taking about a minute too long.

Bang, bang, bang! She beat against the door again.

Something crashed inside, and then he called out again, this time with a little more oomph. "One second!"

She didn't care. She wouldn't be kept waiting. Not after what he'd done.

Bang, bang, bang!

"Goddammit, I said hold on," he grumbled while swinging open the door. Her eyes went wide as they shifted from his bare chest to his barely-there black boxer briefs that left little to the imagination.

Hmm . . . what was I doing here again?

She stared at him, practically salivating.

"Did you need something?" he asked, rubbing his face. His hair stuck out every which way. He had sleep in the corners of his eyes and what Miri could only surmise was dried saliva below his lip. But damn, he looked good.

She blinked twice, then shot her gaze back up to his. "I . . . I . . ." Her cheeks grew rosy, but then she quickly snapped to attention. "What did you do?"

Rafa ticked his head to the side. "What are you talking about?"

"Last night. What did you say to my team when you were all getting hammered?"

Rafa scrunched his face then held his head as if trying to recall the evening before.

"I said lots of things last night, but I don't know what specifically you're referring to. Care to help me out?"

"Jerry and Rahim. They said they were taking your advice, and they left this morning."

Recognition flashed in his eyes, and then he casually scratched his head with one hand while rubbing his rather firm-looking stomach with the other.

"Hmm . . . are you sure it was me?"

"Oh please, Rafa. Spare me." She rolled her eyes and folded her arms. "They said you started talking about os protetores da lua and how they're going to find us out here, chop our heads off, and eat our hearts."

"Okay, I *know* I didn't say all that."

"Really? Because clearly you don't remember a whole lot about what you did or didn't say last night. I mean, jeez, Rafa, you reek of booze. How much did you drink?" She waved her hand in front of her nose.

"I don't know that, either."

"You know, it's one thing to try to convince *me* to leave, but it's another thing to go behind my back to my crew. I tried to convince them to stay, but they were already packed and had a boat waiting to take them back to Caracaraí."

"Why didn't you tell them about the lidar?" he asked, turning the tables on her. "We had a deal. You were going to give the crew all the information so they could make *informed* decisions on whether to stay."

"Because I don't really even know what Vautour's found, if anything. Besides, they need to believe that we actually have a chance."

"Don't you think they deserve to know what we're up against? We're not talking about another contestant on *The Amazing Race* here." Now *he* was the one folding his arms, which did wonders for his pecs.

"I know that. But I didn't want to unnecessarily scare them more than they already were."

"Scare them? We had a *knife* pulled on us. I think the bar for scaring the crew had already been set."

"Right, and I told them about it. Besides, it's been two weeks and nothing else has happened."

"Well, you didn't tell them about os protetores and how dangerous they are."

"The protectors aren't dangerous," she retorted.

"Yes, they are. They're murderers."

"Murderers?!" Miri blurted out, then gave a chuckle. "Where the hell did you hear that?"

"Everyone knows it."

"I think your sources are faulty. There's no evidence that os protetores pose any danger to the outside world. All they do is try to throw unsuspecting explorers off the trail."

"Interesting choice of words there," Rafa said, narrowing his gaze. "*Throw* them off the trail."

Miri rolled her eyes. "It's a figure of speech. I don't mean literally. Jeez, Rafa. Sounds like you've been watching too many action movies."

"Movies?" Rafa laughed in disbelief. "This is serious."

"Well, if you're too scared to be here, then you can go, too," she said, turning to the side and waving her hand dismissively.

"I'm not leaving you out here."

"I don't need you to protect me." She snapped her head in his direction.

Rafa pushed away from the door, taking a step closer. "It's my job to be here."

"Yeah? And it's mine, too," Miri said, squaring up to him.

Without realizing it, they had moved closer to each other. She was now only a foot away from him, challenging him to continue. The last time they'd been in this position, on the boat,

she'd ended it by kissing him. This time, kissing wasn't an option. And frankly, with the way he was talking to her, she didn't
want to kiss him.

Not really.

"You need to call this whole thing off," he said.

This *again*?

"No." She glared up at him.

"No?" he asked, putting his hands on his hips. "Do you
think you actually look menacing right now?"

"Do you think you can intimidate me into leaving? I told
you: back off."

"You're the one who came to me yesterday."

Miri had no response. But when they'd found the stone
table, her body had naturally reacted to his, pulling him close
even when her mind told her to stay away. And at the fire, he'd
bewitched her with his eyes and his sexy smile. She'd missed his
laughter. Missed his touch.

She needed him to back off, because she wasn't sure she
could trust herself to do it.

"That's . . . that's because . . ." The right words escaped her.
"That's because I can't focus when I'm around you. You're a distraction!" she blurted out.

He laughed again and took another step toward Miri. So
close she could smell the scent of his aftershave from the day
before, even through the alcohol. So close she could feel the
heat from his body.

"And I think it's funny that you think *I'm* the distraction,"
he said with a devilish look in his eyes.

Miri gaped, her mouth like a fish out of water, unable to formulate her thoughts into words. "I . . . I . . ." She bit her lip,
hating to reveal her cards before he revealed his, but it didn't

look like there was any way around it. "Yes, a distraction. Look, this expedition is important to me and . . . and . . . you're getting in the way."

"I'm a distraction?" he repeated. "You look at me with those hungry eyes. Taunt me by biting your lip as you stare at me. Those same lips that *you* kissed *me* with, lips I desperately want to kiss again. And now you stand here, challenging me, wearing those cutesy, ridiculously thin pajamas that have the nerve to say 'Sweet Dreams' when there was nothing *sweet* about my dreams last night, and you want to call *me* a distraction? Pringles, you are the very definition of a distraction."

She could sense the wetness building between her legs, soaking through that ridiculously *thin* fabric. She fought to keep from covering herself. From showing any weakness.

"Don't worry, it won't happen again." She forced the words out, despite not wanting to say them. But she needed to. She took a step back. "I want you to know, I asked Anissa this morning about sending you home," she continued.

Rafa straightened up. "What? You can't fire me," he said.

She scoffed.

"I know. That's what Anissa told me," Miri said, looking away. "Some crap about how it could impact whatever story you end up writing. And the fact that *technically* you were hired by someone else, so I'd have to convince them to convince your boss to pull you off the job. But you being here? You're interfering with the expedition. You're supposed to be a casual observer and . . . and . . ."

"I'm a distraction."

She took a gulp, and then her face turned bright red as she turned her head to both sides, checking to make sure no one was watching.

"No one can see us, if that's what you're worried about," he said.

"I know. I just . . . I just don't want people talking, is all. Last night by the fire . . . that was . . . that was embarrassing. People are already wondering if I can hack it, and if they think all I'm doing out here is fucking around with you, then they'll be even less inclined to view me as a leader."

"They were only teasing."

"Teasing or not, it's not okay. This is my job, Rafa. They are supposed to respect me. But regardless, nothing you can say is going to stop me, even if everyone else bails, yourself included."

"Nothing? What if I told you os protetores know where we are and are on their way to hurt us?"

"That story is completely made up. There are absolutely no accounts of os protetores harming anyone."

"What if that's because they hold on to their secrets?"

Miri rolled her eyes. "Now you're taking me for a sucker who believes in boogeymen and ghost stories. It's not going to work, Rafa."

He crinkled his nose and twisted his mouth. "All right, what if I told you Vautour already made it to the Cidade da Lua?"

"Then I'll want to find it to assess the damage. Try again."

His eyes narrowed at her, then, like a light had flickered, he perked up. "What if—"

With a swift movement, Miri stepped forward, placing her index finger on his lips. "Just stop."

While her shushing quieted him, a cacophony of warnings sounded in her head. His body was close. Almost *too* close, aside from the fact that *her* body quite liked it. His gaze homed in on hers as their bodies shifted, placing her between him and the doorframe. She leaned her back against the wood, staring up at him with her palms now on his bare chest, open but giving no resistance. His stance with one arm overhead on the doorjamb and one hand holding her waist was the opposite of cooling things off. Miri was hot. *Red* hot. But not as warm as his skin upon her hands.

The air between them was thick with tension, making it hard for Miri to breathe. They stared at each other for what seemed like an eternity. Questioning. Waiting. Challenging the other to make a move. Miri no longer cared that she could smell the booze seeping from his skin, because beneath it, she could smell *him*. Raw. Desirous. She wanted to bathe herself in his scent, spend the entire day in his cabin melding her body into his until they became one. Fuck it all and sink into his heavenly abyss, not caring whether it was morning or night, Monday, Thursday, or whatever the hell day it might be.

Which is exactly why she needed to pull away.

"This isn't quite what I had in mind when I said we needed to cool things off," Miri said, almost breathless.

"Oh really?" His husky voice titillated her core. She fought to keep her hips from bucking against him. "Because all I was going to say was what if I told you the two point five million species of bugs in the Amazon were all descending upon us at the same time?"

He flashed that killer smile at her, the one that sent a delightful prickling sensation dancing over her skin, and they both burst out laughing. She buried her head in his chest, soaking him in as he brought her closer to his body, holding her tightly in his arms. His touch felt so natural. So familiar. God, why did she have to meet him here? Why now, on the very gig her career depended upon?

Long after their laughter subsided, they still held on to each other. Almost like they knew that letting go would be twofold. She wrapped her hands around to his back as he caressed hers with a soft, soothing motion. Words unspoken. Hearts pounding. His gentle strokes the most sensual thing Miri had ever experienced, making it hard not to want more.

"I wish you were wearing pants," she said.

"I wish you weren't," he responded.

She chuckled and closed her eyes for a moment before finally letting go. "This probably isn't helping," she said, backing away and resting against the railing opposite Rafa and the door.

"No, probably not." He folded his arms and leaned against the doorjamb. God, it was effortlessly sexy, triggering every single one of Miri's biological buttons.

"Have you done this before? Hooked up with someone on a job?"

"I wouldn't say we've hooked up, but no, I've never done this. And we probably shouldn't."

"No, probably not," she said, letting her head drop a fraction of an inch before bringing it back up again. "And why not, exactly?" The uncertainty carried through her voice.

His eyebrow quirked up. "Why not? Are you trying to convince me or yourself?"

Me. Definitely me.

"Both of us, I suppose."

Rafa sighed. "Look, Pringles. I like you. A lot. I think that's pretty obvious right now . . ."

Miri couldn't help but glance at his boxers, and *oh boy*. It was obvious, all right. So apparent that she had a hard time averting her eyes.

"But is this," he continued, motioning between their bodies, "going to get in the way of what each of us came out here to do? Because I'm not sure if we can accomplish our individual goals with this . . . distraction."

Yep. That's what she thought. *Sigh.*

"So then how are we going to make this work? Our *working* relationship that is," she asked.

"I don't know. What do you have in mind?"

"I want you to stop trying to convince me to leave," she said.

"Nope. I can't do that. Not when I think you're in danger by staying here."

She sighed again. "Fine. But you can't meddle with my team. *I'm* responsible for them, not you."

"Okay, then *you* need to not put them in danger like you did when you went after Vautour's guys."

"I didn't mean for you, Felix, and Logan to follow me—" She tried to protest, but Rafa cut her off.

"Don't do that. Don't pretend like it would have been okay for us to leave you. I may not be one of your crew members, but this is a team. There was no way we were going to watch you sail off with those guys. You putting yourself in danger puts everyone in danger."

"All right. I won't put my team in danger."

"Any other boundaries we need to establish?"

She bit her lip. *Focus. Focus.*

"Well, I . . . It bears repeating. We can't let this . . . this thing between us go anywhere."

"Right. Anything else?"

"And you should probably put some pants on because . . . it's . . . it's distracting," she said with a slight smile.

Rafa hung his head and laughed, then lifted his hands over

his head, grabbing on to the top of the doorframe. Miri's eyes shot in every direction, grazing over his physique.

"Okay, that isn't helping," she said.

"Sorry," he said, bringing his hands back down to his sides. Though his smirk said otherwise. It was a dirty move. But she'd be lying if she said she didn't like it.

"I should probably get going."

"Yeah, and I should probably shower. Got to wash the booze off."

Miri stared at him, not moving. Imagining her hand grazing the band of his boxer briefs along his smooth, taut abs. Picturing Rafa climbing into the shower. And envisioning her naked body pressed against him while he massaged shampoo into her hair from behind.

"Pringles?" he said.

With a quick shake of her head, she broke out of it. "Good. I'm glad we got all this settled," she said.

"Definitely."

"Well, I, uh . . . I need to check on the rest of the crew and make sure no one else has quit overnight."

"Sounds good. I'll see you at the meetup spot in, how long?"

"In thirty minutes."

"Right. See you there."

Miri gave him a smile, then turned to walk away, when Rafa called out one more time.

"Oh, so you know, I'll probably be taking lots of pictures today, what with finding that stone table and all. Don't mind me if it looks like I'm staring. Pretend you don't even see me."

A tiny laugh escaped her. "Like that will ever be possible." She smiled at him once more, and he was unable to stop the beaming smile on his own face. "And, Rafa . . . please put some pants on."

. . . .

THREE DAYS.

They spent three days at the stone table with absolutely no further progress.

They'd arrived back at the stone table the day after the initial discovery, this time bringing with them some additional tools to start excavating the table and roping off the rest of the area in a grid so they could accurately mark any other finds.

Hour upon hour, they painstakingly removed the moss and grime from the rock, revealing a beautiful almost-blue stone underneath. But it took time and patience. So, day after day, they returned. Another twelve inches uncovered here. Another several pounds of dirt sifted there. And not a single find.

There was no evidence of human existence in the area. No pottery. No jewels. No clothing. No tools. While the slab itself was beautiful, it didn't make up for the fact that nothing else about the spot gave any indication that this was *the* mesa de pedra.

Miri studied the gold medallion each night, staring at the piece for hours. Trying to figure out how it could possibly be a clue. But just like the stone table, it gave her nothing.

By the fourth day at the site, Miri finally came to a conclusion: the medallion *wasn't* a clue. At least not one that could be used in the present spot. She had that epiphany only after coming to another realization: this *wasn't* the mesa de pedra.

"All right, everyone, let's go ahead and start packing up," she announced after another grueling four hours in the hot, muggy jungle. It smelled like rain. It was treacherous enough when it was dry. Last thing they needed was to get stuck trekking back to Florestacasa during a downpour.

Anissa glanced at her watch. "It's still early," she said. "What time are you thinking we'll be back tomorrow?"

"We're not returning tomorrow," Miri said, garnering confused looks from the entire crew and Rafa, who'd spent the last few days off in the corner of the site, scribbling in his notebook.

And that's *all* he'd been doing the last few days—lounging in the Amazon like the rainforest was his sofa, furiously writing in the leatherbound journal. Miri couldn't remember the last time she'd seen him pick up his camera. Not that there was anything to take pictures of anyway.

Rafa closed his notebook and sat up, studying her intently to figure her out.

"What do you mean we're not returning?" Felix asked.

"Oh! Day off?" Logan followed up.

Good question. She hadn't quite figured out her next steps. But she'd promised Rafa she wouldn't withhold things from the team, so she told them the truth.

"I mean, we're packing up and moving on. This site isn't proving fruitful, so I think it's best to start looking elsewhere."

"Where are we going next?" Brian asked.

"I'm not sure yet. I think . . . I think I need a couple of days to sort some things out," she said.

"A couple of days?" Brian said. She couldn't really blame him, but he was starting to sound like Jerry. "What are we supposed to do in the meantime?"

The group started whispering to each other and talking under their breath. Shit, she was losing them. The forest throbbed in her head, closing in on her with the cacophony of their voices echoing against the rock wall. What was she supposed to say? Where were they supposed to go?

We should have left when Jerry and Rahim bailed.

She has no clue what she's doing.

What a fucking waste of time.

I can't believe I signed up for this.

Everyone's going to laugh at us when we come home empty-handed.

The jungle started spinning around her. Ready to swallow her whole. Her gaze shifted from person to person, all watching her. Waiting for a response.

Sweat started dripping down the side of her face. *Did it just get hotter out here?* She tugged at the top button of her hiking shirt, pulling at it to waft in some air. Anissa. Felix. Logan. Rafa. They all stared at her. Faces twisting. Concerned.

"Uh . . . why don't you all head back for now? I'm going to . . . uh . . . I need a walk," she said before immediately rushing past the rock wall and back into the rainforest.

The group didn't try to stop her, but their voices followed, clamoring in her head. Demanding answers. She covered her ears, but she couldn't quiet the clatter. She needed to think. WWCMD? If she could just get some distance between her and the noise. A buffer from the racket.

"Pringles! Wait!" Rafa called from behind.

No. Not now. She didn't care to explain what was going on. Mostly because she didn't know *how* to explain it. So she picked up her pace, pushing through a mess of vines twisting and tangling around her limbs as she tried to meander through. The forest floor and understory were thick. Almost making it impossible to see what was in front of her with the spate of trees, palms, and philodendrons.

"Will you slow down? Where are you even going?" he called out, grunting as he tried to keep up with her.

"I'm fine. You can head back," she hollered over her shoulder, not slowing down.

"You shouldn't be out here alone. What if something happens to you?"

"I'm just getting some fresh air for a few minutes."

"Well, what if you get lost?" he asked.

She growled to herself, her irritation bubbling up. Why wouldn't he leave her alone? Couldn't he see that she needed some space?

"I'm sure I'll be able to find the right direction," she said.

"The right direction? In the Amazon?" he asked with a laugh that was the equivalent of *you've got to be kidding me.* "Come on, Pringles. We literally walked in circles for days before we happened upon the stone table."

"Happened upon?" *Pfft.* Now she was aggravated.

"Oh, I'm sorry. How about stumbled upon? Is that better?"

A giant ball of fury soared through Miri's body.

"I *said,*" she exaggerated, her voice angry and loud as she continued walking straight, "I *know* where I'm go—"

Miri was cut off as she walked face-first into a wall of rock blocking their way, practically hidden by moss and leaves. She quickly brought her hand to her forehead.

Ouch.

And a second later, Rafa came through the brush and ran right into her. She would have been pissed if she hadn't liked it so much, the feel of his hands bracing himself on her waist, as they stood face-to-face with a wall of rock blocking their way.

"You were saying?" he said into her ear.

She shook free from his annoying hands, ignoring the tingling sensation of his breath on her ear.

"I'm fine. I need to get around this wall is all," she said as she inspected the barrier firmly planted in their way. In one direction, there was a steep drop-off. In the other, the wall extended as far as the eye could see. Perhaps she could walk around it, but she couldn't tell if that meant walking a hundred feet or a thousand. The remaining options were climbing up and over, skirting around the drop-off by clinging to the side, or turning around. But turning around meant admitting defeat.

"This is silly. Let's go back," Rafa said, clearly hoping she'd agree.

But nothing could stop her.

Without any more hesitation, Miri took option B, grabbing hold of whatever knots or protrusions she could as she climbed around the side of the rock wall.

"Pringles, what are you doing?" Rafa asked with a sigh, his exhaustion palpable.

"What does it look like I'm doing?" she said between grunts.

"Okay, Miri, that's enough. You're not proving anything to anyone except that you're willing to get yourself killed to prove your point—whatever point that might be."

"I'm not trying to prove anything. This is the way I wanted to go."

Miri didn't need to see his face to know that Rafa was rolling his eyes, exactly as she'd be doing if the situation were reversed. But WWCMD? Put a boulder in Corrie Mejía's way and what is she gonna do? She's going to tackle it, not let it tackle her.

Miri could do the same.

She moved an inch at a time, ignoring Rafa's protests. Miri

was no expert, but she'd partaken in a few climbing adventures in her day—at the climbing gym. But whatever. It still counted. So what if those involved harnesses, pulleys, and other equipment, all of which were absent in the present situation?

Her heart pounded and her limbs shook. *You can do this*, she repeated over and over. The only thing Miri had to grab on to now were vines hanging on the rock face. Vines that could snap at any minute.

"Come on, this is dangerous," Rafa said. "Look. Fine. You know where you're going. But let's take another way. How about it?"

"This is nothing," she grunted. "It's just like the climbing wall at the gym."

"You mean one of those walls with the perfectly placed, brightly colored hand- and footholds and thick, giant mats below to cushion the ten-foot fall?"

Miri glanced at the ground below her. Big mistake. The drop was a good fifteen to twenty feet and, as Rafa pointed out, *not* protected by plush padding. She quickly snapped her head back to the rock face, no longer able to ignore the sweatiness of her palms.

Except she was in it now. She'd have to keep climbing, whether to make it around the boulder or make it back to Rafa.

She carefully twisted her head back toward Rafa. Oh damn. He was farther away than she thought. He had a worried look on his face, though it was no match for the fear swirling in her stomach.

He scooted to the face of the wall, reaching out his hand for her. But he was still much too far. Six, seven feet at least to reach his hand. "Here, take your time," he said, motioning for her.

Miri repositioned her foot to get more leverage, then reached her hand onto a nubby piece of rock jutting out from the wall.

"That's it," he said, coaxing her back toward him. "You've got this. Now go real slow."

He spoke calmly to soothe her nerves.

"Yep, keep going. Deep breaths," he said.

He smiled at her, his face soft and gentle, and she smiled back.

"See?" he said, holding out his hand. "You can do this. That's because you're a badass—"

"Ah!" she screamed out as her foothold gave way.

"Miri!"

Rafa reached out for her, but it was too late. She went sliding down the rock face, trying to grab on to anything that would stop her, but it was no use. *This is it. This is how I die.* The thought flashed through her head as she tumbled to the ground, pain zapping her from all angles before she landed on her side with a thud.

She groaned, slowly opening her eyes to a blur of greens and browns. Unable to focus, she brought her hand to her head, rubbing the side. *My glasses!* Her hand shot to the ground, searching for her specs without luck.

"Miri! Miri! Are you okay?! Miri, answer me!" Rafa's panicked voice called from above, peering over the edge to spot her.

"I'm alive," she called back, her voice shaky.

But even without being able to see her injuries, she knew she was *not* okay.

"Stay there. I'm going to find a way down," he said.

Stay here? A tiny laugh escaped her lips. As if she had any other choice.

She inspected her body as best she could. Thankfully, nothing seemed broken. But her pants were ripped. Her hands, forearms, and knees were bloody. And her confidence was totally and completely shot.

A rustling of leaves sounded above her, directing her attention to the wall of dirt and vines to her side.

"I'm coming," Rafa called as he slowly descended into the gully or whatever the heck it was that she'd gotten herself into. She watched as he lowered himself with ease on a vine that must have been wrapped around a tree up top.

"Sure, take the easy route," she joked. At least she still had her sense of humor.

When Rafa was a few feet off the ground, he jumped down, then hurried to Miri's side.

"Are you okay? Did you break anything?" he said, examining her arm.

"I'm fine," she said, twisting her arm to check for scrapes and bruises. "Nothing's broken that I can tell. Just the ole pride."

He let out a long breath. "You scared the shit out of me."

"I scared it out of myself." Her eyesight was good enough that she could see his features, although the definition was a little fuzzy so she couldn't be sure of his reaction, she decided to clarify. "I mean, not literally."

He laughed and hung his head, setting her at ease. "You really are something," he said. "Come on, let's get you cleaned up."

Rafa searched through Miri's backpack for a first aid kit, and then got to work on her wounds. She winced as he applied antiseptic to her raw flesh, but he continued working all the same.

"Here," he said, handing over her glasses.

The lenses weren't *too* scratched up, but it would be annoying hiking back with her vision impaired. Thankfully, she had another pair back at the resort. A little tip she'd learned several digs ago after accidentally dropping them down a dig pit.

"You picked one hell of a place to take a tumble," he said as he glanced around at their surroundings before getting back to her scrapes. "That rock wall you were trying to scramble around almost looks like a face."

She didn't care, though. She didn't want to take in the surroundings. Really, she wanted to forget about the whole thing and get the heck out of there. She wanted to get *away* from Rafa, not have him even closer, being nice to her and treating her wounds while she was out there acting like a stubborn child who got their little baby feelings hurt.

They continued in relative silence until he finally broke the ice. "Why do you keep doing things like this?"

"What things?"

"Taking risks. Doing dangerous things. What's your obsession with being *badass*?"

"Why *can't* I do those things? Corrie does them all the time."

"You're not Corrie."

His words stung.

"Well, she had to start somewhere. Maybe this is the start of *my* journey."

"Or it could be the end of it," he said pointedly, sucking the remaining ounce of confidence out of Miri. "You're lucky you came out of this with only a few scrapes and bruises. It could have been much, *much* worse."

She pulled her bottom lip between her teeth, biting hard to keep from crying. He was right. Even she thought she might have died as she was falling.

"What is it about this expedition? Why is this so important to you?" he asked, eyeing her curiously.

Miri's entire body deflated. *Guess we're doing this.*

"Do you ever feel like you're always waiting for your life to start?" she asked. "Like you have all these things that you want to do, but you wonder if you'll ever be able to do them? There's always something, or someone, in your way?"

"What are you waiting for?" he asked.

She turned to face him. "I was waiting for an opportunity like this. A chance to prove that I could be a badass. That I could lead an expedition and make some great discovery. I want to do something amazing. I want people to see me and be like, *Damn, she's fucking rad.*"

Rafa snickered. Ouch. She wasn't trying to be funny.

"What? Why are you laughing?"

"It's nothing. I just love when you say things like 'rad.'"

She frowned. "Well, I'm not trying to be funny."

"I know you're not. That's why it's so refreshing being around you."

"Tell that to the other half of the team who've already quit." She folded her arms and looked away.

"In case you don't remember, I believe I have, Pringles," he said.

Miri shot a glance at Rafa, who was staring at her with a knowing look. Oh, she hadn't forgotten. *Dr. Jacobs looks good all the time.* She blushed thinking about the night at the campfire. Hearing Rafa talk about her to the others like he'd forgotten she was there.

"Well," she said, pushing the tingling feelings aside, "it's what I want. For people to know who I am, like Corrie."

"It takes time for people to build up a résumé like that."

"Well, I don't have time."

"You're young. You've probably got dozens of adventures left in you."

"Not if I come home empty-handed. And before you go saying you're sure this isn't my last opportunity, let me stop you," she said, putting her hand up. "My boss essentially told me that if I don't come back from this expedition with something noteworthy, I probably shouldn't bother coming back at all."

Rafa narrowed his brows. "That's bullshit."

She picked at some sticks on the ground beside her. "Maybe, but it doesn't change the fact that it's the reality of academia. I haven't done anything remarkable. I'm about as boring as they come."

"Pringles, you're anything but boring."

She rolled her eyes. "I should have quit after that run-in with Hunter and Kevin. I could have blamed it on the fact that we were in danger. You were right. At least that way I wouldn't have looked like a failure. Now if we quit it's going to be because I fucked up. Because I've been leading us around in circles for the last few weeks. I'm going to be a laughingstock. In fact, I've got a couple of new suggestions for the title of your article. How about 'Another Moon City Search Down the Amazon Drain'? Or better yet, 'Rookie Archaeologist Couldn't Find the Moon City Even if It Was Tattooed on Her Ass'?"

Rafa took her hands. "Stop."

"Stop what?"

"This isn't your fault. Stop putting yourself down. You're better than that."

"How would you know? This is the first time I've ever been assigned to lead a dig of any kind. There is no *better* when this is the best it's ever been." She turned away, not wanting him to see the tears welling in her eyes and twisting her mouth into knots. "Besides, look at you. You're an accomplished journalist working at one of the world's top magazines, traveling all over the world, doing so many *amazing* things. I mean, Mr. Larity requested *you* by name. I'm here on a pity invite from Corrie."

"You think my life is so great? Pringles, I *quit* my job a week before I came out here."

Miri ticked her head to the side. "What are you talking about?"

"You're right. *GloGeo* is a dream gig. And I *have* done amazing things. But you asked if I've ever felt like I'm waiting for my life to start, and never has someone so clearly put into words what's going on in my head. I have an apartment in DC, but I'm never there. I don't have any pets because who would feed them? Every plant I've ever had has withered away and died from lack of watering. I've never had a single streaming subscription because I'd go more than half the year without using it. I can't remember the last time I went out with friends because I avoid making plans since I never know when I'm going to have to cancel. Frankly, my friends—the few I have left—stopped reaching out years ago. This has been my life for almost a decade. What's the point of all those adventures if you don't have anyone to share them with?"

"So you quit?"

He nodded. "Tried to, at least."

"What do you mean, tried to?"

"My dad. He's on the board at *GloGeo*. So after I tried to quit, my boss called my dad and, well, here I am," he said, holding out his palms.

"Why doesn't he want you to quit?"

"The prestige. The importance." He shrugged. "I don't know. He used his connections to get me this job in the first place. It's hard to accept that I even earned it. I don't want his handouts, though. I want to make my own path, you know?"

"Doing what?"

"I want to be an author."

Miri furrowed her brow. "But you *are* an author."

"No, I'm a journalist. It's different. I document facts. Tell other people's stories. I want to tell my own."

"Is that what you're always doing when you're scribbling in that notebook of yours?"

He nodded. "Mostly I'm outlining my ideas. I've yet to have the opportunity to sit down and draft a full-length novel."

"And why is that?"

"See my prior answer," he said. "My dad. He thinks life is too important for frivolity. Not when there are great things to do and important discoveries to document. But I don't know, sometimes I think a lot of people feel like they need to accomplish big things to be able to say they made it, but for me, everything I've accomplished at *GloGeo*, all the work I've done to help my father? Those things have brought me pride, but they haven't given me happiness."

"What *would* bring you happiness?"

He paused as if he wasn't expecting she'd ask.

"Having what my parents had," he finally responded. "Even though my mother died when I was young, their love has lasted all these years. My father's sole goal in life is to protect her memory. To protect that which was important to her."

Miri's heart swelled. "That's really beautiful, Rafa."

He smiled and took a deep gulp, like he had a lump caught in his throat. He shook his head. "I don't even know what she looked like. My mother, I mean."

"No?" she asked. She'd grown up with both of her parents,

but their home was full of photos, including of her grandparents who'd passed away before she'd even been born. And she knew what every single one of them looked like.

"She and my father . . . their relationship was a bit of a whirlwind."

"How did they meet?"

"They met here. In Brazil. My father was—" Rafa stopped himself. "My father was here on business. My mother was helping him on a project, and they fell in love. She got pregnant. And, well, you know the rest."

"And not even a picture?"

"Nope. Though my father told me once that I remind him of her."

"I bet she was beautiful." The statement slipped out, and Miri bit back her tongue.

"Oh yeah? Why's that? Because you think I'm beautiful?" he asked, like a fox ready to trap its prey.

"No!" she blurted out as her cheeks reddened. "I was just . . . I mean . . . I assumed . . . you know . . ."

He smiled as she tried to backpedal. "So then you *don't* think I'm beautiful?"

"I mean, I do, or, no. I mean, you're handsome. But I . . . I . . . I mean, yes. If your dad says you look like her, then she must have been incredibly beautiful. Or your dad, I don't know. Maybe he's a hunk—"

"A hunk?" Rafa burst out laughing.

"What?" She looked at him, confused.

"Do people still say that? Call men 'hunks'?"

She stifled a smile and shoved his arm. "Shut up. Quit messing with me. Hot old men are hunks. It's an apt word in the right situation."

"I'm sorry, I'm sorry," he said. "I couldn't help myself."

"Okay, hardy har." She pursed her lips, trying her damned-est to keep her smile at bay, but there was no disputing that she found the situation just as entertaining as he did. "Well, thank you for sharing that with me. I'm sure it can't be easy to talk about it."

"You're honestly the only person I've ever told about it."

"Really?"

He nodded. "This may come as a surprise to you, Pringles, but this job doesn't exactly lend itself to lasting lifelong friend-ships. Aside from my editor, the only person I talk to on a regu-lar basis is my dad. And we don't talk about my mom."

"You should tell him how you feel," she said.

Rafa shook his head. "I can barely talk to him about wanting to write novels." He let out a half-hearted laugh.

"Do you not get along?"

"No, we get along great. He's my biggest supporter. He'll do anything for me. But . . ." Rafa paused. "There are certain things we just don't discuss. My mom is top of the list."

Miri furrowed her brow. "Do anything for you except sup-port you in the career you choose and talk to you about your mother when it's clearly important to you?"

Rafa stared at her for a moment as if analyzing what she'd just said, and then threw his head back, closing his eyes.

Oh shit. "I'm sorry," Miri quickly said. "I . . . I shouldn't be butting into your family business." She jumped up and brushed the dirt off her clothes. "We should probably head back to base camp," she said, rushing to the vine Rafa had used to climb down and giving it a swift tug. If it could hold Rafa's sturdy body, then it should certainly be able to handle hers. She wrapped one hand around the thick vine then propped her foot up high in front of her for leverage. "If we hurry, we should make it back before—" she said as she started to lift herself up.

But Rafa stopped her, placing his hand over hers on the vine. His gaze focused on hers with his eyes narrowed. She'd really done it this time. Put her foot in her mouth one time too many.

"Rafa, I'm—"

"Thank you," he said, cutting her off.

She blinked. Wait? What?

"Thank you?" she asked.

"You're right. My dad loves me. I shouldn't be afraid to tell him what I need. Or . . . what I want."

The way the word *want* reverberated in his throat sent a rumble into her core.

"Good," she said, trying to take the focus away from the nearness of his body. "You should tell him."

"I will. But first, we need to get the hell out of here. Are you ready to head back?"

Miri nodded. "Thanks for rescuing me from my pity party of one."

"Oh, I don't think you can say I've rescued you yet. We still have to find our way back."

Miri smiled and puffed up her chest. "Well then, I guess it's a good thing I know *exactly* where we're going."

"Exactly?" he asked, smiling and raising his eyebrows.

"Okay, maybe not exactly. Come on. Follow me."

CHAPTER

Fifteen

DON'T UNDERSTAND WHAT'S TAKING SO LONG," RAFA'S FATHER said on the phone. "It's been over three weeks. Why hasn't she quit yet?"

Rafa sat alone in his cabin using the satellite phone he'd borrowed from Anissa. He'd just finished telling his dad that two more people had quit since they'd last spoken, but it didn't seem to faze him. His dad was focused on one thing and one thing only: getting Miri to leave. The rest of them, he couldn't care less about.

"I told you. She's tenacious," Rafa said, smiling as he scrolled through photos of Miri on his camera.

"Are you even trying to get her to leave?"

Rafa's smile fell, and he quickly turned off the camera as if his father could see. "Of course I am."

Right?

"We're down to half a crew," Rafa continued. Maybe his dad would take that as a positive, at least. "And we've gone practically every direction possible from this resort. Honestly, Dad, I'm even beginning to doubt the Cidade da Lua is out here."

"Then I guess it's too bad you're not the one who needs convincing." There was an air of annoyance in his father's voice. Which Rafa understood given his promise to Rafa's mother and all, but he really *was* trying.

Or at least he had been.

Truth be told, Rafa hadn't taken any active steps to interfere with the expedition in over ten days.

But how could he sabotage Miri when this was so important to her? At this point, Rafa's best bet was to pray the rest of the crew would grow too weary to continue.

"Have you gotten any word about where Vautour's team might be?" Rafa asked, deflecting from his own ineptitude. "I think Dr. Jacobs is especially focused on getting to the Cidade da Lua before he does."

"Mmm, yes," his dad said, clearing his throat. "There've been rumblings that they've given up."

"Given up? Are you sure? I thought he commissioned some fancy lidar tech to pinpoint the location."

"Lidar is very expensive . . . and very difficult to obtain. If anyone could get their hands on lidar imagery, then there wouldn't be any such thing as a lost city. If respectable archaeologists like Drs. Mejía and Matthews aren't able to get it, what makes them think a criminal like Pierre Vautour could? And even then, you'd have to know where to look."

Rafa furrowed his brow. "Then why did they leave?"

"One of the team members got bitten by a lancehead snake, and they evacuated the entire crew. So if Vautour's what's keeping Dr. Jacobs on this mission, he shouldn't be a concern any longer. Now she's all that's left. Please, Rafa. You have to finish this."

Vautour or not, abandoning this expedition would crush Miri. Miri's voice popped into his head. *If I don't come back from this expedition with something noteworthy, I probably shouldn't bother coming back at all.* If only his dad could get to know her. Then he'd see she wasn't the treasure hunter he made her out to be.

"Dad, what if you're wrong about this?"

"Wrong about what? About Vautour leaving?"

"No. About Dr. Jacobs. And Mom. And os pro—"

"Rafael," his dad said with his commanding voice, "we've already talked about this."

"No, *you've* talked. I just listen and take your direction. And we *don't* talk about things. Why won't you ever talk about Mom?"

"Rafael," he warned again, "that's enough."

"Why? Because *you* said it's enough?"

"What's gotten into you? Is this because of Dr. Jacobs?"

"No, Dad. *I* want to talk to you."

"We can talk when you get home. *After* you've stopped the expedition."

"And if I don't? If I tell you that I won't continue lying to her? If I call my editor to follow through on my resignation?"

"Then maybe you shouldn't bother coming back at all. Don't test me."

Click.

Rafa stared at the phone, silent in his hand. Never in all his thirty-two years had his father hung up on him. What *was* that? *Who* was that? His dad wasn't exactly the warm-and-fuzzy type, but this? Rafa didn't know what to make of it.

But this update on Vautour's crew changed everything. He had to let Miri know.

Almost in a daze, he walked back to Anissa's cabin to return the phone only to find her sitting outside with Miri, passing a bottle back and forth. Anissa sat on a chair and Miri on the edge of the raised walkway. Miri's feet dangled over the side as her arms hung over the lower rung of the split railing, protecting her from falling.

"Well, well, well, if it isn't Snap Snack," Anissa slurred. "We were just talking about you."

Rafa's eyes widened.

"What about me?" he asked.

"Nothing," Miri said, narrowing her eyes at Anissa. "Anissa's enjoying the booze a little too much, is all."

Anissa tsked and rolled her eyes at Miri. "Want some?" she asked, then held up the bottle to Rafa.

He took a tentative step forward, noticing the bottle. That same crap that had gotten him drunk a week ago.

A gurgling bubbled in his stomach, and not the pleasant kind that accompanied being near Miri. "I think I'm good," he said, waving his hand at Anissa.

"Suit yourself," she said, taking another swig.

"I came over to return this," he said, resting the satellite phone atop the railing and then taking a few steps back and sheepishly tucking his hands in his pockets. He'd clearly interrupted something. With the way Miri avoided eye contact, he wasn't sure he was welcome. "I guess I'll leave you to it," he followed up before turning to head back to his cabin.

"You don't have to go." Miri's voice was quiet.

And hopeful.

He spun back around. Both women were looking at him. Anissa, the Cheshire cat. Miri, a timid mouse. Everything inside him screamed to retreat. To go back to his room and figure out how to get out of this mess. With Miri. With his dad. With

GloGeo. But his body floated toward her, and he sat down only a few inches from her on the edge of the raised walkway.

It wasn't exactly the safest place to sit. For many reasons.

A loud splash came from the river nearby and they froze to listen. An animal made a high-pitched squeal as the thrashing continued, eventually subsiding. Likely a caiman capturing its prey.

Miri shifted to take a closer look at the river, and her shoulder brushed against his. He looked back at her, his eyes grazing over her silhouette, accentuated by the moonlight. With the way the moon illuminated her lips, they glistened under its glow, causing a lump to catch in his throat. Slowly, her head ticked to the side, and she brought her gaze to meet his. They stared at each other like they were the only things in this vast rainforest.

"Eh-hem," Anissa said, finally snapping them out of it.

Miri snatched her gaze away.

"So," Rafa said, trying to take his focus off Miri's lips, "what's going on?"

"What's going on? We're drowning away our sorrows. Licking our wounds. Tying one on—" Anissa said, until Miri cut her off.

"Brian just quit," Miri said.

"The other field tech?" Rafa asked.

Miri simply nodded. "He's leaving in the morning." They stayed silent for a moment before Miri screamed with frustration into the Amazonian abyss.

"It will be okay," Anissa said, leaning forward and placing her hand on Miri's back.

"No, everything will *not* be okay," Miri snapped. "I've lost more than half the crew. How are we supposed to continue with only five people? And you two aren't even field crew."

She reclined, resting her back flush against the wooden walkway, and folded her forearms over her eyes. "This is it," she mumbled. "Say goodbye to my career."

Rafa's heart sank. *Damn.*

He reached into the side pocket of his cargo pants.

"Want some?" he asked, offering her the peanut M&M's she had given him that first day at the airport in Manaus.

She twisted her head, peeking at him from under her arms with tears in her eyes, then quickly wiped them away. "You still have them?" she asked with a sniffle.

"I've been saving them for the right moment. This seems as good a time as any," he said with a smile he hoped would make her feel better. "Here," he said, tearing the corner off the wrapper and taking her hand to dump a few candies in.

A faint smile broke across her lips. She took the candy, then sat up before popping an M&M in her mouth. He raised the bag to Anissa to offer some, but she waved him away and pointed at the bottle of booze with a smile and a nod. Good. He really wanted Miri to have them anyway.

"Thank you," Miri said.

"You're welcome," he said.

She sighed, tossed her head back, and looked out into the dense canopy above. The buzzing and whistling of the forest were a nice distraction from the thoughts swirling in Rafa's head. They sat for what felt like hours, passing the bag back and forth, slowly savoring the chocolate-covered peanuts like they needed to be rationed over the whole night. Eventually, Anissa fell asleep, but Miri and Rafa didn't make any effort to move.

"I don't know what I was thinking," Miri finally said.

"About what?" he asked.

"About finding the Moon City. I don't know why I thought *I* could actually be the one to find it."

"Seems you had as good a chance as anyone else."

"Yeah, but you were right. We should have quit days ago." She picked at the wooden railing, tossing a tiny piece to the ground below them. "It's probably only a matter of time before Logan and Felix throw in the towel, too. I can't do this on my own. I can barely even do it now."

She laughed, but it was hollow. "What am I even saying? I haven't *done*," she said, using her fingers for air quotes, "anything out here. God, I'm such a joke."

She folded her arms over the railing and rested her cheek upon them, turning her head away from Rafa. Her words created a pit in his stomach.

"No one is going to think you're a joke for not finding a city that's been lost for hundreds of years," he said, hoping it would make her feel better. "The only thing that's funny about this is that explorers keep trying."

"And if Vautour finds it first?"

"He gave up."

Miri propped herself up on her forearm and faced him. "What do you mean he gave up? Where did you hear that?"

"My boss told me. That's who I was on the phone with," he said. He didn't want to lie, but he couldn't exactly tell her that his dad had a network into the archaeological happenings in Brazil. "He'd heard they were evacuated after a snake bite got one of them."

Miri sighed. But the news didn't seem to faze her.

"What does it matter?" she said, lying back down.

Rafa's head cocked to the side, eying her as she stared at the thatched roof covering them. That wasn't the reaction he'd expected from this news.

"I guess it means we don't need to worry about what Vautour might have done to the city if he were to find it." Rafa then paused, struggling to say the next words. "And that you shouldn't feel bad if you decide to give up."

He had to look away when he said it. The words tasted vile on his lips. Like a betrayal.

But Miri remained silent, her gaze unflinching. Time stopped. Everything stopped. Including her.

"Did you hear what I said?" he asked.

She let out a long breath. "I heard you. It just . . . it's too late. It doesn't matter anymore because this isn't about Vautour," Miri said. "I mean, it is—or, it was—but this is about me. I've been thinking a lot about what you said earlier. About finding whatever it is that will bring you happiness," she said.

He'd been thinking a lot about that conversation, too.

"Oh yeah? What about it?" he asked.

Miri sat up and brushed her hand just under her eye. "Well, you talked about how all of your accomplishments have made you proud, but not necessarily happy."

"Those things aren't mutually exclusive. You *can* find happiness in things that make you proud."

"I thought about that, too. But then I really thought about why I'm here and tried to figure out whether succeeding on this expedition would make me proud *or* happy, and at this point, I think the answer is that it won't make me either of those things."

He tipped his head to the side, wondering what she was getting at. "I thought this was what you wanted?"

"So did I. I want to be a leader, but I want to *earn* that respect, not have it handed to me. I want the success of the expedition to be because *I* made a brilliant discovery, not because someone gave me a piece of paper with a list. I want people to *want* to be here, not just sucking it up because it's their job. If we succeed now, it won't be because of anything I did. And how can I be proud of my accomplishment if my entire team gave up on me?"

"If finding the Moon City won't bring you happiness, what *will*?" he asked.

She stared him straight in the eye, then spoke. "Being content with not being some extraordinary, larger-than-life badass and, instead, loving being me. Sometimes talking too much. Often daydreaming about nothing. Being a *good* archaeologist, even if it means never being a great one. Telling corny jokes. Being known for always bringing the best snacks. And wearing fanny packs like they're going out of style."

She smiled, and it warmed Rafa's heart. Did she really not see how amazing she was? He brushed her hair from her face with the pad of his thumb, wiping away a dried tear stain on her cheek.

"Pringles, everything you just said highlights why you're the baddest badass of them all."

"You think I'm badass?" she said with a smile.

"I think you're everything."

She sucked in a breath and bit her lip. The forest stilled around them, fading into the background as they inched closer to each other. He scanned her face, searching for unspoken permission, before leaning forward—

TH-CRACK!

A roll of thunder boomed through the sky, immediately followed by downpouring rain. The ruckus startled Anissa awake and she practically jumped out of her chair, which forced Miri and Rafa apart.

"Holy shit!" Anissa yelled as Miri and Rafa pulled their legs up from the walkway and huddled under the overhanging thatched roof of Anissa's cabin.

Rafa's heart pounded, but he wasn't sure whether it was because of the thunder or how close he and Miri had come to breaking that invisible barrier they'd built between the two of them. That was close. Too close.

"I'm going to make a run for it," Miri said, motioning toward her cabin.

The walkways between cabins weren't covered, but with the rainfalls lasting anywhere from a few minutes to a few hours, they definitely weren't going to spend the night all tucked in Anissa's bed waiting it out. Luckily, Miri only had to run a few cabins down. Rafa, on the other hand, had to travel several cabins away and would most certainly get drenched.

"Good night, Anissa," Miri said, pulling her in for a hug. Then she turned toward Rafa. "Ready?"

Rafa nodded, and then they booked it with their arms above their heads to cover them—as if that did anything. They weaved along the passageway, laughing as he guided her by the hand, careful to keep them from slipping. But as he started to let go of her hand and continue past her cabin toward his own, a hand pulled back on him. He spun around, and there was Miri. Sopping wet and staring up at him with her hair plastered against her face and her clothes soaked through. The rain poured over them as he pulled her into his arms. She clutched his biceps, like she'd fall if she let go. He could barely see with the rain streaming down his face, but he didn't need to see to know what she looked like. The face that haunted his dreams. That consumed him. He leaned down and pressed his forehead to hers, his heartbeat a stampede of horses over an open plain.

Her hands reached up to his neck. Holding him but restraining from pulling him closer.

"I hope you find your happiness, Rafa," she whispered, almost inaudible above the riotous raindrops.

His lips crashed onto hers as he pulled her firmly against his chest. He wanted her. No, he *needed* her. Not only for himself. He needed her to see how remarkable she was.

Their mouths feverishly feasted upon each other, unable to get close enough. His hands twisted in her hair as her hands wrapped behind his back, pulling down on his shoulders. He no longer held back, wanting to touch her, hold her, and never let go.

He hoisted her up by her thighs, wrapping her legs around his waist, and pressed her back into the side of her cabin. The rain was unable to douse the fire between them—the inferno that had been building over the last few weeks.

With her back pinned against the cabin, he rocked his hips into her center. Her moans coupled with the friction of his cock pressed against her sent a surge of euphoria over his skin. More, he needed more. Without breaking their embrace he walked to her cabin, thrusting the door open, swooping inside, and closing it again in one fluid movement. His mouth continued to devour hers as he lowered her feet to the floor then brought his hands to the button of her pants.

"Is this okay?" he asked, breaking their kiss for a moment.

She nodded with a whimper while licking her lips. He then twisted the button and rolled down the zipper before diving his hand into her panties. Upon feeling her slippery wetness, he pressed his forehead against the door.

"Fuck, Pringles," he said with his eyes closed. His fingers glided effortlessly along her slick folds before plunging inside her, sending her hips bucking against his hand.

With his thumb on her clit, he sank his index finger inside her, feeling her clench around him, before he brought his lips back to hers. She lowered her hand to his waist, gliding down toward his cock and cupping it in her palm and gripping his length. But no. He wasn't finished with her yet.

He lowered his knees to the floor, peeling her pants off one leg at a time, then grazed her thighs with his fingers stretched wide. Her panties were at eye level in front of him and he could see her sweet nectar soaking through the thin fabric. He spread her legs with his hand, then ran his fingers along the crotch of her panties.

"Do you like when I touch you like this?" he asked.

She nodded, her breath quickening.

"Do you know how long I've wanted this?" he asked. She shook her head. "Do you know how badly I want to taste you?" She shook her head again.

He spun her around so she faced the door, pulled her panties all the way to the floor, then pulled back on her hips so her ass stuck out. His fingers danced around her slick opening before he dove in with his mouth.

"Oh God!" she cried out in pleasure.

His tongue lapped at her opening while his fingers reached around front to rub her clit. Miri grabbed the wall to steady herself as if her knees were about to buckle.

But he held her up and flipped her around. She looked down at him, admiring her from the floor. His eyes spoke for him as he dove back between her legs. Eating her. Tasting her.

Worshipping her.

"Rafa!" she called out his name as she released, bracing herself against the wall and tossing her head back.

As soon as her body stopped convulsing, he stood and crashed his mouth to hers, allowing her to taste herself.

But Miri had other ideas. She pushed him backward until he fell to the edge of her bed, then she kneeled in front of him and pulled his pants and boxers to the floor.

"Holy moly," she said, taking him in.

She glided her hands over his length, causing him to suck in a breath, and then kept her eyes on him while putting him in her mouth.

He moaned, gripping the bed to steady himself.

"Fuck, Pringles."

She used her hand to cover more ground, increasing her speed in sync with the increased volume of his moans.

"Oh God," he said, running his fingers through her hair. "You're gonna make me come."

He pulled her from him seconds before coming on his stomach. Miri stayed kneeling in front of him as he relaxed his breathing, his hand still in her hair, and then he pulled her up beside him.

"Come here," he said, bringing her mouth to his.

They sank deep into their kiss, not worrying about the expedition or Vautour. Or anything other than each other.

Sixteen

MIRI HAD BEEN WRONG. WRONG ABOUT NEEDING TO FIND THE Moon City. Wrong about what would happen if she didn't succeed.

What did any of it matter? So maybe she made an important discovery. Maybe she got her name in some prestigious archaeological digest. Sure, it would be pretty rad. But would it prove to everyone she was enough? Would it make her happy?

Possibly.

But was it worth dragging her team along on this wild goose chase? No.

She only wished she'd come to that realization earlier.

WWCMD?

She never would have been in this situation in the first place, that's what. Corrie would have recognized their failure weeks ago. And she'd have admitted when she was wrong.

So at breakfast the next morning, Miri made an announcement.

"I spent some time thinking last night, and it's time for us to head home," she said.

Felix and Logan dropped their forks, the loud clacking on their plates immediately causing Anissa to put her hands on her head as she nursed a hangover. They clearly weren't worried about the noise, however, while they bombarded Miri with questions.

When?

Why?

But what about the Moon City?

What about Pierre Vautour?

She wished she could give them quick, easy answers, but how was she supposed to explain the epiphany she'd had the night before? It wouldn't make sense to them. How Rafa had helped her see her worth. She didn't need awards and accolades to prove herself. Even without any actual discovery in the Amazon, she'd already proved to herself that she was a badass. She'd finally given herself permission to let all her tension, all her insecurities, go, and damn, was it liberating.

When she glanced over at Rafa, however, she was surprised to see that he wasn't elated. Instead, he hung his head, staring at her with apologetic eyes. Like he'd done something wrong. After trying to convince her to leave for the last three weeks, why did he suddenly look . . . disappointed?

Was it last night? Regret? She tried to read behind his eyes, but he gave her nothing.

"With everything that's happened, I think it's time we cut our losses. Like Dr. Mejía said in the recording—there was a very real chance that we'd never find the Cidade da Lua, but no one can say it's because we didn't try. So I want to pack up and head to the airport in Boa Vista tomorrow. Anissa, can you book us plane tickets?"

"Yeah, yeah," Anissa said with her head face down on the table and waving her hand in the air.

"What should we do today?" Felix asked.

Miri shrugged. "Do whatever you want. Just don't get bitten by a poisonous spider or get crunched by a boa constrictor."

"I'll be in my room," Anissa said, standing up and shuffling toward her cabin. "Do *not* knock on my door."

"So that's it?" Rafa asked once the others left the dining cabana. There was an edginess in his tone that Miri couldn't quite place.

"It is. I thought you'd be pleased that I was finally giving up?" She said it like it was a question.

"I mean, I am, I suppose." *Hmm . . . that didn't sound very convincing.* "You're not doing it because of me, are you? Because of last night?"

She eyed him. "Not because of you. I'm doing this for myself. Despite what Berkeley may think, I don't need this. Even if it means I'll never go on another archaeological dig again, I'm not going to be bullied by people like my boss or Dr. Quinn into thinking that I need their approval to be happy."

"And you're sure this is what *you* want?"

"Rafa? I've never been more sure of anything in my life. Now come on," she said, pulling him up by the arm. "I want to go out in the Amazon once more, just with you."

"And do what?"

"I want to take it in. We've been here for over three weeks, and I haven't *seen* anything."

He chuckled. "What are you talking about?"

"Each day, we've walked through this forest looking for clues, but I never opened my eyes. I want to *experience* the Amazon. And what were you saying? What's the point if you don't have someone to experience life with?"

He smiled, gave her a quick kiss, and they went to their

cabins to grab their things before hiking into the Amazon for the last time. Likely Miri's last time ever.

Miri led the way, with Rafa hot on her trail. Butterflies swarmed in her stomach as she thought about what might happen after this, especially now that she was effectively unemployed— or at least would be once she got back to the States. But she didn't care. She was free.

Free from worrying about trying to impress others. Free from pretending to be someone she was not. Her whole life she had tried to conform. People tolerated her, but few truly understood her. Corrie. Anissa.

And now Rafa. He understood her *and* seemed to appreciate all of her quirks.

They traveled along a familiar path—the last thing they needed was to get lost on their final day—stopping to take pictures of the bromeliads and forest mushrooms. Rafa managed to snap a shot of a falcon swooping through the dense understory and capturing a coral snake. They spotted a sloth slowly traversing from one tree to another. They took a snack break beside a shallow stream, taking in the sounds of the water babbling across the smooth stones lining the streambed along with the twittering birds chirping in the trees.

"Before we go back, can we stop by that dumb hunk of rock?" she asked.

"What hunk of rock? The mesa de pedra?"

She nodded. "I know it's not *the* mesa de pedra, but it *was* beautiful. I'd like to see it once more."

He took her hand and smiled, leading her back along the trail they'd traversed over a dozen times by that point. By now, they knew the way. They could probably find it with their eyes closed.

As they reached the ravine, rather than take the long way, they each grabbed a vine, swinging across the understory and through the wall of vines. Miri landed on the stone with perfection, and Rafa landed on the ground next to her. At least she could go home having mastered one thing on this trip.

Miri ran her hand along the smooth rock, noticing all its imperfections and impurities. All the things that made it unique and magnificent.

"Come on, I want to get some photos of you with the stone," Rafa said, stealing her attention.

Miri's body stiffened. "Me?"

Rafa looked from side to side, front to back. "Yeah, you. You don't see anyone else over here, do you?"

"But . . . but why do you want pictures of me now? It's just a rock. And the expedition is dead."

"Because I still have a story to write. And you discovered this hulking thing," he said, patting it with his hand. "It'll be great for the article."

Miri thought about the spread *Archaeological Digest* had featured Corrie in several years back. It had catapulted her into archaeological stardom. Helped her land her job at UC Berkeley. She'd looked so cool in the photos and effortlessly sexy. This article that Rafa was writing for *Global Geography*, maybe it could do the same for Miri. Even without finding the Moon City.

"Okay," she said. "What are you thinking?"

He motioned for her to move closer to the stone. "Stand over there and change up your pose every couple of snaps. I take a lot of photos, so keep trying different things and I'll find one that works."

Miri walked over to the stone and rested the edge of her butt on the corner, then arched her back and cocked her head to the side with her arms crossed in front of her, mimicking a photo she recalled from Corrie's article. "Like this?" she said.

Rafa lifted his brow. "Um, okay. Sure. Just keep moving, though."

Snap!

She then climbed on top of the stone, sitting with one leg bent and the other stretched out like her sister's high school cheerleading squad photos. *Snap!* Then she rested on her side and propped her head up using her arm. *Snap!* She then sat up again, and gave him Kardashian duck lips—they were always on magazine covers, right?—waiting for the next *snap* to change position. And waited. What was taking so long?

"What are you doing?" Rafa said, finally ripping her from her thoughts.

She turned her head toward him, and he stood facing her with the camera in front of his waist.

"We're taking pictures."

"Right, but what are you doing?"

"I'm posing, like you said."

"What exactly would you call those poses?" He furrowed his brow at her.

"I'm trying to look sexy."

His lips turned up. "This is not working the way you think it is."

Miri threw her arms at her side as if giving up. "You don't think I'm sexy?"

Now it was a full grin. "No, I think you're *very* sexy. But that?" he said, motioning toward her with his camera.

"This is how models pose in magazines," Miri pointed out, still kneeling on the stone.

"And what magazines are those? *GQ*? *Sports Illustrated*?

Playboy? Because you know where you won't find models—or *anyone*, for that matter—posing like that? *GloGeo*."

"Not on brand?" Miri asked, wrinkling her nose.

Rafa laughed. "No, definitely not the *GloGeo* brand. Why are you trying to look sexy anyway?"

"I mean, I was actually going for sexy *badass*."

"Well, then. Come here," he said, motioning her toward him with his hand.

Miri crawled to the edge of the stone and stepped off, standing in front of him. He set the camera on the stone then squared up with her.

"Okay, first, shake it off." He shimmied his body and she followed suit. "All right, now, show me badass."

Miri popped her hip, pushed out her chest, and puckered her lips. Rafa shook his head. "No. Look, this isn't a pinup ad. You're not selling a product. Sexy and badass aren't the same thing. You can be both, but they aren't identical. Being sexy is all about desire. Lust. Being badass is about confidence. A give-no-fucks attitude. And having the résumé to back it up."

"But I *don't* have the résumé to back it up, remember?" Miri said, scrunching her face.

"Then fake it 'til you make it."

"Show me."

"Show you what? How to fake it?"

"Show me some poses," she said, motioning to this body.

"You want me to show you how to look like a badass?"

"And sexy. You're a photographer. Show me how it's done."

"I'm not that kind of photographer. And frankly, I'm not really a photographer at all. I'm a journalist who happens to be able to take decent enough photos that sometimes I get assigned to do both."

"Well, clearly I'm doing it all wrong, so I want you to show me how to do it right."

He eyed her for a second, sighed, and then said, "All right. Here, switch places with me."

They spun around so Miri was facing Rafa at the stone. He rested his behind on the stone, then said, "This is badass," as he leaned forward into a half crouch, resting his forearms on his thighs, and looking straight on at her.

Damn. He looked like a boss.

"And this is sexy." He sat up and leaned back, spread his legs wider—highlighting the unmistakable bulge in his pants—and lifted his shirt to reveal his rippled abs while turning his head to the side.

Holy guacamole, sweet baby Jesus.

If Rafa was going for lust and desire, he'd certainly accomplished that—and then some. Miri pressed her legs together as her mind cycled through dirty thoughts.

Of her licking those smooth abs.

Nestling in between those thick thighs.

Rafa taking her on that giant stone. Making love to her.

"Your turn," he said, moving away from the rock and jerking her back to real life.

They switched places again and Miri mimicked the same "badass" pose that Rafa had just demonstrated.

"No, that's the way *I* would do it. Show me that *Dr. Miriam Jacobs* is a badass."

Miri thought to herself for a moment. *Dr. Miriam Jacobs is a badass*, she repeated over and over in her head. *WWCMD?*

She climbed on top of the slab and took a wide-leg stance, folded her arms, and tilted her chin up ever so slightly.

"Yes! Yes! Hold that pose," he said, rushing to grab his camera and taking a few snaps. "Now try something else."

She considered her options, then crouched down with one knee touching the stone top and one bent up, resting her forearm on the bent leg. "Perfect," he said, taking another snap. "Try another."

She scanned the area, then hopped down from the table and walked around to the backside. She bent over the table, placed her palms on the surface like a boss in a boardroom, and stared straight on at Rafa.

"Fucking incredible. You're a natural." *Snap! Snap!*

"Oh yeah? Second career in modeling?" she joked. "So long as no one ever sees my test shots, that is."

"The test shots were fine. You were just trying too hard."

"You think? Well, how about this?" she asked, climbing again onto the stone table and slowly crawling across it toward Rafa. Time to see if she could master sexy after Rafa's instruction.

Snap!

"Relax your face a little. You almost look angry."

"How about this?" Miri laid on the boulder, curling her legs to the side yet arching her back, and tilted her head to look back at Rafa with sweet, innocent eyes.

"Here, wait," he said, climbing atop the stone and standing straight above her. He pointed the camera down at her face as he hovered. Miri turned her head and stared into the camera, searching through the lens for Rafa. Wanting him. Wanting him to want her.

Miri bit her lip as she lowered her eyelids yet never allowed her eyes to leave the camera.

Snap!

He lowered himself to her level, kneeling in front of her. "Let's try a few more natural photos," he said, his voice now soft and quiet. "Here, sit up."

Taking his hand, she raised herself up and sat in front of him. "Am I still not getting sexy right?"

He gave a slight chuckle, then snapped another photo, this time without her posed. "No, Pringles. That's not it."

She looked straight into the lens as if staring through the glass was looking through a window to his soul. "Then what is it?"

"These pictures . . . they're for me." *Snap!*

Miri lifted her hand and placed it on his arm. He took the camera away from his face, lowering it in front of his chest and watching her. Waiting for her to speak.

"Rafa?" she whispered.

"Yes?"

"What's going to happen after this?" Her chest heaved, scared to put herself out there. "After we leave here, I mean. Between me and you. Will I ever see you again?"

"I . . . I don't know."

"We're not just caught up in the moment again, are we?"

He pulled her closer so their bodies were flush against each other. His dark brown eyes searched her own as his thumb swept over her lips, pulling her bottom lip open and seemingly sucking all the air from her body.

"Pringles, I was never caught up in the moment," he said. "You've had me captivated from the second you opened your mouth and fanned out your goods." He winked.

"Oh yeah? Well," she said, waving her hands in display, "how about now?"

Rafa dove toward her mouth, taking her body fully in his hands. Their kiss was raw. Full of emotions begging to be let go. Their tongues tangled together, continuing what they'd started the night before.

She could sink into his warmth. Let his tenderness envelop her. Lie in his arms until the sun came up, talking and laughing all night as she fell deeper into her infatuation.

Miri's hand trailed down his pants, making its way to his dick, his erection threatening to burst through his cargos. She applied pressure as she massaged him from the outside of his pants. Tight and firm, with a combination of long, slow strokes and gentle squeezes. All while she rubbed her own crotch against his thigh.

"Fuck, Miri . . ." he moaned, wetting his lips as he kept his eyes closed and tilted his head back.

She twisted the button on his pants, unzipped the fly, and slid her hand beneath the waistband of his boxers. Squeezing his erection. Pumping it in her grasp. She then guided his hand, palm against her stomach, and slowly he let his hand skim against her skin, down to the wetness between her legs. She moaned as he massaged her slippery clit with his fingers. The pressure increasing in her core as both of their hands moved faster.

He leaned in to kiss her. Miri tilted her head up to him as she closed the gap between them, when something caught her eye behind him.

"Wait! What's that?" she asked, swiftly moving from his grasp and letting his lips hang in midair. He swallowed his groan as she climbed off the stone table toward the rock wall surrounding them. There was something notched into the wall. Something she hadn't seen all those days out in the field.

"What is it?" he asked, eventually sidling up next to her with his hands in his pockets.

He let his gaze follow hers, looking up and down at the rock face. He couldn't see it.

But Miri saw something. She carefully brushed away the dirt from the stone in front of her at chest level near the end of the wall, uncovering a circular indentation in the stone with an unusual pattern of half-inch-long pieces of stone sticking out. The pattern was too perfect. Too rigid. This wasn't the work of nature.

This was the work of humans.

"Do you see this?" she asked. Her fingers glided delicately over the indentations. Feeling the pattern. Studying the angles. "I need my bag!" She jumped up and ran to the other side of the table for her things before rushing back.

She kneeled on the ground, then pulled out an excavation brush and the medallion, still wrapped in fabric. Carefully, she brushed out the dirt from the marking in the wall, taking her time as Rafa stood behind her watching. After every couple of swipes, she blew onto the spot to get rid of any loose dirt. Once it was free of remaining grime and without taking her eyes off the wall, she unwrapped the cloth, revealing the medallion.

"Where did you get that?" Rafa asked, unable to take his eyes off the medallion.

"Corrie sent it to me."

"When? How?"

But Miri didn't answer, too fixated on the wall. She lifted the medallion, holding it near the spot she'd excavated in the stone. Holding the piece as if it was the holy grail, Miri took a few steps forward then cautiously placed the medallion into the stone, turning the pendant until it fit into the rock like the perfect piece of a puzzle.

"Oh. My. God," Miri said, standing frozen in front of the

rock. "You know what this means, don't you?" she asked, pointing at the medallion.

He stared at the medallion stuck in the rock. With the pattern on the back and how it fit into the rock, the carvings of the temple and moon weren't facing upward. Instead, they were turned to the right.

"No, I don't know what this means," he said, lifting his hand to rub the back of his head.

"It means this *is* the mesa de pedra. This proves we were right all along!"

Her smile beamed.

"How did we not see this before?" Rafa asked.

"I guess we were so focused on what was on the ground that we didn't think about what might be up higher."

"So now what?" he asked, looking around as if waiting for something to happen.

It wasn't like placing the medallion into the rock opened up some secret passageway or illuminated a path. It fit in place, but nothing else made sense.

Miri's wide smile fell. "I . . . don't know exactly." She turned back to the wall and stared at the necklace with one hand on her hip and the other massaging her chin. "I need to think."

They stood there for what seemed like hours, pacing, inspecting the medallion, trying to insert it in another orientation, attempting to turn it, but only one positioning worked. They hypothesized about the missing piece of the medallion and whether it may have included an inscription or some other clue. But seeing as they didn't have that piece, it didn't really matter.

As she stared at it over and over, however, the carving came into focus in her mind.

It wasn't a temple with a moon. It was an arrow.

"I think I've got it!" she called out. Without hesitation, she grabbed the necklace and took off jogging into the jungle.

"Pringles! Wait!" he called out, scurrying to pack up his things and follow her.

But she didn't wait. She ran. Ran as fast as she could, eager to determine whether she was right. She pulled out a compass, following it in the exact direction pointing from the stone table, climbing and ducking, weaving and swinging. With a boat coming to get them in the morning, they had no time to waste.

She turned to check on where Rafa was behind her. Thankfully, he'd caught up and was only a few feet back. "Come on!" she said, smiling at him.

She reached out for his hand, giddy and high on life, when a voice called out to them in the distance, stopping them in their tracks.

"Well, well, well, what do we have here?" the voice said, startling Miri and Rafa.

They spun in all directions to find the source of the voice, when a figure emerged from behind the trees.

Hunter.

Her heart went haywire, like a pinball about to break a record.

"I was wondering when we'd see each other again," Hunter said, ambling toward them like he was entering a saloon.

"Stay the fuck back," Rafa said, putting himself in front of Miri.

"You owe me a boat, and one of these," Hunter said, pointing toward his crotch at a knife poking out from the waistband of his pants.

"Sorry, Hunter, we're fresh out of dicks," Miri said from behind the safety of Rafa's frame.

Hunter laughed. "Feisty. Now I know what you see in her. Hey, boss," he called out over his shoulder, "we've got visitors."

Hunter turned back to face Miri and Rafa, tossing them a smarmy smile that sickened Miri to her core. "By *boss*, I assume you're referring to Pierre Vautour?" she asked.

"Bin-go," he said, pointing the knife at her for emphasis on the *go*. "He was really hoping you would have gotten the message by now and given up on your quest, but guess we weren't persuasive enough when we last saw you."

"Yeah, that's because we kicked your asses," Miri said.

Rafa turned slightly and whispered, "You probably shouldn't piss him off."

"Whatever. If I'm going down, I'm at least going down not having taken his shit," she said quietly, mustering a smile with every ounce of courage left in her body.

"Real-life badass, Pringles," he said, smiling back and planting a soft kiss on her forehead.

"How sweet," another voice called out. "Looks like I'm not the only one to have found love out in the Amazon."

Miri turned her head toward the new voice. This one with a French accent and coming from a middle-aged man who Miri could only assume was Vautour, staring at them with his gang of henchmen behind him.

He wasn't at all the beady-eyed Indiana Jones villain she'd imagined. He was quite handsome if she was being honest. The term *silver fox* finally clicked for her. Totally the type of man she'd refer to as a hunk.

But there was something else. Something *familiar* about him. Maybe she *had* seen him before, though she couldn't picture where. Miri wasn't exactly hanging out in illegal market trading forums or on the dark web.

She looked over at Rafa to see his reaction. To see if he was also surprised that *this* was the man that they'd feared over the last several weeks. The look on Rafa's face, however, was quite different than hers. All the color had drained from his face. And his breathing had picked up.

Something was wrong. Something was very wrong.

She opened her mouth to ask if he was okay, but Rafa's mouth opened first as he stared directly at the man.

"Dad?"

CHAPTER

Seventeen

RAFA HAD ONLY EVER KNOWN HIS FATHER BY TWO NAMES: DAD and Jean-Luc Monfils.

Now, apparently he needed to add Pierre Vautour to the list.

Rafa's mind spun. He couldn't even hear the words Miri was saying as she shook his arm, trying to get him to snap out of it. To wake from the cloudy haze that had settled over him. Instead, he stared at his dad, trying to piece together his life.

All the trips. All the boards and committees. He wasn't out there doing great things. He was using his clout as a reputable do-gooder as a cover-up while he was swindling and screwing people over on the side.

Oh fuck.

That meant his father was responsible for whatever it was that had happened to Drs. Mejía and Matthews in Mexico a year ago.

The realization returned him to his senses, and he could finally hear Miri's voice.

"Are you okay?" she said.

"No," he answered honestly.

"What the hell is this?" Miri snapped at Rafa's dad. "Are you . . . are you . . ."

"Pierre Vautour? Yes, that's how most people know me. But not all," he said, casting Rafa a knowing glance. "Hello, Rafael."

Rafa could only glare.

"You're . . . you're Rafa's father?"

"Yes, I suppose I am that as well. But don't worry—he didn't know who I was. Right, son?"

"Don't call me that," Rafa spat out.

His dad tsked. "Rafael, don't be like that. You wanted to talk, and we'll get to that. There's much for us to discuss. So much you don't understand."

Rafa wanted to laugh. So much he didn't understand? Talk about an understatement.

Pierre Vautour was a stranger.

"What are you doing?" Rafa asked. "Care to explain to me how I didn't know my father was a criminal?"

"Don't believe everything you hear, Rafael."

"So then it's not true? You aren't a thief?"

His dad let out an exaggerated sigh and rested against a nearby rock. "When you really think about it, we're all thieves, aren't we? Sir Arthur Evans? Howard Carter? Hiram Bingham? They didn't have any stake in their claims other than that they staked their claim first."

"What about Dr. Mejía?" Miri chimed in. "Unlike you and all those other archaeologists, she was searching for her ancestor's remains, not simply looking for a payday."

His dad ticked his head to the side, as if Miri's comment annoyed him. "And if I remember correctly, her lineage ended up being a fairy tale her grandfather spun her anyway. You can't trust anyone nowadays, can you?"

Rafa was going to be sick. His legs gave out and he fell to his knees. Miri kneeled beside him, making sure he was okay before turning back toward Vautour.

"What do you want with us?" she asked.

"I *wanted* you to leave."

"Well, I'm not a quitter," she growled at him.

"Dr. Mejía surely rubbed off on you. In more ways than one now that I think about it."

Miri cocked her head. "What's that supposed to mean?"

"Well," Vautour stood and took off his leather gloves, strolling toward them. "You're both fiery. And tenacious. And, if I remember correctly, she fell for Dr. Matthews even though he'd deceived her."

Rafa's eyes widened, and he looked at his father, silently begging him not to say anything more. But it was too late. Miri was already staring at him with a questioning look in her eyes.

"What's that got to do with me?" she asked Vautour while looking at Rafa.

"Miriam, I can explain—" Rafa started, but his father cut him off.

"I asked him to sabotage your expedition."

"It wasn't quite like that," Rafa said, reaching his hand over to Miri, but she swatted it away.

"This whole time? You've been working for him, too?" Her beautiful face twisted as she bit back her tears.

"No! I mean, I guess, but I didn't know he was Pierre Vautour."

"Oh, so you were just doing it of your own accord? Is that somehow supposed to make me feel better?"

"You don't understand. He lied to me," he pleaded.

"You mean like how *you* lied to *me*? Like father, like son."

"I'm *nothing* like my father."

Vautour laughed, stealing Miri and Rafa's attention from each other. "We're more alike than you think, Rafael."

"Shut up!" Rafa yelled at him.

"All right," Miri said, standing and moving away from Rafa. "This pseudo family reunion is fun and all, but what now? What are you going to do with me?"

Rafa didn't miss that she'd said *me* and not *us*.

"That depends," Vautour said, taking another few steps toward Miri as Rafa watched from his knees below.

"Depends on what?"

"Depends on whether I think I can trust you to be a good girl who does what she's told."

"And what are you telling me to do?"

Vautour moved into her space so that his words couldn't be missed. "Go home, Dr. Jacobs. Pack up your belongings and gather your team and go home, never breathing a word about this to anyone."

"And if I don't? What if I find the Moon City first?"

"You won't. The lidar images I commissioned have been coming in quite handy. Much better than that piece of scrap metal around your neck," he said, nodding his head in her direction.

"Okay, well, how do you know I won't reveal your identity once I'm free?"

"Dr. Jacobs, Dr. Jacobs," he said, clucking his tongue and folding his hands in front of him. "Do you think I don't know how to keep people quiet? Everyone's got a price."

"Go ahead. You can't buy me off. And I have nothing to hide. I'm clean as a whistle."

Vautour snickered, then tossed a glance toward Rafa. "I see why you like her." Rafa tried to stand, but Vautour's men placed their hands on his shoulders, holding him down. Vautour then turned his attention back to Miri. "It doesn't matter if you're clean as a whistle. Rumor is that you're about to find yourself out of a job."

"So what? I can always get another one," Miri said confidently.

"I wouldn't be so sure about that. I don't know what my son told you about who I am, but I know people. People with influence."

"Yeah, and as soon as they find out that you're Pierre Vautour—"

"What makes you think they don't already know?"

Miri threw her head back, Rafa's dad's words seeming to knock her off balance. It hadn't occurred to Rafa that his dad's identity may not have been as secret as he imagined.

"Everyone has a price," his father continued. "All I need to do is call in a few favors, and then your doctorate will be worth more as a place mat than any sort of job credential. Might as well get a job working at a convenience store."

"Well, good thing I am a convenience store snack connoisseur," she said proudly.

"Does she ever stop?" his dad asked, glancing down at Rafa.

"No," Rafa said, smiling as he admired her confidence and gumption. She truly was remarkable.

His dad took a deep breath.

"I told you, boss," Hunter said, "she's weird, right?"

Miri's smile faded as her shoulders deflated. *Fucking asshole.*

"Shut the hell up," Rafa spat at Hunter, wriggling to free

himself, not that it was any use. He was firmly trapped by his father's men. But he caught what seemed like a flicker of sympathy in Miri's eyes as she watched him struggle in their grasp.

"What about him?" Miri asked, looking at Rafa. "What are you going to do with him?"

"Do you care?" his dad asked.

"No, not really." Her words cut deep, more painful than the clenched hands digging into his shoulders. "Just curious whether you're going to have him follow me out of the rainforest to make sure I leave, that's all."

"Seeing as he wasn't the best with instruction, no, I don't think I will. Why? Does this mean we have a deal?"

Miri looked at Rafa once more, but he couldn't read the expression behind her eyes. With a single blink, she turned back to Vautour and said, "Sure."

"Miri, don't believe him. He's a liar. You can't trust him," Rafa called out.

"You're one to talk, Rafael," his dad said. "You know your way back, don't you?" he asked, pointing at Miri.

She nodded.

"Then go. Go and tell your team he abandoned you in the rainforest. But don't you dare breathe another word of this to anyone."

Miri glanced at Rafa once more as he struggled to break free from Vautour's goons. Then turned and ran.

Leaving a hole in Rafa's heart.

So many things swirled through his mind. He wasn't sure what was worse: that his father was a criminal or the look Miri gave him before she left. The pain on her face. The pain in his heart.

A wave of nausea washed over him.

Everything he thought he knew about his life was a lie. Everything he thought of himself was a lie. Where was he supposed to go from here? Was there really anywhere to go?

For a fleeting moment with Miri, he'd thought he had his future figured out. She understood him. He understood her.

Guess he was wrong.

"Don't look so sad, Rafael. It never would have worked," Vautour said, waltzing over to Rafael like they were going to have a nice little heart-to-heart.

"Yeah, because you lied to me. You made me do this."

"I didn't lie so much as withhold some information, but when it comes to her, let's be clear—I didn't *make* you do anything. I warned you to stay away from her, but the fact of the matter is that you knowingly deceived her, and the whole time, you continued your pursuits."

"It wasn't like that," Rafa protested.

"You don't have to try to convince me. I understand you better than you think I do. I was this close over thirty years ago," he said, kneeling to Rafa's level, putting up his hand and holding his index finger and thumb an inch apart in front of Rafa's face. "*This close* to finding it. She would have told me. She would have told me where to find the Moon City had she not died. I could feel it. I could feel her breaking down, trusting me with the truth of who she really was. She loved me. She *wanted* me to know its location."

Anger roiled through Rafa's stomach, and he clenched his fists.

"You mean, you . . . you tricked my mother?"

Vautour frowned. "Out of all people, I don't think you should judge me for fooling a woman to get what I wanted.

We're the same, Rafael," he said, motioning his hand back and forth between the two of them.

No, they weren't the same. Vautour was a monster. Rafa wanted to ask if he'd ever even loved his mother, but a part of him didn't want to know the truth. Some things were better left unsaid. Though that didn't stop Rafa from being ashamed to be related to him.

"Why am I even here?" Rafa asked.

"Before I parted ways with that all-too-susceptible Mr. Larity, he'd mentioned wanting to bring someone to document the expedition. So I dropped casual hints about your work at *Glo-Geo* and how you would be an asset on this journey. I needed someone on this expedition I could trust."

"Trust?!" A single laugh burst from Rafa's lips. Clearly, his dad didn't know the definition of the word. "Was any of it the truth?"

"I said what I needed to so you'd get the job done. Though based on what's transpired, it seems you weren't trying very hard."

"I did try. Warned her about how dangerous *you* were. But I can't help it that I've been falling in l—"

Rafa stopped himself.

"Oh, Rafael, love?" his dad said, placing his hand on his shoulder. "Is that what you were going to say? That you've fallen in *love* with her?"

Rafa stayed silent. He didn't want his father to know how he felt about Miri. Not after this.

Vautour sighed, almost like he was disappointed, and then stood up. "There's no use in denying it. I could hear it in your voice. I knew you were falling for her."

"I'll do anything to make sure she's safe."

His father smacked his lips. "Why are you wasting your life

on this nonsense? I'm offering you something here, Rafael. You can join me. Come with me to the Cidade da Lua," he said excitedly.

"And why would I do that? After everything you've done?"

"Because you are my son. And I'm all that you have. Once you have what I have, you'll see. This life? It's fucking fabulous."

"What happened to 'do great things'?" Rafa asked.

Vautour leaned against a boulder and folded his arms in front of him. "What makes you think I'm not doing great things?"

"Oh, I don't know. Maybe the fact that you're a crook?"

"Rafael, think of all the adventures we've had. The places we've been. Most people only dream of living this way. Pierre Vautour has allowed me to do those things—allowed *us*. He doesn't negate the good things I've done. If you could only see what I've built. There's still so much to show you."

Rafa laughed. "You're delusional. Raising money to save endangered baby seals doesn't pardon you from extorting people on the side."

"Who do you think runs this world? Money and secrets talk. There is a whole other world out there, Rafael, that you don't even know about. People who'll pay inordinate amounts of money just for a scrap of what we'll find here."

"And that's what you're doing? Selling off pieces of history like a roadside hawker?"

His dad lifted his chin. "I'm not some snake oil salesman. Collectors contract with me for these pieces. I keep whatever is left, sometimes even anonymously donating items to museums. You'd be surprised by the type of people who deal in these sorts of antiquities. These are *good* people. *Respectable*—"

"If it's such an *honest* profession, then why are you hiding who you really are?"

"I'm not hiding," his dad said, taken aback. "Pierre Vautour lives in plain sight. It's just separate from my life in Montreal. Come with me," he said, kneeling in front of him again, "and you'll see. I want to share this with you. You and I, we can find the Moon City together. Share the riches of your ancestors—"

"Boss," Hunter said, butting into the conversation, "you aren't being serious, are you? He can't come with us."

"Says who?" Vautour said, shooting a glance up to Hunter.

"I told you what happened on the boat," Hunter whined.

"You mean when we kicked your asses?" Rafa said, channeling Miri's confidence.

"You didn't kick anyone's asses," Hunter said, taking a few steps toward Rafa before Vautour stood and put up his hand to stop him.

"Enough!"

"Well, how are we going to split the loot with another person?" Hunter asked.

"That's not of your concern," Vautour said. "Your share will be whatever I say it is."

"It doesn't matter," Rafa said, "because I don't want it."

Vautour turned back to him. "You say that now, but once you see it—"

"I don't want anything to do with you!"

Vautour's gaze homed in on Rafa. "I don't have time for this." He then turned toward Hunter. "Take him back to camp. I'll deal with him later."

Hunter grumbled something under his breath before leaning down and yanking Rafa up by the arm. "Come on."

He pushed him forward as Vautour and the rest of the crew stayed behind. They trekked through the forest in silence, Hunter shoving Rafa in the back every so often to get him to pick up his speed.

After walking for ten minutes or so, Hunter finally spoke. "Hope you don't think I'm going to agree to any sort of split with you."

"I couldn't give less of a shit what you think, Hunter," Rafa spoke over his shoulder as he continued walking. "I mean, where did he even find you? Lackeys 'R' Us? You don't honestly think that he's not going to double-cross you the moment he gets a chance, do you?"

"Well, Pierre promised me—"

"Promised you?" Rafa burst out in laughter. "He doesn't give a fuck about promises. God, are you really that dense?" Rafa asked.

"Shut up!"

Rafa shook his head, continuing to laugh to himself.

"He really does have a knack for sniffing out gullibility," Rafa said.

"Speak for yourself!"

"Oh, I am. But if you don't see your own gullibility, then you're an even bigger jackass than I thought."

"I said shut. Up!" Hunter shoved him, hard, causing Rafa to stagger forward.

"Oh, piss off," Rafa said, spinning around to confront Hunter but, unfortunately, connecting with Hunter's elbow in his gut instead. Rafa stumbled back, trying to regain his footing before landing on the ground and hitting his head against the dirt.

Rafa saw stars in his eyes as he slowly propped himself up,

holding the back of his head. But Hunter didn't stop there. Without waiting for Rafa to recover, he hopped on top of him, grabbed his shirt by the collar, and delivered a blow straight to Rafa's face.

"Entitled . . . prick!" Hunter growled between punches.

Rafa struggled to fight back, arms flailing and legs kicking, but he couldn't get in a decent shot amid Hunter's unrelenting fists. Through his blurred vision, he spotted the knife tucked in Hunter's waistband, but when he reached for it, Hunter snatched it from his hands then pointed it at Rafa's throat.

Rafa threw up his hands in surrender. With the knife directed at Rafa, Hunter raked his fingers through his hair with his free hand, his chest heaving as he considered what to do next.

"Who got their ass kicked now?" Hunter said, smiling with his mouth wide open, panting for air.

"That's only because you fight dirty."

"Oh, I'm sorry. Should I have let you have the first punch?" Hunter asked, feigning remorse before scowling again. "Fighting fair is for chumps."

"Fine, you win. Now get the hell off me, will you?"

This conversation was getting old. But Hunter didn't budge, even as Rafa tried to wriggle free underneath him. What the heck?

"I don't think so. I'm not taking you back to camp so you can take what's mine."

Rafa rolled his eyes. "I already told you *and* my dad—I don't want any part of whatever you've got going on here."

"Sure you don't. I take you to camp and you and your dad squeeze me out. I'm not stupid."

I beg to differ.

"You know," Hunter continued, digging the tip of the blade

into Rafa's neck, causing him to hiss, "I could just get rid of you right now."

Fuck. Maybe he wasn't so stupid. Rafa's heart rate picked up and his eyes shifted back and forth, looking for something—anything—he could use to fend off Hunter. But unless the plants surrounding him were poisonous, Rafa was shit out of luck.

"How will you explain my absence at camp to my dad?" he asked, steadying his voice as best he could.

"I'll say you ran away."

"And if he sends someone to find me and they find a knife cut through my neck? How about then?"

Hunter sneered. Clearly he was getting tired of the conversation, too. "Then I'll make it look natural."

"Make what look—" Rafa started, but then Hunter lifted his arm—

And everything went black.

I T HAD BEEN AN HOUR SINCE MIRI HAD BEEN FORCED TO LEAVE
Rafa with his sorry excuse for a father.

And her tears had yet to stop.

The scene with Vautour played on repeat in her head. That
look on Rafa's face when he'd realized his father was none other
than the most notorious man in the archaeological world. The
man who'd been working against them since they'd arrived.

Rafa had no one. Only a mother he never knew and a father
who betrayed him.

He didn't deserve that. No, even after ripping apart her
heart he didn't deserve to have his broken by his own dad. She
couldn't abandon him, too.

Not that she'd ever intended to.

Despite Vautour's commands, Miri had lingered, hiding inside the belly of a strangler fig, waiting for Vautour and his men
to leave. She spied on them from a distance, unable to hear what
they were saying, but their body language spoke loud and
clear—Rafa wasn't on his dad's side. Eventually, Vautour and

his crew went one direction and Hunter and Rafa went another. She kept her distance as she followed behind Hunter, aware that getting any closer would give her position away. It was hard to keep up without revealing her presence, and she lost them. Or at least, she thought she did until she saw Hunter take off running—without Rafa.

Fuck! Where is he? She ran in the direction Hunter had fled, her head snapping every which way looking for Rafa, when she tripped and tumbled toward the forest floor. But as she braced herself for a face full of dirt, something soft and warm cushioned her fall. No, not something. Rafa, knocked out cold on the ground with blood trailing down his dirty cheek from his eye.

"Rafa! Rafa!" she said, shaking him by the shoulders. But he didn't budge. "No, no, no," she said, placing her ear on his heart. *Bum bum. Bum bum.*

Thank God. He was still breathing. But barely. Being unable to rouse him and before her panic set in, she ran back to Florestacasa to get Felix and Logan. Once they returned, Rafa was still passed out on the jungle floor but, thankfully, still alive. For the briefest of moments as Felix and Logan lifted Rafa's arms over their shoulders, his eyes fluttered open. He stared at Miri, groggy-eyed and solemn, and mumbled, "You came back."

Miri managed to pull out a smile before his eyes closed again. He was in rough shape. Almost as bad as Quinn had been.

The guys helped carry him back, asking all sorts of questions Miri didn't have the answers to. She filled in the blanks as best she could, but it only led to more questions.

They made it back to Florestacasa right before nightfall. Felix agreed to do a first watch of Rafa so Miri could shower and change. She took her time, packing her things after she'd showered. By morning, they'd be gone. Never to see this place again, which was fine with her. This forest full of secrets and danger didn't want them there. She saw that now. They were lucky they were making it out at all.

A light sprinkle began to fall from the sky. Within moments, the rain increased to a steady flow. Thunder roared through the trees. The scent of rain filled the air and calmed her nerves. Now she understood why people bought those rainforest sound CDs. It was quite soothing. If there was one thing Miri needed, it was something to soothe her soul. She listened to the rain as it hit the roof of the overhang under which she sat.

She looked out her window toward Rafa's cabin, seeing the light flick on and Felix exit the cabin, bringing with him a chair he set by the door. She'd waited long enough. She needed to find out if he was okay. And she needed answers.

Miri marched over to Rafa's cabin. The rain soaked through her shirt and plastered her hair on her forehead. She wiped her hand over her glasses so she could see, but it did nothing. It actually made things worse. As she approached the door, Felix stood up to greet her.

"What's going on?" she asked.

"He's awake. He said he wanted to shower," Felix explained.

"Are you sure he's okay? He might have a concussion," she said, unable to hide her concern.

"Well, I . . . uh . . . I mean, he seemed okay," Felix said. "I can check on him—"

But Miri cut him off. "No, you go. I'll take the next watch. Why don't you get some sleep?"

Felix nodded, and once he was gone, she stood outside Rafa's door, took a deep breath, then knocked.

The sound of his footsteps shuffled on the other side of the door. A moment later he opened it, staring at her in just a towel.

The shower was still running and, judging by the dirt and blood on his face, he had yet to get in. After everything he'd done—and how filthy he looked—he shouldn't have looked so handsome. But everything about him was perfect. He still had hurt in his eyes, however, and Miri wanted nothing more than to hold him, to hug him and tell him that everything would be okay. Which was ridiculous when she thought about it, because first, everything was not okay. And second, *she* was the one who should get the hug. He should comfort her for what he'd done. Not the other way around.

"I need answers," she blurted out, trying to not let her emotions get in the way of business.

He sighed, exhausted, but not as if he was going to make her leave.

"Give me a minute," he said.

He left the door open, allowing her to follow him inside. She closed the door behind her as he went into the bathroom and turned off the shower. A moment later, he came out still in only his towel, then walked over to his bag, pulling out dry clothes.

"I can wait," she said.

He glanced at her, clearly confused.

"If you want to shower first," she clarified.

"Are you sure?"

What was the difference? A few minutes?

"Yes, I'll wait out here," she said, sitting in a chair off to the side of the bed.

"All right, I'll be quick."

He went back into the bathroom, and seconds later the shower started again. *What am I doing?* She hadn't even waited thirty seconds before changing her mind. No, no, she couldn't wait.

She marched over to the bathroom door and banged.

"I'm sorry, I . . . We need to talk," she said through the door.

He opened the door—*God, still with that towel*—standing next to the sink with a washcloth in his hands. "I thought you were going to wait?"

"I was. I am. But . . . I . . ." She looked at him and all the blood and dirt on his face, then snatched the washcloth from his hands. "Here," she said, entering the bathroom and wetting the washcloth under the shower spray before bringing it up to clean his face.

He turned, resting his backside against the sink. They spoke not a word as she swabbed the cloth across his skin. He winced when she dabbed near his eye, clearly having been punched again. It would be silly to ask who'd blessed him with this most recent marking. She thought about making a joke about whether he'd graced Hunter with a poem, but the remorse in Rafa's eyes signaled he probably wasn't up for her nervous witticisms.

Slowly, she cleaned his face, rinsing the filth from the cloth as needed. Returning him to all his handsome glory.

"Why are you being kind to me?" he finally asked.

She pulled her bottom lip between her teeth, debating how to answer. "You were too hideous to try to have a conversation with, that's all," she said, hoping to get a smile out of him. Something to temper the sadness in his eyes.

The slightest upturn in the corner of his mouth ticked. She'd consider that a win.

"You're too good for me," he said.

"I know." This time she smiled, giving him permission to do the same, but his face remained steady. So she resumed wiping his face in silence, and he finally spoke.

"I didn't know my father was Pierre Vautour," he said.

Miri nodded. Given the way Rafa had reacted when they'd faced Vautour and his gang, that was the one thing she was confident in.

"But you *were* trying to keep me from succeeding. You lied to me. From the moment we got here," Miri said, not as a question.

"Yes," Rafa said, closing his eyes and dipping his head.

"I trusted you." Her words came out shaky and not at all with the confident voice she tried to muster. "I told you things I've never told anyone, and you used that to play me for a fool."

"No," Rafa said, taking both her hands in his, squeezing the washcloth with them and dripping water onto the floor. "I never took you for a fool. Honest to God, Pringles."

"How do you expect me to believe that? How do you expect me to believe *anything* you say? I mean, what the fuck, Rafa? Are you even a journalist for *Global Geography*, or was that a bunch of bullshit, too?"

She snatched her hands away, clenching her fists.

"Yes. Everything I told you about that is true. My job. My resignation. My dad's involvement in *GloGeo*. I learned of this assignment at the same time I tried handing in my resignation. My boss then called my dad, and he convinced me I needed to complete this mission for my mother."

Miri furrowed her brow and ticked her head to the side. "Your mother?"

"He said . . . he said she was a member of os protetores. That they met when he was here over thirty years ago searching for the Moon City, and that she was sent to stop him, but that they fell in love. He said he made a promise to her that he'd spend his life protecting the city and that I needed to carry on her legacy by doing the same."

"Do you think that's true? That she was one of them?"

Rafa shrugged. "I mean, that's what he told me, but now? Well, I have no idea. And I have no way of finding out. Knowing him, or rather, knowing Vautour, it probably was a bunch of bullshit. But I wanted to believe him." He paused and looked away. "You don't understand. Something's been missing my whole life. Knowing who I am. Where I came from. I craved that connection. He knew what I needed to hear. How to manipulate me."

A sickening feeling sank into Miri's gut.

"And is that what you were doing to me? Duping me? Telling me what *I* needed to hear?"

"Pringles, no," he said, clasping his hands tightly in front of his chest. "I told him I couldn't do it. I told him I . . ." He paused and held back whatever it was that was on the tip of his tongue.

"What? What did you tell him?"

"I . . . I told him I was falling for you."

Miri folded her arms and took a step back. His words roiled through her head, mixing with flashes from the night before. His lips. His hands. His eyes.

"Why would you say that?" she demanded, her voice quavering. Her heart couldn't take it.

"Because it's the truth. I tried to stay away from you, I swear I did. But you . . . you consume me. All those things you talked about last night—the incessant chatter, the desire to earn what you've got, the corny jokes, and, my God, your obsession with snacks—I love them three times over. You enrapture me. I know I don't deserve you. And I'm *not* asking for your forgiveness. You can do better than me. But you deserve to know how fucking rad you truly are."

Tears started to stream down Miri's face. "And what if I want *you*?"

He shook his head. "I put you in danger."

"Hey, I thought *I* was the one putting us in danger," she said with a smile. "Don't try stealing credit."

But he didn't smile back. "I'm serious, Pringles. I hurt you."

"And he hurt you!"

"This isn't a one-to-one exchange. My dad's actions don't excuse mine."

"You are not responsible for your father," she proclaimed. "And I'm not excusing anything. But I'm *trusting* my heart because . . ."

She paused, and the room filled with steam as he stared at her. His chest rising and falling. Heavy with his breath, as if he anticipated her words.

"Because what, Pringles?"

"Because I . . . I'm falling for you, too."

The words came out of nowhere. Words that Miri had never spoken before. But somehow, after everything, it felt right to say them to him. Yes, she wanted answers. But even more, she wanted him. She wanted his love. His warmth. His comfort. And perhaps it made her a fool for wanting all those things. But when she looked into his eyes? When she saw his face . . . she knew she wasn't the only one who had been deceived.

All he'd ever wanted was happiness. And all she wanted was him.

Without hesitation, Rafa pulled her into his arms. He pressed her back against the door as he pressed his lips to hers, taking her in. He pulled her wet shirt over her head and it dropped to the floor with a slap. Their hands fumbled, removing the rest of her clothes. His towel fell to the floor. When they'd completely disrobed her, they stumbled backward into the shower. The warm spray hit their skin but couldn't break their lips from each other. She moaned as his lips pulled from her mouth and dragged down her neck. His hand moved between her legs. Cupping her mound, already wet from more than the water. He moved farther down her body until he was kneeling on the floor of the shower, his face level with the apex of her thighs. The water from the shower head pounded against his back. He looked up at her. Those eyes told her exactly what she needed to know.

He drove his mouth between her legs. Slowly licking her soft, slippery folds. Tasting her. Sending enraptured missiles firing throughout her body. With one hand steadying her, he used the other to spread her legs, bringing one leg over his shoulder. He opened his mouth, placing it over her opening. He moaned into her as he lapped at her clit. She grabbed his hair, and he looked up at her once more. Feasting upon her with both his eyes and his mouth.

For a moment, he took his mouth away. And she missed it. She missed the feel of his warmth. Of his rough, ragged, yet talented tongue. But he mercifully returned shortly after, this time bringing his fingers to her entrance and pushing inside her as his mouth returned to her clit, licking it with soft flicks. Faster, faster as his fingers pumped in and out of her. Steadying herself with one hand against the shower wall and the other on his head, she cried out as she came, squeezing tightly around his fingers. Letting the orgasm wash throughout every inch of her body.

Slowly, he removed his fingers and stood before her. And then he kissed her with that mouth. She tasted herself upon him, still wanting more.

They traded positions, now with his back against the wall, and the shower spray hitting *her* back. His hands cupped her ass, kneading her flesh, as she lowered her hand between them and wrapped it tightly around his cock. He moaned in her mouth as she stroked him. But she wanted him to feel everything that she'd felt when he'd made her come. She lowered herself to his erection. With his back flat against the shower wall, he stared down at her. His chest heaved as he watched her drag her tongue in long, slow licks across the entire length of his shaft. She cupped his balls as she circled her tongue along his cock's head before putting him in her mouth.

"Oh fuck," he said, bracing himself against the shower wall.

His head tipped back. But she didn't take her eyes off him, watching him writhe as she pleasured him. She took his length in her mouth. Slowly increasing the speed. With one hand on the shaft, stroking along with her mouth, the other hand massaging his balls, she watched him come undone. He stared down at her again. Staring into her eyes.

"Fuck. This feels too good. I'm gonna come if you don't stop."

That's what she wanted, though. She wanted him to feel good. She wanted him to know that he deserved to feel good. She increased her speed. And he moaned once more before stopping her.

"No," he said. "I want you. I want all of you."

She took her mouth from him and then turned off the water before standing to his level. He kissed her once more, then lifted her body, wrapping her legs around his waist as he carried her out into the main room. Their bodies were dripping wet. Sliding against each other as he carried her before setting her on the clean, crisp white bed sheets. He kissed her once more, and then he looked into her eyes.

"I want to make love to you, Miri," he said. "Is that okay?"

She nodded.

"I want to hear you say it," he said.

"I want you to make love to me. I want to feel every inch of you. I want to know you, Rafa. All of you."

He smiled. Then got up off the bed and walked over to his baggage. He reached inside a zipper on the side pocket and pulled out a condom before returning. Rafa opened the condom wrapper and sheathed his cock with smooth precision. He then kneeled in front of her, open and waiting for him.

"Are you sure? I don't want you to regret this," he said.

"I won't. Do you think you'll regret it?"

"The only thing I regret is not telling you everything else sooner. Telling you how I felt about you."

"Then show me how you feel."

Rafa crawled toward her. With one hand bracing himself on the mattress, the other held his cock at her opening, circling between her slippery folds. Wet. Dripping with desire. He took a deep breath and thrust inside her, and she cried out in pleasure. *My God. So this is what it's supposed to feel like.*

He rocked into her. Slowly at first, then increasing his speed.

He lifted her back from the mattress, pulling her chest against his. Rafa shifted his weight so that his ass was on the mattress and she was straddling him. With his help, she rolled her hips on him. It felt so natural being on top of him, and he stared into her eyes before crying out in euphoric pleasure, his body holding her tightly against him as he shuddered through his orgasm.

And they both came undone.

THEY LAY IN BED WITH A SHEET BARELY COVERING THEIR BODIES as they continued to listen to the sounds out in the forest. The rain had settled, though it still trickled onto the roof. In a few hours, they'd be leaving. For now, they enjoyed being with each other. Touching each other. Learning about each other.

Rafa had recounted everything, starting from the moment he'd first learned he'd be traveling to Brazil up to blacking out after Hunter had struck him that afternoon. It broke Miri's heart hearing him talk about the lies his father had spun and how he'd dangled his mother's legacy as a way to manipulate him. Like Corrie said in her letter: he truly was a smarmy piece-of-shit scumbag. But despite Vautour trying to drive a wedge between them, it only made Miri care for Rafa more.

His fingertips glided against her skin in slow circles, back and forth along her back. She did the same on his chest, with her head resting against his pecs. Her fingers traced along his stomach. She could hear his heartbeat through his chest, growing louder whenever she drew closer to his core. They'd already made love twice. It seemed he was ready for a third time.

They'd talked about family, and love, and sex. Miri buried her head in his chest and smiled. Everything about making love with Rafa was fluid. They moved in sync, as if they'd been together for many years. He knew which buttons to push. Which spots to put pressure on. And she seemed to know all his buttons as well. She'd never seemed to satisfy a man before. She couldn't explain it. Was it Rafa, or was it something else? Was it the two of them together? On paper, they made no sense. But somehow it worked.

"I meant what I said earlier," he said. "About falling for you. I don't know what that means exactly in terms of where we go from here, but I can't say goodbye to you."

Miri stared at him. Although she was naked, she didn't feel the need to cover up like she normally did after having sex. No, she wanted Rafa to see her, all of her, and she wasn't afraid to show him who she was. She wasn't afraid to be vulnerable.

"I meant what I said, too. I want to be with you, Rafa. No one has ever made me feel special. And, oddly enough, also normal. I can't explain everything that happened with your dad. But now, knowing the truth, I know you thought you were doing the right thing."

Rafa sat up and took her hands. "He lied to me my whole life, Miri. And now he's told me this tale about my mother, of the Moon City, and how she saved him. But I realize he was using her the same as he was using me, using her to get to the Moon City. Honestly, I wonder if he even loved her.

"He made me believe I was doing it for her, for my mother. For my mother's people. *My* people. I don't even know what the truth is anymore. The only thing I know is that I don't want to lose you."

"You're not going to lose me."

"I don't deserve you."

"Stop saying that," she said, sitting up. "I'm seriously going to punch you if you say that again, and you know I've got a wicked right hook."

He laughed and pulled her over his waist so she straddled him as they wrapped their arms around each other. He kissed her tenderly, massaging his hands on her back. Slowly, she pulled away, then gazed down at his beautiful face.

"You deserve happiness, like everybody else," she said. "Don't let that sorry excuse for a father make you feel any different. You don't need him. You have me. And Anissa, Felix, and Logan. And once you meet Corrie and Ford—"

"You don't think Corrie and Ford will hate me because of who my father is?"

"You're not your father. Besides, disobeying your dad will probably make her like you even more."

He smiled. "So what now?"

Miri shrugged. "I don't know. All I know is that I don't want to be without you. The world is our snack bar—we can choose to do whatever we want."

He brushed her hair away from her face as he stared into her eyes.

"I like that. Our snack bar." Then he sighed. "We're really going to do this, huh? We're going to leave?"

"I don't think we have any other choice, do we? It sucks that an asshole like Vautour is going to get away with it, that he's going to be the one to discover the Moon City."

"Only because he has the lidar images."

"Yeah. I just wish I would have been able to figure out how the medallion worked with the landmarks," she said, her shoulders slumping and her gaze turning away.

Rafa furrowed his brow. "When are you going to tell me what *landmarks* you're referring to?"

Seeing as they were leaving in the morning, keeping the list a secret probably didn't matter anymore anyway.

Miri sighed. "Corrie gave me instructions and a list of landmarks to the Moon City. It came with the necklace that first night at the hotel. It's why I changed our course so suddenly."

"Do you have it with you?"

"Yeah, I keep it with me at all times."

"Can I see it?"

"Sure, give me a second," she said, hopping out of bed and retrieving her pants from the bathroom. She rummaged through the pockets and then handed a folded piece of paper to Rafa. "Here. This thing has been pretty useless overall."

Rafa studied the list for a few minutes, then handed it back to her. "Well," he said, "I'm not sure this is much help. Where did Corrie get this?"

"From the investor," she said, taking the list and setting it on the nightstand beside the bed without looking. "He apparently gathered this intel on an expedition last year when he'd been working with your dad."

Rafa's mouth twisted. She hated speaking about him at all. She wished they could forget him, but that was unlikely to ever happen.

Rafa glanced at the list sitting on the side table again, then focused his gaze, his eye catching on something.

"What is it?" she asked.

"This right here?" he said pointing at the words *rocha cara de macaco* on the paper. "What does that mean? Macaco means 'monkey,' right?"

"It means 'monkey-face rock.' Why?"

"We saw that. The wall that you were trying to scramble around. When I was cleaning up your leg, I said, 'That rock looks like a face.' Don't you remember?"

"I was a little distracted, if you don't recall," she said, wrinkling her nose and not particularly caring to relive that memory.

"Right. But what if that was it? What if that was the monkey-face rock we are looking for?"

Miri sat straight. "Oh my God, yes! The medallion. Look," she said, grabbing the medallion and showing it to him. "Remember when we were at the stone table and I started running right before we ran into your dad?"

"Pringles," he said, tipping his head at her, his voice half-joking. "You say that like I could *ever* forget."

She smiled. Good point. "Well, I went that way because look at the medallion," she said, running her finger along the etchings on the gold piece. "The moon and the temple almost look like an arrow. And these notches in the back fit perfectly when they were placed in that indentation in this orientation," she said, holding up the medallion cockeyed, "like they were pointing in the direction we were supposed to go. If my directional sense is in *any* way correct, then I think we were heading back toward that rock. My gut is telling me there might be another carving like this at each of the landmarks pointing out which way we need to travel."

"Based on where we came upon my dad, I wonder if they even found it yet."

"You don't think . . ." She let the question trail off.

"I'm saying if that's as far as they got, it's possible they haven't made it to the Moon City yet. They were at the very least planning to go back to their camp first."

"Rafa, you aren't proposing that we go back out there, are you?" she asked, cocking her head. "Because he still has lidar images, and all we have is a piece of scrap that's worth less than toilet paper in the Amazon. Besides, we're leaving in a few hours. The boat will be here to pick us up at seven a.m."

"But is that what you really want?" he said, scooting closer to her and taking her hands in his lap. "Because if it is . . . if you want to leave, then I'll go with you and will one hundred percent be there by your side. We can leave and never speak about this place again. Move to Berkeley. Move to DC. Hell, move to Timbuktu. Like you said, the world is our snack bar. But if you're right and that medallion points us to the Moon City, then this would be *your* discovery, Pringles. *You* figured that out, no one else. You *earned* it."

Miri blinked several times and then got out of bed. Her clothes were still wet in the bathroom, so she grabbed one of Rafa's shirts that was sitting on a chair and put it on before pacing around the small cabin.

If she was right, then her wit and intuition had solved the mystery that had been stumping explorers for centuries. Her keen eye had spotted the space for the medallion, something even the others on their team had missed for days.

"Okay, not that I'm agreeing, and I honestly can't believe you're even suggesting this after everything that happened, but what about your dad? I made a deal with him."

"And do you really think he's going to honor that deal?"

"I don't think I want to find out the hard way that he won't," she said, raising her brows.

"I think the hard way *is* you honoring the deal, and then he screws you over anyway. One thing my dad has demonstrated through all this is that he'll do anything to get what he wants. He doesn't care about people. He doesn't care who he hurts."

Miri thought back to the incident that had happened with Corrie and Ford. How Vautour had tried to extort them, and in the end, he still released those photos. And for what? To humiliate Corrie? To get back at her for standing up to him? Rafa was right. What would stop him here? What loyalty did he have to Miri? If he didn't even care about his own son enough not to hurt him, what would stop him from hurting her?

"What makes you think we can beat him there?"

Rafa stood from the bed, still completely naked. Not that Miri minded at all. He walked over to her and put his arms around her. "He might have lidar, but you have this," he said, pointing at her brain. "You're brilliant. I believe in you. If anyone can figure it out, you can, I'm sure of it."

He had so much faith in her. Nobody else had ever had that much faith in her. Not even Miri herself. She wanted to prove him right and to prove Dr. Quinn wrong. She wasn't a joke.

And she wouldn't be labeled a nobody.

Without another word, Miri got up on her tiptoes and planted a quick kiss on Rafa's lips, then rushed to grab her shoes and her other belongings before running out the door.

"Where are you going?" he called out.

"To pack!" she yelled back.

. . . .

THE PLAN WAS SET.

Anissa, Felix, and Logan had been briefed and directed: contact Corrie and see if they could arrange another crew on short notice, alert the Brazilian authorities—and anyone else who would listen—as to Pierre Vautour's whereabouts and identity, and then stand by and await further instructions.

Because as soon as daylight crested the trees, Miri and Rafa set out for the Moon City.

Splitting up wasn't ideal, but they needed to work fast. Once Miri and Rafa could confirm the landmarks, they would send the coordinates for Anissa, Felix, and Logan to follow. But the top priority was to get to the Moon City first. Stop Vautour from looting it. Document what was there. And hopefully, if Vautour had any love in his heart for Rafa and his late mother, plead with him to leave the city be.

It was a long shot, but they had to try.

They retraced their steps back to the stone table quickly, and shortly after that to the monkey-face rock. They'd been right. It was the spot that they had stopped at a few days before. Looking at it in this light, of course, they couldn't have missed it. And there, embedded in the rock itself, was another indentation for the medallion, presumably pointing the temple symbol in the direction of the next landmark.

Hours passed as they trudged deeper and deeper into the jungle, bogged down by almost impassable tangles of vines and the muddy, saturated ground. Places that no human had likely been in hundreds of years. If the protectors existed, they weren't out here. The canopy was so thick, it was almost as dark as night. But keeping with the direction on the compass, they pushed onward, climbing higher into the rainforest. However, after following the compass for miles and miles, Miri was starting to think they'd still somehow made a wrong turn when a rumbling sounded in the distance, the thunderous roar growing louder the farther they went.

"What is that sound?" Rafa asked.

A waterfall. "Lágrimas de jaguar," Miri said. *The tears of the jaguar.* Miri knew before they even saw it. They were getting close and yet again, Miri was right.

"Come on, follow me," she said.

They picked up their pace, heading toward the loud sounds. The closer they got, the surer they were that it was a waterfall, and soon they could barely even hear each other speaking if they were more than a few feet apart. They pushed through the sea of vines to an outcropping deep in the forest. There it was— river falling from a rock that looked like the head of a jaguar with water spilling out of holes that could be in the place of a jaguar's eyes.

"This is it," she said, calling out over the booming flow. "There." She pointed to a boulder beside the edge of the water-fall with a circular depression the size of the medallion cut in the surface.

They crept to the edge of the outcropping to see what was below them, presumably the lake of giant water lilies, but as they reached the edge of the rock, movement below caught Ra-fa's attention. He grabbed Miri and pulled her to the ground so the two of them were lying flat on the dirt.

"What are you—" she started to say, but he covered her mouth.

"Shh," he hushed her, as if anyone could hear them over the rushing falls. Then he shimmied toward the edge of the rock to look down below and waved her over.

There. The other team, resting along the river. Campfire roaring. Men playing cards.

And there was his father, sitting on a camping chair outside of a rather luxurious tent and sipping from a mug. Examining what appeared to be a stack of images and comparing them to a map.

"Look at them," she said. "They're not even in a rush." What a dick.

"Why would they be? They think their competition has gone home."

Miri turned her gaze from Rafa and glared at his father and his team.

"Assholes."

Rafa snickered. "Don't make me laugh. We don't want them to hear us."

She smiled.

"Let's take them," she said.

"Take what?"

"The lidar images." Miri gave him the slyest of grins.

"Have you lost all common sense? No, we're not going to take the images. Do you want to get yourself killed?"

"He won't even see us. And I doubt he'd *kill* us."

"You're joking, right? The images are *literally* in his hands. Unless you've suddenly discovered how to become invisible, he will see you. Besides, we don't need them. We have the medallion."

"Yes, but if we could get the lidar, we could slow him down, or maybe even stop him from finding the Moon City altogether."

Even Rafa should be able to acknowledge it wasn't a *bad* idea.

Okay, well, yes. It was a bad idea. But if it worked? Well, then it would be fucking brilliant.

"I appreciate your badassery and all, but we didn't exactly cover covert Navy SEAL operation skills as part of our training," Rafa said.

"I'm used to people underestimating me. People not noticing me. Ignoring me."

"This is slightly different. We're not dealing with a Dr. Quinn situation here. We're dealing with a team of what," he said, turning back to count, "six or seven rugged, burly men. You will stick out, I guarantee it."

"But no one will suspect it. They think we've gone home, Rafa. Look at them, without a care in the world. These aren't people moving with a sense of urgency. They think they scared us off. And besides. Look."

She nodded her head toward the camp, back toward his father, and right there, sitting on the chair that he had occupied moments earlier, were the photos. Out in the open. He'd left them, not worrying who might get their hands on them.

Arrogant.

Rafa shook his head. "No, no, no, no. I'm not letting you do this."

"And I'm not asking."

"I thought you learned your lesson after the boat thing."

"Well, your father lit a fire under my ass, and I want to show him he can't mess with you. I won't allow it."

"And what about me? What should I do?"

"Head there," she said, pointing past the bottom of the waterfall. "I'll get the images and meet you there."

Rafa's jaw dropped. "What? No, absolutely not."

"I'll be fine."

"But what if something happens? I won't be able to see you from there. I won't know if I need to run in and save you."

"Then don't think of it as you needing to save me. Think of it as me saving you. Here," she said, planting a quick kiss on his lips.

Without waiting for him to respond, she got up and hustled away, scrambling along the side of the rocky falls as fast as she could without drawing attention *and* before Rafa could change her mind. Going down into the camp was foolish, but she wouldn't be intimidated. She'd been letting others dictate her whole career. Tell her she wasn't good enough. Disregard her like she was insignificant.

Well, fuck that.

Miri relished the thought of being a thorn in Vautour's side, ruining his attempt at finding the Moon City and divulging his identity to the world. Then he'd see how *insignificant* she was.

And she'd show him that he couldn't treat people like disposable objects. This was payback for what he'd done to Rafa.

She quickly made it to the bottom of the waterfall. Vautour was nowhere to be seen. He was probably in a tent, relaxing, plotting the evil demise of some other poor sucker. Or, more likely, trying to figure out a way to off his crew once he found the Moon City. Pierre Vautour didn't exactly seem like the type to share his treasures.

Taking her time so that no one would hear, she crawled along the edge of the camp. The ground was wet, soaking through what were supposed to be waterproof pants. But as she'd already learned at the airport that first day, they were definitely *not* waterproof.

Most of the men were down by the water, sitting around a firepit. Cooking something, not at all concerned that Miri and Rafa might be hot on their tail. She scanned the site. Searching for the chair that Vautour had been sitting in. There, at the edge of the camp. Near the tents. And still sitting smack in the center of it were the photos.

This was too easy.

Miri crawled along the forest floor, underneath tall ferns and elephant ear plants. She looked back and forth, making sure no one was coming. But right as she was about to spring from the understory, Vautour emerged from his tent and grabbed the folder, taking it back with him into his private quarters.

Crap.

She debated scrapping the whole idea, heading to the meetup point. But just then, a commotion came from outside the tent area, a couple of the guys arguing over a game of cards. Hunter, of course. Another one of the guys was yelling at him for being a cheater, but the disturbance was loud enough that it caused Vautour to exit his tent to check to see what was going on. Giving Miri the perfect opportunity to sneak inside and take the images.

She stuffed the photos into her bag and then slowly crawled away. Once she was a safe enough distance from the tents as she dared, she got back on her feet and ran as fast as she could toward the spot she'd pointed out to Rafa, hoping that he'd be waiting for her when she got there. They probably should have formulated a better plan, but Miri's habit of acting first and thinking later had gotten the better of her.

Eventually, Miri slowed down, then opened the folder. Inside were about a dozen lidar images and a map with various locations circled and crossed out. It seemed Vautour was still trying to pinpoint the exact location on a map. Who knew how he'd even obtained these images? Not many people had access to lidar technology.

Miri scoffed. Money could buy anything.

Suddenly, a rustling came from beyond the trees. She quickly closed the folder and held it tightly against her chest, backing against a wide tree.

"Pringles?" Rafa whispered. "Is that you?"

Miri ran out from behind the tree, "Rafa!"

He ran over to her, grabbing her in his arms and murmuring in her ear. "Thank God, you made it."

"Did you really think I wouldn't?"

He smiled. "Honestly, Pringles, at this point, nothing about you surprises me. Did you get it?"

She lifted the folder, waving it in the air.

"I don't even know what to say," he said with a grin.

"Then don't say anything. We need to go."

They headed in the direction the medallion had pointed to at the waterfall, eventually coming upon the lake of the giant water lilies. Once they found the next medallion marker, they skirted around the lake, making sure that Vautour and his crew wouldn't see them. It had only been thirty minutes or so, but it was only a matter of time before Vautour and his team would be back on their scent.

So Miri and Rafa moved at double time, stopping only to give Anissa and the others updates on their location. The ground was a muddy mess after the rain from the evening before, however, making it difficult to run through the brush. It was hot, humid. Miri's clothes were soaked through. Her hair was matted against her forehead, yet when she glanced at Rafa he still looked as sexy as always.

They ran for several miles, slowed down only by the darkness descending upon the forest. They'd never hiked this late at night—never once it got dark. Darkness meant trouble. Trouble out here meant danger. Jaguars. Reptiles. Vampire bats.

It was one thing to camp with a group of twelve people. It was another thing entirely to camp with just two, especially when they couldn't risk a fire. Fire would be a direct beacon for Vautour and his men.

"We need a break," Rafa said.

"Just a little farther."

Rafa's hand pulled back on her arm. "We're not going to have any juice left in us if we are too tired to keep going. We need to rest."

Begrudgingly, she stopped. She knew he was right, but dammit, she wanted to keep going. "Fine. But I'm not bothering with the tent."

"It's not safe without it," he said.

"It'll waste time. We can take turns keeping watch."

"Fine, but you sleep first."

"Only for an hour." They couldn't spare much longer than that.

They searched for a tree that would provide them with some sort of protection, finally landing on a giant kapok tree. Its roots curved around them, almost like a hug. Rafa rested with his back against the trunk, and Miri nestled in between his legs. He put his arms around her, holding her tight. She felt warm and comforted in his embrace.

Safe.

One hour. Just one hour and then they'd switch. And another hour after that, they'd get moving again.

PRINGLES, I'M GOING TO NEED YOU TO WAKE UP."

Rafa shook Miri's shoulders. He'd let her sleep way longer than she had asked, but she'd needed it, as evidenced by the fact that he was having a hard time waking her. It was still pitch dark. But they couldn't wait any longer. His father was coming, he could hear them.

"Miriam!" He shook even harder as he called her name in a whispered panic.

She stirred. Under any other circumstance, he would have thought she looked sweet. But not right now. Not when they needed to get going, and fast.

"Mmm. What is it?" she murmured. "Is it my turn to keep watch?" Her voice was sleepy. He wanted nothing more than to wrap his arms around her and keep her safe for the rest of the night. Let her sleep. Let her dream. But they didn't have time.

"We have to get going. They're coming."

As if his words sent a bolt of lightning through her body, Miri zapped awake. She sat straight up. Her eyes were wide.

"Where?"

"There," he whispered as he pointed off into the distance. They were still far enough away, but they were getting close. Their voices grew louder. His father shouting at his crew to hurry. He'd recognize his father's voice anywhere, even hundreds of yards away, deep in the Amazon rainforest.

"Come on, we have to go," Rafa said, taking her hand.

They grabbed their things and crept through the rainforest, careful not to make any noise. With Rafa's father's team close behind them, they couldn't use flashlights, having to rely only on moonlight, which was sparse through the trees. They moved much slower than they had earlier in the day. Rafa's heart pounded. He had no clue what his father would do to him if they caught up to them.

They stopped a few times so she could check her compass. They had probably gotten far enough away from Vautour, but Rafa still blocked the light from her flashlight anyway as she hunkered behind a rock or a tree.

"This way," she whispered, taking him by the hand and pulling him in the direction of a large Wimba tree.

The giant trees lined the trail in two tight rows, almost like they'd been placed there, planted perhaps, rather than grown in the wild. The space between the trees was almost like a road. A road full of roots and vines that they had to climb over. But nothing else was in their way. They moved as quickly as they could over the roots. It would have been much easier in the daytime. But as he found out after spending the last week and a half with Miri, taking the easy way wasn't in her vocabulary.

They neared the end of the trail of Wimba trees. There was a clearing. A clearing that led to a bridge made of vines, hovering over a deep ravine.

"I think this is it," she said. "The bridge."

He smiled at her, and she smiled back. Her smile instantly calmed his nerves.

"Come on, let's cross."

"This looks like something straight out of *Indiana Jones and the Temple of Doom*," she said, inspecting the sturdiness of the vines driven deep into the ground.

"I sure hope not. That would mean not just a bunch of bad guys behind us, but a float of crocodiles below."

"I think we're more likely to see black caimans," she said, grinning.

"So in other words, this is exactly like *Temple of Doom*."

"How about you go on out there and start jumping around like Short Round and let's see what happens?" she joked.

"Do I need to change your nickname to smartass?"

"Nah. I'm good with Pringles."

He leaned down and gave her a quick kiss on the lips. "All right then, Pringles, let's do this. I'll go first."

The setting may have come straight out of a movie, but the bridge itself was nothing like the one in *Temple of Doom*. This bridge consisted of just three thick vines, almost in the shape of a triangle. Two for handholds, one to walk on, all being held together with other, thinner vines along the way. It looked sturdy enough, but it still was really only a bunch of vines wrapped together out in the middle of the Amazon rainforest. And was probably hundreds of years old . . .

Rafa took one step out onto the bridge, steadying himself with his hands on the "rails," and then he shook. The bridge wobbled, but it didn't fall. *Well . . . here goes nothing.*

"Hold on to your potatoes!" she called out with a laugh, channeling her inner Short Round.

He shook his head and laughed, then took another step out, shuffling his feet along the vines. Slowly, he moved across until he was hovering over the middle of the ravine. There was no going back now.

"Wait until I get to the end," he called back to Miri. Who knew if it could hold both of their weight?

Rafa looked ahead at the remaining span of the bridge and back again. *This is long.* Then he glanced down. *Really fucking long.*

The bridge drooped under his weight, but he kept going. Almost there. *Hmm . . . what's that weird groaning sound?*

"Do you hear that?" he called to her.

"Yeah, what is it? Do you think it's an animal?"

"I don't know. It's like a creaking. Like . . ." He paused. Oh no. The vines. The vines coming unwound. "Shit! The bridge. It's going to collapse."

"Rafa!" she screamed.

The bridge sagged farther. He only had seconds, really. The vines started to unravel, pulling out of the ground from the far end where Miri stood. He realized that he had only one option: to keep going. He scrambled as far as he could toward the opposite end of the bridge before it gave way from under him, leaving him hanging from the vines against the side of the ravine. He hit the rock face with a thud but held on tightly.

"Rafa!" Miri screamed out again. "Are you okay?"

"Yes," he grunted as he used all his strength to pull himself to the top of the cliff. Once he made it over the edge, he lay flat on his back and looked up at the sky, panting. That was close.

He turned back to look at Miri on the other side of the ravine. Well, damn. This just made things a lot more complicated.

"Stay there," he called out. "I'll look for another way over."

"I don't think we're going to find any more bridges."

"Maybe we can climb down."

Even from the other side of the ravine, however, he could see the face that Miri was making: it was a terrible idea. Besides, the cliff walls were steep. And making it to the bottom meant crossing the river where black caimans were a real possibility.

"We don't have time for that," she said. "What about that?" She pointed over to a tree that had half fallen over the ravine. The trunk didn't cover the distance, however.

"You're not going to push that over the rest of the way, if that's what you're thinking."

"No, I think I can make it."

"Make it? Pringles, what are you—"

He didn't have time to finish his question before Miri was in a full-out sprint, running up the trunk of the fallen tree.

Goddammit. Why doesn't she ever listen?

But as she reached the top of the trunk, she lifted her arms, grabbing on to a vine that hung from a tree on the other side. And like she'd practiced so many times, she swung from the vine and landed feet first at the edge of the ravine with a thud, like a fucking superstar.

"Let's see Vautour and his crew do that!" she said with a wide grin.

He ran over and kissed her. "Please tell me you don't do things this risky when you're back home."

"Would it change anything if I did?"

Rafa smiled. "Absolutely not." He kissed her again, this time with more passion than the last. *God, I love this woman.*

The realization hit him like a refreshing blast of warm, tropical air. He could spend a lifetime kissing her. A new life that he wanted to start as soon as they got the hell out of this jungle.

"Look, here," she said, locating a stone with a circular indentation at the edge of the cliff where the vine bridge had ended. She placed the medallion in the spot, and the arrow pointed northwest. "Come on. We've got to be getting close to the porta do coração da árvore." The last landmark.

As they distanced themselves from the ravine, they pulled out their flashlights. With the vine bridge destroyed, it would be hard for Vautour and his team to make it over to the other side. Miri was right. Rafa doubted his father would be swinging from vines the way she had. It would take them a long time to cross, if they were able to at all.

The only landmark remaining on the list was the entrance: a door through a tree. They kept straight, consulting the compass to ensure they were going the right direction. Climbing over rocks. Dragging their feet through muck. Ferns whipping them in the face as they tried passing through.

They held their hands in front of them, swatting away leaves and branches as they made their way deeper into the forest, when suddenly, a thick wall of foliage blocked their passage. An impenetrable wall. There was no skirting around it. No getting through. This wall was made of thick tree trunks, spanning as far as the eye could see.

Miri ran her hand along the lush covering, looking for a way through before she stopped at one tree in particular. She ran her hands along its thick bark. Tracing every curvature with her hand. Feeling it.

"What is it?" he asked.

"I don't know. This one feels . . . different. Not like a tree. More like stone."

She pushed on the tree, and it gave way.

A door.

CHAPTER
Twenty-One

MIRI STEPPED THROUGH THE DOORWAY BETWEEN THE TREES. Once through, her eyes widened, her jaw dropped, and she froze, staring at the most magnificent thing she'd ever seen.

A ten-foot-tall, countless-feet-long wall made of rough-cut bluish stone blocks that sparkled under the moonlight in the middle of the Amazon rainforest. A wall that would have likely crumbled long ago if not held together by the roots and vines growing up and over it. And positioned before them, an entry made of two dilapidated wooden doors barely hanging on to their hinges.

The Cidade da Lua.

"Holy shit," Rafa said, coming up beside her.

"Told you so." She looked over at him and smirked. She'd done it. She'd found the Moon City.

Dr. Miriam Jacobs. Nobody extraordinaire.

"Should we go inside?"

She nodded and took his hand. They walked tentatively toward the wall and pushed through the gate. Beyond the entrance, structures made from the same glistening blue stone lined the city. Some sort of luminescent gemstone, no doubt. Lapis lazuli, perhaps? Or hackmanite? Miri was no minerology expert, but whatever it was, it was exquisite.

The rainforest had not been gentle on the city, however. Although it appeared untouched by humans for centuries, the buildings suffered from weather erosion and an invasion of plants. Smaller structures, likely the homes of the villagers, made of materials like wattle and daub, had all but crumbled near the city's entrance. The larger structures toward the center of the almost-square-mile area constructed out of the luminescent stone seemed to have fared better, although a full-scale excavation would almost certainly involve reconstruction. Reconstruction that would inevitably involve assumptions, guessing, and interpretations.

It was larger than she had imagined, although much of the space in the middle remained an open thoroughfare toward a temple at the center of the city. A ball court, perhaps? Or a place for celebrations? It was hard to tell given the condition of the many buildings dotting the vicinity, but based on Miri's research experience, an area this size could have likely housed a few hundred people in its heyday, providing everything its residents needed and more. An amphitheater. Terraces for gardens. The structures shared foundational characteristics reminiscent of those from other ancient civilizations, such as the Inca.

But this city was distinctly not Inca. The Inca hadn't made it as far as Brazil.

The city wasn't as grand or opulent as those found in other ancient civilizations. There was no giant temple like the one found in Tikal breaking through the tree canopy. Nor was it a city like Machu Picchu, ascending high above the clouds.

Perhaps that was the reason the city had gone undetected for so many years. But its simplicity was breathtakingly beautiful.

Rafa and Miri took their time as they explored each of the buildings on their way toward the temple. They were careful not to disturb anything. Rafa took photos, capturing the lives of the people in the city exactly as they had left it. The buildings hadn't been destroyed through an invasion but rather—as evidenced by the caches of withered food, clothing set out to dry, and half-woven baskets and other trinkets inside the homes—abandoned. There were no bodies. No human remains. As if the people of the Moon City had departed in haste, leaving behind all their belongings and reminders of home, like a cast of the day they'd fled.

"It's a little eerie, isn't it?" Rafa asked.

Miri nodded. "These people. What must have happened that they left in such a hurry?"

"I'm a little worried about what we might find."

Or who might find us.

They headed toward the temple, no taller than a two-story building, climbing the stairs worn away by the rain. She ran her hand along one of the steps, feeling the grain of the stone beneath her fingertips. The mineral deposits in the stone had an enchanting glint in the moonlight. This was what people were talking about when they said the city was only visible in the moonlight. It wasn't some special coating. Truth had been overtaken by legend. It wasn't that the city was invisible during the day, but there was something magical about finding it in the night, something magnificent about the way the moon hit the stone. Casting a sparkle throughout the dark sky.

They entered the temple. The roof had partially collapsed in one corner of the room, providing light for the rest of it. A table sat in the center, likely used for religious ceremonies. Intricately woven baskets on the floor held beautiful textiles. She wanted to pick them up to examine their artistry. But they shouldn't be disturbed. Not without proper equipment to document and preserve everything properly. So for now they only looked as Rafa took his photos. He snapped a photo of her.

"What are you doing?" she asked.

"Capturing the moment when the brilliant Dr. Miriam Jacobs found the Cidade Perdida da Lua." He snapped another photo.

"Do I look like a boss?"

He smiled from behind the camera and clicked again.

"A badass boss. Come here," he said, setting the camera down on the table.

"Can you believe it?" she said, looking toward the ceiling and spinning in a circle.

"Yes," he said without hesitation, causing her to shoot a glance back at him. "You never gave up. Even when everything, and everyone—myself included—got in your way. You *earned* this, Pringles. I'm sorry I had any doubt, even for a second." He pulled her into her his arms and brought his hand to the back of her neck.

"You doubted me?"

"Well, not you so much as the existence of this place. If this didn't seem like such a holy room, I would totally take you on this table right here."

She pulled his face toward her. She could kiss him forever. Their tongues tussled together. Their hands worked their way around each other's bodies. Their lips broke free from each other.

"I can't wait to write this story about you," he said.

"I can't wait to spend my life with you." She kissed him one more time. Then pulled away and reached for the satellite phone in her bag. "We should probably let Anissa know where we are so she can send the authorities before Vautour gets here."

"It's a bit late for that."

Miri and Rafa jumped, snapping their heads toward the doorway of the temple. There stood Vautour and his henchmen. Though Miri couldn't help but notice the look on Hunter's face, a mixture of shock and nervousness.

Vautour stepped into the room, clapping slowly. "Congratulations, you found it. And all you needed to do was to steal the lidar."

"I didn't need those goddamn images. I figured it out all on my own," Miri said proudly.

But Vautour looked at her and narrowed his eyes. "Cute," he said.

"How the hell did you get here so fast?" Miri asked.

"Wouldn't you like to know?" he responded.

Miri looked around, then back at Vautour. Was he for real? "Yes. That's why I asked."

"Spunky," Vautour said, ignoring her question and walking around the altar toward Miri. "But did you really think those were the only copies?"

Ugh. She frowned. Of course he would have had a backup. How could she have been so naive?

"Though I have to hand it to you," he continued, "you've surprised me."

"What's that supposed to mean?" she asked, folding her arms.

"Well, given your rather paltry résumé, I wouldn't have taken you as being bold enough to sneak into my camp and take the photos right from my tent."

"Don't act like you know anything about me. You're not as smart as you think you are."

"Oh," Vautour said, making an amused face, "but you think you know me?"

"I know you're a shitty father," Miri spat back.

Vautour glanced at Rafa and then glared at her. "Is that what he told you? My gâté *son*?"

"Fuck you, Dad," Rafa said.

But Vautour narrowed his eyes at Rafa. "After everything I've done for you?" his dad asked.

"You did those things for yourself," Rafa spat back.

"I also know you're a crook," Miri interrupted. "We already alerted the Brazilian authorities that you're here."

"You broke our deal," Vautour said, glaring at her. Miri could practically see the veins pulsing in his neck.

"We're not going to let you steal from this place. These artifacts," she said, turning and waving her hands around the room, "they don't belong to you."

"Nor to you."

"I'm not here to take anything. I only wanted to study this place. Learn about the people who lived here so maybe we can find out what happened to them and protect their legacy," she explained. "I want to save it from people like you."

Vautour sighed as if he was bored.

"Dad, don't do this," Rafa pleaded. "If you ever loved my mother . . . if you ever loved *me* . . . please, just go."

Vautour stared at Rafa, his face softening as if recalling memories deep inside him, before turning away and throwing up his hand.

"Find somewhere to put them," he commanded of his team.

The room broke out in commotion as Vautour's men ran at

them. Rafa struggled to get away, but Hunter punched him right in the gut. Rafa hunched over, crying out in pain as Miri tried to flee, but there was no helping it. The guide who'd been on the boat with Hunter and Kevin, Sérgio, grabbed her by the arm and led her into a different area of the temple. Two men carried Rafa close behind. They took them to a room covered in stone, with just a sliver of a window in the wall opposite the door.

But as Sérgio placed her in the room, he whispered in her ear, "Open your eyes, senhora. Look for the moon."

She looked at Sérgio and tried to see his face, but it was too late. He was already gone, and seconds later the other men were tossing Rafa into the room as well, closing the door behind them. Rafa landed on the stone floor like a pile of bricks, moaning as he held his stomach. She rushed over to him and examined him for bruises and scrapes.

"Are you okay?" she asked.

He groaned. "I'm beginning to think being around you is dangerous for my health, Pringles," he said while eking out a smile.

She smiled back at him and kissed him on the cheek before helping him assess his injuries.

"We really got ourselves into it, didn't we? Do you think we're going to die in here?" he said, raising his head and scanning the room.

"Not if I can help it."

She stood up and surveyed the area, feeling her way along the wall. Pressing against the doorway where they entered.

"I don't think that one's going to budge."

"I know, but Sérgio said something to me," she said, scouring the room for a sign.

"What do you mean, he said something to you?"

"He told me to open my eyes. To look for the moon."

"What the heck is that supposed to mean?"

"I don't know, but I'm wondering if maybe . . . maybe he's a protector."

Rafa eyed her curiously. "Do you think?"

"He *is* a guide for Vautour's men," she said with a shrug. "Who knows how they found him? What if he's trying to help us?"

She walked the perimeter of the space, running her hand along the cool stone blocks, feeling for something—anything—that would give them a clue, when something glinted in her eye.

There. Something looked different on the wall across from the window, where the light hit. She followed the light with her eyes. A shimmer in the stone. There it was. A small moon shape.

"What is it?" Rafa asked.

"Look. A moon," she said, pointing toward the spot. Just like the rock outside, it glimmered in the moonlight. This was what Sérgio wanted her to see.

She traced her finger along the crescent shape and pushed, but nothing happened. As she felt along the curvature, however, she felt a notch in the wall. She put her hand inside, finding a lever. She pulled it with all her strength and it clicked, opening a passageway through the wall.

"Jackpot!"

Rafa hopped up and joined her. Stairs led through to a tunnel with a soft glow coming from the bottom. It could be a way out. Or it could lead to more trouble.

They slowly crept down the stairs in single file. As they neared the bottom and heard voices, they stopped.

"It's my dad," Rafael whispered.

Miri nodded. She whispered back, "Let's go slow."

They hugged the wall and continued down the stairs, inching closer and closer toward the voices. A soft radiance lit the steps, the glow of fire. At the bottom there was a short hallway that led to an open doorway. Their only option.

They crept toward the opening and peered into a room the size of an Olympic swimming pool with a twenty-foot ceiling, lit by torches along the large stone block walls. And in the center of the room sat a trove full of gems and gold. The blaze from the fire reflected on the cache, illuminating the room with an almost blinding light. No wonder people had been searching for this place. There had to have been hundreds of thousands of dollars', possibly millions', worth of treasure in this room in today's dollars.

"Pack up as much as you can," Vautour commanded from the center of the room, directing his men to load duffels full of valuables. "And remember the deal. You fill my bags first. Whatever's left, you can take."

The men laughed and cackled as they jammed their packs with riches. Holding up various pieces to the light. Cramming their bags with everything they could. Talking about what they were going to do with their money once they got home. There was so much that it wasn't possible they'd be able to take everything. But still, to see them taking things, stealing things . . . They weren't taking it for research. They weren't taking it to preserve the memory of the city. Greed compelled them. They were pillaging the Moon City for their own gain.

Rafa tapped her on the shoulder and pointed to a doorway at the far end of the room. There was no way they'd be able to get over there without being seen. Miri shook her head.

"I'm invisible, but I'm not that invisible," she whispered.

"No, silly. I'm going to create a distraction and you run that way. Toward the exit."

"No, you'll never get away."

"I'm not asking," he said with a warm smile. "You've saved me. Now let me save you. And like you said. He *probably* won't kill me. On the count of three. One . . . two . . . three!"

Without hesitation, Rafa ran into the room, startling Vautour and his crew. The men dropped their bags and came running after him.

"Get him," Vautour screamed. The commotion was intense. Sounds of priceless artifacts crashing to the ground echoed as they scrambled through the room. That was her chance. They were distracted. Miri ran to the other end of the room, toward the opening.

"There she is!" someone screamed.

She didn't bother turning around to see who it was. She just kept running, running until she couldn't run anymore. The temple's passageways were winding and narrow. Its was like a maze, and she couldn't find her way out, but she just kept going. Her heart thumped so strongly she thought it was going to explode from her chest. Scared not only for herself but for what was happening down below with Rafa. She hoped he was safe. But it would all be for nothing if she didn't get out of there.

Finally, there was daylight. The sun was coming up. And there was an opening to outside. She ran through the exit and down the stairs of the temple. She ran so fast, she missed a step and tumbled down the final ten steps, hitting the ground with a thud. Her whole body ached. Slowly, she pulled herself back up, but when she tried to stand, she collapsed, and she screamed out in pain.

"Fuck!" she yelled, holding her ankle. She may not have been that kind of doctor, but she knew a sprain when she felt it. But sprained or not, she needed to keep going. Using every ounce of strength she could muster, she carefully stood, holding her leg, and limped toward the city gate.

"Stop!"

Miri froze at the sound of Vautour's voice. She slowly turned and looked up at the top of the temple. Vautour's commanding presence loomed over the city like an emperor preparing to address his subjects. He stood at the edge of the top step, staring down at her, knowing she had no way out. Under normal circumstances, Miri might have had a chance. He was still a good fifty feet and two flights of stairs away. But these circumstances were anything but normal.

Still, Miri couldn't help but glance over her shoulder to estimate how long it would take her to reach the city walls.

Right then, Rafa appeared beside Vautour, struggling, with his arms held behind his back by Sérgio. Blood trickled down his cheek, and his shirt was torn and twisted. Rafa tried to hold his head high, pulling his mouth in a tight line. But his fear was palpable.

"Do you really think you're going to survive out there on that foot?" Vautour called down to her.

"We made it this far, didn't we? Let him go, and I'll gladly take our chances again," she yelled back, nodding her head toward Rafa.

"Why do you care so much about him?" he asked.

"Why don't you?" she replied.

"He's my son. Of course I care about him."

"Really? Then how could you leave him for dead out alone in the rainforest yesterday?"

"Alone? He ran," Vautour said, his voice confused.

"Is that what he told you?" Miri asked, pointing at Hunter standing off to the side.

Vautour turned toward Hunter. "What is she talking about?" he asked.

Hunter looked back and forth. Then, with a swift movement, he pulled a gun from the back of his waistband underneath his shirt, pointing it at Rafa and causing everyone else to take a step back.

"What do you think you're doing?" Vautour growled at him.

"Take another step and I'll shoot him," Hunter said, brandishing the gun.

Rafa shirked to the side to shield himself, still in Sérgio's grasp.

"Pull that trigger and you won't make it out of this jungle alive!" Vautour shouted.

"I think I'm done letting you call the shots," Hunter said. "Now *I'm* the one in charge."

"That is incorrect, senhor." Sérgio let go of Rafa, took a step toward Hunter, and put a knife to his neck. "Put the safety on and toss the gun down to the bottom of the stairs," he commanded.

He motioned at Hunter with the knife. Hunter grimaced as he did as he was told, clicking the safety on the pistol, and then threw it all the way to the ground, not far from Miri's feet.

"Now go over there," Sérgio said to Hunter, gesturing toward Vautour.

"Fuck off, old man," Hunter spat back.

Right then, another man came from beyond the temple, pointing a knife at Vautour. Moments later, three more emerged.

"What is this?" Vautour asked.

"We're os protetores da lua," Sérgio said of himself and the other four men who'd appeared.

Miri smiled. So it was true. All of it. The Moon City, the protectors.

And Vautour was finally going to get what was coming to him.

"What are you going to do, kill us?" Vautour asked.

"No, senhor. We're not murderers. I know the lies that you've spread. I know who you are. You were the one who took our Andressa." Sérgio then looked at Rafa. "Your mother."

Rafa squeezed his eyes tightly, holding back his tears.

"She trusted you, and you took her from us," Sérgio said, rounding Vautour so he faced him head-on. "We're going to take you to her family so you can pay for what you have done to her."

Vautour laughed. "You think I killed her? She died in a car accident," he said.

Sérgio shook his head. "She loved you. Turns out you're like every other caçador de tesouro who's scoured the Amazon for the cidade. And as for the rest of your crew? We'll be taking them to the authorities."

Suddenly, Vautour lifted his arms, struggling, grabbing for Sérgio's knife and knocking it out of his hands. There was an all-out flurry, everyone running, scrambling, wrestling with each other. Hunter lunged at Rafa, but Rafa managed to side-step him at the last second, sending Hunter tumbling down the steps. He collapsed at the bottom of the stairs close to Miri and looked up at her. Then at the discarded pistol ten feet away.

They both dove toward the gun, but he got it first. However, as he struggled with the safety, she stood and swung her fist, landing it squarely on his nose. He screamed out, dropping the gun, and she quickly grabbed it and pointed it back at him.

"Don't even think about it," she said.

She glanced around at Rafa barreling down the stairs toward her, taking her eye off Hunter for only a second. When she turned back, however, Hunter was gone.

She lowered the gun and handed it to Rafa. "I couldn't shoot him even if I wanted to."

Eventually, the ruckus up top settled. Os protetores had all of Vautour's men tied up. But Vautour had somehow managed to escape.

"Find him. Don't let him get away," Sérgio said, as two of his men went off looking for Vautour and Hunter.

Rafa pulled Miri into his arms.

"Are you okay?"

She nodded into his chest. "Yes, but I sprained my ankle."

He took her face in his hands and stared at her. "I love you," he said. "And to be clear, I'm not just saying that in the heat of the moment."

She knew. Because she felt it as well. "I love you, too."

They sat on the temple steps as the protectors continued to look for Vautour and Hunter. But after an hour, they came back empty-handed. His father would likely get away again. Lucky bastard.

The protectors eventually led Vautour's men out of the city in handcuffs tied to a rope. Thankfully, nobody had gotten seriously hurt in the scuffle. Sérgio approached Miri and Rafa on the bottom step. He looked down at them and smiled.

"Why did you help us?" Miri asked.

"You're not here for treasures. Not to take them, at least," Sérgio said.

"But why did you let us make it this far? All of us, I mean," she asked.

Sérgio sighed. "To be honest, senhora, we didn't think you'd make it. Two of you? Alone? We underestimated you. But them?" he said, motioning toward Vautour's crew. "Well, the Moon City won't stay hidden forever. These new technologies and photos? We needed to see if they would lead people to this place. And now that we know, we must find other ways to protect the city."

"How?" she asked.

"I don't know yet, senhora."

"Well, if I can, I'd like to help," Miri said. "I think I'm going to find myself with a *lot* of free time soon, so if there is anything I can do, please tell me."

Sérgio smiled and nodded, then he looked at Rafa. "You are not like your father."

"Did you know my mother?" Rafa asked.

"Yes, Andressa Silva. Her family still lives in Manaus. You look just like her."

Miri nudged Rafa in the side. "See. I told you she was beautiful."

He took her hand and squeezed it.

"What now?" she asked.

"Well, I can't let you go. Not knowing what you know."

"Are you taking us to jail?"

"Oh no, senhora. That's not what I mean. But I can't let you take this." He held up Rafa's camera.

Miri's heart sank. She understood what the protectors were trying to do. But taking the camera meant no evidence that they had found the Cidade da Lua. It meant everything she had accomplished would be forgotten.

It meant she'd still failed.

Her shoulders slumped. But as if Rafa understood what was going through her mind, he turned her shoulders toward him.

"Miri," he said. "You did it. You did it when nobody else thought you could. Who cares if no one else knows the truth, so long as you do? Besides, I know the truth. And you are fucking incredible."

He was right. So what if nobody believed her? She had something even better. Better than her name on a placard in a museum. Better than fame, fortune, and glory.

She had Rafa. And her integrity.

And she was a fucking badass.

Epilogue

Seven months later

THE DISCOVERY OF THE LOST CITY OF THE MOON
By Rafael Silva

I never wanted to be famous.

Yes, I wanted to explore the world and have my name listed as the author of articles in various magazines and publications, but fame? No. Unless you're in the journalism and publishing world, people rarely remember the names of the authors of such articles.

Unfortunately (and if you're reading this), by now you probably have heard of me, no thanks to my father. But in case you haven't, here's a one-paragraph bio of the highlights: My name is Rafael Silva (formerly Rafael Monfils), the *Global Geography* journalist on the most recent—but certainly not last—expedition led by Dr. Miriam Jacobs to the

Cidade Perdida da Lua, the Lost City of the Moon. My father is Jean-Luc Monfils, or as I recently learned, world-class artifact thief Pierre Vautour. I was sent by my father to sabotage Dr. Jacobs's mission in the Amazon rainforest under the guise of needing to protect the city, while, unbeknownst to me, my father was leading another team through the very same jungle so they could pillage the Moon City's riches for themselves. Gun and knife fights, jungle chases, kidnapping, lies, deception, and other vine-swinging adventures ensued. If you want all the nitty-gritty details, I'm sure you can read about it in the dozen or so newspaper articles already covering the topic. Dr. Jacobs and my father both found the Moon City. It sits practically untouched, thanks to the vigilant efforts of os protetores da lua, the Protectors of the Moon. The city's bounties are plentiful. Its beauty unmatched. And while we left the Moon City with most of its treasures intact, Pierre Vautour got away. Or, at least, we think he did.

Now that you know who I am, here are the answers to the most frequent questions I've received in the months since I returned:

How did you not know your dad was Pierre Vautour?

Do we ever really know who our parents are (or any other person, for that matter)? Relationships are built on trust. Jean-Luc Monfils was a well-respected man, undertaking various philanthropic endeavors. I trusted that the person he portrayed himself to be was the person he actually was. All of his nefarious acts were hidden from me, so I never saw him in action. I didn't go to bring-your-child-to-work day, though I'm not sure that's much of a thing in the underground-artifact-smuggling world anyway.

Are os protetores da lua actual guardians?

Os protetores da lua have been guarding the Moon City for centuries, although more in a figurative sense. They are not standing at the gates of the city with spears and armor. There is no directory of os protetores da lua members. Instead, they blend into society. Listening for whispers of another Moon City expedition. Posing as Amazon guides who are unsurprisingly unable to point treasure hunters in the right direction. Sending archaeologists on wild goose chases. But always in a peaceful way.

But if you think you're going to search for the Moon City after this, beware. The Amazon is no place for the faint of heart, after all. If you don't manage to get lost or succumb to the torrential downpours, heat, or plethora of creatures that could off you in a single bite, prick, or attack, you still must contend with os protetores da lua, and while they are not violent and they are not murderers, they will do anything to protect their ancestors' home.

Is Dr. Miriam Jacobs the next Dr. Socorro Mejía?

In my opinion, this is an unfair comparison and a bullshit question.

First, the only reason they're being compared is because they are successful female archaeologists. Second, each of these women is her own person and amazing in her own way. Why the need to compare? But if you really want to know what I think of Dr. Miriam Jacobs, I'll tell you right now—she is the raddest (sorry, inside joke), funniest, most badass woman I've ever met.

Full disclosure: she's also soon to be my wife, so I might be slightly biased.

But in case you don't want to take my biased word for it, keep this in mind: the Moon City has been the subject of many an Amazonian expedition. Yet in less than a matter of a few hours, Dr. Jacobs figured out the mystery that has been stumping people for hundreds of years. I'm not going to tell you how she did it. But using her research, she found the Cidade Perdida da Lua. So if that doesn't inform you of how brilliant she is, then that's on you.

Did your parents ever genuinely love each other or was your mother just another pawn in your father's schemes?

You may have read that my mother was a member of os protetores da lua and that she was posing as a guide to throw my father off the scent of the Moon City. That is true. You may have also heard that she and my father were supposedly lovers (I came from somewhere, after all), but that perhaps he was merely tricking her to get information.

Assuming you know all that, then to answer your questions, seeing as my father has managed to evade the authorities and I'm writing this article revealing his identity, I'll probably never know the truth because he'll probably never speak to me again. I'd like to think my father isn't pure evil, though, so unless and until he confirms otherwise, I choose to believe that at least some part of him cared for her for more than the secrets she kept.

So what about all of the other players in Pierre Vautour's web? Dr. Bradley Quinn, Hunter Johnson, etc.? Where are they now?

Well, Dr. Bradley Quinn is off living in some remote cabin in middle-of-nowhere Saskatchewan, excommunicated from the archaeological world. Hunter Johnson got away, and if the universe is at all fair, then he's probably rotting somewhere alone in the Amazon. The other gang of criminals are getting to know Brazilian prison up close and personal.

As for my father, Jean-Luc Monfils is dead. To me at least. But Pierre Vautour? Who knows where he is. Now that people outside of the criminal underworld know what he looks like, however, he's bound to get found someday. Or maybe he'll have to live in hiding for the rest of his life, never having to pay for his crimes or the pain he's caused. An unfair punishment in an unfair world. But I'm of the personal opinion now that not all that is lost needs to be found.

Did you really find the Cidade Perdida da Lua? And if so, where is it?
Believe me. The Cidade Perdida da Lua exists. We have proof if we ever truly need it.

But are we going to tell you where it is?

No fucking way.

. . . .

THE *GLOBAL GEOGRAPHY* EDITOR IN CHIEF, LUCA CHIBONELLI, SET THE paper down, then removed his reading glasses as he looked across his desk at Rafa on the other side of the Zoom screen.

"Hmm . . . well, it's not so much a *GloGeo* piece as it is a human-interest story, but it's entertaining as hell. You know I can't print this, though, right? Not in *GloGeo*," he said.

"I know," Rafa said.

"Then what am I supposed to do with this?" he asked, lifting the pages.

Rafa shrugged. "Do whatever you want with it. My assignment was to accompany the expedition to the Moon City and write an article about it. That's what I did."

"Well, I'm not quite sure it counts as an article. And when you asked for time off to write and to recuperate after what had happened in the Amazon, I didn't think this was what you'd give me after seven months."

"I'm sorry if it's not up to your standards, but I'm sure you can understand that my life has essentially been turned upside down. It's a little hard to focus after finding out your father is a wanted criminal who's been lying to you your entire life. But I met the terms of my employment contract. If you don't want the piece, then I'm posting it on my social media tomorrow."

Mr. Chibonelli chuckled to himself. "You've got balls. So what's with Silva?"

"It was my mother's surname. I think my reasons for changing it are probably self-explanatory after reading that," Rafa said, pointing at the papers on the other side of screen.

Mr. Chibonelli nodded, tapping his fingers on his desk. "So, is all of this true?"

"Every last word."

Mr. Chibonelli's mouth pursed, and he nodded, taking it all in. "Gun fights and ancient protectors, huh?"

"Yep."

"And you have proof?"

"I do." Rafa gave a single nod.

"What sort of proof?"

"I have photos that are tucked away for safekeeping. Photos of the Moon City. Of os protetores da lua. Photos of a room in the main temple full of riches beyond your wildest imagination.

And the medallion. The investor has that, though. Os protetores da lua agreed to let us take it if we helped protect the city."

"You know, to lend credibility to your piece, you should include a few of those photos."

"Absolutely not," Rafa said, folding his arms and leaning
back. "I swore to os protetores da lua that I won't use those
photos unless I have to."

"And you don't think preserving your credibility is one of
those moments where you have to?"

"No, sir, I don't. I honestly couldn't care less if people don't
believe me."

"I see. So where is it?"

"Where's what? The photos?"

"The Moon City?"

Rafa laughed to himself and shook his head. So predictable.

"I'm sorry, Mr. Chibonelli, but I can't tell you that. I made a
promise, and I intend to keep it."

Of course, that didn't mean that the Moon City wouldn't get
found eventually. Or even that Vautour or Hunter might not reveal its location. Though the chances were unlikely, seeing as
they were too busy hiding from international artifact-smuggling
charges. People would always be searching for the Cidade da
Lua, and inevitably someone else would find it, especially with
the continued deforestation of the Amazon.

But for now, the secrets of the Moon City would remain lost.
And Rafa would carry on in the footsteps of his mother as a
member of os protetores da lua.

"Well, it certainly makes for one hell of a story. When will
you be back in the office?" Mr. Chibonelli asked.

"It's all in your email."

"What email?"

"The one I just sent you," Rafa said, motioning to the screen. "Check your inbox."

Mr. Chibonelli's face looked away from the camera as he clicked around on his screen. Rafa watched as he read the email, Mr. Chibonelli's face turning from confused to agitated.

"What's this?" Mr. Chibonelli asked.

"It's my resignation letter."

Mr. Chibonelli eyed him curiously. "I can see that, but why? Being on this expedition could open doors for you. You know that, right?"

Rafa shrugged. "Open doors how? By people trying to earn my trust in the hopes that I might slip up and tell them the location of the Moon City? And you said it yourself—it's one hell of story. For all anyone knows, I *did* make it up."

"Well, fictional or not, the art of storytelling is a talent not everyone has. Your account may not be true, but frankly, I don't care. Mystery. Intrigue. Lost cities. Stuff like this sells."

"Which is why I'm going to pursue a career writing fiction. You may not care if this story is a lie and may have no qualms about presenting it as fact in *GloGeo*, but I do. My whole life has been a lie. Everything I have I got because of my father. I don't want any part of him in my life. This job included."

"Rafael, this article might not be up to your normal standards, but you're an award-winning journalist. Your father didn't give you that," Mr. Chibonelli said, exasperated.

Mr. Chibonelli would never understand. Yes, Rafa had won countless awards. Been to dozens of amazing locations. Seen and done things that most people could only dream of doing.

But those things were only made possible because of his father. Fruits of the poisonous tree.

"It's time for me to make my own path. To figure out who I really am."

"Time to find out who you are? Rafael, where are you going to—"

Click.

Rafa looked up at Miri standing at the side of the table with her hand shutting his laptop screen and a devilish smirk on her face.

"Hey, beautiful," he said, smiling back at her. "You know you cut off my boss, don't you?"

"Whoops." Miri tilted her head to meet her raised shoulder. "Oh well, he's your ex-boss anyway."

Rafa let that sink in. Ex-boss. He let out a long breath, running his hands up his face and through his hair.

"Are you having second thoughts?" she asked.

"Not a single one. Come here," he said, pulling her arm and bringing her onto his lap for a kiss. "Mmm, do we have to do anything today, or can we stay in the hotel room all day and make love half a dozen more times?"

"Well," she said, lifting her head to look at the ceiling, "we're supposed to meet Sérgio for breakfast and then head to Avó Isadora's for an empanada party, but if you want to explain to your avó why you are canceling, then by all means," she responded with a flare of playful sarcasm.

This was their second visit to Brazil since the Moon City expedition ended. The first had been arranged by Sérgio so Rafa could meet his mother's family. After spending a lifetime with no one but his father, it was almost overwhelming to suddenly come into a family with a grandmother, five aunts and uncles, sixteen cousins, and countless second cousins. But whenever he didn't know what to say, thankfully Miri would jump in and

save him, always finding an abundance of words to fill the silence and leaving the family in stiches with her hilarious stories.
They seemed to love her as much as he did.

Almost.

Everyone commented on how much he looked like his
mother. After finally seeing a photo of her, he had to agree. As
Miri had predicted, she was beautiful. And based on what he'd
learned about her from his avó and his aunts and uncles, her
beauty wasn't only physical. She had been kind and caring,
beautiful on the outside and within. It gave him some consola-
tion that perhaps his father hadn't only been attracted to her ties
to os protetores da lua. Perhaps he really *had* fallen in love with
her. That's what he liked to tell himself, at least. Why he still
cared about his father in any way was a mystery. But those were
emotions he was still unpacking in therapy.

On this weeklong trip, they'd delve further into os protetores da lua. In order for the Moon City to remain protected,
they needed numbers. With Rafa's newfound fame, he wouldn't
be able to hide in plain sight like the other protetores, but he
could still do his part to honor his mother. And protecting the
city was one of Miri's top priorities with her new career endeavor.

"Right," he said, remembering the schedule for the day. "I'm
telling you, we need Anissa to come on these trips to keep
things in order."

Miri laughed. "Well, when we head to the ribbon cutting
next month, you can ask her to be your personal assistant."

"Hey, you're the one with the busy schedule now that you're
launching the Institute. Plus, with your requests for speaking
gigs and interviews all over the world, you probably need an assistant, not me. I'm unemployed, remember?"

Miri's efforts to open the Archaeological Preservation Institute—a nonprofit dedicated to protecting archaeological sites and drawing attention not just to artifacts but to the *people* who lived in these areas—had garnered lots of attention. Her TED Talk on safeguarding the Moon City and the use of lidar in archaeological exploration had more than three million views in only two months, and it left people clamoring for more. People wanted to hear her talk. They wanted her to go on and on, fascinated by the way she expressed her passion. At first, she had been surprised by what Rafa had dubbed *Pringles Fever.*

But he wasn't. Miri's confidence when she spoke on the things she cared about was palpable. So she turned that new-found confidence into action, bringing with her Felix and Logan, who said she'd led them on the *best damn adventure of their lives.*

They even got her a coffee mug that said "World's Greatest Boss."

"I'm sorry we've been on the go so much," she said.

"Sorry? What for?" He eyed her curiously.

"Well, we haven't even settled into the new apartment yet. And you haven't had any time for writing lately."

Rafa smiled and tucked a loose strand of hair behind her ear. "There's plenty of time for that. You're doing great things, remember?"

"I know. And I'm really excited about everything going on with the Institute. Like, seriously. I'll never forget the look on my boss's face when I told him I was starting my own nonprofit and taking with me all the funding people had pledged after the expedition." She smiled thinking about it. It was a badass move. "But," she continued, now with a slight pout to her lip, "I want to buy you a plant."

"A plant?" He cocked his head, grinning at not knowing where this conversation was going. Yet another one of the things he loved about her.

"You said before that you've never felt settled in a home, and that your plants always withered away and died. So I wanted to get you a plant as a housewarming gift for your office, though one of those self-watering plants you only need to water once a month, just in case."

"Just in case?"

"Well, I mean, I don't want to get ahead of ourselves. You *said* it was from lack of watering because you were never home, but, hey, what if you just have a black thumb?" she teased.

He pulled her in for a kiss, unable to keep from smiling as he did so. "You want to buy me a plant," he said, as if it was the most romantic thing he'd ever heard.

And frankly, it was.

"Well, *I* want to get back because I got something special for you, too," he said.

"Oh yeah? Can I know what it *is*?" She looked at him sweetly, twirling her delicate fingers through the hair on the nape of his neck.

"It's an international snack subscription box. A new box will come every other month with treats from all over the world."

Miri's eyes lit up and she gasped. "You know snacks are my love language."

"I do."

"You really *do* love me, don't you?" she said playfully.

"With my whole heart. I'd get you all the snacks in the world if I could."

"Would you slay for snacks?" she asked, then she perked up. "Oh! Are you my snack slayer?"

Rafa laughed. "I don't think that means what you think it does."

But she didn't care. She smiled from ear to ear anyway, proud of her joke.

"Well, I'd do anything for you, too. I'd even give you a job," she said. "You can write the copy and design the marketing brochures for the Institute."

He shook his head. "No, Pringles. I'm done taking handouts. Even if it's for a good cause."

Her mouth turned down. "Even if it's for me?" she asked, batting her eyelashes.

Rafa wrapped his arm around her and stared at her.

"This isn't fair. You know I have a soft spot for Pringles." He smiled, and she smiled back at him.

"Oh yeah? What kind?" she said with a waggle of the brow and a shimmy of the shoulders.

"Hmm . . ." he said, looking up as if he were debating. "*Probably* sour cream and onion."

She teasingly elbowed him in the stomach. But as he went to play-wrestle her, she jumped off his lap, laughing as he chased her around the hotel room. He finally cornered her, both of them huffing and puffing.

"You've got nowhere you can go," Rafa said. Her back was to the wall with no way around him. She scanned her surroundings, assessing her options. Curtains draped over the tall, wrought iron canopy bed frame. Beside it sat a nightstand and a chair.

"Lâche pas la patate!" she called out, sprinting toward the chair and running over it and the side table. She then grabbed the curtain hanging from the bed frame and launched herself into the air, swinging above the mattress like she'd mastered on those vines—and ripping the curtain from its iron rod and landing on the bedspread flat on her back with a crash.

They both burst out laughing, and Rafa crawled across the king-size bed, moving the curtains covering her face and hovering over her.

Her eyes watered from all the laughter, and God, he loved this woman.

"You know we're going to have to pay for that," he said, unable to stop smiling.

"Yeah, but it was pretty badass, wasn't it?" She looked proud of herself. And, honestly, Rafa was proud whenever he got to say that she'd picked him.

They deserved each other.

"No, Pringles. But it *was* pretty fucking rad."

Acknowledgments

I did it! I wrote another book! I used to think writing a book was a solitary feat, and much of it is. Stories swirling day in and day out through an author's head. The writer toiling away, alone at their computer (or paper). But most books, including *this* book, would not be here without the help and support of a fabulous pub team, amazingly talented author pals, family, friends, and, most importantly, readers.

First, to the entire team at Berkley Publishing. I hit the jackpot with my editor, Sarah Blumenstock, and assistant editor, Liz Sellers. You both helped pull this book out of me (and convinced me to add at least another dozen Pringles references) and made it what it is today. As Miri would say, you're pretty rad. Thank you to my publicists, Kristin Cipolla and Chelsea Pascoe, and marketers Jessica Plummer and Hillary Tacuri. I'm so grateful for every opportunity you've presented and for keeping me organized! Thank you to the editing team: Alaina Christensen, production editor; Christine Legon, managing editor; and Courtney Vincento, copyeditor. Your fine-tuning is nothing short of magic. Thank you to PRH Audio and my foreign rights teams and publishers. Hearing my books come to life and seeing them all over the world is amazing. And to Camila Gray, cover artist, and Emily Osborne, cover designer—you knocked this one OUT OF THE PARK! How did you manage to create a cover that rivals the cover for *ROTLH*?! I'm in love.

To my agent, Jill Marsal. I'm so excited to see what the future holds. Thank you for your wisdom and direction.

To the best damn CP I could have asked for, the charmingly bonkers Jen Comfort. Sorry for the version of this you had to read. I am now forever indebted to you and will be the Christine to your Phantom for eternity even though I can't hit those high notes as well as you think I can.

To Melora François, thank you for your feedback, for your artistic talents, and for just being an awesome friend. Miss you, now please move back here!

To the rest of the Ponies, Jas, Elle, Kate, Lin, Kelly, and Alexis: I'll cross state lines and oceans for all of you (and if you don't all stop moving far away, I'm going to have to!). Love you all.

To the Complicated Cats with Hearts of Gold, Jen Comfort, Rachel Runya Katz, Ava Wilder, Alicia Thompson, Rosie Danan, and Regina Black: thank you for the serotonin, whines, advice, and general awesomeness.

To the Berkletes: I'm forever grateful for this group. I'd truly be lost in this industry without you. I hope to eventually meet all of you in person. Someday . . .

Special thank-you to Jenna Levine. You've helped me so so much over this last year. I'm forever yours. Faithfully.

Thank you, Sarah Hawley, for being the bestest conversation

partner for my launch. You helped make it such a special day, and I'm so so lucky you are within driving distance.

To the amazing authors who blurbed *ROTLH*, Ali Hazelwood, Priscilla Oliveras, Alana Quintana Albertson, and Jen Comfort (Jeez, Jen! How many acknowledgments do you need?! JK, love ya!); and those who blurbed *this* book, Christina Lauren, Adriana Herrera, Jenna Levine; and Alicia Thompson: thank you so much. Blurbing is a huge time commitment, and I cannot thank you enough.

To my friends and family: your support has been incredible. I thought, "Oh, maybe some of them will buy my book and just keep it on the shelf." But you bought it *and* read it! I'm still hoping to convert some of you into hard-core romance fans. Let me know if you need more recommendations. ☺ Thank you in particular to LB for ALWAYS being there for me and checking me on that twenty-five percent; and to Natalia, Meredith, and Charli for helping me pick out book event outfits (and thanks, Meredith, for upping this book's orders to two hundred copies).

To my parents and siblings: I'm sorry if my books are too spicy for you, but I'm not sorry to have you as my family. Thank you for continuing to support my dream and for telling everyone you know (and sometimes even people you don't know) about my book.

To the readers: the coolest thing about this whole publishing biz is hearing from all of you. Hands down. I am still blown away whenever someone tells me how much they love my books. I'm humbled whenever you stop by my table at conferences. Thank you for reading, posting, telling others about my books, helping with my cover reveal, and supporting the genre. It's because of all of you that I get to do this.

Finally, back to that initial thought, that writing is a solitary feat. I might be the only human in my office when I'm writing, but I was never alone drafting this book. To my furry companions, Gus and Henrik. Thank you for always being with me, even if only in spirit.

TEMPLE of Swoon

Jo Segura

Discussion Questions

1. Miri likes to take risks, but they don't always pay off. Between all the wrong turns, accidents, creepy-crawlies, and bad guys, do you think it was brave of Miri to keep pushing on in the quest for the Moon City, or do you think she was selfish for putting her team in danger? Would you have handled any of those situations differently?

2. Much of the reason Miri continues the expedition is because she is afraid of returning home a failure and disappointing her mentor, Dr. Mejía. Do you think her fears are grounded, or does Miri put this pressure on herself? Do you think there was any specific point during the expedition when Miri should have given up? Why or why not? Do you think there are other reasons that Miri stays on the expedition?

3. Rafa's reasons for accompanying the team are both professional and personal. Was his personal goal more valid than

the expedition team's? Once he started having feelings for Miri, do you think he should have come clean about why he was really there? Should he have quit the expedition without telling her about his connection to the protectors? Was Rafa ever justified in his deception of Miri? How would you handle a situation where you and a person you care deeply about have opposing interests?

4. By all accounts, Dr. Socorro Mejía is the most badass archaeologist of her time. For this reason, Miri and many of the other expedition crew members idolize her, even going so far as trying to emulate her. What traits and characteristics do you find admirable in a person? Are there any traits in others that you try to emulate?

5. Miri believes in the need to preserve archaeological finds to better understand the people who came before us. Do you agree? If there was a real-life expedition to the Moon City, what do you think should happen to the city and its artifacts after discovery?

6. Rafa questions whether his father ever truly loved his mother—or him—or if they were just pawns in his schemes. What do you think and why? Can someone like his father actually care for others?

7. Miri deems herself a snack connoisseur. If you were traveling to a remote location in the Amazon and could bring a few snacks from home for comfort, what would you bring? How would you feel if that snack became your nickname? (Jo would bring Flamin' Hot Cheetos, potato chips, and

Sour Patch Kids, and she's not mad about any of those as nicknames.)

8. Very Serious Bonus Question: Jo's passing reference to the Teenage Mutant Ninja Turtles in *Temple of Swoon* has sparked a serious debate—Who is the hottest ninja turtle? (Trick question because there is only one answer, and it's Michelangelo.)

PRAISE FOR *RAIDERS OF THE LOST HEART*

'*Romancing the Stone* meets *Indiana Jones* in this thrilling adventure romance'
Entertainment Weekly

'Heartbreak, redemption, and steamy narrative drive a true enemies-to-lovers tale'
The Seattle Times

'A thrilling, page-turning story that will take readers for a wild ride. *Raiders of the Lost Heart* is as unique as it is compelling—a dash of academic rivals, a pinch of second-chance romance, a sprinkle of intrigue, a most badass female lead, and a whole lot of archeological shenanigans in a beautiful Mexican setting! Jo Segura delivered the ultimate enemies-to-lovers adventure rom-com!'
#1 *New York Times* bestselling author Ali Hazelwood

'Sexy, escapist fun and delightful in every way'
Jenna Levine, *USA Today* bestselling author of
My Roommate Is a Vampire

'Adventure, intrigue, and steamy romance! Jo Segura skillfully weaves all three—and more—in this delightful debut!'
Priscilla Oliveras, *USA Today* bestselling author of
West Side Love Story

'This book has it all! Passion, adventure, and so much swoon! Perfect novel for anyone who grew up wishing they could accompany Harrison Ford on a quest! Obsessed!'
Alana Quintana Albertson, author of *Kiss Me, Mi Amor*

'An adventure romance so steamy you'll need to rinse off in a sexy jungle waterfall after reading'

Jen Comfort, author of *What Is Love?*

'Segura's rip-roaring debut is sure to put her on the map'

Publishers Weekly

'With its well-crafted, interesting characters and intriguing story-line, this debut novel will fly off shelves'

Library Journal (starred review)

'Segura balances action-packed adventure with enjoyable romance tropes: Instead of 'just one bed,' there's 'just one tent.' Corrie is a likable heroine, and she and Ford have enough chemistry to keep readers turning the pages. A fun, fast-paced adventure rom-com with plenty of steamy scenes'

Kirkus Reviews

'It's a hopeful sign of good things to come, both by Segura and possibly the genre as a whole: There's been a dearth of adventure romance novels for far too long, and *Raiders of the Lost Heart* is a thrilling addition to the canon that will hopefully kick off a new wave of the subgenre'

BookPage

The jungle is about to get even steamier . . .

'The ultimate enemies-to-lovers
adventure rom-com'
Ali Hazelwood

Available now from

PIATKUS

Do you love contemporary romance?

Want the chance to hear news about your favourite
authors (and the chance to win free books)?

Kristen Ashley
Ashley Herring Blake
Meg Cabot
Olivia Dade
Rosie Danan
J. Daniels
Farah Heron
Talia Hibbert
Sarah Hogle
Helena Hunting
Abby Jimenez
Elle Kennedy
Christina Lauren
Alisha Rai
Sally Thorne
Lacie Waldon
Denise Williams
Meryl Wilsner
Samantha Young

Then visit the Piatkus website
www.yourswithlove.co.uk

And follow us on Facebook and Instagram
www.facebook.com/yourswithlovex | @yourswithlovex

PIATKUS